A Sword of Ice

Copyright

This book is a work of fiction. Any reference to historical events, people or places are used fictitiously. Other names, characters, places and events are products of the author's imagination, and any resemblance to actual events or places or persons, living or dead, is entirely coincidental.

Hardcover design and typography image by: moonpress.co

Paperback design by: storywrappers

Edited by: Lisa Nieves-Taylor

Map design done in: Wonderdraft

This book is for all you queens out there.
Fix each other's crowns.
Together, we can do great things.

Fae Elementals Glossary and Pronunciation Guide

Kingdoms, Cities, and Landmarks

Illyk: *Eel-ick*
Tuath: *Two-ahh-th*
Dana: *Day-nuh*
Vellm: *Vey-mm*
Ielwyn: *Eel-win*
Teg: *Teh-gg*
Orknie: *Orc-knee*
Lake Degara: Lake *Dig-are-uh*
The Arcana: *Arc-ay-nuh*
Lywyth River: *Lee-with*
Tir na Faie (also known as the Feylands): *Tier Nuh Fey*
Ley Line: *Lay Line*
Castle Aileach: *Castle I-lick*
Terrlyn: *Tear-lynn*
Porir: *Pour-rear*
Herria Mountains: *Hair-ree-uh*
Verdt: *Veer-dt*
Ojor: *O-joar*
Wyrshl: *War-shell*
Seirz: *Seer-tz*

People

Shula Azzarh: *Shoe-luh Uh-zarrh*
Piriguini: *Peer-ee-gween-ee*
Ryker Valda: *Rye-curr Vahl-duh*
Clay Valentino: *Clay Valen-tee-no*
Julius Darah: *Jewel-ee-us Dare-uhh*
Valerio Ashera: *Vahl-eer-rio Ah-sheer-uh*
Weylyn Xanth: *Way-lynn Zanth*
Uric Adriel Nova: *You-ric Ay-dree-el No-vuh*

Orna: *Or-nuh*
King Amos Ashera: *Ay-mose Ah-sheer-uh*
Emperor Robert Laurel: *Robert Lore-rel*
Mairin Valda: *May-rin*
Iona Wylde: *I-oh-nuh Wild*
George Apidae: *George Eh-pihh-day*
Temair Beston: *Tim-mare Best-uhn*
The Kurreen: *The Core-Reen*
Malika: *Muh-lee-kuh*
Veles Riel: *Veh-less Real*

Terms

Esses: (Pronounced like S. S.) A derogatory term for the Fae. Originally Seelie Scum, later shortened to S.S., then 'Esses'.

Mana: (Pronounced Mah-nuh) The word to describe the Fae entity/deity/god. It is magic, nature, and the elements, as these are holy amongst their race.

llyk
The Lagnh Sea
Gyshapur
Kaym
Vellm
Bazra
Kayron
Valley of the Dead
Barrenhorn
Telshaw
The Arcana
Myrim
Ielwyn
Badfa
Ojor
Mountains
Wintshore
Loren
Castle Aileach
Crystal Forest
Lywyth River
Tuath
Minn
Bridgertown
Hiel Lake
Seirz
Arcancliffe
Covenglen
Vallart
Solle
Dana
Port Bay
Zaen
Teg
The Arcana
Lake Degara
Port Lays
Clyhr
Orknie
Eul
Porir
Terrylyn
Verdt
Wyrshl
Isles
Ley Line
The Iron Mountains
Crimson Court
Western Waters
Gold Court
Tir na Faie
The Feylands
Jade Court
Sombhra Mountains
The Seelie Court
The Pool
Elin Ocean
Obsidian Court
Naches Forest
Sapphire Court
The Unseelie Court
Nymph Island
N
W
E

Trigger and Content Warnings

A Sword of Ice is an adult fantasy book that contains dark and **graphic** scenes such as:

Sexual themes

Misogyny

On-page animal abuse in the following chapters: 5. *Something Cold and Familiar, 30. The West Isles*

The sexual assault of a side character in *Chapter 3. A Promise in an Alleyway.*

Alcohol and drug consumption

Sexual harassment from a boss in the workplace

Graphic violence

Gore

Post traumatic stress and trauma

The death and loss of loved ones

Grief

Racism towards the Fae in a fantasy setting

The genocide of the Fae in a fantasy setting

Near-drowning in a main character's past

If such material offends you, please do not pick up this book and/or proceed with caution. Remember, your mental health and well-being always comes first.

A Sword of Ice is book two of six in the Fae Elementals series and does not end in a cliffhanger, but must be read in order. It is in 3rd person point of view, and while each book will follow the story of a different Elemental, there are still scenes and POVs from other characters, including the villains.

The Fall of the Fae

The sweet, tangy scent of mangos and coconut juice suffused the warm air. Saltwater lapped against the shoreline, the foam of the waves cooling the crisp, white sand beneath her bare feet. Meanwhile, the sun beat a relentless rhythm against Iona's skin.

The muscles in her arms ached, her fingers were stiff, and her head jarred with each heavy *thwack* of her blade against the shell of a coconut.

Thwack.

Thwack.

Thwack.

In a fierce succession, she split each one open so the juices fell into a sturdy wooden bucket beneath her work table. Only when it filled to the brim did she stop chopping to bend and hover over the milky white substance. The smell of the juice had always been a soothing balm to her senses; it reminded her of a soft blanket, and it let her know that her hard work was paying off.

More importantly, the sweet aroma of fruit drowned out the sharp odor of fish.

Iona placed her palms over the bucket, fingers spread wide, and let years of instinct take over. Magic spread through her veins, bright blue tendrils of it glowing against her ebony skin, streaking like stars just across the surface of her body and into the bucket.

The juice began to cool until it became slush; white like snow and just as cold. Smiling to herself, Iona grabbed a coconut half and filled it with ice, doing this for each one. Once they were all perfectly aligned on the table, she poured in mango juice.

As quickly as she made them, they sold out to Fae passing by on the beach, looking for something to soothe away the waves of heat.

Being the only ice Fae in the Jade Court was a lucrative business for her and her family.

Living at the edge of the Herria Mountains and not further inland meant they, like others in the area, were deemed to live simplistic lives, away from the nobles and their courts. Yet even if they weren't awash with jewels and fine garments like the High Lords and Ladies, Iona's family was rich in other ways, and they were just as integral to the Jade Court as the ruling noble family on this side of Tir na Faie.

The palace needed food, after all, and Iona Wylde came from a long line of fishermen and fruit exporters. Coconuts, mangos, bananas, and pineapples were hauled into carts by her father and brother and taken to city markets twice a month.

And fish.

Iona really hated fish.

So, instead of helping her brother and her father by tossing nets out on their little white boat, or her mother and sister by pulling fruit from palm trees, Iona did this.

She sold coconut and mango flavored ice to passing Fae.

Sometimes, she sold out within a few hours of starting, when the sun was high in the sky and the heat became almost unbearable. At the end of the day, when the last of the Fae walked away from her little stand, her brother and father rowed back in, and her mother and sister joined them on the beach, Iona would make five flavored ice bowls and sit with her family to watch the sun dip across the line of the sea.

It was a perfect life. Even with the current discord at the Ley Line and tensions between humans and Fae filling into a tighter, more confined space that was ready to burst at the seams. There was happiness at the Jade Court, because the Seelie King swore there was nothing to worry about.

And the King of the Fae would have no reason to lie.

Iona swiped the back of her hand against her forehead, smearing the dripping beads of sweat away. Silver curls plastered to her temples and the back of her neck; the heat was almost suffocating.

The courts in Tir na Faie lived by their own rules and their own sense of time. Each court was separated by magical barriers like the Ley Line that kept the humans and the Fae apart. But these barriers were different, keeping weather and seasons restricted within a single court.

And the Jade Court? It was always blistering.

Iona rubbed at the back of her neck and looked up to stare up at the expanse of bright blue sky. Clouds drifted towards her, billowing white that roiled slowly into darker shades of gray.

It took a moment, her brows furrowing and lips pressing into a tight line, before the stench hit her. Her bare feet scraped against sand and rock as she stumbled backwards, heart beating wildly up her throat, as if she could somehow run away from the approaching darkness.

Living so long near the sea had given Iona quite a good idea what storm clouds looked like. She knew hurricanes, tsunamis, thunderstorms. She'd lived them all, and this was nothing of the sort.

Ash rained down across a once blue sky and coated her slick skin, clinging to sweat and the sticky sweet juices of fruit. Fingers sliding against her arms, she tried to swipe it off, but every space she cleaned only stained gray again.

"What—"

Her skin began to tingle like the sensation of bugs crawling over her body, of spiders digging sharp, unforgiving fangs into her skin. It *burned* like fire. Like acid. And when she inhaled it into her lungs, she choked.

"Iona!"

She whirled at the sound of her name being shouted to find her mother and sister stumbling down the slope of sand. Their feet tripped them up, and in their attempt to steady one another, they both came crashing down in a tangle of limbs against the ground.

Iona ran to them, dropping to her knees in time to rub circles across her mother's back as she coughed into her palm. When she pulled away, it was stained with blood.

"Ashwood," her mother rasped, pushing aside the long braids from curtaining her face, smearing blood against herself in the process.

Iona curled her fingers into her palms, shooting a look to her sister. If there was ashwood burning across the skies that could mean only one thing.

The humans had crossed the Ley Line.

The ground shook as the realization struck them. Air that only moments before had flittered with the warm spray of salt was now tainted with something denser, foreign, *vile.* Yet recognizable just the same.

Iron and ash.

And then Iona's father and brother were there, grasping tightly at their oars, wearing the colors of the Jade Court; greens and browns and whites, like the ocean along the horizon and the sand at their feet.

They weren't warriors, and yet they breathed the unbridled violence of an entire army.

Iona watched with detached emotions. Her heart pounding, her palms sweating, her magic splintering inside her veins like glass meaning to crack. Her father bent to her mother's level and whispered low in her ear.

There was a sort of sorrow at watching them together right then. At the way his silver hair brushed against her darker braids as he leaned in for a kiss goodbye. Their final kiss, before he ran off with fishermen and farmers to push the humans back just enough until the Fae armies arrived. A tan hand cupped an ebony face and pulled it into a fierce kiss that would be burned into Iona's mind forever.

There were many moments of that day she would remember forever; she just didn't realize it until it was too late. When she looked back, she would recall small details, like the bronze shade of her brother's hand in her darker one as he gripped her tightly in a final farewell. The flash of fear in her sister's eyes as she wrapped her arms around the two protective males of their family and whispered a prayer to Mana. The blood smearing her mother's hand. The sound of wet coughing. The taste of ashwood on her leaden tongue.

She recalled the bigger details, too. Details that chased her in her nightmares once it was all said and done.

The screams of the dying. The terror of waiting with the women when she wanted nothing more than to fight. The soldiers, tearing through homes and conquering. Iron and blood, fire and ash.

They'd been doomed from the start.

When Iona finally picked up a sword and fought back, she didn't last either. She fell to the sand on her back, staring up at the ever-blackening sky as ashwood drifted across Tir na Faie, gasping in breaths that wouldn't come.

She'd woken sometime later. Blood and blisters coating her body, gasping in agony as she pushed herself to her feet and stumbled against bodies lying in the sand. The bodies of her family, of her blood. Sorrow was a heavy thing in her chest as she realized she was the last. They'd left no survivors.

It took ninety-eight years since the discord started for the humans to best the Fae. Ninety-eight years for them to travel through Herria Mountains and catch the Jade Court unaware.

They came with their iron and their ashwood.

And they watched the Fae fall.

Dirty Fae Secret

102 years later...

Dreams of icy waves pulling her to her death kept Iona tossing all night. Memories of another time. Of war and bloodshed, of the screaming song of battle and unrelenting pain. Of loss and fallen courts, and the final battle that pushed her face-first into the vicious hands of an ocean that would see her dead.

She hadn't died with the rest of the Resistance in those early years of the war. Mana had been forgiving, had given her a second chance at life.

A broken, fucked up life.

But life just the same.

One she was determined to live. She'd decided that the moment the ocean spit her out on the shores of human lands. Grains of sand, ice, and rock dug into her cold, shivering skin. A cold she'd never felt before invaded her senses, pressed down deep to her bones, making her teeth clatter together in hard movements that jarred her skull.

But Iona pushed herself up on her knuckles, to her knees, and finally, to her feet. Her legs had threatened to buckle beneath her, but she planted her heels firmly in the ground and looked at her surroundings.

She'd come from courts of saturated skies and sparkling water. Of lush, vibrant jungles bursting in blooms of exotic colors and scents. Of relentless, beating arms of the sun enveloping warm skin. Of sea glass protruding from the shoreline, winking against the rays of light, and of selkies and merfolk breaching the waves to sing their songs.

Skies in white and gray greeted her when she looked up. Smog threatened to choke her lungs, laced through the frosty air with flecks of iron that chipped from surrounding buildings. The waters were black, the shores gray, and the water tasted like putrid fish against her lips.

She'd always hated fish.

Iona had landed in the kingdom of Teg that day. In the city of Porir just along the coast, where she'd been ever since. She'd built her life among humans, rented a cheap room in one of the few wooden buildings left in Illyk along with other illegal Fae immigrants who hid from the emperor's soldiers.

It was in Teg where she dreamt of her death every night. Where nightmares suffocated her and filled her with images of her family lying in blood and sand, ash coating their still bodies. Every night her legs tangled against her old, torn sheet as she struggled to breathe until she realized where she was.

Tonight was just another one of those nights. Where her nails dug through the skin at her throat, where her lungs choked on imaginary water that no longer took up residence in her body. She woke up to tears drying a sticky pathway down her warm cheeks, her family's names on her lips, memories burning like painted photographs behind her eyelids.

Heart pounding against her chest, Iona stared up at the splintering ceiling of her room, counting the lines spider webbing across the rotting wood. The routine was the same every night. Focusing her breaths, counting lines she already had memorized. She could close her eyes and trace the pattern against her bedding with exact precision a thousand times just to calm her racing heart.

When the anxiety finally ebbed, Iona opened her eyes and let loose a soft breath and with it, the tiniest sliver of magic, causing a cold cloud to puff in front of her face. Pushing herself up to a sitting position, she stretched her arms over her head with a yawn. It was early; even without windows she could tell. It was in the sounds that filtered through the walls and front door.

Her neighbors were up, banging through their own rooms with stomping footsteps and shouted words.

Just another day in paradise.

Kicking the sheet from her legs, Iona got up to begin her day. She cleaned her teeth after a quick breakfast of bread and fruit, then wiped her body down with a damp rag. Afterwards, she slipped into her work uniform; an ugly pant jumpsuit in gray tones, and looked into the only mirror she owned. A broken fragment that she'd fished out of the garbage on a side street.

Her tight, silver-white curls surrounded her head in a cloud, and she re-arranged them as best as she could, pulling them down and over the tips of her pointed ears.

She'd seen Fae surgically alter the tips, hiding the evidence of their heritage to blend in with the humans of Illyk. Many of her neighbors in the building had done so, while others, like Iona, couldn't seem to let go of that part of their pasts.

Sometimes, hiding what she was felt futile. If only because Teg was one of the most corrupt kingdoms in Illyk. Fae migrated here in abundance and hid in the slummiest parts of Porir. It was the poorest city, overrun with old buildings and rusted iron that had seen better days. Soldiers patrolled the streets with death and emptiness in their eyes. They passed by Fae every day, accepted bribes, money, and favors in exchange for their silence.

As long as the guards of Porir were kept happy, the Emperor of Illyk would not find out about them.

It was why Iona hadn't altered her ears. It was why she hadn't left this terrible kingdom. Even being in a cold, icy wasteland of a city where poverty overrun it like shadows snuffing out the light, it was better than death. It was better to be a dirty little secret of Illyk than being hauled into the infamous camps to be burned alive for what she was. Or worse, as it were.

This was her home now.

Tir na Faie was gone.

Sighing at the melancholy turn of her thoughts, Iona grabbed a thick fur coat and pulled it on before stepping out of her room. When she'd first rented the place, they'd called them apartments, but they weren't big enough to even be considered that.

Each room measured at about ten by ten feet, with a rusted, indoor toilet and a small tub that released murky water. In the grand scheme of things, a shitty room was a luxury in this fucked up world she was now in, so she didn't complain.

Even if she hated it.

The stench of musk, wood, and burning herbs assaulted her nostrils as she stepped out into the hall, closing her door behind her. She caught sight of one of her neighbors crouching against his front door, legs splayed out on the floor, a joint with dried hallucinogen herbs between his fingers, the tip burning.

"Hey, Rey." Iona tilted her head up in a nod.

"Afternoon, pretty thing." His accent curled with each puff of smoke, lazy and unfeeling. It was the cadence of the Unseelie, altered over time, but recognizable to Iona just the same. It was the pitch in his tone, the way every word danced from his tongue to a wild beat.

"It's morning, Rey."

"Hmm. Is it?" His head thunked against his unstable door.

She wasn't surprised he didn't know what day it was, since he'd been in that same exact position the previous night.

The Unseelie Fae was clad in tattered, drab clothing, square patches barely hanging on by meager threads. His jacket was thrown haphazardly over his shoulders that smelt stale like the very smoke he inhaled. Long hair tied behind his head, greasy strands touching his cheeks.

His back was hunched slightly to accommodate his paper-thin wings; they trailed against the ground like a thin, old carpet. Moth-like in appearance, they sported holes and tears, revealing thin bone and tendon underneath.

"On your way to work?" he asked. His voice was gravely, like crunching rocks beneath shoes, and the sound matched his lazy disposition.

"Unfortunately."

He pulled the joint away from his mouth and smirked. His parchment-colored skin looked paler than usual, shadows marring his eyelids, dark eyes bloodshot. "Tell Petey I said hi."

Iona scoffed at the sarcasm in his voice. "Tell Belinda I said hi."

Her retort had him snorting and pressing the joint back to his lips, taking in a drag. "She kicked me out last night. Won't open the fuckin' door." He thunked his head against it again. "I got nowhere else to be."

She had the urge to reach out and ruffle his hair, but she curled her nails into her palms instead. "Hope she doesn't leave you out here too long. Take care, Rey. And good luck."

He didn't reply, but he acknowledged her words with a flick of ashes against the floor.

Her teeth ground together, and she forced herself to turn away. Dumbass was going to catch the entire building on fire one day with his carelessness. A part of her relished in the idea of watching this shit-stain burn. The more logical, less bitter part realized how stupid that was. Regardless of how she felt, this was her home now. Like it was home to others.

Burning the place to the ground would definitely *not* be such a good idea.

Her booted feet hit the stairs leisurely, stepping out to the cold, iron clad streets.

She could feel its poison in the air, but the snow overpowered it. She was so used to the iron by now that she was sure she would die at the age of three hundred, instead of living the long lifespan she was meant to.

Some Fae could live up to be five thousand years old. Her father had been eight-hundred. Her mother nine-hundred and fifty-two. But longer lifespans had been before the fall of Tir na Faie. Before they'd been forced to the human lands, where the iron in the air branded death into their lungs.

Iona remembered those first few months. She'd coughed blood at least twice every week until her system grew used to the poison.

It was the way of things.

Mithridatism, it was called. Named after an ancient, human king, it was the act of slowly ingesting non-lethal amounts of poison to accustom the body. Yet it did not make the Fae immune. If anything, it only killed them slowly. An already dying race suffering with iron and ashwood in their bodies. As if they hadn't suffered enough already. As if they *weren't* suffering enough already.

Iona felt good just to be alive, but sometimes she wondered if others felt that way or if she was just too optimistic that things could still change.

She'd lived through dark times in Porir and had witnessed those who suffered even darker circumstances. She'd lived every day to watch the lights diminish from their eyes. They may have been alive, but they were still Porir's dirty little secrets, trading sex and slivers of their souls to survive another day.

That's what it was. Survival, not life.

And yet, despite all the darkness in the world, Iona still believed in Mana and in the hope that someday, she would live again.

They would *all* live again.

Porir City Zoo

The winding roads of the city were laced with ice and frost. Snow slowly trailed from the sky, coating the ground in a thin, ashy layer. Winter was here, and in only a few days, Porir would be knee-deep in the cold.

Winter was always the harshest month, though Iona was sure winters in Teg could never compare to the winters in the northern kingdoms like Ielwyn and Vellm. It was still cold, just the same.

The soles of her boots created enough friction to keep her upright instead of sending her sprawling against the ground. It was one of the first things she learned when she came to Porir: invest in good shoes.

The city was quiet this early in the morning, save for the whistling wind and the occasional footfalls as the citizens made their early morning commute. Iona's ears perked up from beneath her hair, eyes scanning every inch of the street. Besides being known to harbor Fae, Porir also harbored criminals of all kinds, and one could never be too careful.

Catching sight of a soldier, Iona tensed on instinct. Leather and steel armor covered his body, making him look bulky, and an iron sword gleamed at his hip as he patrolled the streets. There was a wobbly swagger to his step that let her know he was drunk, or high on the street drugs the criminals here sold like she used to sell flavored ice.

Iona didn't allow herself to relax until she passed him without incident. She recognized him as one of the soldiers who went into her building to collect debts in exchange for silence, and though she'd already paid her tithe, she was nervous. The soldiers could decide at any time that they didn't want their meager favors and could turn them all in. Every day was like living on the edge of your seat, worse yet, at the end of the chopping block and waiting for the blade to drop.

She walked a few more blocks as the sun rose overhead, illuminating the city in soft tones of white, gray, and black. Industrialized businesses rose up, smoke pluming from towers to blacken the sky. Zigzagging through streets and broken down, tattered buildings, Iona finally made it to the other side of the city, closer to the coast and to her job.

The Porir City Zoo.

The building spread out in a circular shape across the terrain, with tall, iron fences and rusty tin walls. Built like a prison, with dozens of side-by-side cages and glass domes that held animals both common and rare.

Circling the building to the back entrance for employees, she procured her thick iron key. It singed her fingertips every time she touched it, leaving behind the imprint of light scars against her skin. She slipped it into the lock, opened the gate, and pushed her way inside.

The myriad of smells were overwhelming to her sensitive senses. Shit, piss, hay, and *fish* mingled with iron and steel. She should have been used to them by now, but she gagged every time they collided through her nostrils.

Despite the odors, Iona was just glad to have stable work, something she'd fretted about when she'd arrived. It would have been hard to blend in as a human without a job or a place to stay. She was lucky she'd gotten hired at the zoo. A lot of places required thorough checks to ensure humanity, which left a lot of Fae either jobless or dead.

Some of the Fae in her building were turning tricks, becoming prostitutes, for the soldiers and homeowners. It meant the humans could use them whenever and wherever the need struck them. To keep themselves safe, to have a home.

Things could have been much worse for Iona. She was lucky to have landed here instead of in a lonely soldier's bed.

It wasn't the best work anymore, but it was honest and rewarding, if a little sad.

She made her way straight to Petey's office to let him know she'd arrived. The owner of Porir City Zoo liked to dock pay and threaten letters to the emperor if she was late. The asshole.

Rapping once on his door, she pushed it open and found him sitting behind his desk, a bottle of ale in front of him. As per usual. She tried not to sneer at him like she really wanted to.

"Morning, Petey," she greeted in a bored tone.

He swallowed back the contents in his bottle and belched loudly. Petey reeked of piss, ale, and week-old food. Being in close proximity to his stench was worse than the animals housed behind cages.

"Iona, just the Fae I wanted to see."

She didn't react to the malice in his tone but felt it as easily as if he'd pressed a blade to her throat. Petey liked to remind her who had the upper hand by making veiled threats about her heritage. Even just mentioning what she was aloud was laced with wicked promise of perdition.

In his late fifties, he had bald patches along his scalp and wisps of stringy, dark hair. His skin was tough and flushed pink, his eyes beady, with a gut that hung over the edge of his too tight pants.

She never would have stepped foot in the zoo looking for a job if it had been Petey in charge of the place at the time. No. It was his father whom she owed her life to.

Henry was a sweet, human man with a strong constitution and warm smile. He'd been twenty-two when they'd met; Iona had been seventy-seven. Taking a single look at the tips of her ears, Henry had known what she was and had taken her in anyway. He'd given her a job at his family-owned zoo, along with a wage that would pay enough for her rent and food.

He'd been kind, had treated her like he would a friend. She'd watched him grow old, get married, have children. His skin shriveled before her eyes until he was no longer the vibrant youth he had been. As he aged and she didn't, he eventually treated her like a daughter, as if she wasn't older than him.

He'd cared about the zoo, too.

There had been a time when it had been a thriving place, when the animals had been healthy instead of the malnourished skin and bones they were now.

Iona had been heartbroken when he'd died and pissed when Petey had driven his father's legacy into the ground. After his father perished at the age of ninety, Petey had inherited everything. That meant he'd inherited Iona and her secret.

And he used it against her every chance he got.

She would have left. She'd *wanted* to leave when the only person tying her to the city was gone. It hadn't been that simple of a task. Not when she'd required funds to do so and Petey had cut her pay, leaving her feeling like she was trapped in a suffocating place, her heart filled with both uncertainty and hope. And all the while, she'd waited for a sign from Mana. For a hint that it was time to leave this life behind and do what she felt, deep in her gut, she was meant to do.

But there'd been no sign, and so in Porir she stayed.

"What's up, Petey?" She stepped deeper into the room, stopping in front of his desk. Her arms crossed against her chest and she made an attempt to hold her breath to not inhale his scent.

"After you finish your rounds, I'm gonna need you to clean out the empty glass dome, the one with the pool."

That spot had been vacant for years. The last animal they had enclosed in there had been a black bear before it had been rehomed.

Iona had been sad to see the creature go, but a lot of times the animals at the zoo were shipped off to other places that could better care for them. The unwanted, less rare animals were kept here. It was worse now, because they were trapped, starving, without hope.

Like her own kind, in a way.

"For what?" she asked.

His expression shuddered for a second before baring the anger underneath. It transformed into a leer that she recognized all too well. Petey always looked at her lecherously, but because he knew she was physically stronger than him, he never touched, and so she pretended not to notice. He was no danger to her in that aspect. No, the most perilous thing about him were his threats and his arbitrary rage.

"I'm the boss here. I don't see why you're questionin' me."

"Just wondering, Petey. I'm not questioning your authority." Although, she really thought someone should.

He smiled, though, seeming satisfied with that answer. "Got a new animal comin' in. Need it ready for tomorrow."

They hadn't had new animals in years. Not since his father died and Petey ruined his pride and joy.

"Really..."

He must have heard the skepticism in her voice because he glared, slamming his fist down on the surface of his table. "Why the fuck are you questioning me, Esses scum?"

A lightning flash of rage struck down her spine at the term. It was a derogatory word invented by the humans to describe the Fae. Originally, the words had been *Seelie Scum*, shortened to S.S. and eventually, Esses.

Iona should have been used to *that,* too. Mana knew the soldiers that came to collect each month had called her worse, yet it still made her grind her teeth, made her magic respond. It rushed through her blood, banging against the surface of her consciousness as it attempted to get out. It felt a lot like anxiety did in those first few moments after she opened her eyes in the mornings. Shaking fingers, pounding heart, troubled breathing.

She traced the image of her splintered ceiling against her pant leg, shoving her magic aside and relaxing her posture, even as Petey spewed more venom.

"You're fucking lucky you still have a job after my father died. I could turn you into the fucking soldiers. I could send a letter straight to the fucking Emperor of Illyk. Is that what you want?"

The conquering Emperor of Illyk, otherwise known as the biggest Fae hater in the empire. It was his fault she was hiding in the first place and had been for the past seventy-five years. All the rumors she'd heard of him were bathed in blood and cruelty and suspicion. Fae parts were mounted above his throne, a testament to all he'd accomplished, while he still actively sent his soldiers looking for Fae to trap them in his iron camps.

She knew very well what the emperor was capable of. She'd been there on the one hundred and twenty fifth year of the human-Fae discord. When his armies had finally taken possession of the Seelie Court and had destroyed the royals, along with the Fae Resistance she'd been a part of.

"You know it's not, Petey," she replied tightly.

"You're lucky you have an actual job. You should be *thankful* I let you shovel shit. Would you rather suck my cock? Huh?" He reached beneath his desk and she heard the rustle of his clothing. "Is this what you want, huh?"

"No." Humiliation heated her cheeks, but she kept her expression unreadable while her fingers thrummed rapidly against her thighs. She was Fae. She had her pride, and the old, violent part of her urged her to reach out and crush his head between her hands. With her strength, she could do it within a few minutes. But she didn't live in the same world where the Resistance had her back, where she was in Tir na Faie. Where she could openly use her magic. Because even though the humans knew what she was, it still didn't mean she could *be* what she was.

"Then get the fuck out and go do what you're told."

Without a sarcastic rebuttal, she turned and walked out of his office, careful not to slam his door or give a hint of her aggravation.

A part of her knew the only reason he was being a dick was because she'd been equally bad when he started growing up to be an ass. She'd been snarky and rude, if only because she hated his leering gaze, his comments, and the way he treated his own father.

He was a prick, and that hadn't changed. Now he was just a prick who controlled her future, so she bit her tongue and just did what he told her to do. Even if doing it killed a little bit of her soul inside. Even if obeying him felt like a betrayal to her very pride.

Sometimes, she just didn't have a choice.

As she made her way to gather her supplies to begin working, her anxiety eased in bits and pieces, and her magic settled, burrowing deep in her chest. It would come out again, just like it always did, but she was the master of her emotions, not the other way around.

Iona tilted her head up to the sky. Her nose twitched with the sharp bite of cold, a sensation she felt deep down in the marrow of her bones, and she smiled. Sending out prayers to Mana had become as part of her daily routine as tracing patterns along her thighs. So she closed her eyes and she *prayed.*

For a better world.

For happiness.

For hope.

And because Mana was always listening, Iona knew that someday they would come true.

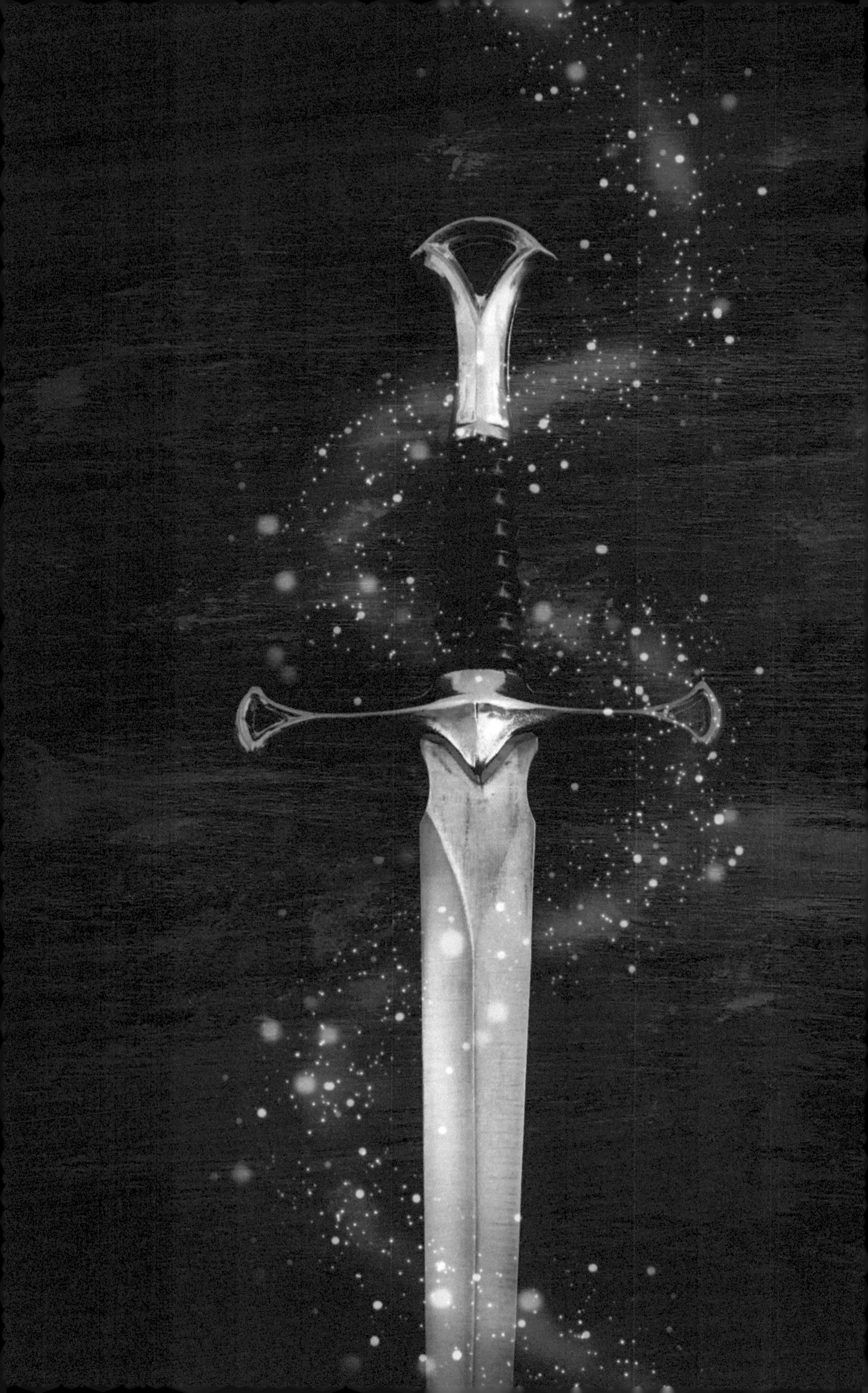

A Promise in an Alleyway

Iona spent most of the day clearing out the glass cage for whatever animal Petey planned on importing. He didn't tell her; he didn't tell anyone, and she knew the other five workers in the zoo had asked with as much a burning curiosity as she felt herself.

Once hay was stacked inside, the pool cleaned and refilled, and the ground swept spotless, the sun had already set beneath the smog covered sky and it was time to leave. Iona packed up the tools for the night first, sighing when she reached the shed only to find everything piled in messily.

She knew, perhaps better than anyone, the toll this job could take on the mind. It wasn't an easy thing, to watch starving animals waste away with little you could do for them other than shovel their shit and refill their bowls with meager meals. The zoo was a dump, the animals all but corpses. Yet it still infuriated her to see the other workers throw everything in the shed without structure.

Henry had thrived on order. Iona had never been the *tidiest* in her youth. She had dedicated her time to having fun and flourished in mischief and chaos. They were traits that still lived inside her, but they'd been brushed softly aside by Henry to make room for more.

"Who says you can't enjoy chaos and order in equal measure?" he'd told her as he taught her the proper way to store the shovels. His slender, almost artistic, fingers were strong at the time. They didn't waver while working with a careful precision, showing her how to organize the contents in the shed.

He'd taught her that it was alright to enjoy the messy side of life, to have a good laugh. So long as you knew how to pick up the pieces of destruction afterwards.

There was something to be said about human wisdom. She'd been older than him, had likely lived a significantly more brutal life than he could ever imagine, and yet his advice had always enraptured her.

Unfortunately, once Petey took over, that particular lesson hadn't stuck with the others like it had her. There'd been a time when more workers had blessed the zoo. Better animals, *healthy* animals. Then Henry died and Petey took all the hard-earned money from his father's legacy to buy ale, prostitutes, and drugs. He'd fired workers, leaving on only a select few, and single-handedly ruined a once-beautiful place. Along with all of Iona's plans for the future.

Iona didn't have it in her to let everything Henry created die. So she kept his memory alive in little ways. Like reorganizing the shed, even when the hour grew late and it was dangerous to walk the streets after dark. Darkness brought trouble, but if she could snuff out the grimness of this place by doing something as simple as arranging the materials, she would.

The truth was, Henry reminded her of the father she had lost so long ago. Mischief shone in his eyes, along with something protective, caring, and gentle. Her father had similar eyes and it was like there was a reflection of her father's soul inside the human man and it was her job to keep them both alive.

She worked meticulously, just like she'd been taught, the iron of some of the materials inside dulling her senses. So when she closed the door and stepped backwards, she hadn't sensed him. Iona rammed into a chest, a miasma of ale and piss clinging to the air around her.

She jerked away before Petey's hands could come down on her and whirled. Her back collided with the door of the shed. Her heart thundered and her fingers tapped her thighs. His image became clearer in the darkness, but she didn't need to actually see his eyes to know they were bloodshot. His breath reeked of stale ale and bread.

"Petey." She was glad her voice came out normal. She wasn't frightened of the human, but she valued being cautious. Because of the way he looked at her. Because she knew how dangerous humans could become within a single instant.

His teeth flashed in the dark. "What are you still doing here?"

"Organizing the shed."

He leered, scrunching his nose with distaste. "Just like fucking Henry."

Iona hammered faster against her thighs and bit the inside of her cheek to avoid spewing her own venom at him. She hated that she couldn't anymore. Back when Henry was in charge, she had been free to say what she wanted, because he'd valued brutal honesty above all else. Things were different with Petey. If her livelihood didn't count on keeping him content, she would've frozen his head off his shoulders years ago.

"I am finished for the day," she said, wrapping her fur coat tighter around her body. A body she was glad was covered in bulky garments with the way his eyes flicked over her figure. "See you tomorrow, Petey." She side-stepped, not giving him her back until she was far enough away where she could hear his footsteps if he decided to advance.

She left, taking time to breathe. Puffs of vapor clouded in front of her mouth with every deep breath she took. After closing and locking up the zoo doors behind her, Iona made her way home, rubbing her palms against her arms.

The darkness was alive around her. The city seemed to come to life late afternoon and partied well into the night. It wasn't loud, but there were familiar, distinctive sounds that she'd come to recognize. Like street urchins running away from whoever's pockets they pilfered, prostitutes with heeled boots clicking against the ice, the clank of steeled helms rattling, or the soldiers' sheathed iron swords hitting leather uniforms with every step.

Iona was alert to every noise, as always. She was only a few blocks away from her rented rooms when unfamiliar *familiar* sounds greeted her from between two buildings. Her feet skidded against the ice and she stopped, angling her head towards the noises. The alleyway was dark, but she saw the figures as clearly as she heard the sounds.

Sniffling, tears, slurping, grunts.

A chill sliced down the length of her spine as the figures became clearer, muffled groans and grunts becoming words that made the hairs on her arms stand. Vile. That was a word she'd use to describe what the soldier was saying. What he was doing.

"Please..." a female voice pleaded. A voice Iona recognized. She'd heard it muffled behind the closed door from across the hall. It had greeted her in the mornings through the still-foggy haze of sleep. But there was such sorrow in it now, followed by tears and sniffling. "I can get you the money, if you just give me a little more time."

"Shut the fuck up, Fae bitch. I gave you weeks. Now, do what I came here for."

The rustling of clothes, a grunt. There was no mistaking the sight of thrusting hips into an open, unwilling mouth. The gags, crying through slurps. Every grunt was a whisper of violence in the night. The way the soldier's nails curled into her long, bright green hair as he set an unrelenting pace.

Her pale green hands slid to the wall behind the soldier, palms bracing against crumbling brick to hold herself steady as he shot down her throat. Her nails curled against the wall, cracking, bleeding. And when he finished, he slumped backwards, his own hands pressing against her shoulders and shoving her away unkindly.

A look of disgust marred his features, and she turned away from the expression. For a split second her pale eyes met Iona's and widened with shame.

Belinda.

She swiped a hand against her lips, and Iona wondered if there was any way she could ever get rid of the taste of the human soldier off her tongue, or if it would burn like ashwood in her throat. If she could ever get rid of the memories of this night. Of a night of promises that gave life for just another day. Because that's what this was. A promise of life. A promise that she'd live to see tomorrow.

That she'd live another day to kick Rey out of their rented room, while he waited at the door, smoking, hoping she'd open it for him so he could stay for the night before they woke up and did it all over again.

Iona tried not to think about Rey's broken wings against the floor, or the hopelessness in Belinda's eyes, or the sounds of her crying as the soldier found pleasure in her body in exchange for protection against a much bigger threat.

Iona forced her gaze away, and though she knew she'd already sent her daily prayer out to Mana, she decided to send another out as she walked away from the scene. Not for her. Not for the world. Not for Tir na Faie.

But for Belinda, and the tears that glassed over pale green eyes, and the decisions she'd been forced to make in the shadows of an alleyway.

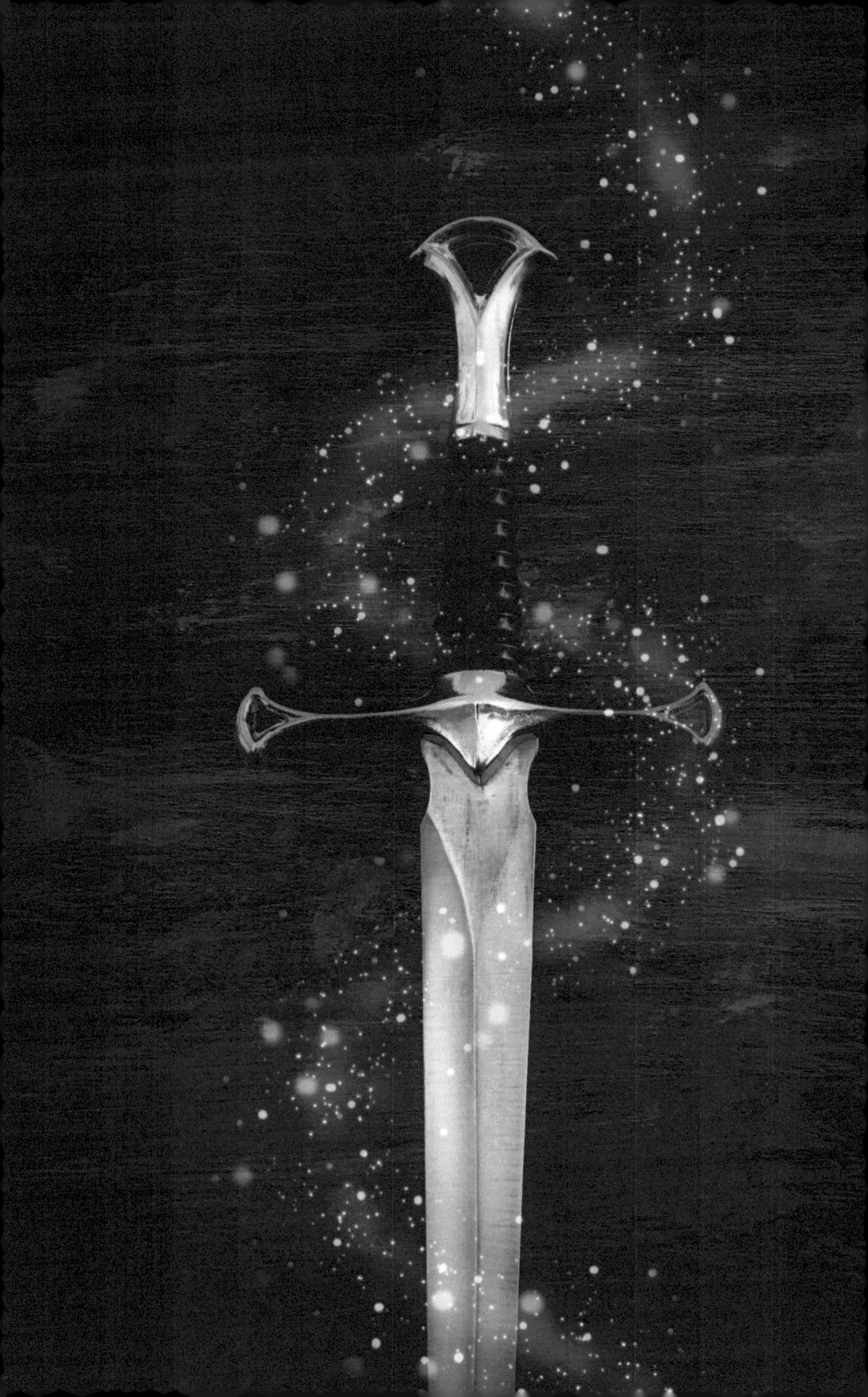

Scars and Stars

When she stepped into the hallway, Iona caught no sight of Rey on the floor. All that was left were a pile of ashes and a half smoked joint propped against the wall, as if he'd kept it there in case he found himself in the exact same position as the night before and needed an emergency smoke.

Her heart grew heavy as she made her way over to her door and opened it. She cocked her head to the side and listened for any sign of another body. Even though she locked her door, she wanted to be sure. There was nothing, so she closed and locked up and stepped into her room, shouldering off her fur coat.

She discarded her clothes as she went, piling them around her house. On the back of a chair. On the floor. Beneath her bed.

When she stood naked in the middle of her room, she turned to look at herself in the mirror. Her curls were frizzing above her head, hay and sticks caught between the tight spirals. They still covered her ears, though, and she shoved them aside to get a good look at the tips. They pulled back and up, like the sharp points of arrows.

After inspecting them, she let her dark eyes trail across the rest of her body in the single broken shard. Ebony skin expanded against her tall, strong figure. She wasn't shaped like other women. She wasn't soft and supple but muscular and *strong*. She prided herself in her body because it was a testament to what she was and all that she had been. A warrior, a hard worker. The muscles of her thick legs reflected that.

There were other things besides the ears that reflected what she was, too. She turned, exposing her bare back to the reflective glass, revealing the cutting slashes of scars trailing down her spine.

A shade lighter than her skin, the scars started at the base of her neck and went down to her tailbone. The scars looked like stars; five adjacent figures trapped in circles down her spine.

She remembered the day she got them.

She remembered the pain.

Agony had splintered throughout her body, a sensation that had nothing to do with the frozen ocean that spit her out against the shore.

She'd stumbled away from sand and ice, hiding in the shadows of Porir. An unforgiving monster, the ice. It had her shivering as the cold seeped through her bones. She may have been an ice Fae, but she'd been used to the blistering, heated confines of the Jade Court, and she could still feel the cold if it was not of her own making.

For days she'd wandered, the Resistance and their failed war a plague on her mind. It was in those moments that her usual levity dissipated, and her own depression slipped through the cracks in her wounded soul. A dissonance between her heart and mind began, leaving behind broken bits of the past until she couldn't pick apart the happiness or the tragedy at all.

Weeks passed of no food or water. And when the first wave of pain hit against her spine, she'd fallen to her knees, the impact jarring against her entire body as something against her back burned so hot, it felt *cold.*

The pain pervaded up to her skull and she tried to hold back her screams. Tried to bite her tongue, but only managed to choke on the copper of her own blood. She didn't know how long she laid against the frigid ground, her cries barely muffled against the pavement. Blood and spit pooled from her mouth, her nails cracked as she clawed against the floor, drumming her fingers to the rhythm of every slicing pang of her skin.

It had felt like someone had taken a shard of ice to her back and began to carve at her flesh.

And it didn't stop. Even when the first flares of agony died down, it hurt to move. The wounds tugged and blood pooled against her dark skin. She lay there for what felt like hours, but it could have very well been minutes.

That's when Henry came upon her. She was vaguely aware of his footsteps, even when they appeared into her blurred line of vision. She didn't know anything beyond the screaming of her body. When her mind finally cleared and she realized it was a human staring down at her, she wished for death. It would have been kinder than the pain.

But the young human man bent at her level and lifted her as though she weighed nothing at all, taking care with her newly wounded back that bled through her cold, stiff clothes. He took her to the zoo, into his office, and he healed her and let her sleep.

When she woke up, it was to an aching, tender back, brand new scars in the shape of stars, and a human staring at her with kindness in his eyes. That in and of itself was cathartic.

The start of a new life. One she'd been living for almost seventy-five years now.

Iona bent her arm at an awkward angle to reach the scars against her lower back, fingering the smooth edges, as if they'd been carved by an expert hand.

She hadn't realized then what the scars meant. Not until later after the pain was gone and she'd looked into a mirror for the first time to see the crusting, healing flesh.

A gift and a warning from Mana.

That she was the last of her kind.

She knew it as innately as she knew the pattern of her ceiling, the shape of her ears, and the brilliance of her own magic.

That she was the last ice Elemental Fae of her kind. She wasn't sure what it meant beyond that. Fae Elementals were important to Mana. The favored in the whole pool of gifted Fae, the Elementals were special. What it meant to be the last, Iona wasn't sure. But she knew there was a purpose for her yet. Something that would come in her future. A sign gifted from Mana.

When it did, she would be ready.

She was sure of it.

Something Cold and...Familiar

The next morning Iona left her house to find Rey in the hall again. This time, they didn't speak to one another, and Iona couldn't meet his eyes. If only because if she did, she was afraid she'd give away Belinda's secrets, and that was no business of hers. Everyone paid their tithe in their own way, and she wouldn't fault her neighbor for doing what she had to do.

So she started forward and left to work, arriving early only to find that Petey wasn't in his office.

Odd, she thought. He was always there. Then she remembered the animal that was supposed to have arrived, and she all but ran across the zoo to the domed cage. Only workers had access to the back rooms that led into the cages, and Iona took it eagerly, opening it and stopping short when the roars of rage reached her ears.

Rage and pain, things she was harrowingly familiar with, fragmenting through her heart. A sound borne of her very own soul. That's what it felt like. Beyond that, Petey's rapid cursing, the snap of a whip, and laughter.

It was a cruel song that made her fingers dance against her thighs as she stepped into the cage and gaped.

The last animal they'd held in this cage had been a black bear. A small creature with big eyes that had been taken away after a month of suffering. The creature before her now was a bear, too. Not black or brown, but white.

She'd read about this kind of animal, all but extinct in what was now their world.

Polar bear.

White fur was stained with blood and grime, giving it both a grayish and reddish tinge, but there was no mistaking what the creature was. A black muzzle was opened in a roar as it made an attempt to snap at its jailors with thick, vicious teeth.

Human men surrounded it. A thick, barbed wire net covered the bear's body. They pulled, digging the wire into the animal's skin. Blood pooled out with every hard yank. The bear cried louder each time while the humans laughed and their leader snapped this whip, flaying the fur from its back.

"I thought you said the beast was docile!" Petey yelled over the commotion at another human man.

The one wielding the whip.

The man's words were drowned out as he snapped it against the bear's back again. The agonized sound echoed through the dome, and the bear turned, black eyes meeting Iona's. For a split second, she felt a whisper of something magical flow through her. Of recognition.

In the creature's eyes, she saw suffering and she recognized it as her own. Like all the other animals here, she *felt* for them. Because sometimes, she was as caged, as trapped, as they were. Starving, shivering, waiting for *more*. As she stared into the bear's eyes, she recognized it like never before.

Iona swore it was a whisper of magic.

Of Mana.

The whip came up again, ready to fly through the air. Her feet moved of their own accord, pushing her forward until she got between the bear and the weapon. Her arms came up, her mouth opened.

"Stop!"

The whip came crashing down against her hands. Strikes of pain crippled through her fingers. She gasped, stepping backwards. Her body bumped into the bear and it growled, but Iona didn't move. Even if it mauled her, she wouldn't let them hurt it again.

Blood slid down her wrists, staining the sleeves of her gray uniform. She pushed it aside and felt the anger bite its way up her body.

"Don't," she ordered, the sting of ardor in her voice.

Petey's jaw clenched together tightly while the human wielding the whip looked amused.

"Don't hurt—"

"It's a beast," the human interrupted in the common tongue, a language that had always been universal both in the human lands as well as the Feylands. She recognized his rough accent from the West Isles, the islands to the west of Illyk that traded in prized animals and cruelty. They called themselves the Kurreen, groups that traded in animal skin and tortured creatures like prizes. No wonder Petey hadn't told her a thing; if she'd known he'd been trading with the West Isles of all places, Iona would have been pissed, and she would have reminded him that Henry never would have done such a thing. "It needs to be tamed."

"Not like that."

She hated how humans equated taming to violence. When the humans couldn't control something, they sought to destroy it. To break it. They'd done it to the Fae, and they were doing it to this poor creature. Iona hadn't been able to do much for the first, but she could do something for the latter.

"Iona," Petey snapped. "Back the fuck off."

Her eyes jumped to his, pleading yet infuriated at the same time. "If you hurt it, it will be weak." She decided to use the one thing he loved more than anything against him. "Then how will you earn your money? No one wants to pay to come see a broken animal."

Petey's jaw worked while the human beside him laughed. "You think you can care for it without the whip? Fine. Be my fuckin' guest." The human wrapped the whip around his waist like a belt, holding up his dirty brown leather pants, somehow accentuating his pirate attire. He gestured with his hand, and all his filthy pirates holding the bear down stepped away and filed out of the cage.

Petey stayed where he was, glaring daggers at Iona. As if his stare could pierce through her skull and leave her for dead.

"Then you take care of this fucking beast." He sneered, his lip curling back in a smile that was as malicious as his heart. "Let's see if he obeys you or kills you first. Get to work." And then he, too, was gone.

Iona took a breath, fingers tracing a pattern against her thighs before she turned and looked at the bear. The energy seemed to have gone from him, and he was sprawled against the hay-covered ground, wire weighing him down. He looked warily up at her, with big, dark eyes and blood against his body.

Iona held her palms up, forgetting for a moment that they were covered in blood, hoping he wouldn't develop a sudden craving for flesh and bite her.

"Hi," she said with equal caution. "My name is Iona."

The bear's eyes held her own, and again she felt that surge of magic. Of something cold and... *familiar* that she couldn't quite place.

Her magic lived inside her body like a separate entity. Like a thread of her soul that responded and moved with her. Staring at the bear tugged on that but also *added* to it somehow. She knew Mana was trying to tell her something; she just wasn't sure what.

"I'm going to clean you up, if that's okay." She started forward, and when the bear didn't lunge or growl, she began to work. Peeling the wire from his frame as carefully as she could, Iona winced every time the barbed wire came off his skin and made him bleed. She hated hurting him more, but she needed to get it off completely.

It bit into her own flesh, but she ignored her discomfort. Once the net was off, she tossed it to the side.

"Can I clean you? Would that be okay?" She knew others would find it odd that she was asking an animal for permission, but just because he was an animal didn't make him any less intelligent than anyone else.

Mana lived in every soul, connected every living thing by threads. Mana lived in this creature as surely as it lived within her, and she knew that he would understand those words.

The bear let out a soft whine and lowered his head on his paws. Permission. That's what he was granting her. So she moved quickly, grabbing a bucket and filling it with clean water and soaking a sponge inside. She hauled the supplies over to the bear and began wiping his body down with gentle strokes.

It took hours of cleaning and dressing his fur with healing salve, but when she finished, his coat was white. Missing patches and covered in scars and fresh wounds, but clean nonetheless.

"All done." She wiped her own hands down on her uniform and took the blood-and-water-filled bucket to dump down a nearby drain. She could feel the bear's eyes on her. Watching, contemplating, but it didn't move.

She tried to remember everything she could about polar bears. They lived in colder climates, thrived in them. Even if it was winter in Teg, she didn't think it was cold enough for him. Had he been in the northernmost parts of Ielwyn, he probably would have been content.

This climate was likely too warm.

Iona got an idea and looked around, making sure no one was nearby. When she was sure she was safe, she held her wounded palms out at her sides and called on her magic. It responded within seconds, sending ruptures of cold against her fingertips and outwards. She was careful to keep the magic confined within the dome, making it colder, making the temperature of the water in the pool drop, not until it froze, but was close to freezing.

The bear's head lifted as the air shimmered with frost. Iona's breath clouded out of her, getting colder and colder. Once she felt it was chilly enough, her eyes shot open and met the bear's. He tilted his head to the side.

And she felt it.

The connection. It flowed gently into her, nestling like a bird in its nest right next to her threads of magic, and she recognized the familiarity. Because she'd heard of it before back in Tir na Faie. Back when magic was alive and thriving.

It was alive then as Iona realized what gift Mana was giving her in this creature. What they recognized as they stared into one another's eyes. A bond as important as magic itself, of companionship and respect.

Familiar.

Iona had found her familiar.

The WANTED of Illyk

Weeks passed by in which Iona fell into a blissful work routine, spending most of her time with her newfound familiar. Due to the new, rare animal, the zoo found itself filled with a plethora of unknown faces from surrounding cities. Everyone wanted to catch a glimpse at a polar bear. A creature who could very well have been the last of his kind.

Even though her familiar thrived under the attention and the income he brought to the zoo gained him favor in Petey's eyes—which meant buckets of fresh fish—Iona could still see the sadness in his expression. She supposed she understood. It didn't matter how many buckets of food she hauled in, how cold his water was, or how popular he became. A cage was still a cage, sometimes with different bars.

At least they had each other, and soon they'd both be free. Those words had become a part of Iona's daily prayer every night as she cleaned out his space and set the low temperature for his pool. She would whisper them to him like a promise. And every time she did, his dark eyes would widen, and his tongue would dart out to slide against her cheek, and there was comfort in that. Comfort in each other.

Iona would fall asleep every night for the next three weeks feeling content and at ease.

But sometimes happiness was as fleeting as the whispers of summer in Teg.

That morning, Iona emerged into the hallway, prepared to leave for work, when she first saw the changes in the building, heard the whispers that made her stop.

The hall was filled with neighbors, some she'd only seen in passing or heard through the thin, crumbling walls. They were staring at those walls now. Not the rotting, molding wood, but at the long sheets of parchment spread over it.

Iona stopped and *stared*, memorizing the harsh, slashing lines of the painted faces of Illyk's most wanted. Different faces stared back at her, of humans and Fae alike, each with their crimes branded beneath their cutting features. Fae sympathizers. Fae criminals. Fae magic wielders.

Iona tapped her fingers against her thighs as she took in the images before her. A skilled hand had obviously done these images, and she could feel the very hatred behind each brush stroke like it breathed life to the characters. Whoever had painted these had turned the Fae into monsters. Monsters she knew they probably *weren't.* Gifted with long canines and malevolent glares only because of their race, not because they really were.

Except one.

Among the wanted of Illyk, in the sea of monstrous Fae faces, a single one stood out. Simply because she was different, not painted to look like a horror from nightmares or old stories, but like a regular, beautiful Fae.

The female was depicted with long, flowing hair, soft features, and cutting, intense eyes. Beneath her face were the words, *WANTED: Alive and Intact.*

A shiver worked its way over Iona's body.

"When did they come put these up?" someone whispered.

"I didn't hear them. It must have been last night."

"I heard marching on the streets."

"I heard they're bringing reinforcements to Porir."

Iona jerked away, trying to drown out the sounds of their worry, but when she turned, she came face to face with Belinda.

The last time Iona had seen the green-skinned Fae had been weeks ago. The memory of seeing her on her knees, taking what the soldier forced, made her skin go cold all over. That night seemed burned in the depths of Belinda's pale green eyes, chased away by something else. Fear. It permeated from her pores, and her fingers fiddled with the hem of her coat, twisting the material.

"Iona," she breathed, a quiver of uncertainty in her voice. "You're friends with Rey."

Friends was a very loose term. Iona didn't really have a surplus of friends in Porir but acquaintances, people who owed her favors. Belinda didn't need to know that.

"Yeah..."

"I—I didn't let him in last night. He was sitting out here in the hall. If they're right and soldiers came in to put up the signs, they would have seen him and—" She broke off, pressing her palm to her lips as if she could hold back the sob that already pushed its way past.

Dread curled low in Iona's belly.

She didn't want to believe that anything bad had happened to Rey. If the soldiers got him, she would have heard it, right? It had been just outside her door. Surely she would have heard a struggle.

Unless there'd been enough iron to dull everyone's senses... Unless Rey had been too high to fight back...

But Belinda didn't need to hear that, either. There was enough fear wafting out from her that Iona couldn't bear to add more on, because she knew the Fae wouldn't be able to handle it.

So she smiled her warmest smile, even while her nails dug patterns into her pants. "I'm sure he's fine, Belinda. He probably went for more hallucinogens or something, but don't worry."

Belinda gave her a tight nod, and Iona wondered if the Unseelie Fae could hear the lies in her voice. She tried to disguise her own worry as much as she could with a happy smile and dancing fingertips, but when Belinda moved, Iona's eyes couldn't help but stray towards the spot where she would usually find Rey.

Empty.

With nothing but ash and a rolled up, half-smoked joint as evidence that he'd ever really been there at all.

Iron Bracelets

The wanted posters went on for miles, glued to every available space of every building and every house of the city. There was nowhere Iona could walk where she wasn't assaulted by the image of glaring, monstrous faces.

She was glad when she finally emerged from the shadows and into the zoo. Each poster she passed had felt like a bright sign pointing towards her own culpability for merely existing. Unfortunately, it didn't seem like something she could escape because when she made it to the zoo, it was to find the exact thing she'd been running from, staring her in the face.

Taking deep breaths, she made an effort to ignore them as she went into her familiar's cage. She needed to clean it out and drop the temperature of his water before she got on with her other labors.

Her familiar burst out of the water as she approached, spraying her with prickles of cold in greeting. His black muzzle opened, lips pulling back and tongue lolling out in a happy declaration.

"Hey, big guy." She bent down, holding her palm out so he could nuzzle her hand with his snout.

She didn't name him. Not in the way humans named their pets, simply because a familiar wasn't a pet but a gift from Mana. A companion. They didn't deserve to be treated so commonly. It was an integral rule of the Fae. Familiars and mates were treated with reverence and respect, and if familiars wanted a name, they would let their Fae know.

"Let me get everything cleaned up for you."

He replied with a ginger lick to her skin that made her giggle before she stood up and went with the motions of cleaning his glass tank. She scooped up manure, hauled out buckets of fish to toss into his water, and spread fresh hay against the ground.

In the midst of cleaning everything up, Iona heard a door open, followed by the stocky footsteps and a presence that reeked of piss and ale.

She didn't turn around. "Hello, Petey."

"Just the Fae I've been looking for."

His slimy voice rolled down her back, making her grip the handle of the shovel tighter before she straightened and turned to meet his leering gaze.

"What's up, Petey?"

Today he was wearing a thick, brown fur coat that made him look even bigger. Dark leather boots decorated his feet, and his legs were pressed tightly against thin pants that were ready to burst at the seams.

"You've seen the posters all over the city, I'm sure." He smirked. There was a lot of evil to be conveyed within a single smile, in the look of someone's eyes. Iona knew true evil and malice. She was familiar with it, if only because she'd stared down into souls on a battlefield back when she'd been in the Resistance.

Petey portrayed a fraction of that, so Iona wasn't afraid of him. Why would she be when she'd battled on the fields of the Seelie Court and had watched her race fall? When she'd held the weight of a sword and shield in her arms. When she'd stared down iron swords, suffered through unimaginable wounds, and heard the screams of her sister as she was dragged through bleeding sands.

He was a bug on the entire scale of things she feared.

"I have." She leaned her elbow against the shovel, folding her body to ease the tension in her back. "Lots of wanted Fae out there..."

His smile widened even further, his lips tilting up comically. "I got a visit from a couple of soldiers last night."

"Yeah?" She straightened and leaned the shovel against a wall and turned back, slipping her hand into the pocket of her jumpsuit. If only because she didn't want him to see the nervous rhythm her fingers beat against her leg.

"By order of the Emperor of Illyk, all business are now required to distribute iron bracelets to their employees." He reached a meaty hand into his coat pocket, pulling out a band of thick iron. He waved it around, and Iona's eyes followed the movement of their own volition. "Do you know what this means, Iona?" He lowered his hand.

Iona shrugged her shoulders, a delicate move that hid the coldness she felt inside like a spreading river through her veins. "Care to enlighten me?" She wondered if her hatred and sarcasm imbued through the words she spoke. Judging by the harsh flare of his eyes, she would say yes.

"It means you can kiss your old life goodbye. No coming and going as you damn well please. It means soldiers will be posted here checking for employee identification and iron bracelets. They're ferreting out the Fae, and it won't be long until they find you." Each word he said was punctuated with short steps towards her until his stench was overwhelmingly penetrative.

She wanted to gag but bit the inside of her cheek and held her breath instead.

Petey stopped, close enough in proximity to touch, and she watched as his gaze softened into vestiges of humanity, something she'd never known he was capable of, something she thought he'd long since lost. "It doesn't have to be that way, though, Iona." He was a few inches shorter than her, but somehow still managed to look down on her with condescension. "My father cared about you..."

Her throat tightened at the mention of Henry. She wanted to scream at him, tell him he had no right to speak about him in such a caring tone because he'd been an ass when Henry was alive. And she could smell the bullshit spewing through his words and his pores.

Asshole.

"Because he cared about you so much, I'm willing to help you out."

Her brows rose, and she couldn't keep the skepticism from her tone. "Really?"

"I can protect you. Get you a fake iron bracelet. You know those are hard to come by these days. They'll never know." He stepped closer.

"You'd do that?" He had never been so giving, so kind. In fact, he was neither of those things, and a bad feeling tip-toed its way down her spine that she tried to shove away.

He smiled again, and the expression seared down to her nerves. Perhaps she'd been foolish not to feel fear, thinking he wasn't a threat because he was weak. In her own arrogance, she'd forgotten something important. That the weakest could sometimes be the most dangerous of them all.

She started to move away, but he was already too close. Petey's hand shot out, gripping her wrist. The quickness and aggression behind it made her freeze momentarily. He stepped into her space, his other hand closing over her breast and squeezing hard enough to hurt.

"For a price," he sneered into her face. The stench of ale was revolting and strong, his breath sour and fanning across her lips.

Iona jerked away from him, but his grip against her breast tightened until she winced. "Fucking let go of me!" Her palm met his shoulder as she shoved him away.

Petey staggered back, growling. "I *own* you, you little bitch. If you don't want your head mounted on the emperor's walls, then you'll get on your knees for me, scum." He reached out again, making a grab for her shoulder, but Iona dodged.

Her back hit the wall and he tried cornering her, oblivious to the shadow that suddenly loomed behind him.

Iona didn't shout out a warning. She didn't say anything, but she watched as her familiar rose on his hind legs and roared. Petey flinched but didn't get the chance to turn around before an enormous paw rammed into his side, shoving him off his feet and away from Iona.

He fell to the ground with a grunt and a curse. The scent of blood was immediate, and when Petey pushed himself to his feet, Iona could make out the tattered arm of his fur jacket seeping through with blood.

Her familiar positioned himself in front of her, blocking Petey from attacking again, but not crowding her against a wall so she couldn't see him.

His glare was murderous.

"Fucking bitch!" he spat.

Iona's fingers slid into her familiar's fur. Holding him steady just as much as she needed to ground herself. She felt like her voice would shake in tune with her pounding heart.

"You're drunk, Petey," she accused softly. "I'll forgive it this time, but I'm not a whore."

He staggered in short, choppy steps, and when her familiar growled, he jumped back. The jostling movement seemed to finally make him aware of the pain in his arm, so he gripped it and hissed. His eyes blew wide as his palm came away stained with blood.

"You fucking *cunt.*"

Her familiar growled.

Petey eyed him warily as he slowly started to make his way towards the door of the cage. His lip pulled back as he stepped further away from her. "You'll fucking pay for this." His eyes flicked between Iona and her bear. "*Both* of you." And then he whirled and ran away, slamming the door of the cage behind him.

Iona didn't breathe until he was gone. Even then, white noise rang through her ears, heart demanding exit through her chest. Her fingers didn't stop running through coarse, white fur. Her eyes became distant. She wasn't sure it was possible to stare at absolutely nothing, but she did it. Was left unseeing until she felt a wet nudge against her hand.

Jolted from the void, she stared down at her familiar, felt the worry in his eyes hit her straight in the chest. So she made sure to breathe a single, deep breath, and she smiled. Her fingers ran against his fur, a gesture meant for the comfort of them both.

"Everything is going to be alright," she whispered.

And for once, she wasn't sure she could believe in her daily prayer.

The Good, the Bad, and Mana

Iona had learned early in life to trust. In the good, the bad, and above all, in Mana. Mana was all-knowing and all-seeing. It wasn't just the elements that made up Tir na Faie, or the threads that connected Fae lives together. It was more than that. It was a mother's love, a father's strength. It was instinct. It was a gut feeling. Signs that something was on the horizon.

For a long time, that instinct had been missing whenever she'd thought of leaving Porir. She could have survived without money eventually, so that wasn't the only thing holding her back. It was that every time she strayed away from the city it never felt like the right moment. Even when her brain screamed at her to move, she could never bring herself to do so, because Mana had not yet allowed it.

The next day, all Iona could feel as she went through the motions was dread. A part of her said she should have stayed within the safety of her own rented room, but a bigger part hadn't wanted to not see her familiar. So she got up, despite the niggling at the back of her head, and she got dressed.

She avoided staring at the spot where Rey once sat, the wood still stained black with ash, his joint still pursed as if waiting for his return. Iona still hadn't heard from Belinda at all, and she didn't ask, out of fear of hearing the truth she already knew, deep in her gut.

She was already outside when she first heard the sounds.

Flashbacks pierced through her mind. A place that was dangerous to venture but hauled her back with merciless claws, until she was no longer on the streets of Porir but somewhere else.

On a sandy beach, clouds roiling dangerously overhead, and the sharp taste of ashwood on her tongue. The ground rumbled beneath her bare feet like an earthquake that could split the ground in two. She found purchase, but her legs were too weak to hold her up. The approaching feel of iron weakened her, and the ash grew denser in the air. She nearly choked on the taste of it but held back her gags.

She breathed through her nose and watched, miles down where sandy beach met mountains being invaded with iron.

Hoards of humans came. Their steeled boots banging against the ground like the drum beats of a war about to decimate. Their weapons gleamed against whatever light was left in the sky, whatever rays weren't blocked off by their darkening smoke.

Iona would remember that sound forever. The first sounds of the marching. Followed by the screams of the dying. It was all like a grotesque song, a deathly wail, a promise of the end.

And the end came that day. It came with blood, ash, and marching.

Iona sucked in a breath, her eyes blinking so rapidly, she felt the sharp points of her eyelashes graze against the tops of her cheekbones like the tip of a knife. Her fingers cramped from how hard she was hitting her thighs. She looked around the street. Humans and Fae were coming out of their homes to look down at what the commotion was.

Iona didn't need to look to know.

She recognized that rumbling as clearly as she recognized her own soul.

Soldiers.

They were coming.

It shouldn't have been a surprise since the wanted posters had all gone up. Someone had put them there and now they were back. Human soldiers by the dozens, if the rumbling was any indication, coming to put their order in Porir.

Iona's feet slid as she broke out into a run, pushing past the gathering crowd and making her way into the shadows. She wasn't sure if she screamed at them to get back inside, to get out of sight, but by the time she made it to the zoo, her throat ached raw as if she'd been shouting. Her chest heaved, and her lungs were desperate for breath.

She doubled over, placing her palms against her thighs as she breathed in and out.

She should have gone home, but she couldn't ignore her familiar.

Iona pressed herself against a wall, dropping her head back to look up at the gray-white sky. Snow drifted down against her cheeks like ash, and when she breathed, her breath clouded in front of her face.

The soldiers were here. In Porir. It wasn't that big of a city, but they'd sent quite a few. Which meant not all of them would probably be bribed like the ones already established in the city for years.

But Iona didn't want to get ahead of herself. She had no idea what was going on and panicking wasn't going to help. Maybe they were just passing through and weren't here to set order to the city at all. Maybe it hadn't been soldiers at all but a parade or a traveling circus of some sort. She took a breath and willed her nerves to calm as she made a plan. She would go about her day as normal until she found out more.

If things appeared dire or if the soldiers stayed, then she would go to George. She had some money saved to pay for a new life, one she would have to fit her familiar into. As far as signs from Mana went, this one seemed to ring loud and clear.

That decided, she went about her day, feeling like Mana was trying to tell her something all throughout. She didn't try to ignore the sensation of prickles along her skin or the hairs on the back of her neck standing on end. She just couldn't quite place what the reasoning for the sensation was. What she should be wary of in the first place. The possibility of oncoming soldiers—if that indeed was what she'd heard—or something darker?

She used a rag to wipe methodically on the outside of her familiar's glass dome. Her hand gripped the scrap of material tightly and scrubbed in circles until it shone. On the other side of the glass, her familiar swam beneath the pool, coming close to make faces at her before he pushed himself off with his paws and swam away, only to come back and do it over again.

Meanwhile, Iona was lost in her thoughts, wiping down the same spot until it gleamed, and she caught her reflection in it.

And, too late, the reflection of someone behind her.

Her heart beat up to her throat and caught. She gasped, turning in time to see the gleam of the iron sword as it arched in her direction. She yelped and dodged to the side. The blade struck against the glass, scratching the surface.

Her familiar bellowed, banging himself against the barrier that separated them to get to her. To protect her from the soldier.

Leather and steel decorated his body in overlapping scales of red and black. She could see his eyes beneath the helm he wore and little else. Shadows and the curve of a smile.

She heard his heart beat, but the proximity of iron dulled a lot of her senses. He took a step towards her and her palm met the glass dome, as if it could keep her upright. It gave her momentum to push herself back on shaking legs.

He swung, the force of the blow was strong enough to take her head off.

Iona watched the swinging blade, her mind working so fast it felt like the human soldier was moving too slowly. She knew what she had to do, what instinct, and therefore Mana, demanded.

Her palms shot out and magic surged. Her veins glowed bright blue against her skin, and frost coated her gloveless fingers.

The human didn't have time to reel back before her magic enveloped his body, coating him from the tips of boots to the point of his sword in hard, blue ice.

He froze, all but a statue in front of her that threatened to topple over. She didn't breathe a sigh of relief, though. Not when her mind was racing, when her familiar still banged against the glass, blood coating his jaws as he tried to break free of his confines.

If one human had come for her, that meant more would follow.

This wasn't what she'd expected from the soldiers. A sweep of the city this fast? They were invading Porir just like they'd invaded the Jade Court.

Realization settled over her as thickly, as softly, as the ashes had all those years ago. She could no longer stay in Porir.

Iona hated to run. Hated how cowardly it was when instinct and muscle memory urged her to stay and fight. But life had changed as quickly now as it had then. She no longer had the luxury of taking her time and making decisions. She had to be assertive, act fast.

And she knew what she had to do.

Taking in a breath, she pressed her palm tightly against the glass, dropping the temperature of the water within.

"Calm," she whispered.

Her familiar settled instantly, but his eyes reflected his distress.

"I will come back for you," she vowed. "I will get us both out of this place. Tomorrow. I promise."

And he howled, a pain-filled sound that cracked Iona's heart as she turned...

...and ran.

George Apidae

The streets that Iona had grown used to seeing nearly empty, occupied with the staggering steps of soldiers who didn't care, had quickly become filled with the marching feet of those who would punish the Fae for existing.

She stuck to the shadows as best as she could, hiding and darting between buildings. At the first sign of leather and steel, she ran faster, quieter. Fear pounded a terrible rhythm in her chest, but she forced it down. There would be time to feel later, she vowed. Now it was time to move without being seen.

She tried not to think about what she'd left behind, or the fact that she didn't feel safe going back to her rented room. A part of her wanted to believe it was mere coincidence, but every time the thought spread through her mind, Mana shot it back down.

Their arrival wasn't coincidence. And it wasn't coincidence that they'd found her at the zoo. Petey had something to do with it, she knew it. And if they'd known where she worked, then he would have told them where she lived.

All of her money, all of her things were there.

Iona wasn't a materialistic Fae, but the money? She needed that for where she was going.

On the northern side of the city of Porir, the buildings were all aligned like a maze. Crumbling, seemingly abandoned structures with hollow insides that pounded echoing footsteps against steel walls.

It was the shittiest part of the city, where criminals came to slither through the cracks and stay out of sight. It appeared all but abandoned, drenched in poverty, where humans littered the streets with tattered clothes that hung from ghost-like frames, and contagious diseases that others avoided. There was no law on this side of Porir.

Which made it the perfect hiding place for Fae who didn't want to be found.

Iona slipped into a building that appeared empty enough on the outside, but that was only for humans who couldn't see past the glamor that enchanted the place. They only saw crumbling roofs and wooden doors with rats scurrying in and out. In reality it was a steel fortress with no windows and a thick door that reverberated when Iona pounded on it.

She wasn't entirely sure how this enchantment held up against the power of iron, and there were only so many secrets the owner would divulge to her.

The door opened on its own after a few moments, as if the magic of the place recognized her essence, and she slid inside. Her eyes adjusted to the darkness as the door closed behind her of its own volition. Small candles sat on the ground leading a trail of light towards a diminutive hallway, like the glowing eyes of sirens enchanting travelers at sea.

Iona followed.

If only because she knew what lay on the other side of darkness.

The candles made way to brighter lights on the other end in the room beyond the hallway. Beams shone from a clear ball stuck on the ceiling. The orange and yellow lights blinked in and out of focus, burning as bright as fire. If Iona squinted, she could make out the fluttering wings of pixies inside.

It sent a shiver down her spine to see them locked away, but Unseelie were ruthless, mischievous. Whoever locked them up had done it for a reason.

The rest of the room was impressive and vast but cluttered. There was so much piled into corners that Iona couldn't discern any one shape from the next. A collection of Fae bones were strung up, the ivory gilded around the edges of the steel walls; preserved wings floated in jars in an array of colors. Black, red, pink, some still fluttering with the faintest whispers of life; fetuses of creatures that had all but gone extinct floated in glowing liquids. What looked like galaxies and streaking stars floated in vials. If she looked closely, she could make out blinking eyeballs set in a crystal ball on a desk to the far right.

Tables were pushed against walls together, holding the furs of satyrs, other Unseelie creatures, and steel contraptions that she couldn't quite make out.

A chair sat in the middle of the room, cushioned like a plush throne. Atop it sat a male, illuminated by the yellow and orange flickering pixie lights. He lounged like a king with long, shapely legs crossed, one over the other.

It all made for the perfect picture, and the first thing Iona noticed was the creature in the man's arms. A single ball with spikey fur that emitted a low, growling noise. Long, boney fingers that housed an assortment of golden rings stroked the thing soothingly. One in particular caught her attention every time she saw it because it was dull compared to the others. It was more coppery than gold and slightly rusted. If she squinted, she could swear the thing was made of iron. Ignoring the thought, Iona's eyes flicked from the hand up to the face.

Lights swayed across bronze skin, giving the male a fiery glow. Clad in nothing but a silk robe that slid off one thin shoulder, it opened at the chest to show the long chains of gold and bone he wore.

Long, dreadlocked hair spanned against his body like thick snakes, covering the pointed ears beneath. He wore a crown of yellow and pink flowers. A dark goatee was scattered around his chin and upper lip, and his lips were tilted up in a smile.

Honey-colored eyes regarded her with mirth, a sentiment that she echoed.

"What the fuck are you wearing, George?"

The Fae smiled and bent to set the creature down on the floor. It rolled away to a dark corner, looking like a dust mite. When George straightened again, he spread his arms wide and smiled.

"Iona Wylde. Come to grace me with your presence." He had a heavy accent that Iona knew came from Nymph Island. George Apidae himself was High Fae, raised on Unseelie land. The accent made him pronounce 'presence' 'pree-ss-aaahh-nts'.

Iona always found him endearing.

"What can I do for you today?" He yanked the bottom of his chair forward, walking with it until he was level with her chest and close enough to touch. His hands spanned across her hips, the touch lasting a brief second. His eyes shone with a bit of Unseelie malevolence that she rolled her own eyes at.

"Why else would I be here?" Her brows rose.

He shrugged his delicate shoulders and leaned back against his cushioned chair. "Why else do the Fae come?" He flashed his canines. "Because I am the black market and the deep web of secrets all across Illyk."

That he was.

If what George did was considered illegal in Tir na Faie before the war had decimated the Fae, then it was even worse now, because he involved himself in all manner of things. He was deep into extortion, rare breeds of animals, forging documentation, and his favorite trade: secrets.

He hoarded secrets like dragons of old used to hoard gold. She wondered if his magic allowed him to expand his thoughts and knowledge out to the world to his network of Fae friends who were just like him. Friends who whispered theories into his ears. Conspiracies about the government and the Empire of Illyk that were so ridiculous, he shared sometimes with Iona. She wondered if there wasn't some truth spun into that deep web somehow.

"So, what will it be? Do you need the heart of an ogre? The tears of a mermaid? The skin of a selkie?" He rubbed his hands together. "My supplies are depleting, though, so it'll cost you a pretty penny."

Iona's nose scrunched up, and she shook her head. "Do people really buy that stuff still?" She could imagine them purchasing it a long time ago, when Tir na Faie had still been strong and independent, rife with magic. But now? There were scarcely any Fae left to purchase these things.

"You'd be surprised at who graces my shop with the need for rare artifacts." He winked but didn't elaborate, and Iona didn't ask.

She didn't want to know who was dipping their fingers into all of this. Humans, that was evident. For as much as they professed to despise the Fae, the richer ones were hypocritical and still fascinated with what they had to offer.

"Well, I don't need any Fae remains. Just a few documents."

George blew out a breath. "Boring," he *tsked.* "Fine. You know my price."

Fuck.

Iona sighed. "I've been compromised, George."

His eyes blew wide. "Yeah?"

"Fucking Petey."

George scoffed and rolled his eyes. "Let me guess; you wouldn't suck his cock?"

Her skin crawled when she thought about it. "You're correct."

"Disgusting. It's a good thing you said no to him. Word on the street is he has a little bit of an itch, if you know what I mean."

Iona made a face. "I don't care what he has or here he sticks his dong. I need papers for me and a certified permit to export a polar bear across any border I wish."

George's eyes were bright, his pupils blown wide as if he'd smoked a hallucinogen joint, but Iona knew that was just his normal appearance. He loved gossip; he loved knowing things.

George whistled. "That'll cost a pretty penny, little Elemental."

"All my money is in my room. And like I said before, I've been compromised."

George pushed his chair backwards, and it scraped along the ground. His palms slapped together, the sound echoing around them. "Rule number one, if you are hiding from the law, never keep your money stashed in the same location you're staying. Who even taught you to lay low?"

Her eyes rolled. "I'll keep that in mind for next time."

His gaze raked over her body. It wasn't sneering or suggestive like Petey's, but clinical, like he could see something beneath her skin that she couldn't. George had never made her feel uncomfortable, despite his profession and quirks that made others recoil. His touch never made her revolt because he always made sure to be respectful in his very light, meaningless flirtations.

Like the brush of a hand across the hips or against her lower back, fingertips against her wrist or hands. It never went beyond that.

She didn't fear he would ask for something she wasn't willing to give. Not because he was above asking; she knew he'd asked those who came begging for favors. He'd just never asked a *woman.* And he would never take what others were unwilling to give freely.

"I like you, Iona," he said.

The words surprised her, if only because he'd never said them before. "You do?"

He smirked. "Of course. Perhaps I even consider you a bit past the line of acquaintance. Not a friend, I don't have friends, but close enough to it."

Her heart beat fast, and she tapped her fingers against her leg. He noticed the movement but didn't comment.

"Because I like you, I'll make you a deal—"

"No deals," she interrupted with the slight narrowing of her eyes.

His eyes flashed with a brief hint of irritation. Iona wasn't stupid. He may have been High Fae, but he was raised with tricksters. He would love nothing more than a deal, and if she accepted, she'd end up accidentally bartering her soul.

His lips pursed and then curled. "Alright, no deals." His fingers reached up to tug at a dreadlock. "Fine. I like you, Iona. So I'll do this for you. Free of charge."

She had a hard time believing he would be so generous. He must have seen the skepticism in her expression. He just rolled his own and yanked his massive chair towards a different table, this one laden with parchment and glasses of ink.

He picked up a parchment, thin and cream-colored, then reached for a quill that he dipped in a vial of ink. Iona watched with a sort of fascination as he let a single drop of ink fall onto the page, and magic flared around him.

Iona still wasn't entirely sure what his magic entailed and what the cost of it was, and he didn't share. Sometimes it seemed as though he could read minds, others as though he could communicate telepathically, and sometimes he seemed like a seer.

How else did that explain the web of theories so strange he weaved?

Whatever it was, she watched as the ink flowed in glowing lines along the paper. Lines made way to loops and trails that spread. When it finished, he went on to the next piece of parchment and did the same.

"All done!" He tossed the quill back into the ink pot. "They aren't glamored, but they're perfect replicas of what travel papers should look like. I also took the liberty of giving you an alias. How do you feel about the name Miralda? Doesn't matter, because I gave it to you anyway. So, here you go; Miralda Tweed, polar bear trainer." He rolled up the pages with quick snaps of his fingers and handed them to her.

She extended her palm and took them. "You have my gratitude."

Now she could get out, before everything got worse.

"Anytime, my dear. And because I feel like this is the last time we'll be seeing one another I want to say, take care of yourself." Something gleamed in his honey depths. Something knowing that she decided not to ponder on.

"You too, George." She started to walk away but stopped, her gaze scanning through the contents of his building. "The humans are invading," she whispered. A warning. Because she cared, and because she owed him that at least. "They might not come on this side, but..."

George chuckled and stood, unfurling his long legs. He took a step towards her, towering over her by a whole head. His dreadlocks swayed with his movements, and she had the urge to reach out and stroke one but stopped herself.

"Don't worry about me, Iona." His fingers brushed along the wrist pressed to her thigh. The touch was soft and comforting. "I'm always five steps ahead of the soldiers."

"Because you're a seer?" she whispered.

He winked. "Can't give you all my secrets, Iona Wylde. Now go. Your familiar is waiting for you." He nudged her, and she had no choice but to leave before she wore out her welcome.

And it wasn't until she was on the other side of the building, door slamming in her face, and her feet taking her away, that she realized what he said.

Your familiar is waiting for you.

She wondered how he could possibly know when she hadn't told him that at all.

A Web of Madness

George, as he was currently known in Porir, watched Iona walk away. Trailing behind her was the thinnest string of light. It glowed a silver-blue and sparkled like water reflecting off a spider's web. Like the ghost of a soul attached to her back, following like a shadow.

The string spread across the floor, digging deep into the earth and fractured into separate strings of light in different colors that spread in various directions. One of those strings cut through George himself, tying him to her.

The threads of life were always weaved in arabesque waves; in different patterns and different ties of destiny. But if there was one thing George's magic had taught him, it was that every single being was connected by Mana.

He could see the strings pulling everyone together as clearly as he could see in the dark. He reached out and caressed the sliver of light that connected him to Iona. A mere stroke of his fingertips, and he was within the confines of Iona's mind, ripping past the invisible barriers and inhaling her every thought, her every memory.

The onslaught of her past was overwhelming but fascinating, and George took every sliver he could get like a starving man. Once he had his fill, he released the strand of her life and leaned back in his chair. Thousands of different colored strings flowed from his chest and broke up into so many different directions.

So many Fae, so many lives.

His fingers slid across the maze of filaments, and he was suddenly pelted with an assemblage of different voices and stories and memories.

They buzzed through his head like a fly caught in a web. After all, wasn't that what his magic was? Just a tangled web of madness and secrets... and he could hear them all.

It was how he knew what was coming. *Who* was coming. And Iona would go with them and change their world.

Not that George particularly cared what the world was like, one way or another. He was illegal, both in Tir na Faie and in the human lands, because he didn't follow the rules. But if there was one thing he learned in his long immortal life, it was that rules were made to be broken.

Even the richest of people, human and Fae alike, broke rules of their own making. His fingers slid down the strings, passing each one by and trembling against the force of them all. Against brotherhoods, the rebels of the north, undercover Fae, and Unseelie in disguise until he touched a single string that he was already so familiar with. It was dark, *evil,* and hypocritical.

He scoffed as he released the strand and it hummed, vibrations echoing through the room like an instrument. If the humans were not capable of following their own rules, then why should he?

The answer was simple.

He didn't have to.

"Fluffy!" His fuzzy creature responded, rolling out from under the table, across the floor, and up his leg until he was nestled comfortably in George's lap, his small body vibrating. "Such a good boy!" His fingers caressed over the creature's curved body.

He had no idea what the fuck Fluffy was, except that he wasn't of this world. Some things, George liked to keep a mystery. Fluffy's origins was one of those things.

"Ready to pack up our little hidey hole, huh boy?" Fluffy purred in response. "I think it's time we took a nice, long vacation, don't you?"

George swept a glance over his things and sighed. It was going to be a real bitch getting everything to move, but he had connections in abundance and that was the least of his worries.

His fingers grasped at his chest for a particular strand and tugged.

"Tudor." He smirked as he felt a slight pull in response. "I think it's time I left Porir for good. Death is on the horizon, and I don't want to be here to see it."

The Final Plan

Iona wished that would have been the end of it, but there was more she still needed to do.

She decided to take a page from George's book and stashed away the important documents in a secret location where she'd get them later when it was time to leave.

It was hard to move around when the city suddenly found itself invaded by competent soldiers as opposed to those who wasted away on piss-poor ale and drugs.

They marched through the streets, banging on doors and pulling people from their homes. Whether they be Fae or human, it didn't seem to matter. They pulled them and herded them out into the streets to test for Fae blood.

Iona witnessed it all from the shadows as they pressed iron against the skin of people. Those who didn't flinch were sent back inside. Those who did were skewered with swords or taken away.

The sight of blood pebbling the streets took her back to another time. When crimson splattered from her wrists down to the sand. The blow that knocked her unconscious, but not before she saw the soldiers take her sister by the feet and drag her away, screaming and clawing at the ground as she begged Iona to help.

She had to swallow back the memories and do something to take the nerves away. She bit the inside of her cheek and pressed her fingers against her thighs as she darted through shadows and found a place to rest for the night.

The sun had long since fallen, and she wasn't finished. There were still threads in the last bit of her plan she needed to weave before she could get her familiar and leave Porir for good. In all honesty, she didn't know what she was going to do or what direction to head towards first. Any plans she'd had before she was forced to revise, now that she had a familiar who wasn't exactly inconspicuous.

Maybe tomorrow she could go down to the docks and buy tickets to travel by boat. Even if her body dreaded the thought, it would be an easier method of transportation than walking through the woods. Without a community at her back, it would be a dangerous endeavor to travel the human lands.

It would be even more dangerous to do anything without money.

All day she'd wanted nothing more than to slip into her rented room and grab her hidden stash of coins. She'd scoped out the place and had found it to be surrounded by soldiers.

Almost as if they were waiting for her.

Fucking Petey, she cursed, using those words like a daily prayer to Mana. *Fucking Petey and his bullshit.* If Henry were alive, he would have been pissed at his son's behavior. Since Mana had taken the sweet, old soul, Iona had enough energy to be pissed enough for the both of them.

Because of his stupidity, Iona was now on the streets, cashing in favors with those who owed her. Those who were still safely hidden from the soldiers. She'd had to move fast, afraid that anyone who owed her money and favors would suddenly find themselves skewered at the end of an iron sword.

Tangling her fingers through her hair, Iona sighed.

She'd been able to collect about thirty golden coins total. She knew she needed more if she wanted to survive and establish herself somewhere far away from here. She had enough money to buy tickets for a boat, but that previous, fleeting idea didn't exactly seem prudent. She was Fae, and traveling with human passengers while she had a polar bear at her side would garner too much attention she didn't need, even with the forged documents.

It wasn't like she had enough money to buy a private boat that would fit both her and her familiar, but she wasn't above stealing one from an asshole of a human to travel by water.

Just the thought of getting on a boat made an ache build in her chest and spread. It had been so long. The last time she'd tasted the water, she'd been drowning on it.

After waking up on the shores of Teg, she'd thought about going back to the Feylands. It was the rumors that had stopped her. So many had claimed that Tir na Faie hadn't only just fallen, but that it had changed completely.

What had once been lands thriving with magic had become a deserted blight. Mana had seemed to have seeped from the Fae's home and made way for the unrelenting soldiers and their iron.

No one stepped foot in the Feylands anymore.

But Iona would. If she had no other choice. And the way it seemed? She *didn't* have any other choice.

Slipping into an alleyway with one exit, she made her way back towards the shadows, dusting away her footprints as she went. The problem about staying somewhere with only one exit was that she could easily be cornered, but there was nowhere else to hide, and this was the safest place right now. It was isolated and hidden well enough in the shadows that she was sure the soldiers wouldn't find her.

Iona pressed herself into a corner, spreading her legs out in front of her. She didn't dare take off her boots or clothes. Not just because the freezing weather or the snow that had drifted down all day and covered the ground like a cold blanket, but because if someone snuck up on her, she didn't want to be caught in a vulnerable position. Everything had to stay on.

Even if she grumbled internally about it.

There was no other choice.

It was a cold, dark night. Iona wrapped her fur jacket tighter around herself and sighed. She wanted to burrow beneath blankets. She'd take her ten-foot by ten-foot molded room over this any day.

Sometimes, she forgot how lucky she was until she lost what she had. And she'd lost so much already.

Sighing, she leaned her head against the wall and let her eyes flutter closed.

Within moments, Iona was asleep.

Stiff limbs made Iona groan as she got up and stretched. Her bones creaked like an old door and her limbs popped uncomfortably. A yawn escaped her and when she blinked her eyes opened, she noticed everything was white.

Winter still hadn't hit with full force, but the snow was inches deep up to her ankles. It was a wonder she hadn't felt anything or died of frostbite last night. She did feel chilly. Her body ached all over, a pins and needles sensation crawling against her skin as her blood circulated and found warmth.

She never thought she'd miss the heat, but she did.

Her boots scrunched under the snow and she winced. It was going to be difficult hiding when she was going to be making so much noise with every step. It was one thing to keep to the shadows, another entirely to leave a trail of noise in your wake.

Oh well.

Iona left the alley.

The soldiers that had invaded yesterday weren't out in packs today. Some patrolled the streets in small groups of twos. She figured they weren't used to the cold, and their steel made them shiver; she could hear the rattling of their bones from where she stood.

She chuckled silently. That could be used to her own advantage if she found herself backed into a corner.

She went about her day, scuttling like a rat running from the lights and chasing shadows. At the docks, she observed, but didn't make herself known. The new soldiers hadn't touched this part of the city yet, but she still wasn't going to take any chances. Besides, hiding and observing in the shadows would tell her who she could steal from.

She didn't want to take a boat from anyone innocent or vulnerable. That meant she wouldn't steal from single mothers or the elderly. But human men who took advantage of another's weakness?

After an hour of watching, Iona finally found her target. A robust human man with a thick, black mustache and glaring eyes. From her position around a building, she could see the meanness emanate from him like a tangible thing.

He shoved a child worker, nearly sending the kid toppling over the boat. She then watched as he grabbed a rope and presumed to beat him until he bled.

That was the one, she thought. That was the one she was meant to steal from.

A gift from Mana, and karma served at its finest, no doubt.

His boat was average in size, a steel thing that looked like it could hold about a dozen people, maybe a bit more. Since it would just be Iona and her familiar? It was perfect.

It wouldn't be such a hardship to steal from an asshole, but she had to be careful about how she did it.

Decided, Iona sent a thank you up to Mana and stalked away. Now, all she had to do was gather her things and go get her familiar. Within a few hours, they would be gone.

And she could say goodbye to Porir City. Her own version of a domed cage.

It would be no great loss. There weren't many memories she treasured here. She had no friends, not really. Henry had been that for her. A friend and, eventually, a parental figure; not a replacement for the father she'd lost one hundred and two years ago, but someone she could always confide in.

Porir hadn't felt like home since Henry died.

Now she had the opportunity to leave this place, and maybe put the plan she'd been sitting on for years into motion. If it all worked out the way she'd hoped, then she would retire back to where she came from. Hopefully there was still a bit of home left in the Feylands. Hopefully there was no credence to the rumors she'd heard and Tir na Faie was still intact.

"Here's to hoping," she whispered to Mana as she slipped into an abandoned building four blocks away. The floor was made of wood and metal sheets that wobbled. She stepped over the cracked floors, counting in her head.

One.

Two.

Three.

Four.

Under the fourth plank, she dropped to her knees and pried it loose, lifting it. Beneath was a thin bag with her papers inside. She double checked to make sure everything was there and slipped them into her coat pocket. She already had her bag of coins on her, now all she had to do was go free her familiar.

Easy, she hoped.

Iona stepped out of the building, but before her boot could seep into the snow, she heard a soft crunch and paused.

Her ears twitched beneath her cloud of hair as she strained to listen. The iron in the air always made it difficult to concentrate her senses completely, but she heard it.

The faint sound of a heartbeat. Of shifting in the snow.

Someone was out there.

Careful to shift her weight, she stepped down. The footfall beneath the snow sounded thunderous and seemed to reverberate in her ears. She paused, and the shifting stopped. She heard a breath hitch and then... footsteps.

She was wedged between two buildings with two exits, one that led out to the street and another that led towards a maze of alleyways and abandoned buildings.

The noise had come from the side that led to the street.

Iona took a step.

Crunch. Crunch. Crunch. Crunch.

She tried to keep her pace as casual and as light as possible, but the footsteps behind her sped up and she was forced to move fast, breathing hard. The footsteps followed.

Iona let out a curse. She turned the corner, catching sight of gleaming steel and red leather in her periphery.

A soldier.

Fuck.

Iona forgot about not making noise completely and ran.

A Clash of Ice and Fire

Every furious slap of her feet against the ground made her ankles twinge with a brief scream of pain. But she didn't stop running, not when the soldier was gaining on her in footsteps that were too fast to be human.

But what else could it be?

No human could ever outrun a Fae. Unless living so long surrounded by iron had weakened Iona more than she thought possible.

She didn't think about that. Instead, she focused, biting the inside of her cheek as she twisted, darting to the right towards a different alley. She put in a burst of strength, her head jarring and lungs wheezing for breath as she picked up momentum.

There was a curse from behind her, in a soft voice that Iona couldn't quite make out. Like the sound of music garbled beneath water.

Her heart beat in time with her heavy, gasping breaths, and that's where she anchored her attention. On the sound of her breaths, and the footsteps of the soldier behind her.

Which was why she didn't realize until it was too late.

A figure dropped from the rooftop, slamming to the ground and making it shake beneath her like an earthquake. Iona's feet skidded back. Snow sprayed, icy bits slapping against her exposed cheeks. The figure on the ground unfurled and stood to a mammoth height.

Clad in a soldier's uniform, leather and steel that were worn just a bit too tightly against his massive frame. The figure's bright green eyes looked at her from beneath the shadows of his black helm. He cut a formidable presence, with bare hands that looked like they could crush her skull with a single squeeze. The too-tight uniform looked like it was bursting, unable to contain the girth of his thick, tree-trunk muscles.

The figure stepped towards her, and for a moment, Iona was too frightened to move, intimidated by his sheer size alone. He stepped into her personal space, and her breath hitched. A jolt of magic surged through her as their eyes met, and then those big hands were encircling her wrists.

The touch of his warm skin against hers had her reacting on instinct. Her knee shot up, connecting to the softness between his legs.

The man grunted, knees dropping to the ground. The jerking movement of his fall made the helm slide off his head and clatter to the snow. His hold loosened and Iona let out magic. Ice pressed against the lower half of his body, keeping him shackled to where he'd fallen.

Green eyes flared and Iona glared. She glared to avoid showing just how surprised she felt at seeing the figure beneath the helm.

Beautiful didn't even begin to cover it. Too beautiful to be human, maybe. In a single glance, she'd memorized all of his features. A rugged, square face and jaw covered in a ginger beard. Long waves of orange were spread like a flame over his cheeks and shoulders.

That single glimpse was all Iona gave herself.

"Fucking dick face!" she spat, and then she was running past him. Footsteps sounded again. Not the giant's, but the smaller soldier, catching up to her.

Fuck!

She'd wasted too much time mesmerized by the soldier and now the other one was merely ten feet away.

Iona knew she had no other choice.

Sliding against the snow, she whirled, shooting her palms out. Magic responded instantaneously. As easy as breathing, ice burst from her fingertips in the shape of dozens of pointed daggers. They flew towards the soldier, whose own hands shot up just as quickly.

And her daggers? They rammed through a sudden wall of fire.

Iona's eyes widened against the blaze as its flickering fingers chased towards her. She cursed and let her powers fly.

Ice and fire met in the middle. Like a bestial dance for dominance, each element pushed, one against the other. They clashed, sending sparks of fire and shards of ice rupturing above them.

Her feet skidded back as the heat pushed towards her, and beyond the fray of magic, she could make out the soldier's delicate hands. Golden bronze, the tips of fingertips danced with green and red flames.

This was no human. But why would a soldier be wielding magic?

Sweat slid down Iona's temples, her teeth gritted, and she pushed with her hands as she took a step forward and her magic... it shattered like shards, ice splintering into jagged edges like the very scars down her back. The force of it extinguished the fire completely, but the volatile use of it exploded, pushing them both back into the snow in opposite directions.

Iona's back slammed to the ground, cushioned by the cold layer of white beneath her.

Her head spun, her magic swirled like a storm in her chest, but she tamped it down, using every ounce of strength she had to shove it back. Her fingers found purchase in the snow as she slowly pushed herself up to a standing position. A grunt of pain left her lips, and her head throbbed, but she gritted her teeth against it and took a deep breath.

A cold cloud roiled in front of her and slowly drifted into stillness.

And Iona watched as the soldier across from her stood. Slowly, those delicate golden-brown hands lifted the dark helmet.

Long black hair came tumbling from beneath it like a long, silk curtain. Iona followed the length of the hair up to the face. A very female face. Delicate golden curves and beauty stared back at her. Eyes that glinted like the burning embers of a fire held a fierce determination.

The helm dropped to the snow and long fingers went up to push aside thick locks of hair behind a pointed Fae ear.

Iona stood as frozen as her magic, transfixed with the figure she recognized from the wanted posters.

She was shorter than Iona, but she held her head tall as she took a step forward. The closer she came, the more Iona felt something. A buzzing through her system that lit every nerve on edge. She gasped, holding the shocked sound in, as the bonds of Mana seemed to echo between them like the discreet touch of a soft hand against skin.

Elementals were rare.

Meeting another was even rarer.

And there was no denying what this female Fae was, how their magic imploded against one another, or how Mana seemed to be pulling invisible strings between them together.

"Hello," the female spoke, her voice a sensual whisper. "My name is Shula Azzarh, and I've been looking for you."

Footsteps sounded behind the woman. Great hulking strides that sent a shiver of both unease and anticipation down Iona's spine.

"*We've* been looking for you," the woman—Shula—said again.

Iona's eyes narrowed, and she could think of nothing else to ask other than, "Why?"

"Because... we are the Resistance."

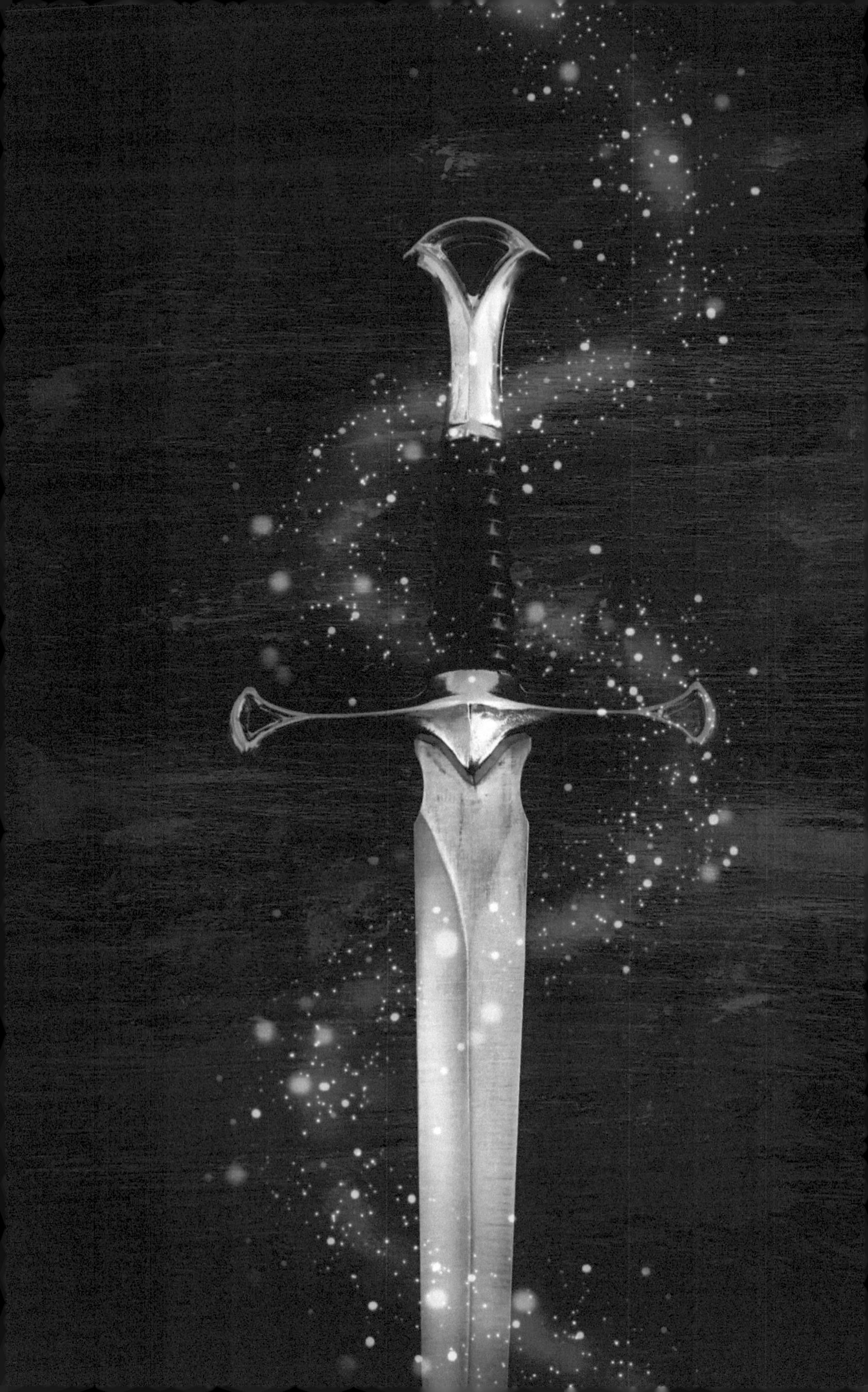

Shula Azzarh

The cold winds of Castle Aileach whistled against Shula's stinging skin. The hidden castle that lay deep in the mountains in the northernmost part of Tuath, on the highest peak, was blanketed in snow and ice. Malicious winds whipped through the sky, making Shula wonder if the unrest was due to the endeavor they were about to go on. Like the elements were warning them of the dangers that lay ahead.

Her hands slid through the tresses of her long, dark hair, pulling the locks over her ears before she caught herself. It was a bad habit she knew she was going to have to break. All her life, she'd been used to hiding what she really was.

First, in the reservation camps. Fae had been tolerated in the small confines, but the Fae who held magic were a taboo in the Empire of Illyk. Then when their hatred for the Fae with magic wasn't enough, they'd ferreted them all out, Seelie and Unseelie alike.

Her parents had died while Shula had fled straight into the arms of an old human woman, whose name she never learned. But that woman had gripped her twelve-year-old hand tightly, taken her through the weaving darkness of the streets of Tuath, and gently pushed her into a run-down house.

Shula remembered the smell quite vividly. It was unpleasant and pervasive, filled with something she couldn't quite place. And underneath the stench of the chemicals and the herbs? Blood and metal.

Candles and oil lamps had lit up the dirty room, the dancing flames reminding her of what lived within her own soul. The light glinted off the scalpels, scissors, needles, and other sharp objects displayed on the table.

She wanted to feel fear, but the loss of her parents overpowered everything else in her chest. All she knew was the agony of her new reality, of a world without her Papa and Mama, and how she was expected to cope with it while hiding from the dangers of the world. The weight of it all was nearly unbearable.

So when the human woman sat her on a table and the man emerged into the room, Shula didn't fight. She'd barely even flinched as the scissors and knife made a slit against the tips of her pointed ears, snipping and cutting off cartilage. Needle and thread sewed them back together when he was done, until the evidence of her heritage was left in nothing but aching skin, black thread crisscrossing and tugging painfully. The wounds behind her ears would eventually become scars.

Shula had taken to growing her hair long, if only so it could curtain the evidence. No one noticed her scars because of her waist length hair. She'd hidden her ears for so long now that it was instinct to keep doing it.

She didn't have to, though; not anymore.

Because she was no longer *with* the humans, and because her ears were *no longer human.*

Pushing the strands behind the tips, Shula smiled to herself, letting her fingers graze the pointed edge. It felt as if they'd never been mutilated in the first place. There were no scars, no phantom pain, no evidence of the difficulties of her childhood marring the surface of her skin.

She had Ryker to thank for that.

Ryker Valda.

Her mate.

He was the one who now bore the scars of her shame and survival. Having used his magic to heal the outer part of her that had been broken and twisted to fit into the confines that Illyk had forced her into, they spread behind his own pointed ears. Just another set of scars he wore on his body like an ever-growing collection.

His skin was covered in them. They bisected along nearly every inch, like jagged puzzle pieces that pulled flesh together on his face, separating a black eye from a white one. Two different colors that stared at her hands as she brushed aside her long hair.

His fingers came down, big hand swallowing hers and giving it a squeeze. It was a gesture meant for comfort, but it was gone as soon as he gave it.

Their relationship had been built from hatred and disgust. Eventually, it transcended into secret glances. Into the quiet but rough brush of fingertips that held on for far too long, only to pull away as if the contact burned far too hot. Like it was forbidden to crave someone so different from themselves.

They might have been stuck in that phase.

It didn't matter that they'd fucked and bonded the night before. The crescent marks of their canines were a bright wound on their necks to prove to everyone that they were officially mates, that they'd claimed one another.

Some habits died hard.

Like fixing hair over ears.

Like avoiding the touch of someone you didn't know how to make yourself want.

With time, she was sure they would grow used to each other and the mating bond they'd both denied for so long.

"Are you ready?" The voice cut through the loud roaring of the wind. Commanding, imperious. Noble. The voice of Amos Ashera, King of Tir na Faie and the Seelie Courts.

A heavy cloak was set over his shoulders, his thick legs spread, and his muscled arms crossed against his chest. His dark, black beard was long and braided, held together with jeweled clips. His eyes held the hint of something dark within them. Dark and desperate and cunning.

It was a look that mirrored his son's.

Prince Valerio walked to his father and bowed. When he stood, the cutting, sharp lines of his facial features were calm. Shula had always thought the prince looked sharp, but there was something infinitely softer about him than his father.

Softer, but no less ruthless.

"We are ready," Valerio answered as he rose.

King Ashera nodded. "Go with Mana, and report back to me when you find the second Elemental." His eyes strayed to Shula, a threat shining in the obsidian depths.

She'd all but declared her loyalty the night before when she'd burst from the woods to save six Fae males she'd grown to think of as friends, and afterwards when she allowed Ryker to heal her ears. She was on their side, ready to take back the Fae pride the humans had all but beaten to the ground.

Even so, he would never trust her.

She doubted royals had it in them to trust anyone, so she tried not to take it personally.

"We will, Your Majesty." Valerio turned from his father, nodding once at Uric, a pale Fae with white-silver hair, covered head to toe in black.

Uric stepped forward silently and Shula watched as he waved a hand through the air, and the air behind him shimmered and glowed. A silver outline appeared, and darkness opened up like a doorway before making way to the image of a distorted mirror.

It was something Shula had become all too accustomed to in the past few weeks.

The portal shimmered and Julius stepped towards it first, unsheathing his sword and hefting his shield to his left arm. He'd go through first for protection, followed by Clay then Valerio. Shula, Ryker, Weylyn, and Uric would bring up the rear.

Shula's bag weighed on her shoulders as she stepped towards the thing. The map of Illyk and six stones in her pocket seemed to burn with promise.

The promise of what should happen if she failed to find the five remaining Elementals.

Destruction.

Death.

The eradication of the entire Fae race.

No pressure... right?

She took a breath and stepped into the portal. Pushing past the surface was like going through a pool of honey. Her ears popped and she made it to the other side, feet stepping on frozen earth devoid of snow. Air devoid of stinging ice.

It was chilly enough, but the lack of vicious winds that had surrounded Castle Aileach made her feel suffocated in her own fur coat and thick boots.

They'd landed just at the edge of the Arcana, a miles wide river that spread from the mountains of Vellm all the way down to Dana, cutting through the human lands of Illyk, in the kingdom of Teg.

As the others stepped out of the portal and it closed, Shula pulled the map from her pocket and opened the fraying slip of parchment.

The night before, she'd used it to track the other Elementals by tossing the stones in her pocket and watching them land on the spaces where each Fae was located. Now, it was like Mana itself burned on the page, showing her exactly where she needed to go.

A thin electric blue line slid from where Shula stood on the map towards the shores of Teg, in a small city named Porir that was just along the coast of the Western Waters.

Her Fae companions had argued right after the pieces fell onto the map. Each on different kingdoms.

Ielwyn.

Dana.

Vellm.

A line that bounced between kingdoms.

And Teg.

Dana had been the closest kingdom to them, but something had urged Shula to choose Teg instead. A nudge from Mana, perhaps? The line leading to Teg had burned brightly and Shula couldn't ignore it.

They had to go to Teg first and find the Elemental there. A feeling of urgency burned at the back of her neck.

"Where to, Fire Dancer?" Clay came beside her, throwing his arm around her shoulders and pulling her close. He smelt like roses and wine and something else. Something fancy. If richness had a scent, it would ooze from Clay's pores in bubbly texture.

His head bumped hers as he looked down at the map. He couldn't see the line like she could, because he wasn't an Elemental. Even though all Fae were tethered by the magical bonds of Mana, only the Elementals could sense one another, and only they had a direct connection to that powerful life force.

"A city called Porir," she answered.

Clay's fingers brushed along her hair, grazing her ears. Shula flinched, an instinctual reaction that had a growl behind them ripping through the chilly air.

A moment later, Ryker ripped Clay away from her, his pupils blown wide with anger. "Don't fucking touch her," he growled.

Clay stumbled and held his hands up. A smirk touched his mouth, showing the dimple on his cheek, like he knew it only made him look prettier.

And he was so, so pretty. One of the most beautiful Fae Shula had ever seen. He had soft, feminine features; plump lips, bright eyes, smooth skin, and lush hair. Everything about him was rich and he knew it.

It was how many females had found their way into his bed. Or so Shula had been told.

Ryker's sudden possessive growling surprised her, but it didn't seem to surprise her Fae companions.

The men all looked at one another with amusement, except for Weylyn, the golden Fae who stayed further from the group like always. He watched like he was waiting for something dark to unfold, secrets he could keep and break apart, all while his eyes gleamed.

"Aw, what's wrong, Ryker? Afraid I'll get my scent all over your pretty little mate?" Clay taunted.

Shula noticed he widened his stance, pressing his feet firmly into the ground to strengthen his core.

"Watch it," Ryker warned, pointing an accusing finger at Clay.

"Afraid she'll see your more animalistic side?" Clay snapped his canines. "Maybe she'll want to fuck a real man instead—"

The words were barely out of his mouth before Ryker roared and attacked. The impact of his body colliding against Clay's echoed throughout the open space of where they stood, making Shula wince. They crashed to the ground in a tangle of limbs and snarling sounds.

Valerio sighed and rolled his eyes. "We're going to be here a while," he murmured, turning to Weylyn. "We're too close to the Arcana for comfort. Scope out the perimeter, report back." His words were clipped, slightly cruel, but they only made Weylyn nod and swagger away.

Shula had questioned the way they'd all treated Weylyn at first, not understanding why exactly they were so indifferent and cruel. She'd soon discovered it was because of his eerie power.

Weylyn had the ability to read the thoughts of others. Around him, nothing was secret, and the sly smirk that constantly marred his face let them all know it. Which meant the Seelie Prince tried to get rid of him as much as he possibly could.

"We need to leave," Shula urged, turning to the prince. "These shores are always busy with travelers."

Teg was already sparse in trees and forestation. Traveling without the cover of the woods was going to make her nervous enough.

"They're going to be a while." Valerio tilted his chin towards Ryker and Clay.

Shula saw blood fly between the two grappling men.

"Break them up!"

Valerio ignored her outburst, and Julius snorted his laughter. She narrowed her eyes at him, and he smirked. "Don't look at me like that, Fire Dancer. The first rule of a mating bond is to *never* get between a Fae male and his mate. It just might be the last thing you ever do."

Shula's eyes rolled.

"It's true, Shula," Valerio said, and she swore she heard a wistful note in his voice. "Fae males are possessive of their mates. Let them fight it out."

She didn't want to admit that the thought of Ryker fighting for her made her stomach coil with a sort of pleasantry. No one had ever fought for her before, save for her parents, so she decided the prince was right, and it was better if they didn't interfere.

They walked for days, trudging through the frosty ground. Pretty soon, white flakes began to descend from the sky and coat the grass in a thin layer. By the time they reached Porir, Shula knew they'd be knee-deep in snow and cold.

As it was, she was trying not to shiver in her fur coat, but her hands trembled so badly, she was afraid she'd rip the map she was holding.

She'd paid more attention to the map than anything else on the whole journey so far. She couldn't take her eyes away from the mesmerizing electric line that led them closer by the hour towards this new Elemental.

Shula wondered what the Fae would be like. Male? Female? What element did they wield? What were they like?

Doubts began to creep in. What if they were like her? Unsure and afraid. What if they weren't? What if this Fae was stronger than Shula could ever hope to be? She wasn't sure what worried her more.

If the Fae was stronger, then what would the others say? They'd have someone to compare Shula to. Ryker would have someone to compare Shula to. Someone possibly stronger, wiser. Maybe this Fae had the pride that Shula had lost and was just now gaining back.

Breaking off those thoughts, she shoved the map back into her pocket and stared forward. She didn't want to think about those things. It didn't do any good to assume, because she'd only hurt herself in the end.

All she could really hope for was that this new Fae would be willing to help them. That they made it there on time. Because *something* was coming.

Shula just wasn't sure what.

The light press of a hand against her back tore her attention away from wandering thoughts. Her head turned to meet Ryker's black eye and saw a brief flash of concern.

"Okay?" he asked. His eye flicked to her hand, which was pulling her hair over her ears.

Fuck.

She smoothed out the strands and dropped her hand into her pocket. "Yeah," she said. "I'm fine."

He frowned as if he didn't believe her. She hated that he could read her so easily, that she'd never been able to comfortably lie to Ryker. Because if anyone understood her, it was him. Even if he didn't accept or like some aspects of her, he understood.

Just like she understood him.

They were imperfect pieces that meshed together and made a whole. Even with different edges and sharpness, they still fit somehow. There was no logical way to describe it.

She wondered if all mating partners felt like this. Like they fit together, but didn't at the same time, a conundrum she was itching to decipher.

"I'm fine," she reiterated, with a lot more conviction in her voice.

Ryker grunted and started forward. She watched his back, her brows furrowed. Ryker... he'd always made her feel insecure, because he'd always been able to read her. There was something about being his mate that left her feeling shy, unsure in ways she wasn't comfortable with and didn't really understand.

They had to figure out a way to navigate their sudden mated status, toe past the lines that had been drawn before and find something new. A different path, a new way to treat one another.

Shula shuffled to catch up with him and when she did, her hand reached for his, fingers clasping firmly between the spaces of his. He almost tripped up at the contact, head snapping to stare at her so hard, she was afraid he sprained a muscle.

She held tightly to him, feeling the raised ridges of scarred flesh against her palm. His touch warmed her, though it didn't settle her unease.

"I'm afraid," she confessed, her voice whispering softly between them so only he could hear it.

His grip tightened on hers, an invitation to elaborate. Funny, how she could feel uncomfortable but understand the silence so perfectly.

"What if this Fae is stronger than me?" She hated giving a voice to her insecurity, but there it was. Like a wound she'd ripped open to let bleed. "You already think I'm weak." She fought the urge to take her fingers to her ears. "What if you see her and—"

Ryker yanked her to a sudden stop, nearly causing a prowling Weylyn to ram into their backs. He dodged, weaving around them with quick, lithe footsteps and went to catch up to the others.

The others who had no doubt heard her and were listening even now.

Her face heated.

"Don't you fucking dare," Ryker growled. "Just don't." She tried to force her gaze away, but he pulled her forward until their chests touched. His other hand came up to grip her chin hard enough to force their eyes to meet. His own were hard, the scars on his face pale compared to the olive, unmarked skin.

"Ryker..."

"You *were* a coward." She tried to look away, but his grip tightened. "Eyes on me," he grumbled. "You *were.* I will not lie to you just because we're mated now. That doesn't mean what I thought then has changed. But it doesn't matter what you were, or what you did. All that matters is *now.* And now? Now you are brave."

Tears prickled behind her eyes, but she refused to let them fall.

He was right, and it was going to take time to get past those thoughts of herself. She shouldn't compare herself to someone she hadn't even met yet.

It didn't matter what the other Fae was like. No two people were ever the same, and she needed to remember that, because no one else would remember it *for* her. No one else would be there to remind her.

Shula had to remind herself.

She was unique.

She was brave.

And she was ready to find the Fae.

The March to Porir

Shula's body slammed on the ground, and the air left her lungs in a single, wheezing breath. She rolled without catching it, using her shield arm to push herself to her feet. Her lungs were screaming at her and her legs were crying in pain, but she got up each time.

Her fingers cramped as she grasped the hilt of the sword, resuming her protective stance as her mouth opened to take in short, choppy breaths.

Julius prowled in front of her, a wicked smile on his face. His long orange hair, which he usually kept tied in a knot on his head, was loose and whipping against the wind, reminding her of the untamable licks of fire. A brown fur cloak was thrown over his shoulders, the hem trailing against his calves with each menacing step he took.

Ryker was big.

But Julius was bigger.

Made of pure muscle that bulged against the confining press of his green and brown clothes, his every blow hurt. Every time his sword clashed against hers or he put the full weight of his body to clash against Shula, she felt the reverberations shake through her skull.

It made her that much more determined to take him down.

"Your arms are still weak. Harden your stance, Fire Dancer," he instructed from across the space that separated them.

"I'm trying," she gritted out.

His smirk withered to a frown. "Try *harder*." And then he was charging towards her like a beastly animal, making the cold ground shake beneath her feet. She waited until he was close before she jumped to the side, her arm groaning as she swung her sword.

But Julius was a trained warrior. His blade met hers in a kiss of sparks that rained between them. He was stronger, and the clashing blow had her skidding back. She tried to find purchase in her feet to avoid falling again.

Julius smirked and she almost didn't see his shield coming towards her. She groaned as it pushed against her own. She swore the brute force made her bones snap. She screamed her pain, tears stinging her eyes, but she didn't give in.

She had more to prove than he did.

When they'd found her, she'd been little more than a scared Fae, too weak to use her own magic. He'd started to train her, honing her into a warrior she never knew she wanted to be.

Fighting was just like dancing in a way, except she couldn't follow the beating of the music precisely. She followed the sounds of his footsteps, the movements of his arms and her lithe feet jumped away as he advanced.

"Stop running and fight me," Julius growled, his eyes flashing.

She'd discovered early on that his Mana gifted magic was his superior strength, and the price of that magic was his rage.

She knew she could use that against him.

Shula smiled over her shield at him and said, "Make me."

He didn't rise to her bait, but he did growl, as if restraining his anger was getting harder with each passing second. "Clay," he called out to his best friend. "The Fire Dancer wants to play."

Shit.

Shula didn't take her eyes off Julius even as she heard Clay prowl near her. The slide of a sword against its sheath. His even breathing.

Her feet slowly edged to the side so she could catch a glimpse of Clay in her periphery. They were circling her, going in for the kill.

Clay was dancing on the balls of his feet, impatient and eager. He was the one who attacked first, running towards her with his sword raised and ready to swing. Shula twirled, raising her shield as the blade of his sword came down against it. She cried out as pain radiated up her arm, but then bit the sound back by gritting her teeth.

As he bounced back, she lowered her shield, swinging her sword. Their blades clanged together, just like she knew they would. She ducked away, dropping her sword. Using her now free hand, she yanked the heavy shield from her arm and swung it at Clay's back. He didn't see it coming, the force of the hit sending him sprawling to the ground.

Shula jumped onto his back, digging her heels into his spine, and leapt over him, diving for her sword just as Julius sprung.

She grabbed the hilt and brought it up in time for their steel to come together. It took every last ounce of strength left within her to hold her blade steady and keep it away from her face.

"Give up, Fire Dancer," Julius growled.

With a cry, she pushed against his blade and rolled. When she jumped to her feet, she felt the heel of his boot slam into her back. Pain zinged down her spine, and then against her front as she fell and hit the ground, tasting grass and dirt on her teeth. The wind left her at the impact and the tears came.

This time, she felt like she couldn't get up.

Her palms dug into a thin layer of snow as she tried to push herself up, gasping for breaths that wouldn't come.

"You're getting better." Julius' voice sounded far away. "But you aren't good enough yet."

The sting of tears was the worst part. Not the losing, but the evidence of her failure burning a path down her cheeks. *That* pain was almost too much to bear.

Julius never went easy on her. None of them ever did. So far, the only one she'd ever been able to take down had been Clay, and sometimes she had a feeling he let her win out of pity.

"Here, Fire Dancer, let me—" She felt Clay's touch against her shoulder. A touch that left as soon as a growl sounded.

Then Ryker was there, lifting her into his arms and turning her. She heard him curse, but everything else started to fade as the pain tried to drag her under.

"Breathe," Ryker ordered, palming her throat.

At the first kissing sting of his magic, she started to push him away. She hated when he tried healing her without warning. If only because she didn't want to inflict this on him. But it was too late. The golden-white glow of his healing magic enveloped her and her lungs opened, allowing her to suck in a breath. Every bruise she'd sustained in the past hour of training disappeared; every cut, every scrape, Ryker took into his own body and winced.

"You fucking shit." He whipped his head in Julius' direction. "You hurt her."

Julius waved Ryker's anger away with quick flicks of his wrist. "Yeah, yeah. Fuck off, Ry. She has to learn to fight somehow."

Before Ryker could retort, Shula pushed herself up from his hold and stood on newly energized legs.

"Again," she demanded.

Julius took a look at her then at Ryker's scowling face. "No, I think that's enough for today."

"I said *again.*"

"No."

She blew out a frustrated breath. "If you're denying me because of Ryker, then I can tell you right now, that asshole has no bearing in what I decide to do."

She heard Ryker's responding growl, felt him stand up. "What the fuck did you say?" he rumbled.

She whipped around to glare at him. "You heard me, asshole."

They were walking on the edge of that blurred line that separated what they were then and now. Perhaps they'd always balance on that delicate edge, unsure if they should fight or fuck. Or drown themselves in both equally.

"You think another round with Julius will help you defeat him?" He scoffed, and the sound grated down her nerves.

"You're such a fucking bastard."

He snapped his canines in a threat.

Julius whistled low. "I am very confused right now."

"Save your strength," Valerio cut in with sharp annoyance. "You will not learn to be a warrior overnight. It took us years to learn the art of the sword and you are trying to cram everything within a few months' worth of work. Now let's go. We have been here too long already. The closer we get to Porir, the better."

Shula gritted her teeth but didn't argue. Only because the Seelie Prince was right. They needed to get to Porir. Something was urging them on; the closer they got, the quicker the feeling built. It was anxiety, twisting at her gut, demanding, urging. And she had to answer the call.

There was a reason Mana wanted them here first.

Shula was almost afraid to find out why that was.

Days turned into a few weeks, and the snow thickened, the cold growing worse, slowing their trek through Teg. When they finally made it to Porir, they were exhausted and too weary to go straight to the Elemental, whose location shone brightly on the map in Shula's hands.

Valerio decided it was best if they all rested, so they snuck into the city. It was a feat that was surprisingly easy to do because it seemed... deserted.

Not that there weren't people, because there were, but it all seemed so dead. No soldiers littered the streets, and if they did, they stumbled across ice, too drunk to care what everyone else was doing.

And the most surprising part of it all?

Fae walked openly.

Shula knew they were Fae because some of them displayed their ears with pride down the streets, even while their posture spoke of anything but. Hunched and walking in sluggish strides, the Fae here looked more like corpses than anyone else Shula had ever seen, even within the reservations from her youth.

Melancholy seemed to shine over this city in a way she didn't understand. If they weren't being forced to hide, why were they so... depressed?

"What the fuck?" Clay echoed her thoughts.

They were hiding in the shadows, the line of them peering over the edge of darkness to catch glimpses at the Fae.

"Must be one of those Fae cities we've heard about," Julius rumbled. "Where they're so drenched in poverty the soldiers don't give a flying shit that they're even here."

They fell into silence after that, and Shula couldn't help but feel a strange sensation settle over her as she took their situation in.

Shula had never been free to walk openly like this, but at least she'd worn a smile on her face. At least she'd danced. At least she'd made friendships, for however long and however fake they may have been. They'd felt real enough to break the confines of her own sad cage at the time.

This was a different type of sadness. A sadness that seemed to bleed into the very bones of the city and spread like a disease. Like the iron that eroded deeply in Tir na Faie.

"Let's go," Valerio whispered, something in his voice that said he couldn't look at this any more than Shula could.

Because if this was what the city looked like, if this was what some of its people looked like, then what of their Fae Elemental? How broken was the Fae?

And how willing would they be to help?

She tried not to dwell too hard on that as they weaved their way into abandoned buildings, finding one that had no homeless humans or Fae, far enough from the street so they would be hidden in the shadows.

They spread out in the building, Weylyn taking first watch like always. He sidled up next to a broken window, peering out of it and listening intently. Shula leaned back against a wall, spreading her legs out in front of her and closing her eyes to sleep.

She must have fallen asleep for a moment, because she was jostled awake the next as Ryker dropped to the floor beside her. She eyed him warily.

"You aren't taking first watch?"

"Do you want me to leave?"

She didn't, but she didn't know how to say that, so she just gestured at the empty space beside her. He leaned back against the wall and closed his eyes.

For a moment she thought he'd already fallen asleep, but she felt the graze of his hand against her wrist.

"Magic," he grumbled.

She tilted her head in his direction. "What?"

"Next time you fight him use magic, too. He knows you've been holding back. That's why he wins. Use skill *and* magic and you'll best him."

Huh. She hadn't even realized she'd done that. Perhaps because when she'd started, she'd separated the different types of training and had never thought to meld the two together.

"Thank you," she whispered.

Ryker didn't reply.

He was already asleep.

Sometime later, Weylyn's urgent whispers woke them up. Shula jumped to her feet before her eyes were even fully opened, her hand gripping the hilt of her sword and unsheathing it.

When she opened her eyes, it was to find the others had done the same.

Weylyn peeked out at the window and gestured that they come look. Reluctantly, quietly, they went. It was then that Shula felt a rumbling on the ground, like the very earth was moving.

She held her breath as she looked outside to where Weylyn was gesturing, only to find a human soldier in the building across from them, gluing long strips of parchment, one after the other, onto the walls.

They were posters Shula had come to recognize almost immediately. She'd seen them often enough around other cities. Most recently, she'd seen one with the image of her own face on it.

Like the ones she was looking at now.

Her face and Valerio's.

"Fuck," she hissed.

"Listen," Weylyn ordered.

Her ears perked up.

The sun had already risen, though the sky seemed perpetually gray. Even with the snow covering the ground to quiet footfalls, there was no mistaking what the rumbling sensation was, or who had caused it.

She'd felt this kind of thing before.

Her eyes cut to Valerio's.

"Now we know why your instinct led us here first," the prince said. "The humans, they're marching to Porir."

Duty to the Fae

"This is a bad idea." Clay shuffled his feet in the rising snow. His breath puffed out in thick clouds.

Julius didn't know how the asshole managed to look so fucking *pretty* all the time. Nose red with the cold, the wind blew his hair against his forehead and cheeks. His eyes were bright in all the grayness surrounding them.

"You scared?" Julius taunted, unable to help himself. He liked fucking with Clay because he was his best friend, and Julius knew he could take anything he threw his way.

They'd been friends for years, before the wars that decimated Tir na Faie had depleted their numbers and changed their world forever. When Clay had still been a pretty little royal, stuck under his parents' thumb, whoring his way through the Sapphire Court out of boredom, and Julius had been a soldier in the court's ranks.

They should have never become friends. By all means, they should have avoided each other because they came from different backgrounds. But they shared something similar that drew them towards one another. An innate sense of wanting more, of having an urge to play, fuck, and fight. It was ingrained in their blood and it had brought them together, making them inseparable ever since.

"Fuck off, Darah." Clay scowled, shoving his hands into his pockets. The black fur cloak he wore did nothing to stave off the cold winds. It pierced through his rich, silk clothes. Garments he kept from his previous life that were still intact.

Julius had scoffed at the sight of them.

He'd always been more rugged, content in wool instead of silk, in leather and steel armor instead of velvet robes and golden jewelry. He was a hunter by nature, and that posh life missed by Clay and the other nobles, like the prince and the king, didn't make sense to Julius.

Sometimes he felt like the king was fighting so he could again have a feast at his table and a golden, gilded palace, instead of to save their race from starvation and turmoil.

But who was Julius to say any of that aloud?

"Try and keep up, little lord." Julius used the nickname because he knew Clay hated it. When his father had died years before the wars, he'd been crowned the High Lord Clay Valentino, favored cousin of the Prince of Seelie. "Our prince needs information, and we're meant to collect." With that being said, he started forward, long strides swallowing up the space between one building and the next. They hid through the shadows, catching glimpses of other hiding faces within broken down buildings.

Poor, frightened faces blurred as he ran, and he tried not to clench his fists or break down walls in his anger.

He knew poverty. He'd been born the lowest of the low in the Sapphire Court, living off game he hunted in Nach es Forest, sometimes fighting the little people of the wood for scraps. He'd had a hard childhood, until he'd been found by soldiers of the Seelie King's army and recognized for his Mana given strength.

They'd taken him in, trained him, given him purpose. To protect. To help others like himself.

Seeing his people reduced to hiding in moldy buildings pissed him off.

They deserved better.

Julius stopped just at the mouth of an alleyway that led off into a main street. Pressing his back to a wall, he peered to the side. The marching had stopped a few hours ago, the ground ceasing to tremble, but there were still soldiers patrolling the streets.

Clay pressed to the other side of the wall, watching in silence.

The soldiers were gathered in clusters, knocking on doors of what looked like homes and rented apartment buildings. When no one answered, they kicked in doors and stormed inside, hauling people out into the cold.

Julius' blood boiled as he watched them herd everyone together. They tore hysterical children away from their mothers, lining them up barefoot in the snow. Then, the soldiers went down the line of people, pressing iron to visible parts of their skin.

Those who didn't move were allowed back inside.

Those who flinched...

His teeth gritted as he watched the iron come down against a bare arm. Julius heard the hiss, saw the flinch, and a moment later the glamor fell to reveal an Unseelie Fae with bright yellow hair and green skin that crawled with vines.

There was shouting, resistance as they tried to tug him away, the slide of a blade, the swing of the sword.

A head toppled to the ground, buried in the snow.

He couldn't take his eyes off it.

Yellow and bright red.

Hair and blood.

"Julius," Clay hissed.

The harsh sound of his whisper cut Julius out of his thoughts, making him realize he was gripping the side of the building, crumbling brick into his fists. He opened his palms and let the debris drop.

Rage soared through him, the price he paid for using even the slightest bit of magic. Sometimes the anger was bearable and other times it was blinding. Overwhelming. It took over every other emotion and sense in his body until it was all he knew.

He felt the rage building, and only a part of it was because of the vibrating magic within his chest. The whole of it was because of what he witnessed as the minutes drug on.

Fae taken, killed without mercy. Humans were spared, even though some of them cried for the Fae they'd known as neighbors, friends, parents, *lovers.*

He tore his gaze away and found Clay staring at him, as if the scene beyond the alley was too horrifying for him to ingest and Julius was the only safe option while blood spilled around them.

"Let's go, little lord," Julius whispered, though there was no levity in his tone. "The prince awaits."

"Is the Fae still alive?" That was the first thing Julius asked as they barged into their hideout.

Shula was leaning against a corner, her hands in her pockets, eyes staring at the ceiling but also through it, as if she were somewhere else entirely.

At the sound of Julius' voice, she looked at him and slipped her hand into her pocket, pulling the map she carried around with her since they'd left Castle Aileach. She unfolded it and stared down, her brown-gold eyes squinting.

Because she saw something they couldn't.

"The light is still bright," she said, looking up and wrinkling her nose. "What's going on?"

Julius raked a hand through his hair. "We need to find them quickly. The soldiers are rounding everyone up and testing them with iron. They either kill or take the Fae away."

"Then we need to find the Elemental before the soldiers can." Valerio paced the ground, a sudden fervency in his movements that came out in short, clipped steps. He paused. "Julius, Uric, Ryker, *Weylyn...*" He turned to the Fae they all avoided and met his golden eyes. "You're coming with me." He turned back.

"Clay, Shula, you stay here until we get back. Shula, tell me exactly where she is."

Julius cut his gaze back over to Shula and watched her puzzled mien change. Her hands trembled, her body went taut, and beneath the parts of her visible skin, he could make out the beginnings of the soft glow of fire. He was familiar enough with her now to know when she was primed for a fight.

"Why can't I go with you guys?" she demanded.

"Because your face is splattered on every wall out in the streets, Fire Dancer," Julius answered for the prince.

She slashed a glare his way that let him know if they were facing off on the field, she'd go for the kill.

"So is Valerio's," she argued.

Valerio waved off her statement. "Your portrait is more recognizable than mine. You are not going."

Shula's nostrils flared. "Then I won't tell you the location."

Oh, shit.

Julius sighed, though a smirk touched the corner of his mouth, and propped himself against a wall, reaching to his holster to pull out his dagger to pick at his nails.

Shula was just getting started.

And he knew it was going to be a while.

Shula felt her anger build in a fiery sensation in her chest. How dare he? He, and all of them, were just as wanted as she was, and she was the only one capable of finding the next Elemental.

She also knew her threat was a low blow. The logical, calmer part of her mind said it didn't matter who found the Fae, as long as they were found. But the part inside her that she equated to *magic*, the fiery part attached to her soul blazed with anger and pride.

She was an Elemental, therefore it was her Mana given right to find this Fae.

Why should she stay behind? Was it because they didn't trust her even after she'd proved they could? Was she not *enough* for them? The insecurities threatened to drag her under, and she gave into it with the sharp rupture of anger.

"Shula," Valerio began, and she could hear the fraying notes of patience in his voice. "There are dozens of soldiers out there. We cannot risk you."

Her hands shook and she crumbled them into the map she held so they wouldn't see how much she was affected by those words.

"I am not your prisoner anymore, Valerio," she spat. "I am just as much a part of this as you all are."

Valerio's dark brows pulled together in a frown. "Of course you are not a prisoner, but that does not mean it is wise to take you with us."

"Why not?" She stepped forward, her voice rising an octave. "I can find the Fae. I can *help*."

She saw the moment Valerio's patience fell apart at the seams. He didn't raise his voice, but he was a prince, had commanded others since birth. He didn't need to shout. It was in the tone of command in his voice, using just the right timbre to sound mocking and belittling at once.

"Are you arguing so vehemently because you really want to help or is it because you want to prove to yourself that you are not as useless as you believe you are?"

Shock reeled her back, had her sucking in a sharp breath. Somewhere off to the side, Ryker growled, but the sound went ignored. She didn't want him to fight her battles for her, not when he'd said the same things about her not too long ago and with much more ire.

Her hands trembled again, and she was sure this time they could see it. "You all said it was my fight, too. You said it was my sacred duty as an Elemental to help save the Fae race. It's why you took me in the first place. Now I am here, willing to help, and you want to leave me behind!"

Valerio growled and stepped forward. His hands closed around the map and he ripped it from her grasp. She let it go before the parchment could tear, but it felt like he was taking something from her. Some integral part of herself that she didn't understand and had been trying to piece through the incongruity of it.

"Your sacred duty was to find the Fae, Shula. You are not a warrior and I will not have you trying to prove to be something you are not. So you will tell me where the Fae is and you will stay here. That is an order from your prince."

His nostrils were flaring and she leaned away from him. For a split second, she was afraid of him, because she remembered exactly what type of magic he wielded and what he could force into her mind at any time. He'd done it once to keep her in line, poured wretched visions into her brain that seemed like reality.

She curled her fingers into her palms and let out a breath filled with smoke and the stench of burning wood.

"Fine," she gritted out. "The map said she was at Porir City Zoo."

Valerio didn't utter another word as he turned and walked away.

Betrayals and Disobedience

The thing about Prince Valerio's order was this: he wasn't *her* prince, and therefore she wasn't beholden to his obstinate request. Just because she had joined the Resistance, it didn't mean she was trading one tyrant for another.

She waited until they were gone, disappearing through Uric's portal before she turned to Clay. He was staring at her warily and with eyes full of compassion.

It's what made betraying him even harder.

"Valerio is—"

"An asshole," she interrupted.

He smiled sheepishly. "Well, I got all the charm in the family and he got all the brood."

Shula blinked at him. "Family?"

Clay slumped into a corner, dropping his head against the wall. "Cousins. Our mothers were sisters. Noble ladies from the Sapphire Court."

Shula's eyes widened. "So, you're actually a lord. Lord Clay..." She broke off and snorted. While she could see him being royalty, she couldn't see him being a good lord of a manor. His demeanor didn't seem to allow the same veneration as Valerio.

"Yeah, make fun, get it out. Julius never ceases to remind me."

She made her way to his side and plopped next to him, leaning back. "Where were you when everything went to shit?" she whispered.

It always seemed like such a personal question. To ask when their worlds turned upside down, who'd they'd lost, what they'd lost.

Shula wasn't old enough to know. She hadn't even lived those times. She'd lived her own brand of torment, she knew what these laws against the Fae caused, the hurt they weaved. But she didn't know all of it because she'd been born into the cruelty.

Perhaps it had been a harsher punishment to watch the Fae's downfall. To know paradise only to lose it soon after. At least her life had been consistent in its despair. At least she didn't long overmuch for something she'd never had in the first place. Not like them.

"In the Seelie Court," he said, a note of melancholy in his voice. "King Ashera called the lords of the courts away from their seats to advise him on what was happening with the humans." He picked at a stray string of his cloak. "My father had died a few years before, which made me High Lord of the Sapphire Court. It was a job I didn't want and was terrible at, but I went because my mother urged me to."

She heard the note of respect when he mentioned his mother. If his mother was all he'd ever had, then it was no wonder Clay loved women. Respected them. She could glean all that from the wistful note in his voice alone.

"Anyway, it's a long story. But while we were with the king, the Sapphire Court fell."

He didn't need to say the words for her to read between the lines. The Sapphire Court fell, along with his mother.

Her heart ached for him.

"I'm sorry about your mother," she whispered, shifting so she faced him.

He smiled. "Me, too."

"And I'm sorry about this, too."

His face registered confusion a moment before her fist whipped out and struck him on the side of the head. He gasped, jerking back, but she struck out again and again until he finally slumped to the ground.

"I'm really sorry." But she didn't have any more time to waste.

When Valerio had taken the map and all but yelled at her, he hadn't given her a moment to explain that the Fae was *leaving* Porir City Zoo.

Even without the map, Shula could find her way to the Elemental. She hadn't told them, but ever since arriving, she'd felt a stirring inside her. Right beside the space that occupied her magic. Something inside her grew restless, banging against the walls of her soul, reaching with phantom fingers to find something that wasn't quite in its reach.

Shula identified it quickly. The part of Mana that tethered her to the other Elementals was reaching out, demanding she find the Fae.

They were close, and she wouldn't rest until she found them.

She slipped her own cloak on and grabbed her sword. She wanted to grab her shield, but figured it would draw more attention than just a sword so opted to leave it. Once she had everything, her features cloaked behind a hood, she left their hiding place and went in search of the other Elemental.

⁂

She followed the tug of her own consciousness, like a thread pulling at her soul, like the will-o'-the-wisps of the forest she'd followed weeks ago. The ones that led to her destiny.

She used every ounce of her skill to move as quickly and discreetly as the snow would allow. But when the world was covered in white, it was hard to hide in the shadows of daybreak.

Her heart thundered, breaking into a faster tune with every furious step she took. A sudden tug was felt somewhere deep inside her and she followed the direction her instinct took her towards.

She turned a corner, caught a quick glimpse of a rushing body. And something deep inside her sang a song of power. Raw and begging, like Mana had slipped inside and whispered the words, *"That's the Fae..."*

She started forward to chase after the Fae and froze as a mirror opened in the air in front of her, and Uric stepped through.

She skidded back against the snow, a curse pushing past her lips as he darted forward, quick and lethal, wrapping his arms around her upper body and yanking her back into the portal.

They fell through darkness a moment before they came out standing on the other side, her limbs thrashing against Uric's hold.

He shoved her away unkindly and she whirled, gnashing her lengthening canines only to realize she was right back where she started. Only, instead of an empty room, she was surrounded by a group of angry Fae males.

"Fuck."

Valerio was in front of them all, and for the first time since she'd met him, anger marred the sharp lines of his features. A murderous, burning anger.

Uric stepped back next to his prince, arms crossed against his chest. Clay stood on his other side, his brown-blonde hair plastered against his temple with blood. She was too cowardly to meet her friend's gaze. She'd rather face Valerio's anger than Clay's hurt.

"I gave you an order," Valerio growled.

"A stupid order."

Uric snapped his canines at her, his black eyes flaring with fury at her reply. "Careful how you speak to our prince, Fire Dancer."

"He's not *my* prince."

Uric took a step forward and there was no pretending it was anything but menacing. "He became your prince the moment you came into our fold willingly. He became your prince the moment Ryker fixed those abominable ears of yours."

Magic surged through her veins and fire danced in her eyes. She saw the reflection of the flames against the marble surface of Uric's black gaze, but he didn't step back in fear. His lips thinned in a challenge.

A challenge that pulsed between them like a living thing.

Ryker's scarred hand clamped down against Uric's shoulder and yanked him backwards, out of Shula's space.

"Uric," Ryker growled in warning.

"Fuck off, Valda." Uric's pale hand flashed and suddenly there was a knife in his hand. He had the blade kissing Ryker's throat, just beneath his thick beard.

"Enough!" Valerio cut in, raising his voice. The command had Uric lowering the blade immediately and sheathing it again. Valerio turned to Shula and she knew she wasn't staring at someone she might have considered a friend in this moment, but at the Seelie Prince. A cruel, unforgiving prince. "When I give an order, I expect it to be followed."

Her arms crossed against her chest defiantly. "You expect us to blindly follow your orders like we're your subservient slaves and you're our tyrant ruler."

He snarled and stepped in front of her. For a moment, she knew true fear that passed as quickly as it came. "Do not presume me to be the Emperor of Illyk, Shula Azzarh. These men follow me and my father because we are just. I give orders and they follow them, because when they are not, someone dies. Be lucky it was not you this time."

The reality of his words were cold as they sluiced over her like water. Still, she felt the oppressive weight of needing to contradict him.

"I was fine on my own. I found the Fae and if Uric hadn't—"

"If Uric had not grabbed you when he did, soldiers would have found you. Did you even notice they were right around the corner?"

She pressed her lips together. She hadn't noticed, and she wondered how *they* had, but kept her lips clamped tightly shut. He'd probably had Weylyn spying in on her thoughts. Insufferable, mind-reading, Fae bastard.

Valerio read the response in her expression easily enough. "You did not. Because no matter what you want to believe you are *not a warrior.* You are a dancer who, up until a few months ago, did not even use her own magic. You do not know how to fight, you do not know how to work as a unit, which is why I expect you to follow my fucking orders when I give them."

He was so close, the edges of his dark hair brushed along her cheeks.

"You are used to being alone. You are not alone now. *We* will handle it. And you? You will stay here and hide. Because up until a few months ago? That is all you were good for anyway."

He stepped away from her, no trace of kindness in him at all. He was nothing but a leader, a noble.

A prince.

A true tyrant, laying heartbreak and havoc in his wake, turning and walking away without caring what he left behind. Tears, shaking hands, and the words that pierced her worse than any sword ever could.

Useful to the Fae

Fucking females, Valerio fumed silently as he stepped out of the portal with Uric, Weylyn, and Ryker. This time, he'd made Julius stay behind to wrangle Shula if she got another stupid idea to go off on her own.

Fucking females.

"Don't bother looking," Uric snapped at Weylyn as he started walking down the alley. "The Fae is long gone by now."

Weylyn cocked his head to the side in a silent question. Before he could use his magic to pierce Valerio's mind, the prince scowled. "We need to come up with a plan. There are too many soldiers, and with our faces plastered against every building, we will be too recognizable."

Silence followed as they all seemed to think, trying to come up with a solution to their problem. All save for Ryker.

Valerio felt the daggers in his bicolored stare that he was sending in his direction.

Valerio sighed and turned to meet his gaze. "Say it," he ordered. Because he knew his healer was itching to snap his canines.

Mated males, Valerio wanted to scoff. *Territorial, defensive bastards.*

"You were too harsh," he grumbled.

Valerio's eyebrow rose. "I merely spoke the same truth you have been telling her since you met."

Ryker's jaw clenched so hard, Valerio was surprised he didn't snap a few teeth. He tore his gaze away from the prince and muttered, "That's different."

"How?" Valerio's eyes narrowed. "Because she's your mate?" He hated saying the words, feeling like they burned on his tongue.

But he didn't want to visit why they did. A single glance over at a smirking Weylyn let him know that the other Fae knew exactly what he was thinking.

Fucking bastard.

"We have an understanding," Ryker said simply.

Valerio didn't bother to ask him to elaborate because he didn't care what kind of understanding they had between them. He was still their prince, and when he gave an order, it should be obeyed.

He may not have been a king, may not have been his father, but he deserved the same level of respect.

"She wants to prove herself," Ryker continued slowly, as if he were debating speaking these words at all. "She wants to be useful to us."

"Her existence makes her useful enough." Uric waved an impatient hand in Ryker's direction.

Valerio shot Uric a look to keep him silenced. They were in too precarious a position to start arguing now. "She has nothing else to prove. Being on our side is enough."

Ryker let out a growl and looked away, his lips thinning together as if he wanted to say more. For a moment, Valerio thought he would hold his tongue, but Ryker spoke again. "I know very well what she used to be and that there is still so much she has yet to learn as a warrior, but I know she can help us find this Fae."

He contemplated words while Uric scoffed at them. "We don't have time for her *feelings*. There are more important things."

Like finding the second Fae Elemental.

Like learning how to be invisible so they could walk freely among Porir without the soldiers discovering them...

He held his hand up and the arguing near him silenced. His breathing picked up and his lips twisted into a smile.

"I have an idea."

A Taste of Blood

Clay pouted against the wall, rubbing his palm over his head wound, smearing the blood further into his light hair.

Julius snorted at him and shook his head. "Can't believe you let her get you."

"Fuck off. She caught me off guard."

Julius laughed quietly. Apparently, the Fire Dancer had got him good. She was a tricky little thing. Better Clay than Julius. At least he wouldn't be the one to incur Valerio's wrath for letting her get away.

And Valerio was a mean son of a bitch when he was pissed.

Even after they'd left Julius and Clay alone with Shula to go hash out their plan, he'd come back with a furious expression. He'd taken them both to the side, telling them what he wanted them to do.

The Seelie Prince had looked Clay in the eye and all but growled, "Can I trust you to do *that* at least?" It had made Clay flush a shade shy of Julius' hair color, much to his amusement.

"What happened was you dropping your guard around a pretty face, just like you always fucking do," Julius told Clay.

"Like you don't get stupid for a pretty woman." He didn't even bother to try and deny it.

"I love women." Julius smiled. "Love what they have to offer. Love what I can offer *them.*" He sighed almost wistfully. The last time he'd had a woman... Fuck, it had been way too long. Years, it felt like, though the reality was that it had probably only been months. Fighting and plotting had taken up so much of his time lately that he almost forgot what it felt like to have a female riding on top of him. "But I don't get stupid over them like you do."

He knew why Clay got stupid over women. Julius loved them, but no one loved them as much as his best friend. It ran deeper than just lust. He actually listened, enjoyed their minds, their thoughts. Julius knew it had to do with his mother, like he saw bits of her in every woman he encountered.

Julius was happy enough to fuck them and leave them, befriend them if they were nice enough. He just couldn't understand why Clay was so invested in

Shula. She was beautiful, sure, he wasn't *blind.* Julius just enjoyed his women a little... *more.* She was Ryker's, besides.

"Whatever. What's taking so damn long?" Clay complained, peering around the corner of the wall. He jerked back. "Shit, soldiers are coming."

Julius smiled, unsheathing his sword. The slide of the metal was music to his ears. "How many?"

Clay peered again. "Two."

"Perfect."

Julius stepped out into the night. His sword gleamed against ice and silver moonlight, illuminating the white of his feral, canine smile.

The soldiers froze at the sight of him.

He couldn't make out their features beneath the helms they wore, but he caught a flash of recognition in their eyes, because he'd tied his hair up to reveal his pointed ears. So they could know exactly who was killing them.

The acrid scent of their fear reached his nostrils and his canines snapped together, anticipation building with every passing second.

The humans stumbled, pulling their swords from their sheaths, and Julius laughed as he brought his own blade up to his face. They watched him like he was a reaper of their own legends. But he was much worse.

At least their reapers took souls and let them move on.

Julius was here to destroy them.

His tongue slid against the flat part of steel. "Come and get me," he urged, his eyes dancing dangerously. "My blade wants to taste human blood tonight."

And so it did.

Julius and Clay came back hours later, well into the night. Piled into their hands, they carried folded, bloody leather and steel, which they dropped to the ground with matching smirks.

Shula tried to meet Clay's eyes, but he looked away and she felt a pang of hurt in her chest. She knew she deserved his ire and indifference after what she'd done. She'd betrayed her friend, had hurt him and escaped.

She needed to grovel to earn his forgiveness, because she knew she'd fucked up.

He was the only one who treated her with respect and kindness, had been since the beginning, and she might have ruined a genuine friendship because of her stubborn need to prove that she could be just as good as any of them or as any Elemental that they were out to find.

She'd created an image of this Fae in her head and it wouldn't leave. She was trying to show up a phantom personality.

Shula had never been this competitive before. Determined? Yes. Stubborn? Yes. Competitive? There were strange lines drawn in the ground with this situation. She didn't quite know where she would fit once they found this new Fae. She was going to help them, but she wasn't sure if she could handle being known as the coward of the group.

She pulled her hair over her ears, paused, then pushed them away so they were showing.

"They put up a fight," Julius said, his eyes dancing with laughter. Blood was flecked on the corner of his mouth and he made no move to wipe it off. "Two uniforms, Your Highness."

Valerio stepped forward, toeing the humans' garments. A tight smile pulled at his lips. "Excellent. The two of you will wear them and find the Fae."

Shula's hands curled in her lap. She was growing all too familiar with anger, but she was frustrated, too. She still felt like it was her *right* to find the Fae. Destiny came to mind when she thought about it.

It wasn't just about impressing them, showing this group of Fae males what she was capable of, but also something deeper than that.

Shula pushed herself to her feet. "Let me go," she pleaded, hating the desperate note in her own voice.

Valerio cut her a glare and just as easily dismissed her. "No."

She stepped towards him, only to be blocked by Uric. She frowned at the overprotective Fae and looked over his shoulder at the prince.

"Please."

"No."

"I will be able to convince this Fae to join our side," she tried again.

"So can we."

Shula scoffed in the prince's direction, making him frown. "What do you plan on telling this Fae?" she asked, pressing her hands to her hips. " *'We are the Resistance!'* " she mimicked, then snorted.

It finally caught Clay's attention. He shot her a look and she shrugged apologetically.

"Sorry, Clay, but that was so idiotic. Nothing any of you could have said at the time would have convinced me."

Valerio's eyes narrowed. "But convince you we did."

"By kidnapping me? You have no idea who you are dealing with or if this Elemental will kill you before you try. And you didn't convince me. I convinced myself."

There was silence, and Shula counted the heartbeats before Valerio answered.

"You do not follow orders. I cannot risk it."

She gritted her teeth. "I'm an Elemental. The Fae will believe me over you."

"No, Shula." His tone spoke of finality and she knew that it didn't matter what she said. He wasn't going to agree.

It seemed hopeless to argue at this point. Valerio was set on his decision, and as much as she wanted to fight it, it was futile. Shula believed she was right, that she could convince the Elemental to join them, just like she knew the prince was underestimating her.

There wasn't going to be another opportunity to slip past them to do it herself, so she turned and settled in for the night. Resigned to do what the prince ordered, she let her eyes drift closed as they spoke in hushed whispers around her, words she couldn't quite make out and didn't care to anyway. She seethed in her own anger, tugging at the end of her hair and curtaining them over her ears while they talked.

Then she felt a presence beside hers. Not Ryker's. She turned and was faced with the bloody side of Clay's head.

"Fire Dancer," he began softly. "Talk to me."

She sighed, shoving her hair away. "I'm sorry, Clay."

His bright eyes were searching and hurt, and she hated herself for that. She didn't want him to doubt their friendship. She didn't want him to think that she took joy out of putting her hands on him, out of hurting him, but she'd seen no other way. It made her feel like scum.

"Why?" he asked. "Are you just trying to prove something? Because you don't have to."

"Maybe a part of me is, but there's something else, too. Finding out you're the last of your kind is *big.* Finding out the Emperor of Illyk is searching for you and wants to *use* you? That's even worse. This Fae, whoever she or he is, is like me. I feel a connection here, and I know they will too, because Mana binds us. It's just... nice to feel like you aren't alone. And I thought I could connect with this Elemental. At least in that."

Clay sighed and gripped her knee, squeezing it. "Get some sleep, Fire Dancer," he urged. "We'll talk more in the morning." He started to stand, paused. "Oh, and no hard feelings about knocking me out. Just... don't do it again, yeah?"

That's how Shula fell asleep.

With a smile on her face.

Cut From the Same Cloth

"You need to let her go."

Valerio's arms were crossed against his chest, and the low timbre of his whispering voice suddenly halted as Clay approached them. Uric cut a glare in Clay's direction, which he ignored, and Julius didn't acknowledge him save for the slightest tilting of his lips.

Clay waited impatiently for a response, his brows pulling tightly over his eyes.

Valerio resumed his whispering as if Clay hadn't even spoken.

"Did you hear me?" he interrupted again. "I said you need—"

"How silly of me to forget that you had been crowned a prince and are now the leader of this group. What other explanation, since you presume to command me so?"

"Cut the shit, cousin."

Valerio blinked and turned slowly. That had gotten his attention because it wasn't always that Clay actually acknowledged the relation between them. While he held his cousin in high esteem, he wasn't as close to the prince as Uric was. They were just too different—blood of their mothers be damned.

They both adored their mothers over their fathers. The two had been cut from the same cloth, but they'd raised two completely different males.

"Let Shula go find the Elemental," he whispered, stepping closer.

"Did the blow to your head render you into a complete imbecile? She is not going. That was an order."

"She can do it." He resisted the urge to turn and look at the Fae in question where she lay, already settled in for the night.

"The only thing she can do is disobey orders. I cannot risk her life or the group's well-being if she cannot follow my orders."

"How do you expect her to follow orders if you don't give her the chance to prove herself?" Clay challenged.

Valerio growled, the warning low and threatening. Clay didn't even blink at the prince's displeasure or at the menacing vibes Uric gave up. He was well aware that the silver Fae's hand grasped the hilt of his dagger, and he had no doubt he would threaten to use it on Clay if he spoke another word.

Clay snorted. "I am not afraid of your growls, cousin. Answer me this; why won't you let her do it? You know she's a fast learner and she's picked up fighting well enough. She's proved she can melt iron and save all our asses, so what's the fucking problem?"

His jaw tightened, but his expression otherwise remained calm and collected. Clay almost wouldn't have noticed, but he caught the way his eyes flicked towards her over Clay's shoulder. And Clay didn't need to turn to know that Ryker had already settled in next to his mate.

"Oh, this is rich." Laughter bubbled from Clay's chest.

"What is?" Julius was already stripping, having obviously tuned out of the ensuing argument in favor of peeling away his traveling clothes, layer by layer, exposing his hulking body to the cold air.

Ignoring his friend as he stuffed a thick leg into the tight, leather uniform, Clay stepped closer towards Valerio.

"We're cut from the same cloth, cousin, just like our mothers were." He smirked and it took that single look to convey everything he wanted to say. He wasn't going to out his cousin in front of everyone. The poor prince probably had enough to worry about, what with Weylyn reading his thoughts every chance he could get. He didn't need that type of betrayal, too.

There would be time to speak of his cousin's reasoning later, when the threat of other ears weren't around to hear his confession. One that had felt all too obvious when he looked close enough. That wasn't important, though. It was important that he got his head out of his ass and let Shula become a part of them like anyone else in this fucking room.

The prince's eyes narrowed with the realization that Clay knew why he was so adamant on keeping Shula right where she was.

"Don't worry, prince, your secret is safe with me. Now, will you let her go or not? She's ready and you fucking know it."

There was a moment of contemplative silence in which Clay smirked, but at the same time held his breath. Then Valerio turned without another word.

Clay tried not to smile too wide.

Because he knew that he had won.

"Wake up." A boot nudged her leg.

Shula's eyes flew open, and she found herself staring up at Valerio and Julius. She blinked away the grogginess and extricated herself from Ryker's hold. She wasn't sure when he'd sidled next to her in the night, hadn't even felt his arms wrap around her.

"What's going on?" She sat up and stared at Julius.

He was clad in a human soldier's uniform, but it looked to be a size too small, nearly bursting at the seams. He looked rather uncomfortable in the whole thing, and even the helm looked like it squeezed his head.

Valerio smirked mirthlessly down at her. "Put on the uniform," he said. "You're going with Julius to find the Elemental."

Shula shot to her feet. "Really?"

"Yes."

Without realizing what she was doing, she threw her arms around Valerio and hugged him close for a second before she was yanked out of his arms by a suddenly awake and growling Ryker.

"Shula?"

"Yeah?" She picked up the clothes, hefting them in her arms.

Valerio's eyebrow rose. "Just try to follow orders this time."

The Strength of Ice

They'd prowled all morning until they finally found the Fae. A female that Julius had caught a glimpse of from far away. She wore gray all over, a pale, drab color that offset the rich, dark color of her skin. White curls peeked out from over the collar of her gray fur coat, hair that hid the evidence of her ears, making it impossible to see if they were pointed or not.

But the moment Shula saw the female, a gasp pushed past her lips.

"That's her," she said.

So Julius watched, and they followed her, splitting up. Because they were dressed as soldiers—soldiers the female was going out of her way to avoid—Julius knew it was better to corner her, catch her off guard. Shula took to the ground, while Julius took to the unstable roofs of the buildings.

That way, he had a better vantage point of the Elemental.

They still weren't sure what kind of magic she possessed, so they had to be cautious. Especially, taking one look at her figure beneath her coat, Julius knew instinctively she wasn't the type to stand idly by.

She was the type of female Julius enjoyed. Strong, capable. Her legs were long and muscular, a body thick with the strength of someone who was no stranger to hard work. She wasn't square, as she gave off the subtle hint of curves, but she was thick in the most perfect of ways.

He waited on a building, peering over the edge and standing on a crouch. The Fae slipped into a building a few ways down, and he saw Shula prowling in the darkness towards her. But when the Fae stepped out, she paused, head cocking to the side.

As if she could hear Shula from around the corner, feet crunching in the snow.

Fuck.

The Elemental burst into a run. He heard Shula cry out softly as she followed. Their footfalls against the snow echoed loudly, and he let out a curse, even as the thrill of the hunt vibrated through his system.

He ran, jumping from one rooftop to the next, praying the decaying buildings would hold his heavy weight. He was ahead of the Elemental while Shula stalked her from behind. She was *fast*, her body darting between alleyways and turning sharply around corners. She caught up near the building where Julius was and she turned, gauging the distance between her and Shula.

Julius took advantage of her distraction and jumped from the building.

He landed on the ground with a thud and a crouch, looming to his full height over her.

She was tall, and he finally caught a good look at her face and her scent.

Smooth, ebony skin, piercing dark eyes, plump lips, round nose, and a slightly squared jawline all made for the perfect face. She smelt like the delectable combination of ice, apples, and mint, scents he associated with his childhood and the freedom of the forest. The sight of her beauty almost had him staggering back. But it wasn't that. Not exactly. It was magic. A magic so unrecognizable it jolted through his system like a bolt of cold lightning down his spine.

He was surprised, but no more surprised than her.

She seemed intimidated by his size and staggered back a step while he pushed forward. His hands shot out, encircling her wrists. The touch sent a zing through his body and he opened his mouth to speak.

He didn't see the blow coming.

Her knee connected to his dick, and he felt the pain shoot up to his throat. A whimper pierced past his mouth and he dropped to his knees, the helm slipping from his head. The impact was jarring, but not as jarring as the pain in his groin. He wanted to reach for it, but a moment later he was struck with cold. His gaze darted down to see ice spreading from the Elemental's fingertips all over the lower half of his body, keeping him pinned in place.

That answered the question of what kind of Elemental she was.

"Fucking dick face!" she snapped, and then she was running past him.

Fuck.

He tugged against the ice, but it kept him as still as a statue, immobilizing his arms and legs.

Footsteps sounded down the alley and a moment later, Shula appeared. She took one look at him, scoffed, and ran to catch up to the fleeing woman.

Double fuck.

Rage boiled through his body, bursting out of him in magic. It surged through him and he groaned, flexing his muscles until he heard a crack as the ice holding him down began to break apart into chunks on the ground.

He groaned, letting that strength take space at the forefront, even while he was consumed by ever-growing rage. The ice broke apart, showering around him like crystalline sparks. He stood and whirled, a growl rumbling deep in his chest. His canines snapped and he tilted his face up, nostrils flaring as he scented his prey.

He was a hunter, and he would find the Elemental.

The angry part of him made him want to make her pay.

An even bigger part of him wanted to see what else the Fae was capable of, because Julius liked his women strong, with a cold bite of fury. Women who could take him down with a single burst of magic.

Or a well-placed kick to the dick.

His rage and amusement swelled in equal measure as he turned and followed after the two women. He went after Shula's familiar scent of fire and confection and the newer, more pleasant scent of apples and mint and ice, and the sound of their clashing raw magic. Of fire and ice warring against one another as viciously as enemies. The two women groaned and cried out as they were blasted back from the collision.

Shula fell to the ground, and so did the other Fae, but she recovered first, standing and watching Shula warily.

Then Shula stood, lowered her hood, and began to speak.

"We've been looking for you."

Julius made himself known, walking up behind Shula. And for a moment, the beauty in the ice Fae's expression halted him. It was gripping, hypnotizing, and a sliver of magic burst through his chest, through his soul, and nestled inside. It became something primal, demanding. Something he'd never thought he'd feel yet recognized right away.

A wildness like the drumbeats and dancing of the little people of the wood he used to revel with in his youth. This was that same adrenaline-filled feeling, and he couldn't hold back the single growl that rumbled in his chest or the savage thought that ripped straight through his mind.

Mine.

Ice clashed against fire, and the ice didn't melt, and the fire continued to burn.

The raw magic of Mana burst through Shula's veins, and when it collided against a strong line of ice, all she could feel was a *connection.* One so fierce, it made her knees tremble and her lip quiver. And it made her strong too.

She hadn't understood what it meant to be an Elemental in this capacity. Not until she had another one so close. Because she felt something like instinct kick to life inside of her. Something fizzled between their strands of magic, and the proximity made her feel strength eddy inside her.

And then it exploded and Shula fell back, colliding against the ground. The breath whooshed out of her on impact, but she scrambled to her feet, trying to appear the picture of calm. As calm as the Elemental Fae across from her evidently was.

She was *strong*. Not strong because Shula was close. She seemed powerful enough all on her own that for a minute, self-consciousness threatened to overwhelm the fire Fae, but she pushed the insecurities away and tilted her head up. Her fingers went to her hair, pushing the strands away from her ears so the pointed tips were visible.

Dark eyes flicked to them for a brief second before settling on her face again. There was a sort of fascination in her gaze and a challenge.

Shula stepped forward cautiously. "Hello," she said. "My name is Shula Azzarh, and I've been looking for you." She heard Julius' steps behind her and amended her statement, "*We've* been looking for you."

"Why?" the Fae demanded. Shula didn't know her name, but she suddenly felt a flicker of admiration for her because of that tone and her ferocity alone.

"Because," she replied. There was so much she could say. So much she wanted to say. So many words that she wished had been said to her but hadn't been. And what came out of her mouth next wasn't what she'd meant. They were words she regretted almost as instantly as she said them, if only because she had mocked Clay for them, and she knew he would mock her as well. "We are the Resistance."

Mates

Iona stared at the two.

Fae.

She should have realized the hulking, handsy stranger was Fae, but his ears were hidden behind flaming hair. He was too big to be human, and he'd obviously broken out of her ice somehow, something very few would have been able to do unless with the aid of magic or superior strength.

As for the female, Shula Azzarh, she was an Elemental. Iona could feel their connection like a vital thing, flowing between the two of them. Even *so*, even when all her life she had thrown herself into executing the will of Mana and following her own gut instincts, she was reluctant.

If only because the Fae male was staring at her like he meant to devour her whole.

"The Resistance is dead," Iona declared. Her voice didn't tremble, but her mind was a maelstrom of thoughts. "I should know. I watched them fall." Right before she'd left the chaos of a lost battle, led to a boat to get her race to safety. Right before the accident, followed by the storm that swept in and she was swallowed by unforgiving wet arms that had deposited her right here in Teg.

"They're alive. Small, but alive." The fire Fae's cheeks were bright, golden-brown skin darkening to a reddish hue.

"Okay, is that supposed to mean something to me?" She didn't want to admit to these strangers that it did. A majority of her life, she'd fought with the Resistance to take her home back. They'd lost, and it was one of the darkest days of her life, to watch everything she loved fall to the hands of greed and selfishness.

Now this fire Fae was here, telling her that what she'd said goodbye to so long ago was alive?

Her first instinct was to pick up a sword and fight at their side again.

But she eyed their uniforms warily. What were a couple of Fae doing wearing the emperor's colors?

"It's a long story," Shula said, as if reading her mind, shuffling from one foot to another. It was a shy, vulnerable gesture, so quick and gone in a flash before she steeled her spine, matching Iona's defensive stance. "The point is, you're an Elemental, and the Resistance needs your help."

Iona scoffed, though the sound was merely for show. The truth was, she didn't precisely know what she should be feeling with these revelations except abject shock. "So we can fight another losing battle?" Shula opened her mouth to argue, but Iona continued before she could. "Look, how do I even know you're telling the truth? Why would I blindly trust either of you?" Her gaze strayed to the orange-headed Fae, who was vibrating with tension, his green eyes swallowing her up in his heated gaze. She pulled back from that, trying to ignore the bite of magic and pull emanating from him, and turned back to Shula. "From where I'm standing, the both of you look like enemies."

A slivering sensation rolled down her back, Mana berating her for all that, no doubt. She always followed Mana's instincts, always. She'd seen what had happened when she ignored it, but even so, she felt wary about them.

Even more so when the ginger Fae stormed past Shula, nearly knocking her to the side, and stomped close to Iona. She gasped at his proximity and stepped back. The anger rolling off his body was a palpable thing and crashed over her body like the waves of a black ocean. His muscles bulged against leather and steel, the veins on his neck standing out, looking ready to snap.

He was pissed. Because she'd kneed him? Well, he'd grabbed her first, and she wasn't going to apologize for that. She tried to stand her ground, but he was too intimidating, too close, too much.

She stepped back until her back pressed tightly against the cold walls of the building behind her.

He loomed over her, everything about him threatening.

"Julius!" Shula snapped a warning, but he didn't listen to his companion.

He pressed close. Their bodies touched, every hard inch of him against every soft inch of her. There was no crevice for wind to blow through between them. He bent. She was tall, but he was taller, lowering a fraction. She caught the flare of his nostrils as he breathed her in. His hand lifted and instinct and fear had her magic shooting out.

A block of ice covered that hand that reached for her. He looked at it, like it was a nuisance, and with a flex of his fingers, the ice broke into fragmented shards around them.

Holy Mana.

Fuck.

Her thighs shifted at that display of strength and she leaned back against the wall.

The male—Julius—seemed angrier, but when his hand lifted again, it wasn't to strike her, but to grip her at the back of the neck and drag her close. Her body, treacherous thing that it was, followed with little fight.

The feel of his fingers digging into her skin should have been a warning, but all Iona felt was a rapid-building warmth flowing through her veins. She stood on the tips of her toes as he tugged her closer until his nose grazed against the tip of hers.

Their eyes met, her palms pressing against his chest, unsure if she wanted to shove him away or keep herself steady as he pulled her closer.

Probably to keep her steady.

Because the next moment, she felt the slamming sensation of magic snap deep into her soul. Something similar to when she'd met her familiar but sharper, more aggressive and demanding, falling into place right next to her soul.

Julius must have felt it too, because it brought a smile to his lips before he growled out a single word that tilted Iona's world off its axis.

"Mate."

And then his lips came crashing down on hers, and all she knew was the taste of his tongue, the scrape of his teeth, as their magic and a sliver of their souls nestled together in an unbreakable bond that was a gift from Mana itself.

The Bonds of Mana

He tasted like magic and smelt even better. He gave off a woodsy scent. Like earth and grass and leather and ale.

He was dominating, and she was aware of everything. Of the way his blunt nails dug into the back of her neck, the way he held her tightly against him while caging her against the wall. Of the scrape of his canines against her lips right before his tongue delved into her mouth, slashing against her own like he was asserting dominance.

She was lost in the sensation for a second. The bond settled between them and she felt it. It pulsed right next to the living fragments of her magic, next to the bond with her familiar, but fiercer. It was more prominent, severe, settling in place like he belonged there.

And Iona supposed he did. A part of him inside her because Mana demanded it. Her thighs trembled, quivered with the sensation of desire that coursed, hitting her like the blow of a shield against the body.

It threatened to drown her in it.

And yet...

Her knee came up, connecting between his legs once again. He groaned at the sudden onslaught of pain, ripping his lips from hers and she took advantage of it, shoving him a few steps away from her.

"First of all..." She heaved, her chest rising and falling rapidly as she regained her wits. "I don't tolerate possessive, angry dominating bullshit. So don't *ever* think you can pull that shit with me again. Mate or not, you do not *own* me, asshole. Got that?"

Julius dropped to his knees, cradling his dick in his palms. He stared at her with surprise through his haze of pain and she glared back. She wanted him to fear her. More than that, she wanted him to *respect* her. Because she was his mate. Mana had brought them together, and that wasn't something she would take lightly, because it meant something.

And she needed to clear the air before things got any further.

"I will forgive you this once because this caught us both off guard. But so we're clear, you do not kiss me to silence me or possess me. If you are going to kiss me, it will be because I give myself freely to you, because we both want to enjoy it. Not for any other reason. You got that?"

He nodded and she swore she saw admiration glowing in his eyes. Good, she thought. If she would have seen anything else, she would have frozen his head. And good luck to him trying to get out of *that*.

She dismissed him by flicking her eyes up to Shula, even when a part of her wanted to keep staring at Julius. To study what Mana had gifted her with. She resisted the urge and focused on the Elemental.

The thoughts that had only moments ago been swirling with confused fervor were now clear. She didn't want to say that a kiss had cleared them, but the bond had seemed to settle, and Iona let the bonds of Mana speak for themselves. Instinct took over, and the answers became so clear.

If Mana had brought these Fae to her, it was for a reason.

She was supposed to speak with them. To go with them.

As if it could hear her thoughts, Mana responded in a burst of magic that shivered down her spine. More specifically, down the scars along her back.

Shula stepped closer, weaving around Julius' body so she was face to face with Iona. Amusement glittered in her eyes, an expression that was briefly replaced with determination.

"So," she began. "Will you help us?"

It was on the tip of Iona's tongue to say yes, but she held herself back. It was like making a deal with George, she supposed. She couldn't blindly go in without knowing all the details first, lest she end up bartering her own soul.

Iona looked around. The sun was high in the sky and they weren't exactly hidden. She turned back to Shula. "Let's get out of here. We're too out in the open."

Shula nodded and held out her hand. A truce of some kind, though Iona didn't say that she'd felt peace the moment fire and ice collided.

Iona placed her hand in Shula's and undeniable magic blasted through them, making them both gasp aloud.

"Our hiding spot is close," Shula said, breathlessly. "We'll take you there."

Iona didn't have it in her to be wary in this because she felt Mana urging her on. There was nothing but this, as she tightened her grip on Shula's hand. Nothing but this connection between them and something else that was Mana-given, too.

Trust.

Friendship.

The signs she'd been waiting for.

The New Resistance

The new Resistance was hiding relatively close to where she'd stashed her papers, merely a few blocks away near the desolate buildings where the homeless dwelled.

Shula led the way while Julius and Iona trailed side-by-side behind her. Iona gave herself about a foot of space between Julius and avoided turning to look at him, even though she felt his green eyes almost penetrative against her own body.

He looked like he wanted to close the distance between them, maybe kiss her again, but she knew his stare might have been equal parts curiosity because that's what she was feeling, too.

"Here we are," Shula announced, staring up at the abandoned building. She went through first, tapping a four-note tune against the door and stepping inside when it opened.

Julius gestured forward. "You first."

Iona stepped inside fearlessly, Julius walking in after her, and once the doors closed, she scanned the room and at the curious faces staring at her.

Her gaze went down the line of Fae males. Shula and Iona were the only females among six men, each more different than the last.

There was a man in the far corner of the room with black hair that was braided down to his waist, coppery-brown skin and golden-bronze eyes that slanted just a bit at the edges. There was something almost feline and predatory about the Fae as he took her in from head to toe, as if he were searching for her secrets with a single glance.

The next Fae was, in a word, *pretty.* The kind of pretty that was too perfect, too refined, and made her want to smash her fist into his face, skew him up and make him look normal. Sandy colored hair, bright eyes, and a smirking smile that would have charmed a snake greeted her. Perhaps the only imperfect thing about him was the dimple on his chin, but even that seemed endearing in a frustrating way.

After him, there was another one, almost as big as Julius but not quite as tall or muscular. Looming in stature, he had a thick beard that did nothing to hide the scars bisecting across his olive-tone face. There was a black cat perched on his shoulder that Iona automatically knew was his familiar. The Fae's two different colored eyes—one white, one black—glared at her for a brief second before going straight to Shula and softened there.

Leading the pack of Fae were two males. One with white hair that hung down to his shoulders in sharp sheets like blades, black eyes, and a grave, judging expression. He was as pale as a corpse, dressed in all black and holding a dagger tightly in his hand. She noticed the way it discreetly pointed in her direction, the tenseness of his body, as if he was readying himself to throw it at any sign of brusque movements.

Julius must have noticed, too, because he let out a low, possessive warning growl.

Iona rolled her eyes and shot him a glare before turning to the final male of the group.

A male she recognized immediately. From the slashing, sharp lines of his face, to the shaved sides of his head and the long hair pulled into a bun at the top.

He wore no crown, not like he had the last time she'd seen him, but she would have recognized him even without one on.

No one could ever misplace Valerio Ashera, crown Prince of the Seelie Court.

"Your Highness." Iona dropped down on one knee; an action borne from years of instinct that apparently was still ingrained in her every action.

It didn't matter that the Resistance had disbanded, had been lost to her for years now. She still had respect for the prince of Tir na Faie, and she would show it.

"Rise," Prince Valerio said with something in his voice that sounded a lot like amusement.

She stood, staring at him with wide eyes. She heard the chuckles of the other males around him, saw the way Shula's brows pulled together on an almost confused frown.

Iona tilted her chin. "I thought you were dead."

Valerio's dark eyes danced with mirth. "Many think that," he whispered. "But as you can see, I am alive."

"Clearly." Her eyes flicked over the small group of them again, brows tugging tightly over her eyes, lips pressed in the thinnest of lines. The scents of each person intermingled through her nostrils. Some sharp, some discreet, some like Julius' comforted her senses. She caught whiffs of confections; of chocolate and the richness of wine. Of the familiarity of steel and foreign scents that tickled her nostrils and made her want to sneeze. "There were whispers that the entire royal family had died."

Valerio observed her, and she knew he was trying to place her, and she knew he wouldn't remember. It was confirmed with his next words. "I am sorry, I do not remember you. Have we met before?"

Iona shot him a smirk. "In a manner of speaking." She stepped deeper into the room and looked around. They'd made the place their temporary home. Shields and swords were propped up in the corner of fine make, though scratched with use. Bags that bulged with supplies were neatly stacked side by side against the rusted wall.

She remembered the days, back when they were fighting to take back what was theirs, of camping across the different courts in the Feylands. Apparently, they were doing that even now.

"I was part of the original Resistance in the wars against the humans one-hundred and two years ago." She looked at his face as she said this, noting the surprise in his expression.

"I am grateful for your service," he replied.

"Are you?" Iona stepped close, not close enough to touch when she knew the white-haired Fae must have been his protector, if the way he wielded the dagger was of any indication. She didn't want to find it buried in her chest if she got too close to the prince. "It didn't feel that way when a lot of us were left to die."

Prince Valerio blinked, the only outward sign of surprise he'd show, she figured. "Were you there when—"

"When the Seelie Court fell? Yes. And when we evacuated to the boats."

She remembered the chaos of that time. When the air was dense with rusted iron and ashwood, burning through lungs. When Fae warriors had been ordered to grab citizens and flee. Not to the Unseelie Courts, where the humans hadn't been able to conquer, and whose hostility was innately known, but to the boats.

Iona had gathered as many as she could. Women. Children. Elderly. They boarded, saying goodbye to the only home they'd ever known. She could still feel the ash coating her tongue, the tears sticky on her cheeks, hear the cries of others in the air as loudly as she could hear the dying.

"It was storming that day," Prince Valerio said. "The humans had catapults. They sent iron balls flying to those boats." His tone was haunted.

Iona felt her fingers tap against her thighs as she was ripped back to that time. When the first ball landed against their ship and wood splintered. When the raging sea dragged them under, which may have been a slower death than to be crushed by iron, but still preferable. She remembered crying out for her family, thinking her soul would be taken with Mana at long last.

"We'd presumed you all dead," Prince Valerio continued, stepping closer.

"Yes, well, so did I. Looks like we were both wrong." To avoid giving in to the burning sensation behind her eyelids, she swept her gaze across the others. "And you have a new Resistance. How... quaint."

Prince Valerio chuckled. "Introductions are in order, I suppose."

She gave a firm nod. "My name is Iona Wylde, Elemental Fae; ice is what I wield."

Valerio gestured to the white-haired man next to him. "This is Uric Adriel Nova. You've met Julius Dara and Shula Azzarh..."

She smirked. "In a manner of speaking."

If he wondered at her tone, he didn't show it, though she could feel the curiosity of the others heavy in their scents. "That is my cousin, High Lord Clay Valentino of the Sapphire Court." He gestured to the prettiest Fae, who sent her a charming, seductive smile that made Julius growl from behind her.

Lord Clay sent Julius a smirk, his bright green eyes dancing as if he knew. It made Iona wonder if mates gave off a certain smell or something that would make their connection that much more obvious. So far, she couldn't sense a difference in herself, except for the eager buzzing of his presence.

"That's Ryker Valda," Valerio continued. Ryker was the scarred one standing next to Shula, the cat on his shoulder. "And that's Weylyn Xanth." That was the predatory Fae with his smirking grin.

"Small group," she observed. "Too small to call yourselves a Resistance."

Uric scoffed unkindly. She glared at him, knowing he was going to be either a handful or a raging dick. Maybe both. "There are many more than what you see here, Elemental."

He said the word 'Elemental' the same way someone would say 'the plague' or 'venereal disease'.

Julius caught on to the tone as well.

"Watch it," he growled, stepping close to Iona. Everything about it was possessive and annoying.

Uric's whole body was taut in the type of way that seemed so natural on him. Iona doubted he'd ever relaxed a day in his life, as he looked prepared to jump on Julius and slice at his throat with the ease of a murderer.

That cold, black gaze darted back and forth between Julius and Iona, sensing what everyone had no doubt only guessed by now.

Julius then confirmed it. "Careful how you speak to my mate."

The collective silence was a painful drumming in her ears.

She shoved her elbow into Julius' side. "Fuck off, dick face," she mumbled. "I don't need you fighting my battles."

Shula chuckled.

"So, what do you all want from me?" She pushed forward before Julius could say anything else or before they could ask questions about what he'd just declared. They didn't need to touch that topic just quite yet. Not that she felt embarrassed about it, but she wanted to discuss that with him in private and not with an audience of curious onlookers.

"We need your help," Valerio began. He didn't even look ruffled, showing just how true of a royal he was by keeping his composure in the face of surprising news.

"Long story short, the Emperor of Illyk wants to eradicate the Fae, and he's looking for us Elementals to do it," Shula interrupted, her voice tinged with a hint of impatience and urgency. "We need to find them before he does and—"

"Stop right there." Iona held up her hand, cutting Shula off from speaking entirely. She noticed how everyone shifted nervously. "Do you have more Fae at your disposal than just this right here?"

"Yes," Valerio answered slowly.

"And you want us to go on a journey and find Fae?"

"Yes."

"Before the emperor does?"

"Yes..."

Iona smiled, feeling a surge of rightness through her body. Mana urging her, pushing her to make a decision. This was what she'd been waiting for. For years since she'd been tangled in the secrets of Illyk she had hoped to find a group like this. Of Fae who would be willing to help the cause and truly set her plans and ideas in motion. With them, she wouldn't have to run away and lie in waiting. With them, she could finally take action and do what Mana had kept her from doing for years. Now she knew why. Mana had simply been waiting for their paths to cross.

"Son of a bitch." Iona chuckled. She looked back up and met confused faces of the Fae. "Alright," she said. "I'm in."

Shula's eyes widened almost comically. "Are you—" She broke off, but Iona knew what she wanted to ask. *Are you sure?* She's the one who tried convincing Iona, why was she so surprised? Perhaps it was the fact that she'd so readily accepted.

"I've never been surer about anything in my entire life."

And the timing was perfect, too. She was leaving Porir anyway, so why not leave with them? The decision was fast, and she didn't have all the details, but she couldn't ignore the feeling of rightness anymore.

"But... why?" Shula asked, clearly shocked.

Iona shrugged. "I used to be a part of the original Resistance. We failed our mission. Every day since then I've been thinking about what could have happened if things had been different. If we'd succeeded. And every day since then I've been stuck in this shit stain of a city, praying to Mana that things would change..." She trailed off. "You were sent to me by Mana for a reason. I don't want to look the other way. I want to do something important with my life again."

Shula's jaw clenched, but the rest of the men smiled.

"Well, that was easy." The one named Clay clapped his hands together. "Then we should probably get going before more soldiers come—"

"No."

He paused, staring hard at Iona. "No?"

"I mean, yes, I'll leave with you, but I'm not leaving Porir without my bear."

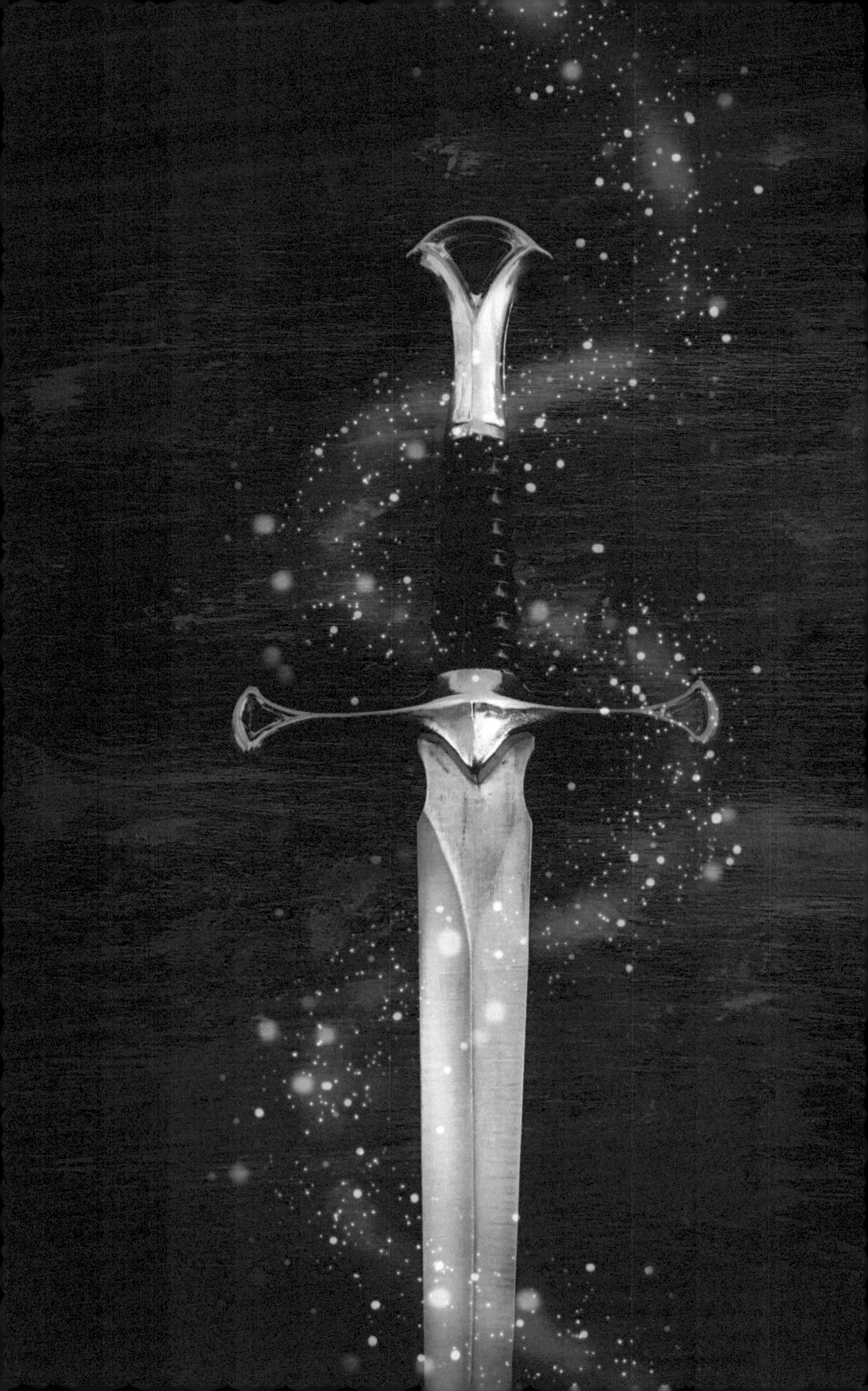

Lovebirds

"Your bear?" Prince Valerio's brows pulled together like he couldn't quite comprehend what she meant. He shared a look with Uric, one meant for best friends who'd known each other for so long, they only needed a single glance to convey their words.

She'd had that with her sister.

Iona was silent a moment, letting them stare, absorbing what she'd said.

"We are in a hurry," Clay cut in. "Can't you just buy a new one?"

She couldn't help but throw her head back and laugh. "Do not be foolish. I cannot replace my familiar."

"Wait, your familiar is a bear?" Clay whistled low, his eyes wide. "Color me impressed."

A smile spread over Iona's face, and a sense of pride. "A polar bear, if you want to get specific."

"Nice!" Clay beamed.

Uric scoffed. "How do you expect us to take a polar bear with us across Illyk in search of the Elementals? That is not exactly inconspicuous." He shook his head vehemently from side to side. "No, we cannot."

Iona pierced Uric with a glare. She already didn't like the Fae male and was itching to just throw her fist to his face to get him to shut up. The only thing stopping her was the sight of his hand wrapped around the hilt of his dagger at his belted waist. Not that she didn't think she could take him, but if she was going to be traveling with these Fae, it would be better not to piss of the prince's bodyguard.

"Then feel free to leave without me," Iona challenged. "Because where I go, he goes."

"Perhaps you didn't understand this is a stealth mission. It is difficult enough traveling with such a large group. We do not need to worry about catering to a polar bear's needs."

Fuck his dagger, she thought as she stepped forward, snapping her canines in threat, a snarl letting loose from her throat. There was a blur of motion before her and the next thing she knew, the edge of a sharp blade was skimming her throat. Her own hand snapped out, fingers wrapping around Uric's wrist.

They were face to face, wearing equally threatening expressions as they faced off. A sting of blood against her neck made her blink and nothing more. She'd been through much worse than this.

"Try it," she dared, a smile curling her lips. "Kill me and say goodbye to my help."

His lip curled back in a sneer to show the gleaming glint of his canines. "What makes you think I won't?"

"You came to find me for a reason. You obviously need me."

His dark eyes flashed violently and a moment later, a muscular arm tore between them, shoving Iona back a step. Then Julius was in front of her, his wide hands shoving against Uric's shoulders. He didn't seem like he'd used force, yet still the other male went flying back, hitting the far wall with a clang before sliding down it in a heap on the floor.

The white-haired Fae snarled and stood to his feet, gripping his knife. Julius let out an answering growl. Iona had half a mind to let them tear through one another. There was no doubt in her mind that Julius would win that battle with his brute force.

But if these were to be her new companions, she couldn't create animosity between them. Her hand shot out and placed over the leather on Julius' arm. He froze, turning to look at her with his flaring nostrils.

"Don't," she warned.

He didn't look inclined to listen to her.

"Enough!" Prince Valerio stepped forward, pinching the bridge of his nose between his thumb and forefinger. He dropped his hand and looked up at Iona with searching eyes. "A familiar is a gift from Mana," the prince continued. "One we cannot ignore, and we will not. Of course your familiar will travel with us, but we must be ever vigilant with a creature that size."

She dropped her hand from Julius' arm and felt a strange tingling sensation as soon as she did, so she brought her digits to her thighs and started tracing out patterns against her pants.

"Where is he, if I may ask?"

Iona stared at Valerio. "Porir City Zoo. He's in a special enclosure."

Uric huffed with annoyance. "And how do you expect us to get in there?"

She smirked and reached inside her pocket, procuring the iron key in her palm. It burned against her skin, but it was a pain she'd grown used to after all these years; she still had the tiny scars crisscrossing against her fingers as evidence.

"How do you have a key to the zoo?" Clay asked, amusement shining in his already bright eyes.

"Because I work there. Rather, worked there. It's a long story, one meant for another time." She pocketed her key. "So are we leaving or what? I had a plan mapped out to get him out of there before you all ganged up on me in the alleyway." There was no real ardor in her voice, rather a bit of affection.

She'd only known these Fae for a short while, but already she felt a deeper connection with them than she had with anyone else in Porir in all the time she'd been here.

"What exactly was your plan?" Prince Valerio sounded amused.

"Get in. Get him out. Leave Porir." She shrugged.

"Good enough," Clay supplied with a chuckle.

"Do we split up?" Before the question was even asked, all the Fae began shouldering their bags that were leaning against the wall and sheathing their swords at the belts on their waists, just beneath their coats.

"We go in together," Prince Valerio decided. "You lead us through the city, since you know it better than anyone. We leave discreetly. There are too many soldiers and we cannot afford to draw attention to ourselves."

"Follow my lead and you won't," Iona assured them. Confidence oozed from her in waves, because this felt *right.* Being around these Fae were the answers to all her prayers.

"Then let's go." The prince started towards the door and the others followed in a single line after him. Ryker and his familiar passed and Shula followed, the fire Fae giving Iona a look she couldn't quite decipher before turning abruptly and catching up at Ryker's heels.

Julius and Iona were the last ones left in the room and he was facing her, as if waiting for her to go through the door first or waiting to say something.

His mouth opened. Closed.

Iona rolled her eyes, yet a smile still tilted her lips. His sudden insecurity seemed rather adorable. Like he didn't know quite what to make of Iona. She wondered if he was the type of Fae to dream about his mate and if she lived up to his expectations or if he was disappointed. If he was, there was no helping it. He'd have to accept the hand that Mana dealt him or leave her alone.

She'd never took the time to dream up of that kind of life, with a mate and offspring, when all that had occupied her mind had been thoughts of war, a past she could never change, and a future that was too far away to be chased.

Yet here her mate stood, staring like he didn't know how to approach her in a way that wasn't with brute force. Because she'd shot him down and kneed him in the groin twice.

She felt the sudden urge to approach him, to kick past the walled barriers for a brief moment to ease his mind. This must have been as new for him as it was for her, and what other way to navigate it than together?

She took a step closer and watched his body coil tightly like he was ready to pounce.

"We got off on the wrong foot," she whispered.

His brows rose, and she took a moment to study his features. She'd gotten a glimpse earlier when he'd grabbed her wrists, then she'd gotten a taste of his mouth. Now she stared at the *male.* Everything about him was virile and strong. From his scent down to his size, to the tiny silver scars across his flushing, freckled skin. His jawline was square and scruff with a reddish-orange beard that barely concealed the smirk or the white flash of canines beneath. His nose was crooked, as if it had been repeatedly broken and hadn't quite healed in the right direction, and his lips... The bottom one was bigger than the top, and she could remember the rough feel of them against her own mouth.

A part of her wanted to feel them again.

But not then.

"Is that what you call kneeing me in the dick?"

Iona snorted out choked laughter and shrugged. "You had it coming."

He grunted but said nothing. Not that they were given the chance to chat anymore when Clay poked his head back inside. "You lovebirds done yet?" he demanded, but there was humor in his tone and his eyes danced inquiringly. "I want to leave this shitty place."

"You and me both, little lord," Iona teased, earning a scowl from Clay and a barking laugh from Julius.

Yeah, she thought. Mana had definitely answered her prayers.

An Empty Cage

Iona slipped the key into her familiar's enclosure and pushed the door open a fraction. Her back was pressed to the wall, as it had been most of the journey towards the zoo, as she slid discreetly between whatever shadows the daylight gave her—rather, *them*—to remain hidden from soldiers and humans.

Not that the human citizens of Porir would ever give them up. At least, that had been before the soldiers had come through. Here, the humans were just as impoverished as the Fae, most all of them living in equally frightful conditions. It was the human soldiers and employers they'd had to worry about. Men like fucking Petey, who she was lucky not to have run into as they slipped their way into the zoo, dodging patrolling soldiers and other workers that she'd once considered almost-friends.

"Stay here." She gestured at the others aligned along the wall behind her. They'd taken a back entrance, darting between bins of garbage and supply closets to stay hidden. Taking a breath, she pushed the door open further and stepped inside the enclosure.

Only to find it empty.

"What the fuck?!" Her feet slipped against the ground as she ran into the glass dome, dropping to her knees at the edge of the pool. Her pants soaked through with cold water, but the pool was still. There was nothing beneath the surface.

Her eyes rose up to look across the glass. There was no one in front of it waiting to catch a glimpse at the rare sight of a polar bear.

The emptiness echoed around her, pounding loudly through her ears like white noise. Her heart was beating in tune to the rapid pulsing of her fingers against her thighs. Her breaths grew shallow and for a moment, she wasn't in the enclosure but on an empty beach with bodies littered at her feet, the silence so loud, it made her choke on her own need to scream.

A lot of people defined loneliness as being *alone*. They didn't know the darker side of it. The side where you were surrounded by bodies devoid of souls, where the loudest sound was the splash of waves against a shore and how even that sounded too quiet in a world where you were used to the noise. Surrounded by death, she'd felt utterly alone, and in a single moment of weakness had begged to Mana, a prayer breaking her lips.

Take me, too.

Those same words echoed through her mind just then, a slippery, fervent thought before she felt a warm hand grip her wrist and she was pulled right back to the moment. Back to silence and a missing familiar, but with a strong palm encircling her skin, thumb stroking against her pulse in calming movements.

She twisted her neck up and met the worried green stare of Julius.

"Iona?" Her name was a tentative taste on his lips.

"He's gone." Her own voice broke and she despised the weakness in it. So she took a breath and pushed herself to her feet, regretting that doing so made his hand slip away from her wrist at all. She squared her shoulders. "My familiar is gone," she repeated much more firmly.

Panic started to rise and she wanted to shove it right back down, but it clawed up her throat, leaving her feeling abandoned. Her fingers traced the pattern of her old ceiling against her pants as she tried to force herself to focus.

She recalled the day Petey had attacked her. It felt like so long ago now, but it had only been three days ago. The way her familiar had rushed to protect her and his menacing, parting words.

"You'll pay for that. Both of you."

Panic was replaced with rage almost instantaneously.

"Fucking Petey," she growled out. Her canines burst against her gums as they elongated, snapping in her fury.

"Who?" She could hear the confusion in Julius' voice, but she didn't have time to ease it. Not when her familiar *was gone.* When Petey had done something to him. She didn't want to even think about what had happened or contemplate all the dreadful possibilities.

"Mana, keep him safe," she whispered right before she broke away from Julius and ran. Her feet carried her with incredible speed, sending her zipping past the others. She didn't give herself time to register their surprise at her sudden disappearance, or that Julius was calling her name.

All she knew was that another human was trying to take away someone she cared about and she couldn't let it happen.

Not again.

And she swore, if Petey had harmed her familiar in any way...

He wouldn't live long enough to regret doing it.

⁂

Her foot connected to Petey's office, the wood splintering inwards, flying apart. The man inside yelped, dropping his bottle of ale as she stormed inside. His eyes widened as he took her in, as if surprised she wasn't skewered at the end of an iron sword like he wanted her to be.

"What the fuck, Io—" He barely got the rest out before she sped around the table, her hand gripping his throat. A single jerk of her arm and he was lifted, his body slamming against the wall as she held him suspended above the floor.

"Where is he?" she demanded.

Petey's face reddened under the pressure of her hold. His fat fingers grasping against her hands, dull nails scraping along her skin as he struggled.

A fucking fool.

She was Fae. She'd never showed off how much more powerful she'd always been than him and because of that, he'd underestimated her. Never fucking again.

She loosened her grip just enough to get him to talk.

"S-s-sold the b-beast..."

"You did what?" she snarled, snapping her canines near his neck.

"I sold the beast!"

The shock of the words had her ripping her hand away as if he'd burned her. He fell to the ground, his legs giving up beneath him. He coughed and spewed, his hands going to his neck to rub away the soreness she'd left behind against his skin.

She staggered back a step until her lower back hit the edge of his desk. Pain seared up her spine, but she ignored it.

"You did what?"

Petey coughed and pushed himself to his feet. His back hunched, and his face was red with rage as he glared at her.

"I sold the fuckin' beast! You were gone for a few fuckin' hours and he was out of control. Bad for business, so I sent him away two days ago." Spittle flew as he spoke, his voice rising and echoing in the confined space of his office.

"No..." Her heart fractured in her chest. How could she not have known? How could she not have noticed the distance between her and her familiar? Why hadn't Mana hinted at what she would lose?

Was this to be her curse? To gain a mate, but lose her familiar?

She turned away from Petey, if only so he wouldn't see the heartbreak slashing across her features like the badly painted portraits spread all across Porir. A sob rose in her chest and stuck there. She wanted to force it down, to calm down, but her head was pounding, her fingers scraping against the wood, digging a pattern on the surface.

"How could you?" she whispered, feeling the first sting of tears against her cheeks. "How could you do that to him?"

Petey shifted behind her. She felt his heat hovering close, the acrid scent of smoke and ale burning through her nostrils.

She felt the energy drain out of her. She tried reaching down into her soul to find the magical space her familiar had occupied. She didn't feel different, didn't feel like something was missing or in pain. That should have been a relief, right? But it wasn't. She felt like her heart had been ripped open, like there was nothing but darkness ahead. The same feeling as drowning, like unforgiving arms were pulling her deeper to her death.

And she *was* drowning, gasping for breath, struggling against the currents of waves of her own emotions.

Petey's hand closed over her shoulder, his grip firm. She was too far gone to shake him off. There was nothing but a roaring sound in her ears and the feeling of choking on water that wasn't really there.

Maybe if she hadn't flashed back to that moment in time, she would have heard the sound of steel sliding against a sheath. She would have felt the pressure Petey placed against her shoulder. She would have had fair warning before agony ruptured through her body as he shoved the blade into her back.

Julius ran out of the glass enclosure after Iona. Her panic splintered through his chest, down the bond they shared. They may not have had a bonding mark, at least not like Ryker and Shula, but it felt as if they'd both already accepted it anyway, and that's why he was feeling her inner turmoil.

She sped away, past the group that waited for them. He wanted to run after her, but a hand shot out, gripping him to a stop. He turned with a snarl pursed on his lips before realizing it was Valerio.

"What?" he snarled.

"What's going on?" His prince looked at him pointedly.

"Her familiar is gone."

"Where is she going?"

He yanked his arm away. "I don't know where she's going." But he was going to find out. Without waiting for a reply or for permission, Julius followed after his mate, following her traces of mint, ice, and apples, following the tug in the space set between the recesses of his own soul.

He hid as best as his big frame would allow in the shadows, but it was hard to have a care when adrenaline and anger pumped through his blood. Not anger at his mate, but at whatever had caused her distress.

He didn't know anything about her life, considering they'd only met about an hour ago, but faced with this, he realized he wanted to slay anything encumbering her. He'd never felt such primal possession towards a female before. But Iona was his mate. She was different.

She was made for him, and he for her.

She didn't know it yet, but he would protect her from all harm. And as soon as they had a moment to speak, he would tell her that he wasn't going to allow her to run from him ever again. Whatever problems she shouldered? He had strength enough to carry for them both.

He made it somewhere towards the back of the zoo, following his instincts. He was aware of the others running much more quietly behind him, of Valerio's hissed warnings, but all Julius could think about was Iona.

Something was wrong.

A gut feeling confirmed when he heard the sound of her shout and the sudden sharp smell of blood flooded his nostrils.

He almost staggered back but pushed forward into a small room with a broken door, just in time to see a human bending Iona over the desk, one hand braced against her shoulder and the other holding a sword.

A sword he had skewered to her back.

Blood pooled against the thick fur of her coat. Her palms were pressed tightly to the surface of the desk, her mouth opened as she screamed her pain.

The sound ripped through Julius' chest, agony-filled and heartbreaking at the same time.

And just like that, he was blinded by his rage.

The sword was yanked out of her body, and the human looked up, his eyes widening in fear. That second was all Julius gave him before he roared and charged. The sword came swinging but with a single brush of his arm, it was ripped from the human's grasp and clattered to the ground.

The human whimpered and stepped away, his eyes darting back and forth, looking for a place to run. He wouldn't find a way to escape. Not when Julius was on the hunt.

Julius' palm shot out, crashing against his face. Julius felt the crunch of cartilage break as his nose smashed beneath the Fae's palm, and then he was lifting his body up against the wall, holding him there like he was dangling nothing more than a doll.

His pathetic cries were muffled behind Julius' hand.

Julius squeezed and the human's eyes bulged in fear. He relished in the stench of it. He would make him pay.

He would make him hurt.

He would make him bleed like he'd made Iona bleed.

"Wait!" Fingers coated in blood clamped down on his leather clad arm and squeezed. He loosened his hold on the human a fraction and turned to face Iona. She stood, her legs wobbling, tears streaming down her beautiful cheeks, and blood coating her fur jacket. She stood tall, even as she trembled, she was brave.

Julius had never seen someone more beautiful.

"Don't kill him," she pleaded.

A muscle in his neck strained tightly and a growl rumbled through his chest. "He hurt you."

"I said don't kill him!" Her nails dug into the leather, ripping it and breaching the skin underneath. He felt the sharp press of her magic, threatening, warning.

"Fine," he conceded, dropping the human unceremoniously to the ground. His legs crumbled from beneath him, and Julius was sure he heard an ankle snap. Julius' foot connected with the sword; an abomination made of iron, he kicked it out of the human's reach.

Iona bent, and he noticed the pull of her features, but he didn't rush to help like instinct demanded. Her wishes were more important than his feral demands. "Where is he?" she demanded.

The human sniveled like the coward he was.

Julius couldn't help himself after that. His foot stomped down on the man's leg and the crack reverberated loudly through the office. Then came his cries.

"My mate asked you a fucking question," Julius spat.

"Fuck! Fuck! Okay, I'll tell you. Gods, please stop! I sold him back to the Kurreen. They took him to the West Isles. Fuck! My leg! My nose!"

"I want a fucking name!" Iona shouted, causing him to flinch.

"Temair Beston, okay?! He's the whip wielder from before! The West Isles! That's where they told me they were taking him!"

"You better pray my familiar is alive and healthy, Petey," she threatened, her voice dark and low. "I put up with you for years because I respected your father. You attacked me, betrayed me, and sold my familiar."

Every word she spoke fueled Julius' anger even more. He kept them close, letting the acrimony ravage through his body, and he memorized every thread of it like he was ingraining the intricate details of a tapestry in his mind.

"I hope Mana destroys your soul, giving you no rest after you're gone," she spat. Cruel, offensive words to the Fae. "In case you didn't understand that, then I'll make it simpler for you. Rot in fucking hell."

She started to stand and the human lunged for her, striking out with his hand, but Julius was there, using his arm as a barrier. He felt the sting of iron cut through leather and embed into his skin. He hissed a single breath of discomfort and the human's hand fell away, leaving the knife lodged into his skin.

The human recoiled at the expression on Julius' face. He didn't bother to pull the knife from his arm as he bent and picked the human up by the head, dangling him between his two arms. The human flailed and cried.

Julius called forth his magic.

And he crushed the human's head between his hands.

His palms smacked together. Brains, broken bits of skull, and blood exploded, staining his borrowed uniform. He didn't care. All that mattered was the asshole was fucking dead.

He turned to Iona, wondering if he'd see disgust in her face at what all he was capable of. Fae were naturally stronger than humans, but he was stronger than most Fae. It was a gift from Mana, and it came at the price of his rage.

His nostrils were flaring, and he tried to keep the irrational anger in check. He grabbed the hilt of the iron dagger and yanked it out of his arm. Blood pooled from the wound and pain shot up his extremity that he ignored.

He could only stare at Iona. At the beautiful picture she made.

It was common for him after a fight to want a strong drink and a hard fuck.

Iona could give that to him, he thought.

Instinctively, he knew that, but he didn't reach for her. She was the one who reached for him. She grabbed his arm and pulled it close, staring at the wound, her head shaking. Dark eyes were glaring at the blood like it was a nuisance.

He supposed he shouldn't tell her she had remnants of the human splattered in her curls, then.

"You fucking idiot," she grumbled. "You had to go and get yourself stabbed."

He blinked with incredulity a moment before his lips curled into a smile of amusement. The rage abated. What usually took hours to leave his body left in an instant simply by looking into her eyes. "Right back at you, mate."

"It's just a scratch." But he could tell that it wasn't just a scratch. He wanted to haul her over and sit her down in front of Ryker, who's gentle herbal smell waited for them right outside the broken door. "I can live with it. Right now, there are more important things that need doing."

"What could possibly be more important than tending to these wounds?"

She shot him a look of impatience and he realized, with a jolt, that he could get used to this. To this banter, the teasing. He'd never wanted a female in his life longer than it took to fuck them. With Iona, he wanted more. It didn't matter that he didn't know her, that she didn't know him.

They were mates, and the rest could come later.

"Finding my familiar is the most important thing. We've wasted enough fucking time already." Her hands dropped to her thighs and began a relentless tapping rhythm. He'd noticed it before but didn't comment on it. "My familiar could be hurt. So don't even try to convince me to stop, because I won't."

He wanted to, but he also recognized the depth of the warrior's stubborn ferocity in her gaze. He recognized it, had seen it before on the battlefield. Duty came before everything else, even ones own well-being. He'd gone through battles with broken arms and infected wounds more often than he could count.

Who was he to deny that to his mate when she was on a mission, when determination burned deep into the depths of her eyes?

"Then what the fuck are we waiting for?" Julius demanded. "Let's go find your familiar."

He almost didn't see her smile because it was replaced just as quickly with anger. She pushed her way past him and out the door, not sparing a glance to their gawking companions.

"Let's go," she demanded. "We have a boat to steal."

Thieving Ultimatum

"Why are we stealing a boat again?" Clay asked for what felt like the tenth time in the past few minutes. And since she'd already answered him every other time, she decided to ignore him just then.

Instead, she focused on the pain thrumming from her shoulder to her back. The tip of Petey's sword had gone through her shoulder, not enough to do lasting damage but enough to *hurt.* Agony radiated and she felt the blood pooling against her clothes, staining her coat. She should have taken the time to at least clean the wound, but she couldn't bring herself to stop at all.

They were at the docks, staring at the boat Iona meant to steal. The others were at her back, staring either at her wound or over her shoulder at the large metal boat.

She felt a hand prod at her side, and she whipped her head around to glare at Clay. "What?" she hissed, more out of pain than annoyance with him, though she was growing quite vexed with the little lord.

"What's the plan here?" he pressed.

"We kill that piece of shit, take his boat, and sail to the West Isles and get my familiar back from the Kurreen." She felt a pang, stronger than even the wound on her shoulder when she thought about what her familiar must be going through.

When he'd arrived, he had been held down in wire, bleeding and fighting for survival. He would land right back into the thick of that violence again.

"Two things. What's the Kurreen, and instead of stealing a boat couldn't maybe Uric transport us there?" Clay asked hopefully.

Iona didn't know the extent of the magic they wielded. Shula was a fire Elemental, Julius had abnormal strength, that much was obvious, but the others? Due to Clay's question, she gauged that Uric had transportation abilities. Useful for other occasions, she supposed. Useless in this one, though.

"The Kurreen are mercenaries. As for having the gloomy bastard transport us? It won't work." She ignored Uric's indignant growl and continued, "The West Isles are said to have iron gates that are a hundred feet tall. Iron weakens magic; we'd be lucky to get within a hundred feet of the Isles, and even if we did, we'd land in the predator-infested waters." She fought back a shiver as the memories threatened to assault her mind. "I don't swim."

She could feel inquiring gazes on her, but she ignored it, intent on the pulsing in her shoulder as it kept her grounded. It served to remind her that whatever torment she experienced would never be half as bad as what her familiar was likely going through. The image of fur flaying from his flesh burst behind her eyes, and she bit back her own groan of pain.

She couldn't feel anything in their bond, having not had the chance to explore more of it before he'd been taken away. She was empty, hollow; could scarcely sense the phantom echoes of his presence somewhere inside her.

"We are wasting time," Uric growled. She turned to look, watching him shift, tilting his body towards Valerio's. She wondered if he even realized he did that; always angled himself closer to his prince. In the short time since she'd known them, it had grown obvious. She swore if she looked hard enough, she could almost believe that it wasn't just a gesture of protection, but something more. "We have a mission, my prince, and this is not it. After we retrieved her, we were meant to look for the next Elemental before the Emperor of Illyk finds them. We cannot traipse across the sea looking for a fucking bear."

Iona grinded her teeth together. She wanted nothing more than to slam her fist straight into his face but held back the urge. Mana should be proud of her restraint, she thought.

"That 'fucking bear' is my familiar," Iona gritted out. "And you don't have to be here. No one is forcing you to come with me."

Uric sneered. He was as pale as death, as deadly looking as the reaper of human legends. Dressed in all black, colors that only made him look nearly translucent, he was little more than a ghost. "As if we had a choice to leave you behind, Elemental."

Iona's eyes rolled. "I have a fucking name. Try using it, yeah?" Then she turned to the prince and she could see him contemplating Uric's words. Her eyes narrowed. "Look, I get you're on a timeline or whatever. But *nothing* is more important than my familiar right now. If you don't want to help, don't, but know that I won't help you, either."

She was skating on thin ice, unsure how they would meet her thieving plot and ultimatum. They overpowered her seven to one, and there was nothing stopping them from trying to take her by force.

Her chin tilted up at the thought. *Let them try.* She wasn't some meek female they could cart around or bind in chains. She had a will of her own, and she would give them chaos if they dared.

She made sure her eyes conveyed that, too.

Prince Valerio sighed and pinched the bridge of his nose then turned to Uric. "She is one of us now. Her mission is our mission. We have to help her."

Uric's jaw tightened in response.

Ha, ha. Asshole.

Prince Valerio turned back to Iona. "But no more detours. After we find him, you help us find the third Elemental?"

"Yeah, sure." She didn't ask questions. The most important thing was finding her familiar.

Shula muttered from behind her. "I wasn't given that luxury."

Iona wondered at that, but before anyone could acknowledge that comment, Iona was darting towards the docks and the boat that would lead them to the West Isles.

"Impulsive," Valerio muttered, watching Iona run towards the boat. "Worse than the Fire Dancer."

Shula glared at him with indignation, but Julius didn't pay attention to them. He was watching his woman. His mate.

She moved with a brutal force, but there was a certain grace to those movements that he admired. The docks were nearly empty, with a few humans hauling baskets of fish from smelly, dark waters. No soldiers littered the place, but he knew that was always a possibility of changing.

He watched, her boots echoing against the wooden docks as she ran towards the boat and stormed up it like she was a queen entering her castle.

Humans shouted, some charged at her and she smiled and dodged their swords, using maneuvers and slaps to disarm them and turn their own weapons against them. She fought through them, tossing them off the side of the boat with vicious kicks against their backs. By the time she'd taken possession of the boat by herself, she was panting, and Julius couldn't help but notice she looked a little weary.

"I must look at her wound," Ryker insisted anxiously, pushing past Julius and making his way to the docks. He'd obviously noticed the same thing in regards to her wound. Normally, Julius scoffed at Ryker's self-sacrificing ways. But he didn't fault him for it this time, considering the one he wanted to heal was Julius' mate.

"Guess it's time to go." Clay slapped Julius on the shoulder, a broad smile on his lips. "Damn, Darah, you found a mate who could kick your ass straight to another life if she wanted."

Before Julius could respond, Shula shoved past them, her every step a stomping aggression as she followed after Ryker towards the boat.

"What's her problem?" Clay asked, brows pulled together as he followed her movements.

"We are wasting time with this," Uric insisted. "Valerio—"

"Enough!" Valerio barked. "We need her."

"We could—"

"No." Uric opened his mouth to argue, but the prince interrupted before he could get the chance. "The same methods we used for Shula will not work on this Fae, and I will not risk her ire. Kidnapping Shula at the time was our solution, but I will not do something so callous again. Iona is willing to help us, all we have to do is this single favor for her."

Uric's jaw clenched with disapproval, but he didn't contradict Valerio again.

Julius ignored them and made his way towards the boat, boarding to find Iona on deck, raising anchor with brusque, impatient movements. She aggressively torqued the handle, shoving against it and huffing.

"Let's go!" she called out. "I want to leave before the soldiers come!"

Julius smiled to himself and went to help his mate. She flicked a glance at him as he took over, using his gift of strength to help raise the anchor quicker.

She didn't thank him like he thought she would. Didn't even look impressed. She was already onto the next task, and once the anchor was up and everyone was on board, she began steering.

Clay swaggered next to her and Julius listened in on their conversation, his irritation at Clay's flirtatious nature growing. "Do you know how to do this?" he purred salaciously.

She shot him a look of impatience. "More than you, probably."

"Jokes on you, because Valerio and I are excellent sailors."

Iona didn't answer. Or if she did, Julius didn't hear. He was already turning away, a frown pulling at his brows as they started to sail away.

To the West Isles.

A Pleasant Distraction

It was hours of smooth sailing. They'd long since left Porir behind until they were surrounded by ocean on all sides. The further they drifted away from the shores of Teg, the clearer the once-black waters became.

And still Iona trembled.

Not from the pain on her shoulder, as that had long since passed thanks to Ryker, who had a healing gift from Mana. He'd touched her shoulder in passing and she had turned to snap at him with prickly defensiveness before she felt searing white-hot magic burst through her body, healing her wound closed.

As the pain had left her, Ryker had grimaced and stormed away before she could see him obviously absorb it into himself. Iona had stared after him. His magic had left her hollow inside. She'd wished she could take that ability of his and bottle it up and lock it away. It was a dangerous magic to possess and instead of making her feel rejuvenated, it made her feel a looming sense of doom.

It reminded her too much of her past and took her back there. To a time before the war had decimated her family. To scrapes and bruised knees and a gentle hand passing over the wounds. Watching them knit closed, leaving smooth skin behind as if they'd never really been there at all.

To distract herself, she'd steered the boat until Clay came over to bother her. By then, her emotions were too high, her fingers desperate to touch her thighs in a soothing tempo.

She'd given up the reins of the ship to Clay and Valerio hours ago after she was sure they knew what they were doing. The boat had several maps stashed away of the entire empire as well as a compass, and other tools so they wouldn't get lost navigating.

She'd left the two males to it so she could go catch her breath. She tried forcing away memories and feelings by keeping herself busy along the deck, but the more she tried, the worse her body shook. Tears prickled behind her eyelids, and she forced several deep breaths to her lungs to keep them at bay.

Iona pressed her forearms against the edge of the boat, staring at the rolling water beneath them. One memory made way for another. Of canons hitting the boat, of jarring impact sending her flying against the water's surface, how it felt like hitting concrete. Of arms dragging her under and hauling her through the ocean until she was spit out by black hands. The sensation of losing all sense of breath.

Then her familiar's pain-filled eyes. The blood on his jaw and fur, the way he'd placed his trust in her hands so easily and she hadn't been there to save him from Petey's wrath.

She should have been there for him. She should have gotten him out before running away. Those papers she'd got from George would be useless, now that she was going to be on the run with the Resistance.

Iona dug her nails into the metal edge and took a deep breath, but it didn't ease her anxiety. She felt her nails starting to chip, and the sound of the rushing water made her groan.

Then, a hand came down on her own, covering it completely in a blanket of warmth that she felt down to her core. Her eyes flew open to find Julius, his thumb tracing circles over her skin.

She was surprised at how quickly it eased her anxiety. Her body welcomed his touch with a sure conviction, and she wanted to lean into his broad shoulder, wanted him to wrap his arm around her for comfort.

She slipped her hand from beneath his palm and stepped to the side, putting much needed distance between them. She could feel his body stiffen beside hers as he likely took a bit of offense to her pulling away, and she forced herself to meet his eyes. They weren't angry, but she swore she caught a glimmer of hurt that he quickly replaced with a hard mask followed by a flirtatious grin. The series of convoluted expressions tore at her chest.

"Relax, Iona," he practically purred. "Your fingers will cramp."

It was too late for that. Those words went unsaid, but she wondered if he could feel them pulsing between the empty spaces.

"I'm just worried." Her fingers went up and pushed aside the curls from her face, exposing her pointed ears. "I can't feel anything down our bond." Not that she would have known how to anyway. She should have spent the time she had with her familiar learning how to use the bond. She'd grown too confident in the faux-pacifism of Porir that she'd forgotten all could be lost within a single moment.

She made a vow to ask Ryker to teach her about the bonds with familiars. He seemed rather in tune with the black cat that perched on his shoulder. It wouldn't hurt to learn from someone who had more experience. If only so she never failed her own familiar again.

"Hey." Julius drew her attention to him again. He didn't reach for her, but it looked like he wanted to. "Everything is going to be okay. We'll get him back." He chewed on his plump bottom lip, contemplating something before he reached out to brush aside an errant curl from her cheek. His touch lingered, fingertips hovering over her skin. He couldn't stop touching her, like it was an intrinsic need, and the crazy part was that she didn't want him to.

"Mana, please will it so." She sent the words up like a prayer.

Julius smirked and she answered with a teasing, tentative smile of her own. His palm enveloped her cheek and he seemed to pull her closer.

Iona let out a soft breath and forced herself to step away from him and the addictive sway of his touch. He scowled, his hand falling at his side.

"I am worried about my familiar," she confessed. She wanted him to understand why she was forcing the distance, but knowing that if he didn't, well, it wasn't her problem. "I was given a gift from Mana, and it's a bond I cannot deny."

"But you'll deny me..." He didn't sound angry about it, though a visceral sadness coated the words.

"Never. I would no sooner ignore the bonds of a familiar than I would the bonds of my mate." His eyes lit up, but he didn't touch her this time, and she was thankful for that. "I want you to understand, though, I won't explore this." She gestured between them. "Not while my familiar is out there suffering. I will not allow myself the liberty of a pleasant distraction. I will not let myself forget him through you. It's not fair to either of you."

Understanding seemed to dawn on Julius. His smile was soft. "Alright," he said. "But no more running from me. Let me help you do this. Let me help you get him back."

Warmth spread across her chest as gentle as any magic. "I would like that."

"Good." He clapped his hands together then. "If you don't want to be distracted with pleasures of the flesh, how about with something else?"

Her brows lifted. "Oh?"

His smile became a touch malicious. "Training."

That she could do. Training reminded her of the past, where good memories and bad collided to form a part of her. Training had always been an escape for her. A way to hone her skills; it gave her purpose and strength to do what she knew she needed to do.

It had been so long since she'd had someone to spar with.

Julius was strong; he'd be the perfect partner.

"Let's do this." She smiled, but inside, laughter threatened to bubble out.

I will fucking destroy you.

A Sword of Ice

Julius stood across from her on deck. He'd shucked his fur cloak and stood in nothing but a simple brown tunic—rolled up at the sleeves—pants, and boots. Iona tried not to be distracted by his arms and the thick dusting of hair across his skin, but it was difficult not to be. Then she caught his knowing smirk and she steeled herself against what she now knew was a purposeful ploy to best her.

If he wanted to play dirty, then she could too.

Her fingers worked at the ties of her cloak as she slowly and lasciviously began pulling it off and tossing it to the side. Next went her leather vest until she was in nothing but her own gray tunic and pants. Her breasts felt heavy beneath the confining fabric, and she knew it was nearly see-through, that he could just make out the sharp jut of her nipples beneath the cloth.

When she looked up, his pupils were blown wide and his nostrils were flaring as he took her in. She smirked and pretended to ignore him as she swept her own gaze around the deck.

They'd garnered an audience, their companions surrounding them and watching with amused expressions. Clay appeared next to her, carrying a sword like an offering. She stared at the blade as he held it out to her and shook her head.

"I won't be needing it."

Clay's blond brows rose, but he remained silent as he stepped back.

She turned back to Julius to find him smirking arrogantly at her. In his hand, he held his own glinting sword, wielding a shield in the other.

"Pretty confident in yourself, mate?" he taunted.

He was a lumbering predator, all bulk and long, prowling limbs that swallowed up a path back and forth, while his eyes sized her up. She knew he was gauging her for weaknesses. Because she was doing the same with him, but much more discreetly.

"Perhaps," she answered coyly.

"Your magic won't be enough on its own here, you know." He held out his sword, as if to emphasize his point. "You'll need so much more than that if you want to best me."

Power flared inside her body, responding to his taunts, brightening her veins an electric blue, filling her eyes with the lustrous hint of ice. "I'm sure I'll manage."

"Well then..." Julius charged.

Iona stayed still as he ran towards her. What he had in eagerness, she had in patience, and she waited until he was close, his sword arched over his head. She darted forward and magic burst from her fingertips on her right hand. It spread, lengthening, taking form, and when his sword came crashing towards her, she met him blade for blade.

His eyes widened with surprise, and she smirked at him over her sword of ice, molded to fit into her palm perfectly. Julius growled and pushed back against her.

Shock reverberated through her system at the jolt of the contact and she weaved and dodged as his sword followed. Steel and ice clashed, causing sparks and biting snow to rain down around them. Wherever his sword chipped, she sent her magic forward, hardening the ice of her newly made blade until it was practically impenetrable.

They parried back and forth, dancing around each other, every blow a striking force that she felt clatter her teeth together. It became evident, by the way she was panting and he wasn't, that he was going easy on her.

Rage flared up.

"Afraid to try harder?" she jested, causing him to glare. He charged and magic shot out from her left hand, coating the ground in slick ice. Julius slid with a cry and she dodged as he pummeled towards her, falling face first onto the floor.

She heard laughter ring out and fought away the urge to take a bow. When Julius stood to his feet and whirled, she didn't give him a moment of reprieve. Ice shot out, encasing his feet to the ground. He looked down at it as it spread up to his knees.

She knew the moment he used his magic. It made his whole body seemed to bulge, bulk up and strain with more muscle. A single jerk of his legs had the ice cracking and he was advancing with furious stomps. She tossed ice liberally in his direction, but the more she tossed, the angrier he seemed to get until he was practically charging for her.

Iona didn't want to run, but it was either that or have his brawny body slam into her. She turned and rushed away, and he chased. She flung magic back at him, but he broke past daggers of flying ice with only his fists, sending shards crunching beneath their feet.

"Fuck, fuck, fuck! Wait!" She threw out a wall of ice, but his rage and his muscles only seemed to increase with every punch. He broke through the wall face first and Iona rammed against the edge of the boat, panting. "Fuck! Julius—"

But he was already charging, dropping his sword and shield as he went. The collision of his body against hers sent the wind straight out of her lungs. She cried out in pain, his arms wrapped around her waist, and then gravity took over and they were both falling towards the water.

Iona didn't even get a moment to scream as they descended. Her mind flashed back to that instant years ago. A collision. Pain. Cold. Water. Dying.

Panic clawed at her throat and her magic reacted on instinct, spreading out beneath her in a viciously powerful instant. She wasn't sure how far it spread, wasn't even aware that it had until both she and Julius landed against solid ice instead of water.

The ice cracked where Julius landed, creating a crater that had him falling into cold water. In her fear, Iona scrambled away from the spreading slits in the ice, fear causing her to choke up. A moment later, Julius burst past the surface with a howl of rage, turning in the water until he caught sight of her. His fingers scrambled against ice as he pulled himself out, soaked and slippery.

"Are you alright?" She found her voice as he sprawled out against the ice. He didn't answer except with heaving breaths and a groan.

Too late, Iona realized the groan wasn't coming from him.

Her eyes widened as the boat collided against the ice she'd spread across the sea. The collision made the entirety of the metal boat shriek, and a jagged, hard edge perforated through the bottom.

It was all Iona could do not to scream as her magic ripped open the bottom of the boat, and it began to sink.

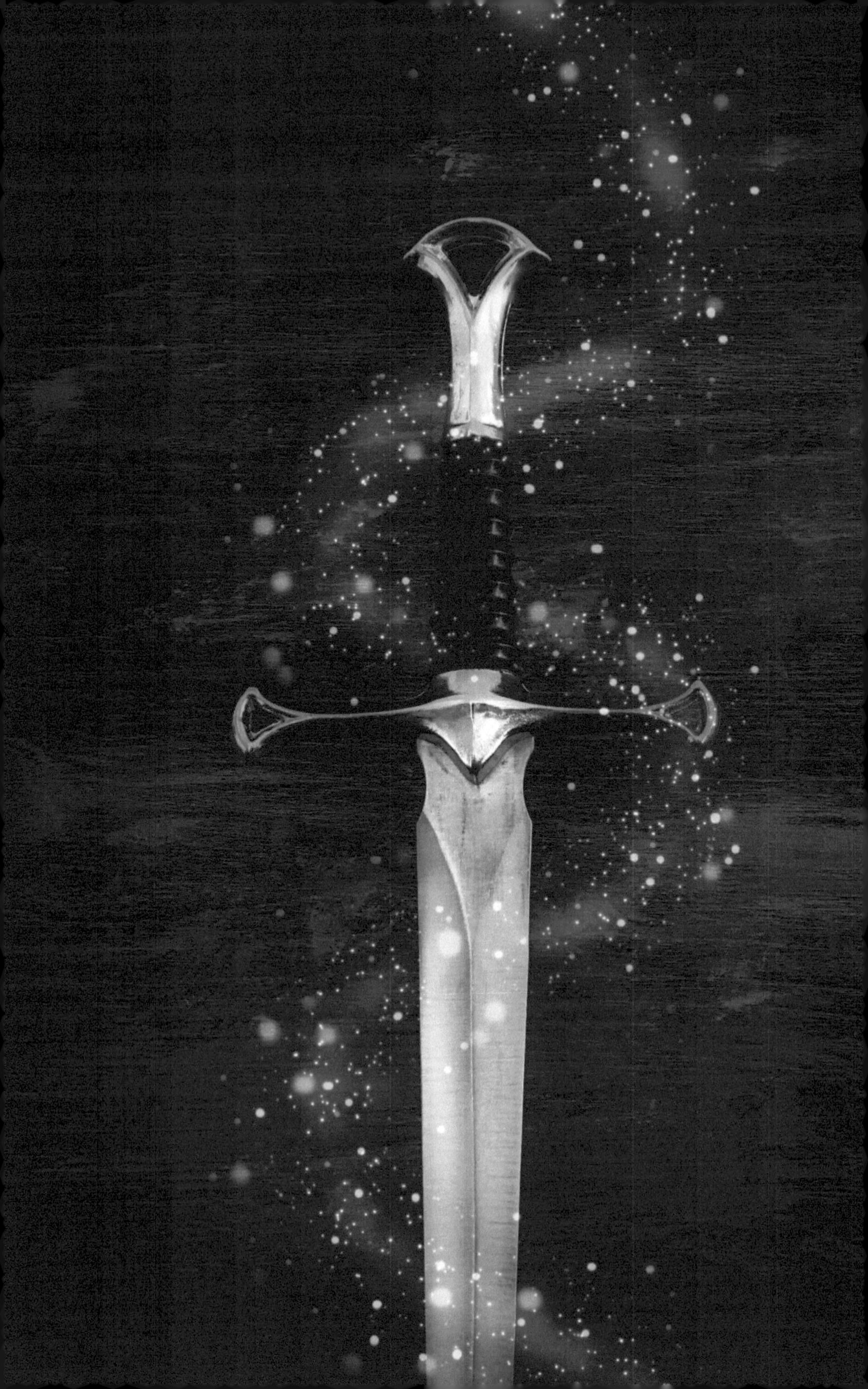

An Artistry in Scars

The boat lurched to a stop and started sinking.

Shouts could be heard from the deck, and Iona let out a curse as she jumped to her feet. She waved her arms over her head.

"A little help!" she shouted.

A moment later, the air in front of her shimmered and opened into a mirrored doorway that Uric stepped out of. She didn't acknowledge his glaring expression but darted through the entry without turning to see if Julius and Uric were at her heels. She burst through the portal on the other side, her feet skidding against the deck.

"Shula! I need your help!" The fire Fae ran on wobbling feet towards Iona, who didn't wait before she grabbed Shula's wrist and tugged, pulling her down to the stairs that led below deck.

A massive hole was dented inwards and water was rapidly rushing inside.

Iona stepped down, knee deep into the water towards the hole. The rapids pushed her backwards, but she gritted her teeth and forced her legs to cooperate. She had to fix this, because in her panic, she'd fucked up. Her heart felt like it was pounding in her throat as the water swallowed her legs, but she couldn't let the fear take over.

Her magic shot out from her palms and she directed it, letting it frost over the hole, slowly but surely blocking out the water. She willed the ice to harden more than the sword had so it resembled gleaming metal until no more of the ocean poured inside.

Even after she finished, there was still the matter of the water up to her waist. She turned to Shula, who still stood on the steps, staring at the pool, wide-eyed.

"Your turn, fire Fae," Iona said with a twitch of her mouth.

"Uh... I..." Shula trailed off and Iona could just make out her golden-brown cheeks reddening.

"You need to turn this into steam, or else we'll never get moving." She waited patiently, but when Shula still didn't move to do anything, Iona's eyebrows furrowed. "What's wrong?"

Shula shook her head back and forth. "I'm not sure if I can do that."

"You're going to have to—"

"No, I mean..." She paused, looking away from Iona, not meeting her eyes. "I don't know *how*. I—I just started using my powers a few months ago." She whispered the words like a sin, like something to be ashamed of.

Iona's own eyes widened. "No shit."

All her life, she'd used her magic. Her parents had encouraged it, but she was obviously older than Shula. Had lived in a different time when magic had been appreciated. She didn't have a childhood memory where she hadn't practiced honing her gifts.

Shula swallowed. "I mean, I can do some things. But I haven't perfected it. Not like you have. And I don't want to—"

"Hey, I'm not judging you." Iona waded through the water so she was closer to the other woman. "And honestly, I never would have guessed. You had such control over it when we were fighting that I just assumed..." She trailed off, observing Shula intently.

Shula was biting the inside of her cheek, and her trembling fingers pulled at her dark strands of hair, covering them over her ears and then uncovering them once more. It reminded Iona of her own finger tapping habits.

Everyone had their own monsters, some more vicious and deadly than others. Everyone had their own insecurities and this was obviously one of Shula's.

"I can teach you." The words had Shula snapping her gaze to Iona. "I mean, I'm not a fire Fae," she amended. "But I am an Elemental. You have good control. I'm guessing you just need to fine tune your abilities?"

Shula nodded.

"Right, so my magic is ice, but it's more than that. It's cold. It's molding shapes."

"Like that sword."

"Yeah. I used to make igloos on the beach at the Jade Court back when—" She broke off and shook her head. That information was irrelevant and brought with it pain that she didn't need. "Anyway, magic isn't just one aspect. Your magic isn't just burning. It's warmth. It's drying water. It's life."

Awareness shone in Shula's pretty golden depths. "Right."

"All you have to do is tell your magic what you want. In this instance, you don't want fire. You want the warmth it brings to dry all this water up. Give it a face, call it towards you. Concentrate."

Shula tugged at her hair again before she released a breath and stepped down, wading into the water beside Iona. She held out her palms, closed her eyes.

Iona waited, while keeping her own magic at the ready just in case. She could feel the waves of concentration coming off the other Fae and held her breath so as to not disturb her.

Shula's veins seemed to spark to life beneath her skin, like rivers of fireworks flickering across her veins, her magic came to life, the tips of her fingers glowing red. She grunted, the veins in her neck bulging.

Slowly, steam began to rise in the water. It heated Iona's legs, and the confines below deck grew almost stifling. Iona's own magic held strong against the boat, the ice solidifying with every pressing wave of heat. Sweat beaded against her face and she lifted her hand to wipe it away. Her curls frizzed against her cheeks. By the time Shula was finished, she was sweating through her clothes and they clung to her damp skin. Vapor surrounded them, nearly suffocating, but at least the water was gone.

Shula's eyes opened and she let out a gasp. Her own hair clung to her cheeks, strands sticking to her ears. She smiled and turned to find Iona chucking off her tunic, peeling the material from her skin.

"You did good." Iona hung her tunic or the rail so it could dry. She turned and caught sight of Shula staring at her back and the raised scars there. She smirked. "An agonizing experience, I can assure you."

"Don't I know it." Shula pushed off her fur cloak then reached for the hem of her tunic, yanking it over her head to mimic Iona, placing it over the rail. Then she turned, pushing aside her waist-length locks of hair to expose her back.

And the scars of flames down her spine.

There were two flames trapped within a circle, starting just at the base of her neck. The artistry of her scars matched Iona's own. As if they'd been carved by the same hand of fate. Shula had two circles, and Iona had five. But Iona's were old scars and Shula's looked fresh, crusted over with scabs and painful to look at.

Shula turned back around, fingering the tips of her long hair. "You know what it means, right?" Her voice shook.

"It means we are the last."

Shula swallowed visibly. She looked... uncomfortable, and for a moment that confused Iona. When they'd met a few hours ago she'd seemed confident in her abilities and now it seemed she was retreating within herself, hiding some integral part of her. Something about her was embarrassed. Afraid.

"We could have children someday," Iona said, her eyes flicking over the mark on Shula's neck. A mating mark. If she had to take a guess, it belonged to Ryker. The indication was there. From the way they'd pressed close to one another. From the way his eyes devoured her with every step. From the way his bicolored eyes flared. Like looking at her for too long hurt and was akin to jumping directly into a blazing fire, only to be consumed whole by her flames. "We might not always be the last."

Shula's eyes flashed with what Iona could only describe as surprise. "If we live that long."

Iona wanted to flinch at the harsh tone of her voice but shook her head. "What I've learned in my life is that it's best to trust in Mana. Mana will guide you if you believe." She paused and her fingers tapped against her thighs. "When I was young," she began softly, "my sister would pray every night to Mana."

It was a ritual of sorts, one that had irritated Iona to no end. Sometimes, in the dead of night while she was trying to sleep, she could hear her sister's voice echoing through the miniscule space of their shared room, interrupting Iona's rest.

She would toss a pillow to her sister's face. "Shut up or get out!"

"Have a care. I'm praying to Mana, and if you want my wishes granted, you'll shut up." And she'd go back to praying and Iona would groan, unsure why it would matter if Iona wanted Mana to answer her sister's wishes.

It wasn't until later that Iona found out her sister never prayed for herself but for others. For their brother's dreams. For Iona's wishes. Their own personal shooting star that streaked through their lives, leaving star dust of hope and faith and a little bit of magic behind.

And she'd been cruel about her voice softening the edges of the darkness.

She swallowed away the memories and forced firmness into her voice. "She said that if you sent your will out, Mana would hear it and turn things in your favor. So the more you say that this life is hopeless, the more hopeless it will be. I try to stay positive, and I pray to Mana that things get better and I know that one day it will. Eventually."

"Do you really believe that?" Shula's voice was quiet.

Did she really believe it? For so long, she'd scoffed at her sister for her habits and her sister had never taken offense. In fact, she'd smile as if Iona's critiques were endearing instead of annoying.

She remembered her sister's daily prayers, word for word, of every day.

Just like she remembered her last prayer, screaming out into a darkening day, with ashwood coating her tongue and iron embedded into her skin, her body coated in blood.

Save me.

Iona's nails dug into her skin, bringing her back to the present. She smiled at Shula, though it felt like a sad twitch of her lips. "I have to believe it," she whispered. "Because if I don't, what else is there?"

⁂

Iona was... well, she was fascinating.

She was everything Shula had ever wished she was and *more.* She was strong, independent, determined, and she radiated a positivity that Shula could only ever find in her dreams.

And she was everything Shula feared she'd be on the journey to Teg.

Iona knew how to wield her magic, embraced both it and the shape of her ears like an honor. She'd been a part of the original Resistance and wanted to help. To fight.

She believed in positive affirmations, that Mana was listening.

She wasn't a bitter Fae and had helped Shula through her own magic.

With every passing second, the more Shula got to know Iona, she wondered if the others would see in the ice Fae what Shula did, and if they wished *she* was more like that. If they wished Shula would have been as easy to fall into their fold as Iona was.

They'd kidnapped her, kept her with them, watched her so she couldn't leave. Shula had fought every step of the way and Iona just... accepted.

It was hard not to compare herself to the other woman when their purpose was the same. Now she had to find out where she stood within their space, where she could wedge herself between them. This woman was as scintillating as her ice beneath sunlight. It was a glow that seemed to be embedded into her personality. Shula didn't feel half as brave as Iona so obviously was.

That didn't sit right in her chest, and her magic stirred in response to her distress.

She turned away from Iona and slipped her tunic and jacket back on, feeling suddenly too vulnerable, too exposed before her. Her clothes became a barrier; if only they could ward off her negative thoughts.

"I'm going up," Shula said, avoiding Iona's gaze, lest the Fae see the truth in her eyes. That she would never surmount to be as incredible as her.

Her feet went up noiselessly and she chewed on the inside of her mouth, feeling Iona's gaze on her back, as if she could see through her clothes and to the scars underneath. No, not the scars. Her very soul. It had Shula panting as she reached the top deck. Her feet nearly slid against the surface as she ran to the edge, gripping the railing tightly. Her breaths were coming out in quick bursts, and the rolling waters beneath them seemed to calm her a fraction.

Everything felt too restraining, too tight against her chest. Like nothing fit, not even *her*, not her own skin against this new person she was trying to be.

She sucked in salty, cold breaths of air when his voice cut through the haze of her thoughts. "What is it?"

She jolted and turned to look at Ryker. At the picture he made in soft wafts of sunlight, the wind whipping at his long hair and beard. His scars seemed much more prominent against the graveness of his expression.

His eyes were flicking over her body as if he was looking for wounds. She wanted to tell him that the only thing wounded was her mind, not her body, but refrained from speaking. The last time they'd talked about the wounds of the mind, they'd ended up arguing.

And she was so, so tired.

"Nothing." She turned back to the sea, her mind dizzy, her stomach in knots.

"You're lying," he accused, stepping close to her and gripping her chin between his thumb and forefinger, pulling her gaze to his. "Tell me."

So much had changed. It was a thought that overpowered her as she looked up at her mate. They'd started out hating each other and now... what they had wasn't quite love exactly. It didn't even feel close enough to be that. But there was a certain admiration and honesty between them that she couldn't deny.

"Everything is different," she confessed. Telling the truth should have felt liberating, like a heavy weight lifted from her chest. Instead it just felt suffocating, like the weight of the truth was becoming even more confining. "She is different. I wasn't sure what to expect but she's so strong and everyone... you all praise her for it while I was condemned for what I thought was my own strength."

Ryker's nostrils flared and he sucked in a breath. "Shula." There was a silent plea in his voice as well as a berating tone. She forced herself to look away again, but all he did was growl and pull her gaze back to him, a quiet command between the two.

Eyes on me.

Like he was quietly protecting her from something. Like he had so many months ago while they witnessed the crueler hands of the Fae torturing a human that had helped kill Orna. He was always trying to protect her in little ways. Healing her wounds, pulling her gaze away from an image that would otherwise be branded into her soul.

But he could never protect her from the cruel truth of herself.

"She's amazing. She's brave. She's tough." *Everything you accused me of not being.* She didn't say those words aloud, but she was sure he felt them somewhere down the bond of their mating mark.

"You will be too," he interrupted.

Those words were like a knife to her chest. *You will be. Will.* Because she wasn't brave or tough or amazing. If she wasn't those things, then what was she besides a burden they had to train? Someone who until recently had been too human, too afraid of her own magic and true self.

She'd hid in the shadows to survive, had fled from fights, had denied herself. She was everything they abhorred in a Fae and they'd always told her so. Now she was with them, trying to leave that behind and fit into something else that wasn't quite right, either. Even if she wanted to be one of them, like a burning need inside her, they would always remember her as what she had been.

Tears prickled at the backs of her eyes, and she registered a brief flash of panic in Ryker.

She wanted to lash out at him, push him away like she always did. But she was trying to leave that scared, partly human girl behind her. "I don't want or need to hear that right now, Ryker," she said, her voice shaking.

"Then what do you *need* to hear?" He said it in such a way that let her know he genuinely wanted the answer to that. Maybe he felt her distress. As her mate, as her *bonded* mate, he would sense those things, her inner turmoil.

And his instincts wanted to make it better.

But she couldn't just give him all the answers. It was like he was asking her how to help fix her when she didn't even know the answer to that herself.

"I don't know." She turned away from him and it broke her heart because it was the truth. She wished someone could help her. Wished someone could tell her what she was supposed to do, how to be stronger and not the coward they all so obviously thought she was. She wanted that with a fire that burned inside.

"Shula... I will do anything for you. Tell me what to do." His timbre was a low growl.

"What could you do?" Her eyebrows rose. "Heal me? Protect me?" She paused, tilting her head to the side. "Love me as I am?"

His eyes flashed and his mouth dropped open, but nothing came out.

Yeah, she thought. *Didn't think so.*

"Do you think we rushed into this?" Her finger slid over the crescent shaped mark on her neck. Touching it left her feeling sensitive, weightless, and a spike of desire shot through her that she quickly tamped down. There was a certain artistry in the scars they both wielded that spoke of so many things that she was almost too afraid to voice.

"What do you mean?" The words were all but a growl, his expression angry, but deep in her chest, in her soul where the bond was nestled, she felt a rising flare of panic not her own.

"Maybe we should have waited for this." She gestured at the bite, between them, voicing the pain. "Maybe... maybe we aren't right for one another and it was just a moment of selfish weakness for the both of us."

His anger spiked. It made her magic swell, but she smothered it. She didn't want him pissed, and she didn't want to hurt him, either. He was her mate, but he shouldn't be burdened with fixing her, just like she shouldn't be the one giving him the answers on how. Just like he should care for her because of who she was and not who he wished she would be. Because that pressure? It built inside her chest like an ache, and all she wanted to do was please him and everyone else. But she was losing herself in it, and there was no way out.

"Is that what you feel?" he gritted out tightly.

Shula's shoulders shrugged. "I don't know. Maybe. Let's be honest, Ryker, we don't really *love* each other. We hardly know each other and what we do know has been all fighting and hatred. Maybe Mana is wrong and we aren't meant to be mates. Maybe we're just wrong for each other."

His rage was a storm inside her chest and she tried to pick it apart, to separate it from her own confusing emotions so they weren't tangled in the same, messy web. She wanted to feel what she needed to feel, not his own emotions, not his rage or panic or betrayal. But even while she picked apart the threads of their feelings, he seemed to latch on, surging inside her so he could feel her own confusion and helplessness.

His eyes narrowed. And she could feel every battle waging between them. His instinct screamed at him to grab her. Maybe a part of her wanted that. To be held and cherished, to be told that she was just as brave and amazing as anyone else.

But Ryker was never one to hold to false promises and hope. His every word had always been honest and brutal, and this was no different just because she was his mate.

"Then run away from me, just like you run from fucking everything else."

The tears slid down her cheeks even as she tried to stop them. She felt his pang of panic at the sight of them. While he hated himself for hurting her, he also didn't feel regret at the words, because they felt honest.

She was burning from the inside, smoke in her lungs threatening to choke her. She took a step back and Ryker went to reach for her. She wasn't sure if it was to change his mind or to say more of the cruel things he was so good at saying.

He didn't get close to her, because her fire shot out and scorched his palm. He cried out and guilt swallowed her whole, but she didn't stop to check his wound. She knew if she touched him, that bond that pulsed between them would overtake her with lust and she'd forget every cruel thing he said, and she didn't want to forget. She turned and ran down below deck.

Iona was no longer there, but the whisper of her magic still was. Shula was alone. She threw herself into a corner, tugging at the strands of hair, pushing and pulling them over her ears and back again.

Her tears burned like rivers of fire, and they tasted like embers on her tongue as she struggled to catch a breath. Footsteps sounded down the stairs, light and recognizable. A moment later she was enveloped with the rich scent of something bubbly and decadent and delicious. Not quite confection, but something smooth and drinkable, like a rich wine and bright flavors that popped in the mouth.

Clay.

He sat next to her and didn't speak, but he grabbed her around the shoulder. The next moment she was in his arms, sitting across his lap while his hand pressed against the back of her head so her cries were drowned out against the front of his tunic.

"You can cry, Fire Dancer. There's no shame in that."

The words opened a floodgate of emotions inside her. She felt Ryker trying to tug against their connection and she slapped him away, building up a wall to block him out. She didn't want him here. Not now. She wanted to grieve and figure shit out on her own.

Heal herself, because no one was going to fucking do it for her.

And Clay? He held her as her mind whirled through those thoughts. He held her long after the tears dried and her face was sticky with evidence of her weakness.

She pushed away from him, settling back at his side. Her head dropped to the wall behind her and she looked up at the creaking ceiling.

"It smells like fish down here," she said, her voice a mere rasp from crying.

Clay chuckled. "It wasn't me, I swear."

Shula found herself echoing the laughter softly. Then she groaned and tugged at the ends of her long hair.

"What am I doing, Clay?"

"I would guess you were letting your emotions out." His fingers clasped against her knee and squeezed. She found comfort in the touch. "Nothing wrong with not wanting to be around those assholes." He side eyed her. "Or one asshole specifically. What'd he do, Fire Dancer? Want me to drain his blood?"

She held back a shudder at the thought of Clay using his magic against Ryker. She'd only seen it once briefly when they were in Terrlyn, a small town in Orknie. A soldier had been hurting Filomena, a young maid in a safe house they were staying at. All he'd done was hold out his hand and magic surged, bursting the guard's veins from the inside. The influx of blood poured from his orifices, making him look grotesque. It even made Clay's own eyes and nose bleed.

All magic came with a price. In his instance, it was blood for blood.

"No," she answered, because she believed he would fight for her honor if she asked it of him. Despite their rocky beginnings, she considered Clay a friend. A best friend, if she was inclined to lean towards that idea, which she supposed she *was.* He'd always been there for her, giving her the emotional support she needed.

She hadn't wanted friends.

He became one just the same.

"What's wrong?"

She sighed and pushed her hair away. "I just don't know where I fit in."

His blond brows pulled together. "Where? Here? With us, you mean?"

"I'm not like you all and it's never been more painfully obvious than it is now. A new set of ears isn't going to change that about me. I think I'm still... human, or as human as I ever pretended to be. And they can all still see it. I see their judging looks. It fucking hurts."

She'd never been so honest with someone else before except probably Fanny. That had ended in disaster, but Clay was different. She didn't know how, he just was.

"Why do you want to please them so badly—?" He broke off, his eyes going wide. "Ah," he said with understanding. "Because of Iona?"

Shula took her bottom lip between her teeth and forced a nod.

"Right. Look, Fire Dancer, I think I get it. Your whole life you've been forced to hide who you are, then to pretend you were something you're not to keep yourself safe. I certainly don't fucking begrudge you for it, but I think a part of *you* still does." She opened her mouth to argue and he shot her a look full of mirth. "Look, let me finish, alright? You've been used to molding yourself, to change so you fit exactly into the environment you're at. You had to alter your ears, pretend to be human and become one. Your goals have changed and now you have to learn to be Fae all over again, right?"

She hated how accurate it was. He'd ripped the words straight from her soul when even she hadn't been able to place them.

"Right," she agreed.

"Now you're trying to fit in with us. Because they gave you so much shit for any decision you ever made, now you're trying to mold yourself again just to fit into our little circle. To be what you think we want you to be."

"How did you—"

"Trust me, I know more than anyone. I grew up in the Sapphire Court, remember? My parents were nobles and they wanted me to be a proper little shit. I tried to force myself out of the image they wanted for me and I became something else. Then my father died and I suddenly had to fit into everything I ever rejected and it was restraining." He shrugged. "So I get it. I understand."

"How did you do it?" she asked. "Fit in, I mean."

He sighed and his lip tilted into a smirk, showing off his one dimple, making the indent in his chin look all the more prominent. "The thing is, I never did."

Her hopes deflated and she sagged against the wall.

"Fire Dancer, what if there's no magical secret? It's not as complicated as we make it out to be. We aren't all the same, but what someone lacks, someone else makes up for it. Think of Julius. He's fucking strong, he's a good warrior, but he isn't serious enough. He has anger issues. Valerio is level-headed, but he's fucking impatient and eager sometimes. Uric is stealthy, protective, but he's blinded by loyalty. Ryker is an amazing healer, but he's so caught up in his past that he can't see past the scars on his face. And Weylyn?" He paused, chewing against his lip. "Well, Weylyn's a giant fucking dick. I don't know what to say about him." Shula chuckled. "And I'm... I'm loyal, I'm clearheaded, but sometimes I get in my emotions and let them take over."

"And me?" she asked in a small voice, almost afraid at what he would say.

He smirked again and tapped his finger to her nose. "I think you're perfect."

She swallowed the lump in her throat. "Be serious. Please."

"Fine. I think you have great power inside you. I think you're determined and kind and fierce, but you're too afraid to realize just how amazing you really are. Does that answer satisfy you?"

She sucked in a watery breath and felt the tears slip from her eyes anew. He said all that with such fervor, like he truly believed she was all those things.

Yet she still asked, "You don't think I'm cowardly?"

"Fuck no, and whoever says otherwise is a fucking idiot and I'll fight them for you. Do you know what strength means, Fire Dancer?"

"It means..." What did it mean? "It means bravery, it means fighting—"

"I'm going to cut you off right there. Fire Dancer, strength doesn't mean just one thing. There are so many different kinds of strength and everyone wears a different kind like a brand. There's the quiet strength of a mother kissing her child's wounds. There's the graceful strength of a dancer twirling across a stage. There's brute strength to punch through a boulder. There's something especially brave in the strength it takes to keep living after you've lost everyone you love.

"We all have some kind of strength in us. Maybe not everyone understands your brand of power yet, but they fucking will. Because you, Fire Dancer, are fucking powerful in your own right. You could move mountains, burn cities, reduce evil to ash, give life and hope to this world that has none." He brushed aside a lock of hair to expose her ears, his fingers grazing them gently. "Having these doesn't make a difference. They're not a reflection of what's in here." His palm pressed to her chest. Right over the rapid beating of her heart. Then he dropped his hand back into his lap and his smile was a radiant thing on his face, making him so much more beautiful. "The next time you ask yourself if you fit in, don't. Because you already do, Fire Dancer. *You already do.*"

Ryker couldn't concentrate. Not on the waves pushing the boat towards their destination. Not on his familiar, curling her body around his legs. Not even on the impending journey ahead. Usually, he was always hyper-focused, and yet he couldn't. Fucking. Concentrate.

The blame for this was the Fire Dancer's.

Shula Azzarh's.

His mate.

She was the culprit who invaded his thoughts with maddening frequency. Where he'd once despised the very thought of her taking up space within him, now things were different. The mating mark pulsing on his neck reminded him of that.

That she occupied a place inside his soul. They were interwoven. They'd sealed their fate. *She'd* sealed her fate the moment she'd let him sink his canines and cock into her.

She was *his.*

And she was *angry.*

Desperately, he reached down their bond, invisible fingers caressing their twining threads. Her presence burned warmly, brightly. It thawed out pieces within him, giving life to what he thought had been dead.

Now that she'd awaken those parts, he couldn't imagine being without her warmth. Without her care. Without her.

But the moment their minds brushed, he felt her build a barrier, higher and tighter than any iron wall.

The rejection stung and grated.

His head snapped in the direction she'd gone. The direction where Clay had followed after. Where she would lean closer to him. And Clay, bastard that he fucking was, would allow it.

Rationally, Ryker knew the two were just friends. Unfortunately, he could no longer rely on that rationality. His thoughts were possessive, feral. He wanted to rip Clay's hands off for daring to touch his mate. The first time, he could have forgiven, but he did it too liberally and too frequently. His fingers trailed against Shula's arm, her hair, her *ears,* every spare chance he got.

Like he was baiting Ryker every time he marked Shula with his disgusting scent. Embers and confection and *chocolate* mingled with the richness of roses and wine.

The only thing keeping Ryker sane was imagining flaying Clay's flesh from bone. For being a barrier between Ryker and Shula. For holding her as she cried.

It should have been Ryker kissing away the tears from her cheeks. It should have been Ryker who she confided in.

Why was it so much easier for his mate to turn to Clay than to Ryker? His fingers twitched, bringing attention to the burn against his palm. He did not begrudge her for lashing out, as it had been accidental. His injured hand rose to his face, over the scars that marred his skin. Was he so monstrous on the outside and within, that she did not feel comfortable enough speaking the truth to him? Was it because Clay was prettier to look at and therefore, easier to trust?

Well Ryker would never be Clay. He would never be pretty and easy-going. He had suffered phantom pains in places that Clay could never imagine, and would continue to do so. He could not change what he was or what he looked like and he did not care to.

But for a brief moment, pain built an ache in his chest and for the first time in his life, he wished...

The door opened once more and Clay filed out with Shula close behind. Ryker's eyes snapped to his mate, but she studiously avoided his gaze. Not before he caught her puffy, swollen eyes. Not before he caught her leaning closer towards Clay as if searching for his support.

Those elegant, unmarked hands reached for Shula, giving her hand a squeeze.

It took everything within Ryker not to gnash his canines or rip out his friend's throat. Every instinct in his body roared in a vicious demand for blood. He would have run forward and yanked them apart. He would have dug his hands into Clay's neck.

He would have...

Had Shula not turned to him then. A brief, flashing expression came over her features. Of pain and hurt and something else even more terrifying.

Regret.

The truth of it was there in a blink before she turned away once more. Feet of space separated them, but the distance had never felt so vast, the space between them had never felt so empty.

And Ryker's heart had never felt more broken.

The West Isles

The West Isles were surrounded by iron, just like Iona had said they would be. Iron eroded from the sand like stone circles in the Unseelie Courts of Tir na Faie. They spread out across the shoreline like a wall to keep intruders out. The docks were more like a long metal bridge. They expanded miles out onto the sea that people walked across and made it to the entrance, a wrought iron gate manned with humans holding lethal weapons.

"Well, we can't go in through there." Iona sighed as she slammed the spyglass closed. They were miles away from the Isles still, and they needed a new route if they wanted to somehow get past the wall. "Go around," she ordered. "We'll see if we can find a place to enter."

"How exactly are we going to get past them undetected?" Uric clipped. "We've seen them, it won't be long until they see us."

"You have so little faith," Iona teased, even while clenching a fist, lest she send it flying for his bastard nose. "Prince Valerio, please turn the boat. We'll circle the island."

The prince didn't question her as he turned the wheel of the ship, changing their course. And before Uric could open his mouth and speak again, she stepped towards the front of the ship.

"Shula," she called out, turning to meet the fire Fae's gaze. Burning embers met hers with determination. Iona didn't know much about the other Fae, but she felt a kinship all the same. There was something just beneath her surface that was primed and ready to prove. Like a fire licking past the windows within a burning building, waiting for the perfect opportunity to erupt. "Ready to create fog?"

A knowing look passed over her expression and her lips tilted in the smallest of smiles before she stepped next to Iona.

"Steam the ice, Shula Azzarh," Iona whispered.

Her hands glowed blue and snow and ice began to form against the surface of the water. As soon as it hit, crystalizing the surface, Shula's own hands shot out and plumes of steam emerged until the ice was melted entirely.

They worked side by side, using ice and fire to create a steam so thick, it clouded around the air like a dense fog, blocking their ship and the whole horizon from the enemy's view.

Shula's hair flapped against the wind, the curling edges sticking to her cheeks, the ends slapping against Iona's own skin. Raw magic vibrated between them, Mana tethering them together as they worked. Iona felt a burst of strength and knew without having to look that Shula felt it, too.

They were stronger together, and their bonds would only grow.

The boat glided through the water, weaving around the Isles, past rocks that jutted out through the ocean.

They circled around the island. It was more dangerous here, where rocks congregated, piercing out like weapons of warning against boaters. But they pushed through, Iona freezing the rocks and Shula melting them until they disintegrated in the water. Once they were far enough away from port, their magic dissipated and the fog cleared enough to reveal caves.

They carved into the walls of black, high cliffs. A waterfall with dark water fell from the top, splashing against black shores below.

"This might have been a place where smugglers came," Iona whispered, almost afraid to break through the eerily echoing sounds of the water. "Back when the things that are now legal were illegal."

Prince Valerio steered the boat close to a cave and a moment later, they dropped anchor. The walls high up on this cliff weren't made of iron, but of natural elements, and were unmanned. Iona didn't know how long it would be that way; she knew they had to hurry.

She turned to look at Uric. "You. Make a portal now."

His lip pulled back in a sneer and she felt a strange sense of gratification in the gesture. He looked like he wanted to argue, but Prince Valerio pressed a hand to his shoulder, silencing him immediately.

She almost cooed at him like a good little dog but bit her lips instead.

Everyone gathered around Valerio at the quick gesture of his fingers and convened in a circle.

"We do not know what we will face when we get there," he said. "I want us to separate in three groups."

Valerio, Uric, and Weylyn.

Shula, Ryker, and Clay.

Julius and Iona.

Those were the groups Prince Valerio chose just before Uric opened the portal. Their plan was simple. Search the island for her familiar and meet back within the hour by the top of the cliffs to come up with a plan.

Once Uric opened the portal, Iona was all too eager to step through it, but Julius gripped her upper arm before she could.

"Wait," he leaned down to whisper, his beard grazing the sensitive skin on her cheek, making her tremble.

Ryker and Shula stepped through first, and then Clay followed.

"Trust me out there, Iona." His fingers came up to brush aside a stray curl. "We work as a team."

Before she could answer, Uric grunted, "Hurry up."

She broke away from him, and his fingers slid down the length of her arm. His hold left a feeling of wakefulness behind. A sense of trust, of unity. The feeling settled even as she stepped through the reflective surface of the portal, pushing through it and landing on the other side.

Her feet sunk into black sand and rock. Her head tilted up to the sky, and when Julius emerged from the other side, she made a face. "The air smells like fish."

His fingers were comforting against her lower back. He wasn't pressing for affection, wasn't forcing flirtations, but was offering stability that she desperately needed.

Iona's whole body trembled with worry and anticipation that she tried to stave off by taking deep breaths. Her fingers tapped against her thighs as she swiveled her gaze around the island.

There wasn't much to see, as they were perched on top of a cliff, but beyond, she could just make out the bustling noise of a small city and feel the restricting pressure of iron coating the air.

"Everyone split up," Valerio ordered. "And make haste." His already dark eyes seemed to darken even further. His nostrils flared, and there was a hint of premonition and warning in his voice. "The air is thick with blood."

The Isles was like a metropolis. A city that burst at the confines with too many people, with too many tastes and textures and scents. It was a marketplace of illegalities, the stalls filled to the brim with things that had once been forbidden.

Ashwood, belladonna, and of course, Fae.

Iron cages hung from stalls and swung back and forth, rattled with the desperate rage of the pixies inside. Blue skinned, with sharp, snarling teeth, they tried gnawing at the iron bars of their prison. In other places, she made out High Fae slaves, their heads shaved and collars clamped around their throats, being walked through the streets like pets.

The Fae weren't the most astonishing things enslaved in the market.

That honor went to the animals.

Creatures were held behind bars like in a zoo, but this? It was crueler.

Tigers with black and blue stripes were corralled into corners by iron spears, evidence of past cruelties prominent over their bodies. Thick black horns had been shorn off into nothing but tiny stumps, and when they snarled, it was to reveal fangs made of iron instead of bone.

Two headed deer in mismatched colors of black and white, magical and holy creatures from Tir na Faie, were laying in a pool of their own blood, their eyes gauged out, their meat being sold by the kilo.

There was a cage filled with horned rabbits, creatures that symbolized good luck, with body parts missing and hanging from knotted rope that swayed with the breeze.

Iona wanted to cry beneath the shadows of her hood, but she held herself straight as they walked through the throng, cloaked and hidden. The only reason they'd decided to wander through the crowd at all was because they were busy, and foreigners walked similarly to how they were, with their hoods pulled over their faces.

This market was what Iona always imagined George to have worked at, but he'd never been purposefully cruel as far as she could tell. His market had never been like this. Everything he sold was already dead and harvested. Not alive and bleeding.

Julius was a formidable presence behind her, and she tried to use him to ground her, to keep her focused. She had the urge to bust down all the cages. She'd always had that impulse at the zoo, because of how helpless and starved they looked, but this was different. These cages were smaller. This was heartbreak in its most ethereal form.

She had to remind herself she was here for her familiar. Just imagining all he was going through made her blood turn cold. Her fingers tapped against her thighs in retaliation against her thoughts. They moved incessantly until she felt Julius' warm fingers wrap around her wrist, stopping the movement. Like he'd sensed her distress and was grounding her.

The touch was gone as soon as her fingers settled, leaving behind that tingling sensation of rightness.

"I think the bigger animals are over here," Julius' voice said gruffly. Even while he calmed her down, she could feel the tension rolling off him. This wasn't an easy place to be. And if they were caught?

The West Isles had always been a place of savage humans and barbarians. Iona had never really been sure what had happened to it after the fall of the Feylands. George had gifted her with whispered theories about what they'd become, about how they'd called themselves the Kurreen and allied themselves with the Emperor of Illyk. They were an island of mercenaries who rode through the desolate Feylands, looking for magical creatures to take back to their island of iron and cages. They rid themselves of the animals, while the emperor's soldiers rid the world of the Fae.

They wove their way through the busy place, Iona keeping her eyes straight ahead to avoid looking at something else that would shoot straight through her heart and distract her.

Small cages and stalls made way for the bigger ones. Animals like elephants and bison, animals that could very well have been the last of their kind. She took a breath, and when they rounded a corner, it was like being hit in the chest. The blows came, painful and unyielding. Her eyes widened and her mouth opened as a painful cry burst from her lips.

There was a cage beyond, so far and yet she saw everything in it so clearly. She saw her familiar trapped in the corner of the large prison. The Kurreen in their pirate attire were gripping spears that they jabbed against his body.

They might as well have been stabbing her.

Every blow to his body was like pain to her own chest. The bond that had been silent for so long was suddenly screaming, the agony ripping through her mind and soul, splintering her apart from the inside.

They were torturing him. Blood bloomed across his once spotless coat and she recognized the net as they threw it over his body and pressed him to the ground. It was the same net they'd used the first time she saw him, and the same asshole wielding the whip.

Iona took a step without realizing it and before she knew it, Julius' arms were wrapped around her middle, hauling her back and into the secrets of the shadows and hidden alleyways where they wouldn't be seen, and where she couldn't see.

But just because she didn't have eyes on her familiar didn't mean she couldn't feel it. That pain, the hopelessness.

Tears broke from her eyes and froze on her cheeks. Her nails dug into Julius' hands as she struggled against his hold.

"Let me go," she gritted out in gasping breaths. "Let me go."

"Iona..." His lips pressed to her ear, but not even the steady scent of him could keep her from reaching him, could keep her calm. "Don't, please."

"Let go of me. I have to get to him. I have to."

"Think about this, Iona. If you go out there like this, they'll kill you *and* him."

She couldn't listen to reason, not when her emotions were running too high, too demanding and aggressive. She had to get to him, if it was the last thing she did. Her magic shot from her body, ice freezing Julius from the bottom and making its way up in painful increments. He grunted against the freezing bite of her power, but he still held her tightly.

He gasped in her ear. "Freeze us both if you must, my love, but I am not fucking letting you go."

Ice cracked with every flex of his muscles. Behind her, his nostrils flared wildly and, pressed intimately to the space at her back, she could feel the savage thudding of his heart.

Her fingers scratched and her mind tried to push away his pleas. Her magic was angry, looking for retaliation. And Julius was taking the brunt of it, breaking it away, even as he grew angrier and angrier. But he didn't crush her beneath his grip. He fought away the rage that consumed him.

"Iona," he growled. "Listen to my voice. Listen to my heart."

He was an anchor holding a rocking boat in place and that sound steadily broke through the haze of her panic. Her fingers dug into his skin, moving instinctively, rapidly clawing through the spider web pattern of her old ceiling. His heart bounced to the rhythm of her finger strokes, pulling her out of that headspace, bringing her back into the moment.

He must have felt when her body calmed because he loosened his hold, and she slumped in his arms and began to sob.

Julius held his mate in his arms as she cried. His arms were the only things holding her upright so she wouldn't crumple to the ground in her agony.

They may not have officially mated, but he could still feel her pain like it was his own, and that in and of itself was akin to dying. The ache spread through his chest, made him anxious. His instincts roared, like a vicious monster trying to break through his body. Both from feeling her and from the aftermath of using his own magic. He wanted to protect her. Needed to do it with every fiber of his being.

And protecting that bear was like protecting her in a way.

He knew what she was feeling. Wanting to rush and smash the humans' skulls down to their toes wasn't something reserved for Iona alone.

He wanted them to pay too.

"We have to be smart about this," he whispered, pulling her back up and turning her to face him.

Frost glittered against her dark cheeks like diamonds, tears she'd frozen in place. He reached a hand up to brush them aside, the cold catching against his dull nails.

She sucked in a breath, her eyes meeting his. They were dark with the barest hint of frost against the black orbs. Like snow was glittering just beneath the surface.

"We need a plan to get him out alive. Do you understand?"

Almost numbly, she nodded.

"Iona." His voice came out gruff, snapping her out of it. Not out of impatience, but because he needed her to focus, not travel to whatever far away part her mind tried to take her to.

Her gaze focused on him. "I'm here," she whispered.

He searched her eyes, making sure it was true, before he continued. He cupped her face between his big palms. His thumbs traced a line against her cheekbones, and he heard her suck in a breath.

"We'll get him back, Iona. We *will.*"

"Promise me you will do whatever it takes."

Of all the promises Julius could ever make, this would be the easiest of his life, and the one he would fight the most to keep.

"Yes." He bent and pressed a soft kiss to her forehead, a surprisingly tender gesture for him, and he whispered against her skin. "And we'll kill anyone who gets in our way."

Tombs of Ice

They met the others back near the cliffs to come up with a plan. Julius fabricated it and Iona listened, trusting him enough to plot out the rescue of her familiar. Under any other circumstances, she never would have confided in anyone else with it.

She could trust Julius.

It was insane that she felt that when they'd only just met, but the dangerous promise he'd whispered in her ear before still echoed in her ears.

We'll kill anyone who gets in our way.

It's what she'd desperately needed to hear. And it felt nice knowing that someone would put as much value on her familiar's life as she did.

She could tell a lot about the way someone treated an animal, and the fact that he was willing to go through these lengths, and not just for her, but for others? She had felt the way disgust roiled from his body with each passing stall. She saw the way his hands had clenched. Despite his own feelings, he'd acted calm, steady, and he'd talked her down from doing something impulsive and destructive.

Now, she would see just how many bodies he left in the pathway to save the other part of her soul.

Once the plan was set in motion, they broke up into groups again, Shula and Iona together and the males heading off in different directions. Before Iona and Shula made way towards the cage where they were keeping her familiar, Ryker stopped his mate with a touch on her arm.

Iona tried not to notice the way Shula seemed to tense near the male. Or the way they were silent, saying nothing. But they did look deep into each other's eyes, silent words of communication passing between the both of them. It seemed conversation enough. When they pulled away and Shula made it to Iona's side, Iona looked to the other Fae.

"Everything okay?"

Shula seemed surprised that Iona would ask, her eyes widening a fraction, the expression quickly veiled by the pressing hard lines of her features. "Everything's fine," she replied absently.

Iona wasn't inclined to believe her, but she didn't ask. Instead they moved forward. They walked in relative silence, the closer they got to the city, the tenser things became. By the time they reached the alley near her familiar's cage, Iona's whole body was vibrating with anticipation and fury.

The Kurreen were no longer torturing him, but men were posted outside of the cage, slumped near it, joking. As if they hadn't a care in the world while the fresh blood of Iona's familiar still stained their spears and whips.

She would rip them apart.

The thought came as vicious as the tidal wave that had pulled her under the depths so many years ago.

Her familiar was in a corner of the cage, his body hunched, bleeding and afraid. Iona's gaze stayed on him for the longest time, willing him to understand that she was coming for him, hoping he could feel her through their bond.

Then he looked up, eyes focusing on the spot where she was standing, and she swore he could see her hiding in the shadows, the expression marring her features murderous and ready for blood. Her whole body quivered with the thrilling thirst for their lives.

She wanted to rush to him. The urge was right there, simmering beneath her blood, demanding retribution, but she had to force herself to wait. Julius had promised a distraction. A safe way to get her familiar out.

But she waited.

And waited.

She tried not to let her impatience show, but her fingers pressed incessantly against her thighs and her breathing grew almost shallow.

Then, almost imperceptibly, there was a shout from the crowded market. Her attention was dragged away for a brief moment to find two figures ramming into each other, hooded cloaks up to hide their faces. But Iona swore she caught the gleam of canines flashing beneath the shadows.

She could just make out Clay's and Julius' voices, rising in challenge. Then the scrape of steel followed by the clang of weapons clashing. A crowd had gathered to watch the commotion and instead of breaking it up, they placed bets and jeered. As if this was an everyday occurrence that didn't bother them. In fact, they seemed to relish in the violence and promise of death.

The West Isles were bathed in violence and blood. It only made sense the people were, too.

"Now!" Iona urged, darting from the shadows.

Shula followed behind her, but she didn't turn to the fire Fae as she made her way to the men surrounding her familiar's cage.

Their eyes strayed to her absently, as they were more focused on the fight beyond, and she didn't lower her hood so they could look into her eyes. She saw them just fine, and that was enough. Her magic shot out and a sword formed in her hand.

They gasped at the sight, tripping over one another as they fell backwards onto the ground. She froze them in place, letting ice coat its way along their feet to keep them pinned in place before she advanced.

Her sword of ice reamed through their flesh, and those who decided to scream found their tongues scorched by Shula's fire. They choked on fire and blood; their silent screams of agony lost to the violence ripping through the air. When the life finally left them, it was their tombs made of ice that trapped their miserable souls in place.

Ice crept up and coated the locks on the cage, and Iona brought the hilt of her sword swinging down against the lock, shattering it to pieces.

She didn't ask Shula to cover her as she went inside. She trusted this Fae, too.

Her familiar stood as she approached, and she tried not to cry at the sight of his body, worse than when he'd arrived at the zoo. Whole clunks of skin and fur were missing, his eye crusted over with blood, and when his mouth opened, two teeth were missing.

A sob lodged up her throat. "I'm so sorry." She held her hands out, slow to approach. She knew what it felt like when people went towards her just a little too fast. How quickly the mind could flash back to a different time of cruelty and pain. She wouldn't cause him anymore.

He lowered his head slightly and she heard a voice through her mind. No, not her mind, she realized. Through her soul.

It was not your fault.

Her eyes widened as she realized what happened. Her familiar was communicating with her. Tears prickled behind her eyes, but she forced those away. Her palms came down against the sides of his face and she pressed her forehead to his.

"It won't happen again. Ever," she vowed.

He rumbled something that sounded like approval or contentment. She didn't know. Because Shula was rushing into the cage, her eyes wide. "Time to go." Her chest heaved with every breathless word.

Iona turned and found the distraction of Clay and Julius was being broken up by soldiers. Soldiers wearing the colors of the Emperor of Illyk.

"Fuck."

"Yeah," Shula said, hand clamping down on Iona's. "*Fuck.* We have to go."

She tugged her out of the cage, and Iona could feel her familiar following behind. Iona dug her heels into the ground, abruptly stopping Shula in her tracks.

"Julius—"

His howl came a moment later. It was a sound of rage and pain. And from where she stood, she saw clearly how the hood of his cloak slipped, revealing his face. His ears.

A hush seemed to collectively settle over the crowd. Everyone stopped, frozen. And then, Clay lowered his hood as well, revealing a feral, beautiful grin that matched Julius'.

As one, the humans charged, encircling Julius and Clay, drawing their weapons and sneering at their ears. Weapons clashed, and they were swallowed up by the crowd.

Panic and rage swelled inside Iona. "We have to help them!" She started towards them, but Shula yanked her back.

"That wasn't part of the plan," she said. "They can handle themselves."

"Fuck that." She pulled herself from Shula's hold and started to run. Just as Julius broke through the throng of humans with a beastly roar. Limbs and blood flew through the air as Julius tore through them with his bare hands.

He was like a boulder, a force of pure strength and fury busting through flesh and bone like he was breaking through brick or her ice. The humans seemed to realize just how dangerous he was, because some fled. Those that didn't charged for him.

Someone snuck up at his back but suddenly Clay was there, lifting his palm up. Iona held her breath and watched blood explode from every orifice of the human.

A shower of gore rained down like a geyser and when Clay turned, she could see the blood dripping from his own eyes and nose. He was the perfect picture of violence and wore a smile so at odds with that destructive power that Iona couldn't help but laugh.

But just as a single wave of attacking humans ebbed, another took its place. They charged, quickly overpowering Julius and Clay.

Her feet flew across the ground as she dove into the fray. Elbows and the slice of swords met her. Her magic shot through her veins like a jolt and she unleashed it. Ice rose from the ground in jagged spikes, splintering everyone apart, piercing through bodies like blades. The air was filled with the scent of blood and the crying groans of the dying. Her magic gave the Fae a moment of reprieve, and Julius' green eyes met hers from across the deadly, glittering beams.

More people herded around them and a certain thrill pressurized through her body, an adrenaline and a bit of fear. But she faced it side by side with her mate. With her friends.

And when the humans charged, she didn't feel afraid. While their swords slashed through her clothes and the iron singed her skin and blood stained against her coat, she was not afraid. Even when it seemed hopeless. They were encompassed, just the three of them. Clay's eyes cried blood until he wobbled on his feet. Julius' rage was blinding, making him useless in fighting strategically.

Where were the others? The thought flittered through her mind like a vicious song, a prayer that a moment later went answered.

Humans screamed as licks of fire cut through the spaces between their bodies, the heat blasting them away like an explosion. The flames burned bright in colors of red and green and purple. There was a roar, familiar, recognizable, and the thrill of bonds deeper than Iona itself. The bonds of familiars. Of mates.

Of Elementals.

Shula stepped through the flames, her entire body glowing scarlet like rivers of lava threading through the blood in her veins. She looked formidable, and a surge of pride welled through Iona's chest.

The fire parted and Iona's familiar tore through the crowd, reaping his own vengeance against the ones that had taken him. Blood and magic flew, and Shula stepped beside Iona. Their magic combined in a single swell of power, ready to be unleashed.

A portal opened behind them, Valerio peeking his head through.

"Time to go," the Seelie Prince commanded. Then he was grabbing hold of his cousin by the back of the collar and yanking him through the portal. Julius shouted at her to follow. Iona was aware of her voice screaming at her familiar to get inside. Only when he did, did she turn to Shula. Together they nodded.

Together, they jumped into the portal.

And together, their magic exploded across the entire island.

A Claiming

They landed against the deck of the boat with a thud. The impact jarred Iona's knees, leaving her whole head spinning. It wasn't that making her dizzy, she realized a moment later. It wasn't the force of her fall, but the whole island, shaking, splintering. The waters rippled as Iona and Shula's combined magic exploded above the cliffs.

Rocks broke off and fell towards them, and for a moment panic set in, and Iona was reminded of the catapults heading for the boat full of Fae. Of the storm that followed. Of the feeling of death.

She wasn't sure if she screamed, but her nails grasped against the deck, clawing as if she could somehow get away from both her memories and the fear of the rocks falling towards her. Memories of the past collided with the present, a force so powerful, she couldn't pick anything apart in the chaos of her own mind.

Her throat constricted, and she couldn't breathe. Like she was being dragged under unforgiving depths to her death. How her last thoughts in that moment had been of her sweet sister.

Only this time, her thoughts strayed to others. To Julius. To her familiar. To Shula. Her friends.

Then a moment later she was hauled up in strong arms, a hand pressing into her abdomen, another closing over her fingers. They gripped, controlling her like an extension of herself, tapping a familiar figure against her thighs.

"Feel the pattern," a gruff voice whispered in her ear. It took her only a moment to refocus her mind, to realize that the one holding her, pressing her back to his chest, was Julius. She could make out the angry flare of his nostrils blowing hot breath against her hair, of the rapid thumping of his heart. More than that, she could make out the gentle yet firm press of his fingers against hers as he forced her to trace that comforting design against her own body.

How do you know?

The question was heavy on her tongue. She tried to breathe, focusing on the web he was helping her trace. Like he'd watched her do it often enough now to know what it meant. That it brought her comfort, it eased the ache in her mind.

When her breathing finally steadied, he closed his hand around her fingers, pushing them into a fist.

"You're okay," he assured, his voice low. It took another moment to realize the boat was already moving and they were leaving the West Isles behind them. "We're safe. You're safe."

His words slowly pulled her back to reality. She took a deep inhale and turned her head, looking at the islands they were leaving behind. From where she stood, she could make out the smoke and still scent the rawness of magic, pluming towards the sky like a promise. Of destruction. Of retribution.

She loathed to pull away from Julius when his masculine scent of leather and woods seemed to ground her, but she extricated her body from his, slowly turning, keeping a grip on his wrists, his hands, just to keep them tethered a little bit longer.

His eyes were bright as he looked down at her, silently asking if she was alright.

"I'm fine." Her voice was a mere croak, and the words ached in her throat. She cleared it and looked around, suddenly embarrassed that everyone else had witnessed that.

But no one seemed to be paying attention. They'd all found something to keep themselves busy, tossing over broken bits of cliff that had fallen on the deck, tying the sails, steering the boat. Though she didn't doubt they'd heard her, she was just glad they weren't openly staring.

She didn't like showing that weakness to anyone. Not even those who were her friends.

She leveled her breaths and forced herself to smile. "We destroyed the island."

"Half of it." Julius' mouth twisted into a smirk.

"Good. That place was deplorable." There was still an ache in her chest, though, tightening it in sharp bursts.

She pulled away from Julius, moving with purpose and determination to distract herself. She found her familiar sitting against the deck, staring at her with his one good eye worriedly. Ryker was next to him, his thick brows pulled tightly over his bicolored eyes. His hands slid across her familiar's body. The black cat was at his feet, weaving between his spread legs and purring.

Iona approached and Ryker turned. He seemed angry, frustrated. "I cannot heal him," he growled. "I'm trying but my magic does not seem to extend to animals."

Magic always had limits. Iron, ashwood, the price to pay, who it worked on. It didn't surprise Iona that his magic didn't work on her familiar. He already bore the terrible scars of others, there was no need to give him more pain.

"I'll heal him."

"I can—"

"It's fine," she interrupted. She was familiar with his kind. The kind of person who wanted to save everyone; they were martyrs. Her sister was the same way.

She tried not to think about that as she smoothed her hands down her familiar's body. He winced and she murmured her apology.

"Come on," she urged. "Let's get you cleaned up."

Because Ryker was hovering, she made him go find a bucket and a rag to clean his wounds, along with alcohol to disinfect them. The boat was bound to have some. After he got the supplies, she sent him away with a growl and a snap of her canines. He begrudgingly left, dragging his feet across the deck like it was just too difficult for him to walk away from the injuries.

She wanted to take her familiar down below deck, but Iona knew he wouldn't fit through the door. She did her best to find an inkling of privacy on the far side of the boat, where she cleaned his wounds.

She winced every time she had to swipe the rag near his opened flesh. Tears prickled every time she added alcohol to disinfect. By the time she was finished wiping him down, his coat was gleaming white again, with patches of missing fur and skin. She wrapped his wounds and willed her magic to surround him so he'd be cold, just the right temperature to be comfortable.

When she finished, she dropped the rag in the bucket and took it below deck, staying there a moment to catch her breath and reinforce the strength of the ice covering the hole on the boat. She needed the solitude to process what had happened. It seemed like everything had unfolded so fast, and she hadn't had the time to fully process. Starting from when Petey attacked her, to finding the Resistance, to her familiar being gone. Then she needed to cope with what she'd witnessed on that forsaken island.

Her heart broke over the fact she hadn't been able to rescue the rest of the animals and Fae there. They never would have fit on the boat, and she despaired to think about what her and Shula's combined explosive magic would have done to the island's residents. Not the vile, evil humans, but to others. To the animals, the slaves.

Had she hurt them? Had they died?

She didn't want to think about the innocent creatures who deserved so much more than to have been forced into slavery at the bleeding hands of mercenaries and pirates. Yet she tried to find comfort in the fact that their deaths would have been quick and preferable to the torture they'd endured.

Still, that wasn't for her to decide. Their souls were Mana's and Mana's alone.

She sighed as she kicked the bucket to the side. Footsteps walking down the stairs pulled her out of her melancholy thoughts. She recognized the heavy fall of them immediately as they creaked under his weight.

She didn't turn to meet him. She just felt suddenly so tired. The desire to sleep forever creaking through her bones.

"Saw you come down here," Julius began quietly. "I just wanted to make sure you were okay."

Iona sucked in a breath and turned to see sincerity in his gaze. She didn't bother forcing a smile, knowing he would see right through it anyway. Instead, she leaned back against the wall and sighed.

"I have had better days."

He prowled closer but didn't touch her and didn't speak. He stared, like he could somehow find the answers of his silent questions in her soul. The secrets of her life she kept tightly bottled.

His presence was grounding, like the roots of mighty trees. She'd never met anyone as steady as him, save for her father, but Julius wasn't like her father at all. He was virile, strong. Her father had his own brand of strength that was different. But he wouldn't have been able to deal with what Iona was now, with what she had become.

Julius could.

He'd lead her out of that place in her mind. He'd memorized the pattern of a ceiling he'd never seen and known to use it as her comfort to yank her out of a past that was sometimes too painful to face.

"Thank you," Iona whispered, her voice echoing through the quiet of the room, making it sound too loud. She wondered if he could also hear her heartbeat. It wasn't rapid, but steady. Like him. Because he didn't make her nervous. But he did make her want, make her *need.* And she wouldn't fight a gift freely given.

"For what?" An orange brow rose. Not mocking, but slightly amused.

"For everything. For helping, for my familiar, for pulling me out of that place..." She swallowed.

She didn't like contemplating the memories that dragged her under, but there was no denying that the past had irrevocably changed her in ways she never thought possible. She wanted to think they were good changes. That despite the mess the war had left behind, she was stronger because of it. Even when she was too weak to resist the pull of memories and nightmares that made her heart pound and her body break out into a cold sweat. Even when she felt like she was drowning and sometimes hated her body for betraying her, she always climbed out of it.

She had to keep telling herself she was strong, even if she sometimes didn't feel like it. Because sometimes, when you said something often enough, when you prayed hard enough, everything you wanted had the possibility of coming true.

So that's what Iona did. She prayed and she hoped, or else she'd truly be lost in her own past. In wars, ashwood, blood, and track marks in the sand, the evidence of a body the humans had dragged away.

"What do you see?" he asked softly. "When you go there?"

A lump formed in her throat. She'd never talked to another person, Fae or human, about this at all. Not even Henry, who had owned part of her heart. She found herself wanting to confide in Julius. Not just because he was her mate, but because she simply wanted to share that part of herself with someone else who might understand.

"It... varies..." She swallowed. "Sometimes it goes back to one-hundred and two years ago. The Jade Court, that's where I'm from." He nodded. "The sky is blue then gray, and the ground shakes as the soldiers invade. Then there's nothing but screams and blood."

And her sister's body being dragged through the sand.

She didn't say that part.

"Sometimes," she continued, "I see the war. I'm back there, watching friends die. Or on the boat that was meant to take us to safety. But more often than not, it's the water. I'm choking on salt and the acrid taste of fish..." She took a breath, willed her suddenly rapid heartbeat to slow back to their normal rhythm. She was safe. She was with Julius. She was safe.

"And your fingers... it brings you comfort."

Her eyes opened, and she hadn't even realized she had closed them. "Sometimes. In my rented room, the ceiling was splintered. Every time I woke up from a nightmare, I would feel frozen in place. Like I couldn't move or breathe. It feels like I'm awake but unmoving, trapped inside my own body, like I'm going to die..." She let out a breath. "The only thing I can ever move first is my fingers. I learned later that I could move them. So while I stared up at the ceiling, frozen in my own body, I could move my fingers, tracing the pattern on the ceiling, and it eventually started to calm me down, pull me out of that... comatose state, I guess you could say."

He was quiet for a moment, tilting his head slightly to the side as if he were contemplating her words, really letting them sink in.

"Sometimes I feel the same," he said. "With my magic." He held his hands palms up, like maybe he could see past the flesh and to the power underneath. "I'm so strong, but to use it, my emotions are taken from me until all I know is rage. It's... overpowering. Like I can't control my own body and something else is taking me over." He pushed out a breath and a smile curved his mouth. "I know a lot about the memories of war, too. I have plenty of them."

She had the desire to reach for him and she let herself give in to that. She placed her hands against his and they closed. She could feel the pulse against his wrist, steady just like him.

"What calms you down?" she asked.

"Your voice." His answer was almost automatic.

Iona snorted. "No, seriously."

"Seriously."

"We just met."

"I know that."

She stared at him, eyes narrowed and unbelieving.

Julius' fingers slid down her cheek. "Only time used to calm me down. I would have to live through the rage until it ebbed. And then I met you. We have a bond, and even if we aren't mated, I can feel a part of you in me, and your voice is like a light, tugging me out of that dark place."

Her breath hitched, and this time, her heartbeat sped up. Not from nerves, but from excitement, from desire. Her thighs shifted as if she could stave off the sensation of wanting that coursed through her.

But Julius was a Fae. He could smell it. His nostrils flared, indicating that he did. Iona wasn't embarrassed. Let him scent how he made her feel. He was her mate, and she hadn't felt such a strong attraction to anyone else before.

Just like she'd never truly *felt* for anyone else before.

It wasn't love; they didn't know each other well enough for that. It was a rightness. Like this was where she was supposed to be.

She'd never been more sure about anything in her life than she was about Julius Darah.

She didn't have to hide what she felt, even if it was in the slick that coated along her pussy that ached for him.

"It's the same for me with you," she confessed, her voice just a little breathless. "You're a very... grounding presence."

It was his turn to snort. "I am the most impulsive fucker you'll ever meet." Slowly, he pulled his hands away from hers and she missed his touch as soon as it was gone. "You'll realize that soon enough."

They seemed to be parting words. Like he was prepared to go back to the deck and leave her again to her thoughts. The idea of him leaving didn't sit well in her chest.

She'd told him she wouldn't deny him. That when they found her familiar, they would revisit *this.* It suddenly felt wrong to let him walk away. She didn't *want* him to walk away.

There was a pulse of magic between them, and it urged her to reach out. To take. Accept.

To *mate.*

"I want you," she blurted, causing his whole body to go rigid at the words. But they were said with a firmness, a rightness, an honesty.

His green eyes flared, and for a moment they looked like the flickering flames of Shula's magic. It made her smile.

He mistook the smile for something else. "Are you joking with me right now, Iona?" he demanded. "Because—"

"I'm blunt," she interrupted. "I know what I want and I go for it. If there's something I learned early in life, it's that it's too short for games and for dancing around your desires. You are my mate. I want you. You want me. Why wait?"

His jaw clenched. "Be sure, Iona," he whispered darkly. "Because if you say you want me, then I plan on claiming you. Fucking you. Bonding you. You'll be my mate in every sense of the word."

She stepped forward and pressed her palm against his chest and said the words she'd been itching to say since they first met.

"Then claim me, mate."

A dam seemed to break between them, and suddenly there were no barriers. No reservations. Julius growled and bent. His mouth covered hers, stealing the breath from her lungs as he staked claim to her lips, devouring her with his tongue and teeth.

She moaned and pressed her body to his, his big hands spanning across her hips to keep her pressed tightly in place, like he could somehow inhale her body into his, making them one soul, one heart that beat in two separate rhythms but fit together just the same.

He growled against her mouth, the vibrations rumbling from his chest to hers, pulsing all the way down to her clit. His thighs pushed against her own as he forced her to step back until she collided against the wall. The aggressive feel of his hands pushing her against a solid surface made tingles sear through the scars down her spine, a sensation of desire all on its own.

Iona gasped against the graze of his teeth against her lips, arching into him with every touch of his fingertips as they traveled to the front, massaging their way down her thighs.

Every touch left an erotic trace trembling in its wake. Her legs shook, her pussy cried out, and Iona wanted to feel the delicious slide of his skin against hers, of the friction that would tilt her over the edge of desire.

She found herself thrusting against him, groaning as she found the slightest bit of relief against her core. But it wasn't enough. It wouldn't be enough until he claimed every inch of her.

Iona wrapped her legs around him, pushing herself up with her heels so her center was level against his cock. It strained against his pants, begging to burst free. She rubbed against him, moaning into his mouth.

He pulled away, nipping at her chin.

"What are you doing?" Julius' breaths came out in heavy pants.

Iona opened her eyes to see his glittering with amusement. She rubbed against his shaft. "Isn't it obvious? I want to be fucked. Claimed."

"You will be." He kissed his way down her neck, and she felt the first nip of his canines against her flesh, pressing down further to the sharp ridges of her collarbones. A teasing hint at a claiming that had yet to happen.

"What are you waiting for?" she all but begged, grinding herself tighter against him.

"I want to take my time with you." He pressed an open-mouthed kiss to her throat, trailing his tongue against her pulse. "I want to *savor* you."

She growled, a sound borne of frustration. "Savor me later. It's been so long and I—"

"I will wipe the memory of each and every bastard that came before me. I can promise you that, mate." His voice and touch took on a possessive tone that made a thrill run through her blood. Because it was spoken like a promise, like a vow. She didn't tell him that she forgot any and everyone else the moment their mating bond snapped into place. No one else existed for her but him.

"Can you?" she teased. "Because I don't think—"

His snarl cut her off and he dove for another kiss. Rougher, aggressive, demanding. He tried to dominate her with a swipe of his tongue. Like he wanted so steal the words right from her mind and prove that he could make good on his promise.

But Iona was just as demanding, just as aggressive.

Her hands pawed at his clothes, tugging at the ties of his cloak and shoving it off his shoulders. It fell into a heap at the floor, making a slight swishing sound. They were too close together, with too little space to tug off his shirt, so Iona reached down and yanked at the ties of his trousers and slid her hand inside.

She cupped his dick, wrapping her fingers around the hard, velvety texture of him. He was so thick, she couldn't wrap her fingers around him fully and groaned as she imagined him inside her, stretching her to completion.

She gave an experimental tug and he groaned deep in the back of his throat, hips jerking against her hand.

"Fuck," he rumbled. "Fuck, that feels so good." His hand fumbled between them, easily reaching into her own pants to caress the slick folds of her pussy.

She cried out as his thumb pressed against her clit, teasing slow circles around it, just enough to let her feel the friction but not enough so she could get off like she wanted to.

"Fuck, Julius, make me come. Fuck, I'm so close." She jerked her hips against him, begging to be tossed over that edge, but he jerked his hand away and slid her off his body. Her feet touched the ground and she would have wobbled, but his hands grasped her hips, holding her in place against the wall.

"No," he demanded. "I get to say when you come."

Oh, the poor, delusional bastard, she thought with a smile. If he thought he was in charge, he had another thing coming.

Her hands slid up the hem of his shirt, feeling her way up the hard ridges of his abdomen. When she reached his pecks, her nails scraped across his nipples and with a quick work of her feet and hands, she had him turned, pushing his body up against the wall. She stood on the tips of her toes, forehead grazing against the sharp hairs of his beard.

"You don't command me, Julius," she purred while her nails traced patterns against his skin. "Only I command me." Then she was dropping to her knees in front of him, her hands tugging at the waistband of his pants, pushing them down his strong thighs.

His cock sprung free, bobbing up, the head glistening and purple. She leaned forward without preamble and took the head into her mouth, swirling her tongue around him. Above her, Julius hissed and then groaned as she took him deeper into her mouth, hollowing out her cheeks so she could take him to the back of her throat in one suck.

"Iona..." His hand tangled into her silver curls, gripping and tugging her closer. She breathed through her nose, allowed him a few seconds to take control as he forced her against him. Up and down, he found a vicious rhythm. Her tongue sucked and licked the underside of his dick, her hand coming up to cup his balls, which were pulled back tightly.

"Fuck!" His roar seemed to rumble through the entire room. He grabbed her by the shoulders and ripped her away from him, pulling her straight to her feet and shoving her back against the wall. It was a dance between them, a fight for dominance.

When he knelt in front of her, he yanked off her boots and pulled her pants, peeling them from her legs until she was bare before him. His canines snapped, nipping against the soft flesh of her inner thighs, grazing over every inch of her skin until his face was level with her soaking folds.

She braced her hands against his shoulders and bit her bottom lip. He looked up at her through bright lashes, a mischievous grin splaying on his mouth. A mouth he brought close to her pussy. His nostrils flared as he inhaled the scent of her.

"A fucking gift from Mana," he said, grabbing her thighs and spreading them wider. "I could bury myself in your juices all fucking day." Then his tongue darted out and licked her from the bottom up to her clit, where he grazed his teeth against the bundle of nerves, sucking it between them.

Iona cried out, bucking her hips against his face. He tortured her, his tongue and teeth driving her up the heights of pleasure while his hand thumbed across her skin and up higher, sliding against her folds right before he plunged in.

She cried out loudly, not caring if the whole fucking boat heard her. She worked her hips against him, riding the digit and his tongue, aching for release. But he pulled back, and a protest was on the tip of her tongue before he grabbed her by the backs of the thighs and pulled her down. They fell to the floor, Julius' body rocking the boat, and her straddling his face.

"Ride my face," he ordered, his beard scraping against her thighs.

She groaned and obeyed, rolling her hips against his mouth as he lapped up her juices, swallowing down the evidence of her need. He sucked one fold into his mouth while he worked his finger inside her, stretching her tight channel until her thighs trembled and all but clamped against his face.

He growled against her, the vibration pulsing her clit. She was close, so close to the edge. She was coming...

Julius pulled away and she groaned in frustration, reaching down to dig her fingers through his hair, tugging furiously. "If you don't make me come right fucking now..."

He chuckled and pushed her down the length of his body.

"Julius..." she complained.

He sat up and she ended up straddling his waist. He reached for the hem of his tunic and pulled it over his shoulders, baring his delicious, muscular body to her. Her fingers itched to explore, but he began to wiggle his pants off, and she shifted to help him toss everything off until he was naked beneath her. Then his fingers went to her cloak and top, nearly ripping the material in his haste to get it off of her.

When she was bare above him, he laid back against the floor, his pupils flaring with desire as he took in her body. His gaze roved over her appreciatively, stopping at her breasts, and then going higher to meet her gaze.

"You're perfect, mate," he growled, his hands gripping her hips and setting her over his erection. "Perfect for me." He pulled her down gently, so his cock teased the entrance of her folds. "I can't wait to sink my cock into you. Can't wait for your screams to rock this fucking boat."

"Do it," she challenged, dropping her hips so the head of him pressed into her a fraction. "Make me yours. Make everybody on this boat *jealous* and desire what we have." She pushed down against him and his head dropped back against the floor.

"Fuck, yes, Iona. You're perfect, you hear me? Perfect."

She placed her palms against his chest and rolled her hips, pushing all the way in. His hips rose to meet her, plunging to the hilt inside.

"Yes," she gasped. "Fill me up. Fuck me, Julius, fuck me now."

And then he began to move at a savage rhythm. He didn't relent, didn't slow down. He grabbed her hips and moved her up and down, using her against his dick. She was so full, so incredibly full. Every time he pulled her down, her clit slapped against his flesh, making her ache and cry out, writhing against him and desperate for that friction.

He swelled inside her, his nostrils flaring like he was angry and aroused in equal measure. She cried out, sure she was screaming his name with each thrust.

"Come for me." He slammed her down against him. "Come."

Her body had been on the precipice since they started, and at his command, Iona fell, slumping against his chest, thighs tightening around him, as she rode of the wave. He pumped in and out of her, prolonging the sensation until he swelled and cried out, bursting and releasing his seed inside her.

Still he moved his hips, trying to drag the pleasure out for as long as possible. One hand reached up and tugged her towards him where he took her mouth in a rough kiss before breaking away and nipping her neck.

She felt the bite of his canines a moment later, sharp teeth piercing past the barrier of skin and digging into her flesh. Her body soared, pleasure and pain mingling together. Magic erupted into cresting waves around them, and she felt the first soft sprinkles of snowfall against their skin. Her magic responding to the overwhelming sensations.

Her own lips pressed against his pulse, and she felt her canines lengthening in her mouth. They grazed the tender flesh at his neck.

"Yes," he breathed, begged.

Who was she to resist?

Her teeth sunk into him and magic exploded all over again, his taste erupting against her tongue. He was all leather and woods and ale. He was summertime, grass and sunlight bursting against her tongue in a flavorful explosion. She groaned as she felt their bond settle into place. A sliver of him nesting inside her, a part of his soul intertwining itself with hers in a tight, firm, unbreakable knot.

And a sense of rightness washed over her again, even as he pulled his teeth from her and trailed his tongue across the new wound on her neck and she did the same. His hips jerked against hers one last time and his body slumped a moment before he rolled them to the side.

He was still hard inside of her, and he pulled her closer, brushing aside the curls from her cheeks. His smile was radiant, and she could feel their bond solidified by everything that just transpired between them. She answered with a smile of her own and they didn't speak. They didn't need words. Just this. Just each other.

Julius pulled her into the crook of his arms and that's how they fell asleep.

Mated.

Bonded.

To the sound of each other's steady heartbeats.

The Price of Love is Agony

The next morning, Iona slipped off to the deck to check on her familiar. Even though the air was chilly and bit against her skin, she left the cloak off. The crescent marks on her neck burned in the best of ways, and she wanted to show them off. For the first time in a long time, she felt giddy with excitement. Hope was an awning thing, something she'd only ever thought about in her daily prayers and now felt more tangible.

She smoothed her hands down against her familiar, checking and redressing his wounds and talking to him about little nothings. He paid attention, but he didn't speak into her mind again. Not that she'd expected him to. She was just glad his eyes were a bit brighter today and that he seemed to be feeling better, despite the raw wounds still on his body.

An hour into talking, and she felt the air on the deck shift. It charged with electrifying energy that bolted through her nervous system like a strike of lightning. She knew it was Julius before she turned and saw him strut across the deck, his chest puffed and a smile pulling widely at his mouth as he preened.

He turned and their eyes caught, though she was sure that he didn't know for a moment where she was. He changed course and walked right over to her, not stopping until their chests brushed. Then his hands twined behind her, hands grasping her ass as he picked her up, aligning them like they'd been last night.

"Morning," he growled.

Iona's hands slid up his shoulders, her thumb grazing across the crescent marks on his own neck. The action made a low growl emit from his throat, a sound that brought her satisfaction.

"You were gone this morning. I didn't get to give you this." Then he kissed her, devouring her so thoroughly like he had last night. She couldn't help the groan that came out of her throat. He whirled with her still in his arms and walked across the deck.

She broke away. "Put me down, brute. I have things to do."

He feigned a hurt groan but did as she asked and when they turned all eyes were on the both of them.

Iona especially felt Shula's burning like the magic of her fire

"What?" she cocked her head in the fire Fae's direction.

Shula's face reddened and she stammered, "N-nothing it's just that..." Her eyes lingered on their matching crescent marks, the evidence of their mating bond. "So soon?"

Iona's brows raised. "Why would I wait?"

The Fae tugged at the ends of her hair, pushing them over her ears. "It's just... you've known each other for so little time..."

Iona waved her off. "We're Fae. We have plenty of time to know one another. We live long life spans and are all but immortal."

"But what if you regret it?"

Iona's eyes narrowed onto the other woman's shoulder, right where her own bond mark should be but was hidden beneath her clothes. It felt like she was asking more for her own benefit rather than Iona's. Still, she answered.

"I won't regret it."

"But how do you know?"

"Because I trust Mana, and Mana would not have gifted me with a mate I did not want. Mana is an all-knowing force that sees hearts and destinies, and it works in mysterious ways. I trust that this is a gift, a bond I'm meant to cherish for the rest of my life. Time doesn't matter here, only magic and that his soul matches mine."

Shula looked away, her eyes going straight to Ryker's, only to find him staring back at her. Her face reddened even further, and she stood abruptly and walked in short, quick steps towards the door that led her below deck. She went down and didn't emerge.

Iona couldn't help but feel like she'd said something to upset her.

"What did I say?"

Julius chuckled, though the sound held no joy and pressed a kiss to her temple. "I'll explain later," he whispered.

Ryker watched Shula go, but he did not follow. Even while every instinct in his body, his soul, screamed at him to go after his mate, to hold her, comfort her, vanquish what ailed her, he resisted. How could he vanquish her demons when he was one of them?

He hated that he didn't understand what she wanted from him.

Hated it even more that she felt like their bond had been a mistake.

It hurt him, gutted him worse than any wound on his body had ever inflicted.

The words he'd spat out hadn't helped either, but they were true. She was running, just like she always ran. Ryker didn't know what else to say or do that would make her want to stay. He knew something was wrong, with him, with her. They were both so deeply buried in their own anger and insecurities, but it was a hole they couldn't break out of.

"You're a fucking dumbass."

Ryker turned to Clay, who was staring after Shula as well. A possessive growl rose up in his chest. He didn't want the Fae looking anywhere in her direction.

He wasn't really sure what to make of this new, primal, obsessive part of him that demanded Shula be his and only his. He'd felt a whisper of it before they bonded. Now it enveloped him with demanding, angry fingers.

He knew what a mating bond was, what it entailed, and he'd done it. Because he'd wanted to. Because he believed in Shula more than she believed in herself. Because love was selfish, and he wanted to remember what it tasted like. In that selfishness, he'd forgotten it was agony.

"Fuck off," Ryker growled.

Clay pierced him with a look of anger, something very surprising since Clay was hardly ever serious about anything except whose skirt he could chase next.

"No," he grinded out. "I'm not going to keep fucking quiet. Shula is my friend."

Ryker's temper flared and he snapped his canines in Clay's direction. He didn't even flinch, but Ryker wanted to rip him apart suddenly.

"Fuck off with that," Clay growled. "She may be your mate, but you obviously don't know a damn thing about her."

Ryker froze, feeling as though he'd just been gutted. "I know her better than you."

"Oh, really?" he mocked. "Doesn't seem like it. Do you even know why she's so pissed at you? No? Let me give you a hint. You keep trying to turn her into something she's not because of your own skewed, fucked up ideals about what it means to be a real Fae."

"I do n—"

"Don't stand there and fucking deny it. You think a Fae isn't a real Fae unless they're fighting or being a giant asshole and a martyr like you."

Ryker clenched his teeth, but he had no reply to that. Nothing Clay would listen to, at any rate. And he didn't owe the other Fae an explanation, besides. Shula was *his* mate. He didn't need advice from Clay or anyone else on how to handle their problems.

"You're not even fucking listening." Clay shoved him, jostling Ryker out of his thoughts.

He jerked towards him, his eyes wild with anger. "What the fuck do you want me to say, Clay?"

Clay's palms collided with Ryker's shoulders, shoving him back. His anger was a patent thing now, showing in slashing lines of his pretty features. "I want you to realize what a dick you're being. You still think deep down everyone is like Mairin, don't you?"

The pain of hearing her name came suddenly. The scars holding the leftover, smooth bits of his face together pulsed with a phantom agony that never quite seemed to ebb.

"What if she was still alive?" Clay continued, his voice knives that cut through his skin in slow increments. "Would you give her shit for what she did?"

Ryker roared and reached for Clay, grabbing hold of the front of his jacket to bring him nose to nose. "She's *not* alive, and that's the point." It was why he wanted Fae to be strong, why he healed them. Because if he couldn't save her, at least he could save everyone else.

"No, the point is, she's fucking *dead* Ryker. It's been *years.* Shula isn't Mairin. She's your mate, even when you don't fucking deserve her."

He shoved him away with a snarl. "You don't know what you're fucking talking about."

Clay threw his head back and laughed. "Don't I? Who the fuck do you think she goes to when she's crying over you? Who holds her while she sobs over a mate who treats her like shit?"

Something stabbed through Ryker's heart at those words. At the fact that his mate went somewhere else, to someone else instead of him. To Clay of all people. This fucking pretty boy bastard. He'd known, but having Clay taunt him with it made it that much more real.

"Stay away from my mate."

"No. You get no say in who I see or in who she sees. You don't get to treat her like shit and then claim her in the same breath. It doesn't work like that, and if you think it does then maybe she needs a new mate. Someone who can appreciate her."

Before the words were even fully out of his mouth, Ryker charged, ducking low and grabbing Clay across the waist, sending them both sprawling in a heap across the floor. His fists flew, each impact a song of his rage, as if trying to silence the heavy implication of Clay's words.

"Shula is *mine*," he snarled. He felt Clay's blood against his knuckles, felt his own scarred hands split open, but he couldn't stop.

Clay grunted and kicked with surprising strength, sending Ryker flying. He landed on his back with a whoosh of breath and quickly pushed to his feet to face Clay.

"You push so hard for her to change. You demand more, more, more. Hasn't she given enough? She joined us, changed her ears, saved all of our fucking asses, and still it's not enough for you. You want her to be what you think she should be, because Mairin's death has you so fucked up you can't appreciate her for who she really is."

Everyone had turned to stare at them, to listen in to their argument, but Ryker didn't care. He was blinded by the words being hurled at him, one after the other. His chest heaved, his canines were snapping, and all he wanted to do was rip Clay's throat out.

"Fucking self-righteous hypocrite. As if you were a fucking gift from Mana. You are *nothing*, and you've given her nothing, changed nothing for her like she has for you. No wonder she can't even talk to you. She may be your mate, but you don't fucking deserve that title."

Ryker went after him again. They met in the middle, a tangle of fists and violence. Blood flew across the deck, and Ryker absorbed the blows with grunts and feral cries, hitting Clay back with all his rage the words provoked, the hurt they caused.

But even as every blow struck against the sensitive skin of Clay's face, Ryker wasn't sure if he was punishing Clay...

...or if he was punishing himself.

Ryker took a hit to the nose and he retaliated with one to the gut. Clay grunted and then Ryker felt the raw sting of magic flood through his system. It was a subtle tug at first, followed by something sharper. Like his blood suddenly stopped flowing. His heart suddenly began pounding. Blood began to slowly drip from his eyes.

He jerked away from Clay, whose own eyes were crying tears of blood.

The price of his destructive magic.

Crimson pooled from Ryker's ears. He grew weak, stumbling backwards. A vessel in his eye broke, his vision was tainted red...

Valerio cut in between the two of them. "Enough!" he barked.

Clay lowered his hands and just like that, the pressure in Ryker's body eased, but he ached all over. And because his magic didn't work on himself, he would have to deal with the pain. He tried to ignore the part of him that said he deserved it, but it was strident.

Clay swiped the back of his hand against his face, wiping away the blood at his cheeks. He glared at Ryker and spat out one last knife to his heart.

"No wonder she doesn't want you anymore."

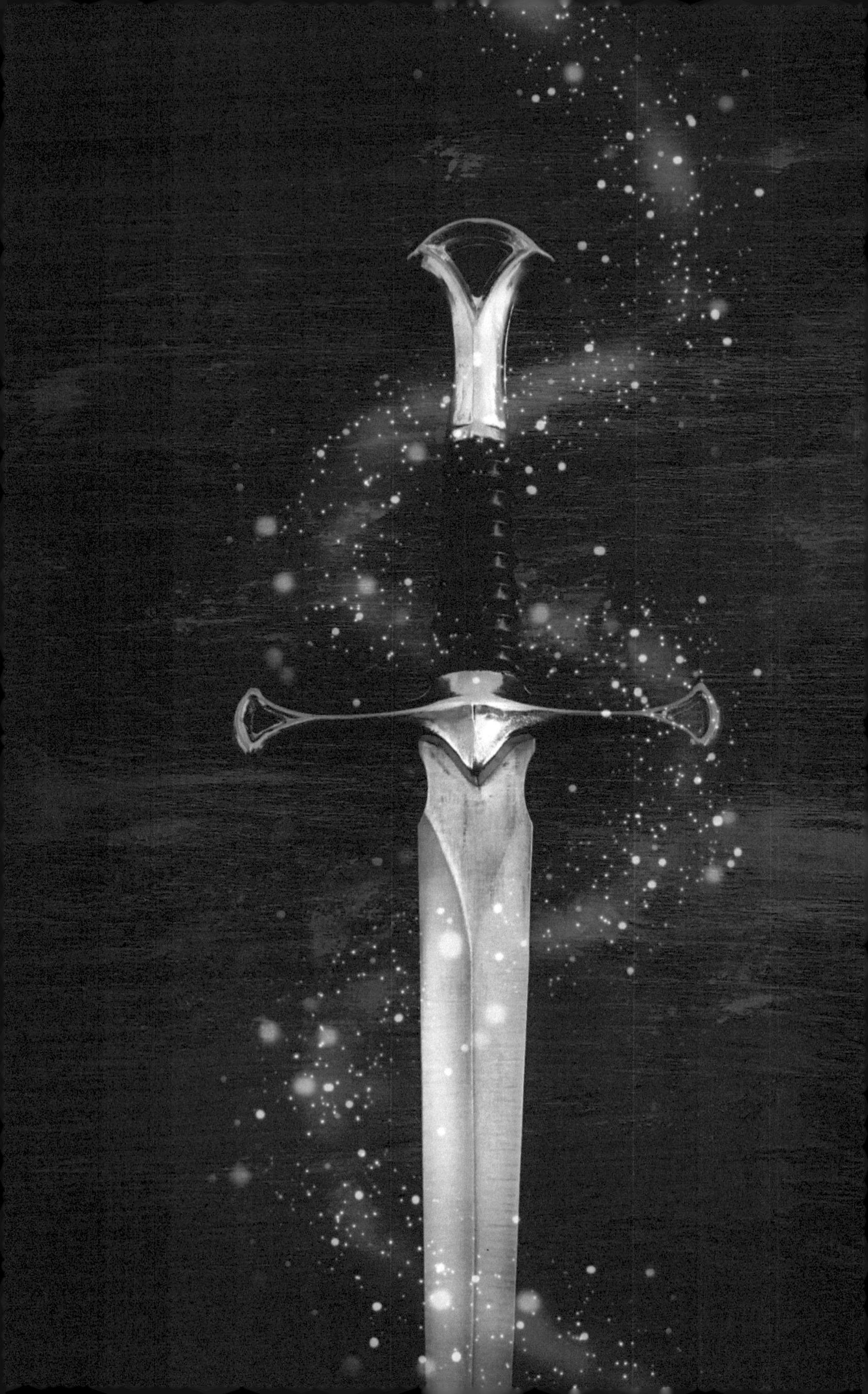

A Healer's Impulse

After the fight between Clay and Ryker, things on the boat became strained. Shula didn't come up from below deck, and everyone grew focused on sailing and leaving the ocean behind. They had a mission to accomplish and now that Iona was done holding them back from it, she figured they were impatient to move along.

Days on the boat blurred together in seeming silence. The tension was like a dense fog through the air that Iona nearly suffocated on it. She was on the deck, trying to dispel that energy, leaning against the barred edge and staring down into the water when she sensed another's presence at her side.

She turned with raised eyebrows to meet Weylyn.

The Fae was eerily silent. He always moved like shadows, always blending into the background so most times, Iona found herself forgetting about him entirely. He didn't look as formidable as Uric and Valerio, or as friendly as Clay, as strong as Julius, or as brooding as Ryker.

In fact, he was on the lithe side, with an unimpressive muscular frame, but passably tall height. He didn't appear threatening, but there was a gleam in his golden eyes that was almost... malicious, mischievous. There was something about him that seemed to be layered more deeply beneath his golden-bronze skin and almost laconic demeanor.

His thin lips twisted into a smile, a gesture that seemed almost cruel and knowing. He stared and Iona stared back, meeting his golden eyes until his seemed to penetrate hers, like he was looking so deep into her soul, he could rip it straight out of her chest.

She shifted just as those golden eyes rolled to the back of his head, and his whole body froze. Iona looked side to side, but everyone was busy, and no one was paying attention. She looked back at him and stepped close, reaching her finger out to poke his chest.

He didn't move.

"What the *fuccccck*?" she sang low. "Can I help you?"

As soon as the words were out of her mouth, he blinked, his eyes going that golden hue again and his smile grew even wider as he took her in. Like he knew some secret she didn't.

"Okay, this is weird." Iona stepped back from him, feeling the hairs on the back of her neck suddenly stand on end. "What do you want?"

"I think the real question is, what do *you* want?" His voice was as eerie as him. With the musical lilt of an accent.

Iona didn't always recognize the accents of the Seelie and Unseelie Courts, but his was... it was magical. Curling, low, with the slightest hint of dark seduction laced in between. His scent suddenly reached her, tickling her nose. Like something spicy with the slightest undercurrent of sweet she couldn't place.

"What are you talking about?" She wondered if she should just punch him in the dick and be done with him for the day, but she couldn't deny she was curious.

His long fingers spread out across the ledge, tapping a slow, recognizable rhythm. It was the one she pressed against her own thighs. Except, Weylyn seemed to be making a mockery of it.

"There's a reason you joined the Resistance. Old and new." His fingers stopped tapping and he cocked his head to the side, his long, black braid swaying with the breeze. "And it is not because you like to fight."

Her blood went cold and her heart pounded up to her head, making her dizzy.

"There's another reason, isn't there? A selfish reason..."

"I don't—"

"Know what I'm talking about?" He smirked and she wanted to punch his teeth in. "Lies. You see..." He shifted towards her, his fingers edging closer along the ledge. He invaded her space, his scent so strong she wanted to sneeze. "I know *everythin—*"

She didn't let him get the rest out, because her arm was darting out, her knuckles colliding against his face so hard, she felt his teeth split her skin. The sting of it hurt and she jumped back, waving her hand in front of her and wincing.

Weylyn groaned as blood gushed from his nose and split lip. His hand rose to try and staunch the flow. "You—you broke my nose..." He sounded genuinely surprised by that, and maybe even a little proud. Like no one had ever dared do such a thing before. Perhaps they hadn't.

"You deserved it. Now fuck off."

He didn't move but to cup his nose and try to stop the blood flow. His eyes were wide and staring at her with fascination. Or maybe he was contemplating her murder. She didn't know and didn't care.

He'd never get that far.

"What part of fuck off don't you understand?" Magic responded inside her, cooling her blood, surging through her veins until she glowed like bright lights. Fingertips frosted over and snow began to swirl around them like an approaching storm.

Like ash.

Weylyn dragged his foot through a thin layer that frosted over the floor. He dropped his hand and blood dripped over it.

Blood. Ash. Sand. Marks through the ground. Screams for help.

Iona took a breath and it clouded in front of her. Her throat felt hoarse as if she'd been screaming, but she knew it was only because of the memory of that day. Of the burn of ashwood on her throat and tongue as she cried for her sister right before the blow came that would knock her unconscious.

"Fuck off, lapdog." A voice cut through her memories, growling and as penetrative as the herbal scent that came from his body.

Ryker appeared next to her, giving her a side view of a glaring black eye. His arms were crossed against his chest as he glared at Weylyn, like he was daring him to say something that would give Ryker a reason to break his nose all over again.

Weylyn seemed to recognize the challenge in the other Fae's gaze. He smirked and whirled, his long braid slapping against his back as he walked away.

Once he was gone, Ryker turned to Iona, his eyes flicking down to her hands and the split skin on the backs of her knuckles. He stared at her wounds and she stared at his. The twin black eyes and split lip he sported was the only evidence left of what he and Clay had done.

She wondered what it was like to heal others but never yourself. If it hurt as much as other wounds when he absorbed the scars.

"Let me take a look at that." He nodded at her hand.

She fought the urge to cover it. "I'll be fine." Her fingers flexed as if to prove a point. She was Fae, and while Fae could heal faster than humans, that didn't by any means make them immortal. They had longer life spans, better senses, and magic, but they still bled. They could still be hurt.

Could still die.

"I insist," he urged.

"So do I."

His brows drew together and that black eye narrowed. The white one had no pupil, no iris, though she felt the disdain in it just the same. "Humor me," he said.

Iona sighed. She knew what healers were like, and he wasn't going to give up. Besides, it was just a little wound. It didn't matter.

"Fine," she conceded. "Where to?"

"My things are below deck." He turned, giving her an indication that she should follow, even if he didn't say the words. She sighed and walked after him, waving her bloody knuckles in Julius' direction as they passed.

His green eyes were dancing with gaiety, likely because she'd punched Weylyn in the face, and there was no hint of jealousy. She was glad of that at least. She'd seen Ryker's jealousy. It wasn't a pretty look on Fae males, the possessiveness they got with their mates. Besides, Ryker was already mated to Shula, even if they seemed to be avoiding one another.

She followed him below deck where he grabbed a wooden stool and kicked it over to her. "Sit," he growled, before going to his pack and rummaging through it, pulling out what smelt like salve. He grabbed a rag and clean water and kicked out another stool to sit across from her. It groaned under his weight as he took a seat and leaned forward.

Iona held out her hand and waited with bated breath as he began swiping the rag over her bleeding knuckles.

"Fucker has sharp teeth," she complained as he traced over a particularly tender spot.

"He deserved it." Ryker cleaned the rag and began swiping again.

Iona observed him while he worked. He was methodical and tender, despite the sheer intimidation of his size. He wasn't as big as Julius, but he still cut a formidable figure. Only slightly smaller and less muscular, but it was the mystery behind his scars that made him look eerie and somewhat dangerous. They slashed across his face, pulling his expression into a perpetual frown. And that white eye?

The gentle hum of white and yellow magic pulled her from her thoughts. She looked down and watched his fingertips glowing as they spread salve across her knuckles. It left a tingle in its wake as she was enveloped with his healing magic. Where his fingers trailed, her split skin disappeared.

She sighed. "That always skeeves me out," she confessed.

Ryker's eyes flicked up to her. "You've seen healing magic before?"

A lump caught in her throat. She almost didn't answer, but the words came out of her anyway. "My sister..." Big brown eyes flashed in her mind. Black braids, dark skin, a charming, caring smile. "She had healing magic." She hated talking about her sister in past-tense, all but confirming she was dead. It hurt to think about. "She always had a good sense for broken things."

Broken bones, broken skin, broken hearts...

"It's a gift and a curse," Ryker rumbled. "I can sense pain and injuries from miles away. Like an itch falls over my skin that I need to scratch. Even broken, dead bodies can demand to be healed sometimes." His fingers hovered over the scars of his face, and she wondered if he even realized he was doing it, if they hurt, and she wanted to know their origins.

It wasn't her place to ask.

"The dead start to rot," he continued in a haunting voice. "I feel it, and my magic demands that I heal it."

Iona's brows pulled together. "Won't that rot you, though?"

Ryker grunted but didn't answer, even while his fingers scrubbed over the length of his scars before lowering. She figured he was a man of few words and even more secrets, and everything he'd just told her was rare for him. But then, "So magic runs in the family."

Iona found herself smiling as she recalled the simpler times. Before the war. "In us females, at least. Me and my sister were the only ones."

Ryker's lips twitched. She almost swore it was a smile he wore. "An Elemental and a healer. Rare."

Iona shrugged. "It was our norm. You kind of remind me of her."

His brows rose.

"You know... without all... that..." She gestured at his body with her free hand. "I mean in personality. She was always fixing broken things too. I think it's inevitable with healers; an impulse, really."

Ryker pulled away from her and his hand went up to his face, hovering over the scars. "Was her price—"

"No," she interrupted. "She didn't feel their pain or take their scars. Her price was her energy, her own health."

Sometimes she'd come home limping at night, wheezing. Her skin would be stuck to a skinny frame, her movements would be lethargic, like a living corpse, one foot in the grave already.

Until her father made her put an end to it. No more healing. Because her sister would have killed herself to save others. Kind of like Ryker.

"All magic comes with a price," Ryker murmured.

"Not mine." Her well was endless. She held up her hand and let a layer of ice coat it like a glove. "I pay nothing for this. Mana has given me a gift. The gift of a life without a price."

Ryker stared at her. "Not yet," he whispered. "But you'll pay a price soon enough."

Before she could ask him what he meant by that, footsteps came down the stairs, followed by the smell of smoke and steel and violence with the undercurrent of something soft. Like a blanket.

Uric appeared at the bottom of the steps, his white hair shielding the sharp angles of his cheekbones. His pale skin had a hint of color from the cold and with the black clothes clinging to his body, he looked even paler.

He looked like a baby bird, she thought with amusement.

His glare cut in her direction as if he'd read her thoughts. "Prince Valerio wants to speak with you." He turned and bounded back up the steps, calling down a harsh, "Now!"

Iona pushed herself to her feet. "Thanks for this." She waved her hand in his direction. "I appreciate it."

He nodded but otherwise didn't say anything as she walked away.

A Web of Lies

Valerio was at the helm of the ship, his hands on the ledge. His hair whipped against the wind, black strands like slashing shadows of knives against his skin. His black eyes were focused on the waters beyond. He was surrounded by his Fae companions, all of them huddled close and looking at the approaching shores.

Iona could make out blackening sand and almost sighed at the thought of being back in Illyk. The ocean made her more nervous than a land built of iron ever could.

Valerio turned as she approached. He didn't smile, and she didn't bow. The grave lines of his features were all she needed to know that this conversation was going to be a serious one.

"You called for me?"

"Yes. I wanted to speak with you about what to expect once we make it to shore."

Iona nodded. Her whole body was rigid as she waited. Then she felt Julius' grounding comfort at her back, and his hands came to rest against her shoulders. She loosed a breath, enjoying the woodsy scent that pervaded her nostrils. He smelt sweet too. Like ale or mead. It reminded her of the sweetness of her flavored ice she used to sell, and she smiled at the memory. At him.

"You're distracting her," Prince Valerio accused Julius.

"I'm listening," Iona argued with an eye roll.

Prince Valerio sighed before continuing. "We need you and Shula to locate the next Elemental so we can head there immediately."

"Right." Iona gave him a firm nod.

"We need to plan out a way to get there without being caught. It will be much more difficult now that we have a polar bear following us..." He trailed off as his gaze went to her familiar. It wasn't with disdain, but Iona still felt herself begin to bristle regardless.

"How many more Elementals are we looking for here?" she asked, diverting the subject from her familiar.

"Four more." It was Shula who answered, her voice soft yet firm. "According to The Seer, we're the last left."

"*The* Seer?" Iona felt her eyes bulge. She swept her gaze across her companions and for a moment, she felt almost overwhelmed. The Seer was a thing of Fae legends, told around campfires, whispered in the middle of the night. And for a second, she realized how little she knew about them and their journey. She'd been so desperate for their help in finding her familiar, knowing that Mana had put them together for a reason, that she hadn't let them finish their explanations about where they were going and why.

She supposed now was the time.

"You all have a story to tell," she mused. "And I'll hear it."

They all shared glances among themselves that were almost conspiratorial. Then they looked toward her. She thought Prince Valerio would speak, that he would be the one to tell her what she needed to know. The one who opened their mouth wasn't any of the males, but Shula.

"I was twelve when my parents were taken from me by the emperor's soldiers," she began. "Shortly after, I met an old human woman who gave her life for my own and found Piriguini's Circus for the first time. It's where I stayed hidden, where I was betrayed, and it was where the soldiers found me again ten years later."

She spoke and Iona was hypnotized with her every word. Within the next few moments, Shula Azzarh painted a picture of what life had been like at the circus, about what it had been like to be betrayed by a human named Fanny who had once been her friend. She spoke about a mysterious Brotherhood and their catacombs, about the sigils on their floors that matched the ones on their own backs. About water that burned down her throat like fire, rituals, robes of white and red.

Then she spoke about meeting the Resistance. About being held against her will by them. At that, Iona couldn't help but throw a glare Prince Valerio's way, for the blatant disrespect they'd all so obviously shown Shula when she'd been little more than scared and clueless herself.

But Shula kept talking. About Orna and Des, and her friendship with the two mismatched mates, Fae and human.

"They loved each other," Shula whispered, and Iona could see the tears glistening in her eyes that she refused to let fall. "Anyone with eyes and a soul could see that."

Iona's hand went up to cover Julius' on her shoulder. She may not have had love, but she knew one day soon she would. With him.

"Then they died." Shula's words were cutting, full of pain and rage in equal measure in such a way that Iona could feel them glide down to her own soul. Her magic hummed and vibrated, and her heart pounded as Shula continued.

There was more, so much more to their journey that Iona hadn't even realized or thought of beyond those first moments they'd met. Even now, it was hard to fathom that they'd gone to Tir na Faie and had survived.

For a moment, she was heartbroken to hear that her home really was what all the whispers claimed to be. They'd gone to the Jade Court, just past the Herria Mountains, now known as the Iron Mountains, its name lost in time because of the humans. Her home was reduced to little more than a deadly trap for all Fae who entered.

Then she spoke of The Seer, a creature trapped between the iron bars of their own cage and the prophecy they spoke.

"We're a direct tie to Mana," Shula explained. "We are the pillars of the magical balance in the world, all of us Fae connected by invisible threads. Our lives are tied to Mana's, and we are an essence of Mana. The Emperor of Illyk wants to find us all and use us to sever the threads and wipe us all out."

Shula was looking at Iona expectantly. Like all of this information should shock her. Like she should have been appalled, doubled over and gasping.

Iona merely stood there, gnawing at her bottom lip, her fingers tapping against her thighs. She only stopped when she felt Julius' hand cover her own; her breathing and pulse steadied as his presence settled her completely.

"So George was fucking right."

Shula blinked.

Behind her, Julius' chest rumbled. "Who the fuck is George?"

Iona sighed and stared up at the sky. She had visited George quite a few times for favors and things, and each time he'd spoken to her of prophecies and conspiracy theories that he pulled from deep in his web of connections. Of the Fae, of the camps, of the *emperor...*

"George is my supplier," she explained. "He forged paperwork for me in case I ever needed to flee Teg." She held them enraptured with attention. "I'm not entirely sure what his magic is, but he has connections everywhere and was always spewing what I assumed were conspiracy theories, but now I know they make sense."

"What are you talking about?" Prince Valerio questioned, dark brows pulled together.

"The Emperor of Illyk isn't real."

Shared shock rippled through her companions.

"I know it's hard to believe—"

"It's fucking impossible to believe," Uric cut in with a glare. "What nonsense are you spouting?"

"Have you ever seen the emperor?" Iona countered. "Has *anyone* ever seen him?" When no one spoke, she crossed her arms against her chest. "Exactly. He's little more than a fairy tale that has been whispered about for two-hundred years. Humans don't live that long, but do you know who does?" She stared from face to face, watching as realization started to sink in. "Yeah, the Fae."

"Wait a minute, back up." Clay held his hands up, looking confused, and with good reason. He'd been confused when she'd heard the story, too. "What do you mean?"

"There are rumors spreading through George's dark web of secrets that the Emperor of Illyk isn't real. In the sense that he's what he says he is. He's been whispered about for years, passing decrees about the Fae, though no one knows where he lives, no one has seen him... There have been no ascension ceremonies to crown any new emperors... Because there aren't any. The web thinks he may be Fae."

Uric snarled. "What nonsense—"

"Oh, shut up," Iona snapped. "It's a theory."

"A stupid theory."

"You were raised in the reservations." Prince Valerio turned, regarding Shula. "Have you heard of this before?"

Shula shifted her wait from foot to foot. "The humans always seemed focused on teaching the Fae out of us. They taught us to read and write in the common tongue, they taught us about their gods, and they fed us a false version of history in which the Fae were the monsters." Her expression became sad. "The only reason I never believed the stories or fell into that trap was because my parents whispered the truth to me at night when no one else could hear.

"They claimed discord had already been happening between the human lands and the Feylands, and a soldier didn't rise until the war was already well underway. They said he rallied every human kingdom of Illyk to march against Tir na Faie and when he successfully conquered, they crowned him Emperor of Illyk."

"What else was said about him?"

"Only that he was from Orknie originally. There was never really a lot of information on him as a person or what year he rose up."

"Exactly!" Iona snapped her fingers at Shula's words. "Just think about it for a moment!" Iona gestured in Uric's direction. "No information on who he is, but he's from Orknie. Before the war, humans and Fae migrated between the Ley Line all the time. He could easily be Fae. If you can't believe that, then maybe you can believe this: what were some of the first laws he passed? He rounded up the Fae into reservations and who were the first he took?"

Shula's eyes widened. "Fae with powers."

"And why is that?"

"To put them in his camps and kill them?" Clay supplied, scratching at his blond mane.

"Not kill them. Experiment on them." Something in her heart clenched painfully as her past tried to assault her. Screams and ashwood and bloody drag marks in the sand...

Her fingers worked in a frantic rhythm against her thighs once again.

She closed her eyes and swallowed the rising lump in her throat, loosing a breath. When she opened them again, she forced herself to say, "The theories say that he took the Fae with powers to the camps and that's where they conducted their experiments."

She knew it sounded far-fetched when it was first heard. When George had first told her, she'd scoffed and laughed in his face. But she'd laid awake for days after in her rented room, staring up at the splinters in her ceiling, running the possibilities of it being the truth in her head over and over again.

The more she thought about it, the more sense it had made.

"Why would he experiment on the Fae?" Clay asked the same question she'd gone back to ask George herself.

So she gave him the same answer George had given her.

"To harness their powers somehow. Because he wants them for himself." She looked at Shula then, staring long and hard as if she could picture the threads of Mana that bound them together. "Why else would he want the Elementals? We are the most powerful Fae in existence, precisely because there is no price to our magic. The Emperor of Illyk wants that for himself."

"The Seer said—"

"He can wipe us all out. I know. How do you think he plans on doing that? I think he means to do it by absorbing Elemental power. Imagine the catastrophe if one man has the power of six Elementals within himself? It would be devastating."

Iona waited patiently as they absorbed this information. It had taken her much longer to get used to the idea. That those who had been on that beach with her one-hundred and two years ago had been stolen. Dragged away to camps because of the magic that lived inside their veins.

She'd been one of the lucky ones.

She'd stayed up night after night. Not even sleep would come, and her fingers had cramped from their frantic movements against her single sheet as her mind raced. Migraines had plagued her as her brain tried to absorb the information. As her soul tried to come to terms with everything she'd learned.

About her people and their suffering, and how she'd been helpless to stop it. It was only thanks to Mana she was able to keep a hold of her sanity for so long. At least, until she met the newer Resistance.

Now there was no doubt in her mind things would get better. That there was hope for her people.

Prince Valerio sighed, closing his eyes. When he opened them again, there was a deadly flash of *something* beneath his depths. "You have given me much to think about, and much to report to my father," he said slowly. "In the meantime, we go on to find rest of the Elementals before the Emperor of Illyk can."

He started to turn away and Iona felt dumbfounded by his response. That was all he had to say about it? He was their leader, the leader of the Resistance, and she'd just dropped the information that could change the course of the war forever.

"Our people are in those camps!" Iona argued before he could fully turn from her. "As our prince, it is your job to get them out!"

It felt like everything stilled then. Their breaths, the waves, Iona's heart...

Prince Valerio turned slightly, the slashing lines of his brows cutting over angry eyes. His thin lips were pressed into a firm line and he didn't speak, even if his body language and eyes did the speaking for him.

He was pissed.

But so was she.

He was her prince and he deserved respect and reverence. Iona was merely a fisherman's daughter, a poor girl from the Jade Court who, if not for this, would have otherwise never had crossed the Seelie Prince's path. Yet she deserved to be heard. After being silent for so long, she needed to say it. And after missing for so long, he needed to hear it.

"They are being tortured for their magic, either to prolong the emperor's life or give him more power, and you will turn your backs on those who cannot help themselves?"

She felt Julius' hand reach for her shoulder, pulling her back. It was how she'd realized she'd been stepping closer to the prince, her voice rising in anger. Uric had discreetly slid to his prince's side, his blade clenched tightly in his hand as if he meant to protect Prince Valerio from Iona.

She took a breath, though it did nothing to calm her, and stepped away from him.

"They deserve to know their prince cares enough to free them," she said. "As a royal, it is your mission—"

"My mission," he interrupted, his voice dripping colder than her ice, sharper than a blade, deadlier than the sweet scent that emanated from his body. "Is to ensure the safety of the Elementals. Not to prove or disprove a theory given to you by someone named George." He sneered the name, like it tasted too human on his lips.

"But—"

"I am prince and commander of this group."

Magic pulsed around them, darkening, frightening. Images and shadows flicked around the edges of Iona's vision. Her heartbeat sped up, her fingers twisted into the material of her pants as she moved them. Fear was prominent, suffocating, and she felt herself begin to hyperventilate.

"I will reiterate only once more." His voice rose like thunder booming. His features changed, shifted, and he became something akin to a monster. "We are going to find the Elementals, not go on a useless chase through the emperor's iron camps. As soon as we make it to shore, you and Shula will lead us to the third Elemental." He stepped forward and Iona flinched, an involuntary whimper prying from her throat, and she hit something solid behind her. "And you will not ever fucking question my authority again."

A Prince with Too Much Heart

Madness crept along the edges of Prince Valerio's mind. It was a weakness he would not show, and even as it threatened to cripple him into fragility, he walked away with his back straight, pulling the images of shadows and monsters back into himself.

He hated that he had to be this type of ruler. A ruler who used fear and magic to be obeyed, but it was what he was becoming. What he'd always been. A mere boy among men, like his father and king so cruelly liked to remind him.

He tried to tell himself it was for the good of the entire group. They could not afford to go on a wild chase across Illyk at the behest of Iona, because of a conspiracy theory they didn't even know was true or not.

And she was pushing. In his experience, those who rose and pushed for their own selfish reasons without thinking of the consequences could become mutinous. He'd had to shut down her ideas as quickly as they formed.

Not many understood what it meant to rule. The needs of the many always outweighed the needs of the few, and he'd been given his orders, besides. Orders straight from the king. To find the Elementals. Beyond that, nothing else mattered.

Not even his people, locked away in iron camps.

His steps almost faltered as he stormed below deck, the darkness creeping in, making his movements faster, more eager as he rushed to be alone.

Fuck!

His foot came in contact with a wooden stool and kicked it against a wall where it tore to pieces like the vestiges of his own sanity.

Fuck!

His entire body trembled until he felt like he was losing control of everything. The price he was forced to pay for using his magic was temporary insanity and he never knew in what form it would take hold. Sometimes it was in bouts of anger and violence, sometimes hysteria, and sometimes he would lie there in a comatose state until his mind slowly returned to him.

This time, he felt it in violence and hysteria.

Laughter bubbled up in his throat even as he automatically reached for the second stool and picked it up with his trembling fingers to smash it against the wall. Broken bits pelted against his face, but he barely felt it beyond the uncontrollable sway of his body.

His hand curled into a fist and he smashed it against the metal of the boat, splitting his knuckles open. He hit it again and again. Blood and skin flew, and he laughed as his bones began to crack against the boat.

And then he felt a strong pair of arms wrap around him from behind, pulling him away from the destruction of his hands. Valerio was hauled to a steadily breathing chest. Soft strands of white hair tickled his cheeks and he struggled against the hold, doing nothing but making the Fae behind him grip tighter.

"Let me go, Uric," Valerio ordered between manic laughs.

Uric did not listen.

"Calm yourself, my prince."

Uric was used to these displays. The two Fae had been together for so long, they knew one another's moods, their pasts, and knew how to care for one another when the use of magic took its toll.

"I am no prince!" Laughter roared from his chest that he knew would embarrass him later. "No one heeds my demands when I only want to protect them from a worse fate." He struggled, slipping one arm free that he used against Uric, punching against his friend.

"They do not know the cost of being royal," Uric supplied. "They know nothing except their own foolishness."

Valerio felt his body begin to sag against Uric's as the energy began to leave him though the need to wage violence still thrived in his chest.

"What if she's right?"

That was the worst part of this whole thing. What if Iona was right about it all and the Fae were not being killed but experimented on by humans?

Now Valerio had the suspicions to investigate in order to confirm or deny those claims, but he could not. Because his orders were to find the Elementals. He did not think one life was more important than others, especially when they had so little Fae left anyway. All Fae were important, Elementals, Seelie, and Unseelie alike. He did not want to pick and choose who to save, or what life to place over another.

The Elementals were important, but so were the Fae trapped in camps. Being a royal meant he was forced to prioritize who he was going to save. It meant hiding behind the shadows of King Ashera and following orders he did not like because to disobey a king meant death, even if it was his father. His cruelty extended even to Valerio and if he died, he'd not live to help those who needed it another day. There would be no one left to temper the king's erratic moods.

"How can I call myself their prince if I am not willing to save them from such a fate?"

The urge to destroy slowly abated from Valerio's body. The trembling ceased until he regained his full senses. That was when he became aware of his position. Of Uric pressing Valerio's body tightly against him, rubbing soothing circles against the panes of his abdomen with one hand.

His pillowy yet sharp scent invaded Valerio's nostrils, and it brought with it a certain level of comforts that only best friends could.

"You do not know if what she speaks is the truth," Uric said quietly, his voice fully pulling Valerio from the mania. "We would risk a lot if we followed that theory only to discover it was not true. *We cannot risk it.*"

His words severed the doubts, and yet the guilt still did not ease.

Valerio sighed and straightened, pulling away from Uric and turning to face his long-time friend. Those black eyes were filled with worry, and Valerio tried easing it with a smile.

"I am fine."

Uric didn't look convinced. He reached out and touched him, his grasp warm and... caring.

Valerio breathed in through his nose and when he let it loose, he opened his eyes. Uric's stared back at him, the depths telling a story that Valerio did not want to hear. It was a vulnerable expression, born from a weak moment. Uric was otherwise unreadable, kept his emotions tightly locked away behind blades of steel as sharp as his scent.

It was only in these rare moments when the two found themselves alone that Uric dared drop those defenses to look at Valerio like he was more than just his prince. More than just his friend.

It burned something inside Valerio's soul, something painful. Because he knew what the look was, what it meant, what it longed for.

It was something he could never return.

Valerio pulled away from Uric and watched his friend's expression fall. He did not like feeling like a cad, did not like feeling like he was hurting the one Fae who cared more about him than any other. But the heart was a fickle thing and had the ability to misinterpret the touch of a friend for something more.

Valerio would not do that.

"You are right," he said firmly. "We cannot risk it."

Uric's perfected hardened expression slammed over his features. A tightness pulled at his whole body. Like he could read Valerio's mind, knew what he was thinking, and a part of him hated his prince for it.

"I need to speak of this to my father, regardless."

As if summoned, or waiting at the top of the stairs for this moment precisely, Weylyn stepped down. His golden eyes glittered with mirth over a broken, bruised nose that Ryker hadn't bothered to heal. Not that Valerio blamed him.

"The king wishes to speak with you." He smirked in Valerio's direction, and the prince had to fight not to grit his teeth. Every interaction with Weylyn was slow torture. Yet he was forced to put up with him.

Valerio didn't need to respond, didn't need to give his permission. Weylyn's golden eyes flared, rolling to the back of his head, and his magic reached out, pulling Valerio in.

Weylyn's magic was an aggressive force. It felt like his subconscious was being pulled through a dark tunnel, suspended in nothingness. He wondered if this was what Weylyn felt when he used his magic, if he paid the price with his inability to move, see, or hear anything on the outside. He never asked but knew the Fae could read the question from his mind anyway.

Then he heard his father's voice ringing out loud and clear, like an echo through his mind.

"You have found her, then?"

He likely already knew the answer thanks to Weylyn, but Valerio answered anyway. "Yes, Your Majesty. We found the Fae Elemental."

There was a pleased hum on the other end of their connection. "And where is the next Elemental?"

"We do not know yet, Your Majesty," Valerio answered, his own voice echoing oddly across black air. He sucked in a breath, debated on whether or not he should mention what Iona said. For a moment, he was glad that only Weylyn could read his mind in this state, and not his father. "The Elemental did, however, give us distressing news."

"And what news is that?"

Valerio told his father what Iona said, about the theories that, once he said aloud, did not seem all that far-fetched. By the time he finished, a part of him was itching to look for the Fae in the camps and save them.

He cleared his throat when his father did not reply. "Perhaps they could—"

"No."

His voice had Valerio clamping his mouth closed.

"I rue the day your mother gave birth to such a foolish child."

Valerio felt the words like a blow, though they were not new to him. His father always insulted him, and even more so Valerio's mother.

The Queen of the Seelie Courts had not been his father's mate, and so there had been no love between them. Their marriage had been a contract and nothing more, a female of noble birth given to the prestigious Ashera line. As if that should have made up for her happiness. It hadn't. And in the end, it was what got her killed.

Sometimes, Valerio thought it was a good thing he was the spitting image of his father, or he would have faced death that day too.

He'd been a child, sent off to the Obsidian Court to stay with the noble family there. It was where he'd met Uric, where Uric had been given to him like a gift from a strange pale family as was tradition with the nobles.

Every prince needed a lord at his side, a guard, someone of prestigious blood. Uric was the last born of his family. They always said he would not amount to much, so they'd discarded him to become the Seelie Prince's plaything at a young age, without knowing the two would become the best of friends.

Uric had been there with him when they'd gone back to his own court only to find his mother gone.

"I gave you orders. You will not change them or I will flay the flesh off your back, boy."

Boy. King Ashera liked to call him that. To demean him, make him feel like he'd never amount to half the king that his father used to be.

People respected him. Listened to him. Feared him.

While Valerio found it difficult to control one little group.

"Yes, Your Majesty," he answered, though the words felt hollow.

"I refuse to repeat myself. I will not keep reminding you what your duty is. You will find the fucking Elementals like I asked, and you will bring them to me. Nothing less, nothing more. I do not care how those miserable Fae in the camps help our numbers. They are not important. The Elementals are. And once we have them, we will use them against the human emperor, and I will take great joy in watching him die."

Then his voice was gone, and Valerio's conscious was slammed back into his body. He blinked his eyes open, sucking in a heavy breath. Rage flew through his emotions, mimicking the hysteria and violence from earlier. He stared at Weylyn, but the Fae was already turning away and prowling up the steps.

Valerio watched the Fae go with a curse stuck in the back of his throat. Saving the Elementals was the smartest decision. That much he knew with certainty, and yet when his father said it with such hatred and cruelty, it left a sour taste in his mouth.

Valerio always felt balanced between doing what was forced on him and what was right. Because the decisions a king made were not always the right ones. He never tried to lean too much to one side or the other, out of fear of what he would become. That he'd be too kind and virtuous, too cruel and careless.

His father tried to shove him on the same side as him, and Valerio always told himself it was what he wanted, it was his legacy that would be cemented into the new world they meant to forge after the war was over.

Still, it felt wrong. Like cruelty didn't particularly belong within the spaces of his heart. He could scream and use his magic to pretend to be cruel, to be feared and drown in the sorrows of the decisions afterwards.

His mother and Uric always said his heart was too big. What he called love, his father called foolishness.

What made his father a revered, vicious king made Valerio a kind, sympathetic prince.

The fool prince.

The *hearty* prince.

The *wrong* prince.

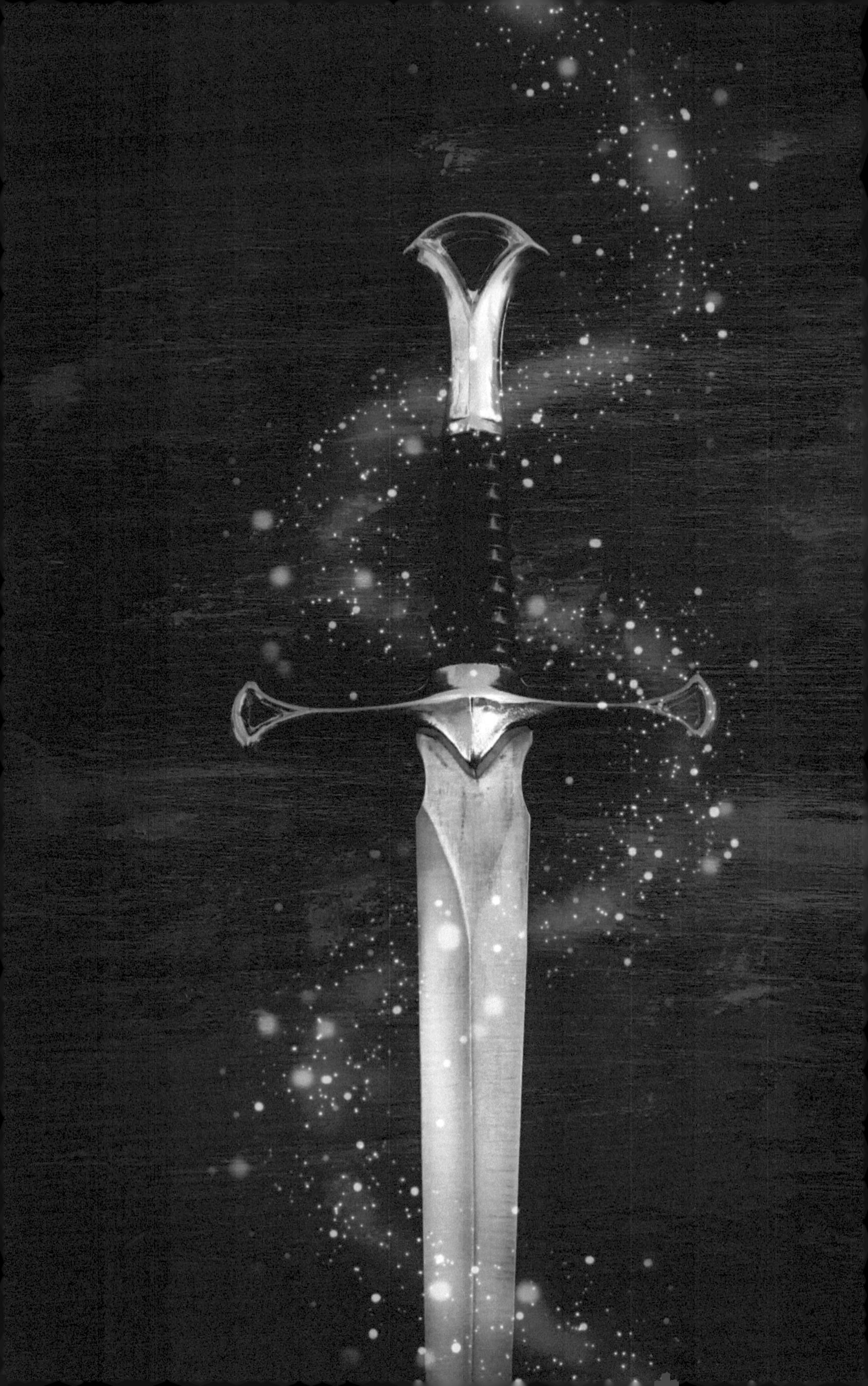

The King's Bitch

Iona fell into Julius' arms, slumping against the hardness of his chest. His fingers engulfed hers, helping her to tap a familiar pattern against her thighs. But not even that could help the fear that was still lodged in her throat.

Images of shadows and death faded from her vision as Valerio walked away from her. He took his magic with him, but the feelings it had provoked remained the same.

"Fuck," Julius cursed from behind her. As if he knew tracing wouldn't work this time.

Iona took in a breath, but it was hard to catch air into her lungs. Beneath her panic, she felt the stirring of her magic and two bonds. Julius' and her familiar's worry mingled in with her senses, overwhelming her entirely.

Then Shula was in front of her, the fire Fae's eyes compassionate.

"His magic is a bitch," she whispered, her dark brows furrowing into lines of anger. "He did it to me once, too."

Her hand reached out to touch Iona's clammy skin on her cheek. The female's palm was warm and reassuring, and the bonds of Mana shoved away her recoiling senses and made her feel stronger. A zap passed between the two Fae, like a current of electricity.

Iona wasn't sure she would ever get used to the sensation, but it made her feel better just the same. The panic ebbed, her breathing returned to normal, even if her heart beat a wild rhythm in her chest.

She let loose a breath. "Thanks."

Shula pulled her hand away. The touch had been sisterly almost, with a bit of tentative affection behind it, though she looked embarrassed as she dropped her hand to her side.

"He's a dick," Shula said. "But..." She chewed on her bottom lip. "I think he's right. The camps are brutal." Her golden-brown eyes sparkled as if fire lived within her depths. "We would be outnumbered. It wouldn't be safe. Best to hide, you know?" She gave Iona a tight-lipped smile which wasn't returned, then she walked away.

They all did, leaving Iona and Julius alone.

Julius turned her in his arms, his big hand cupping her cheek much like Shula had. "Are you okay?" A crater formed between his brows; he was frowning so hard.

"I'm fine." A lie. She didn't feel fine. Physically, perhaps she was alright. Mentally, she could be better. But her emotions were working on overtime, pounding through her with angry fists.

She needed Prince Valerio to agree to go to the iron camps and free the Fae. She couldn't explain it. Mana was urging her to do it, telling her it was the right choice. The *only* choice.

Yes, she knew how dangerous of an endeavor it was, but everything was dangerous these days in Illyk. Being alive was just as perilous as storming an iron camp. At least they could do some good while they were living illegally in Illyk just by breathing.

At least they could save others.

"Talk to me," Julius insisted.

Iona's hands reached up to grab his bulging biceps. "How can we not save them?" she asked quietly.

His thumb stroked against the apples of her cheeks, the touch tender. "I know it's hard, but our prince has given us orders."

She swallowed the rising lump in her throat. She thought for sure he would have agreed with her and didn't know what to do knowing he didn't. She needed someone on her side. At least one person.

Her hands fell and she stepped away from him. For a moment he looked panicked due to the distance she placed between them. She couldn't find it in her to reassure him. She knew inherently that they would not always agree on things, that opinions were as different as every corner of the world. Iona didn't begrudge him for not taking her side, but she did want him to understand.

"Let me ask you this, mate," she said ferociously. His eyes flared at the word, at the reminder of what they now were to one another. As if he could ever forget. Maybe she'd done it to remind him they were now a team. However alone they were both used to being, he could not shove aside her words like they meant nothing. "What would you do if it was me locked in that place?"

Green eyes and nostrils flared. He seemed to grow bigger, stand taller. "I would punch the camp to the fucking ground."

She smiled a bit sadly at him. It was just the answer she'd been expecting. "Yet you would not extend that courtesy to others."

He opened his mouth, and she knew he was going to make excuses, defend his prince, but she didn't need to hear that right now.

So Iona turned, and she walked away.

When they were a few miles from the shores of Teg, near the border where it met Orknie, they dropped anchor. It wasn't smart to park ship near the shores where any human could see them and get the authorities involved. They had to make it close enough where Uric could portal them from the boat and to a secluded woods area in Orknie.

Everyone had packed their things and shouldered massive packs against their backs. Since Iona had left with nothing, all she had was her hand digging into her familiar's fur, the other one clasped tightly against Julius'.

She could feel the tension reverberating through her mate, but she did nothing to soothe him. Iona was just as anxious, if not more than he was.

It was a new adventure, a new stage in her life, something she wasn't used to. Traveling all of Illyk out in the open with other Fae, her mate, and her enormous familiar was a dangerous call for attention. But she knew this was the right thing to do. Mana had decreed it.

Little tendrils of magic let loose from her palm, sending cold all over her familiar in preparation for their journey through warmer weather than he was used to.

Once Uric opened the portal, they were ushered through and made it to the other side. Orknie's grounds were frosted over, but not covered in snow like Teg further north. Iona took a deep breath and stared at the sky. She'd never been outside of Porir before. For years that had been her life. Now things were different.

The skies weren't as dreary or as gray, though that may have been due to the fact they were surrounded by nature. The grass alone was a shock to her system. In Porir, there were nothing but crumbling streets and torn-apart structures. Tree roots didn't touch the city; instead of branches, it was metal beams that twisted towards the sky; instead of grass and earth, the ground was littered with crumbled brick and trash.

It was like being in some new, surreal world that made her chest compress.

"Let's make camp," Valerio ordered once everyone was through the portal. "In the morning, you two will tell us where the next Elemental is, and we will journey that way."

Iona cut a glare to the prince that he didn't see.

"Where are we exactly?" she asked Shula, who had pulled a crumpled map from her pocket and was studying the lines with crumpled brows.

"Just outside of a town called Verdt." Her finger pressed against the spot she'd indicated, and Iona cast a quick glance at the map, her mind whirling with thoughts.

Everyone busied themselves with setting up camp, and since Iona had nothing, no tent or blankets, she decided to go speak with the Seelie Prince. She needed to convince him that going to the iron camps were in their best interests.

She pulled away from her familiar and Julius and approached Prince Valerio.

He didn't turn to greet her as he spoke. "The answer is still no."

She grinded her teeth together at his utter dismissal. "Prince Valerio, if you'd only—"

He whirled around and she closed her mouth. "I distinctly remember giving an order. What makes it so hard for you to understand?"

His body seemed to quiver with deadly promise. It made her fearful for a single moment. She had to remember who she was talking to. Their world had become a shitty place and the courts were scattered, but he was still a prince and still commanded fear and respect.

"Please hear me out."

He held up a hand. "I have heard you out, and yet my orders remain the same." He looked at her with a glare, daring her to contradict him once more. Only she knew she wouldn't like the repercussions. "And if you do not like my orders, then feel free to leave."

It was a challenge, one he knew she wouldn't face. Because as much as they needed her, she needed them, too. She doubted he would ever let her go anyway. Even if she tried—which Iona wouldn't—he would stop her, keep her against her will just like they'd done with Shula.

"Can you tell me why you won't consider it?"

"I do not have to explain my decisions to you."

Her eyes narrowed on his stiff shoulders. "Your father is making you, isn't he?" She didn't need to be involved directly in his inner circle to know that he was following King Ashera's orders. He'd as much as said so before, but she never imagined what the strict confines of royal life were like, even for a prince.

He cut her a glare.

"How much power do you really have?" she challenged. "As a prince of the Seelie Court and the king's only child, I would imagine you had much more power than you do." She didn't like speaking to her prince this way. The words burned on her tongue, but she didn't think he would listen otherwise. "You're little more than the king's bitch, aren't you?"

He snarled, his rage showing in the snapping of his canines. A vicious gesture that he pulled back within a second, his eyes widening as if he were surprised he let himself do even that. He took a breath to calm his obviously fraying nerves.

He cracked his neck from side to side and glared at her. "You will not goad me into anything, Elemental. My father is king and his word is law. Only fools disregard it."

Iona scoffed. She should shut up, but she couldn't. She was too riled up, too pissed that he wasn't listening to reason. "Your father must know how beneficial it would be to this war to save those in the camps. We've been nearly eradicated. We need Fae."

"The Fae in the camps are dead," Valerio argued, and she wondered if it was because he really believed that or if he was trying to convince himself.

"They are not. They're there, and they need us."

His eyes narrowed. "How do you know?"

"Because Mana told me!" She couldn't hold back her shout. It echoed harshly through the trees and burned out her throat and at the backs of her eyelids. She was aware everyone had closed in to listen now, but she didn't care that they had an audience. He would hear her, either way.

"You want me to believe that Mana speaks to you?" Valerio mused, his brows raising over burning eyes. "You?" He said it with disdain, as if Iona was worth nothing.

She knew better.

She was an Elemental. Favored of Mana, with power that surpassed even the prince.

"Mana speaks to me," Iona repeated firmly. She didn't need him to believe it, because she knew the truth. "There are Fae in those camps. Which you'd know if you did your job as prince and actually tried to save them from those places, instead of cowering in fear."

"Careful with those words, Elemental," Valerio warned on a low growl. "Remember who you are speaking to."

"I thought I was speaking to the Seelie Prince and not the coward before me."

She felt the blade kiss her throat before she saw the blur that was Uric at her side. He growled, menacing, moved like a shadow. She swallowed and felt the edge dig into her skin.

Roars sounded through her bonds. Her familiar growled and Julius was suddenly there, his own sword pressed to Uric's throat.

"Release my mate or I'll sever your head, Uric." Julius would make good on that promise, too. She didn't need to look into his eyes to know. She felt his emotions through their connection.

"Enough!" Valerio growled.

The command had Uric and Julius both dropping their arms. She didn't look at the prince's bodyguard or reach a hand up to her throat where she felt a thin line of blood dripping.

"The fact of the matter is, we need numbers," Iona tried again in a much calmer voice. "The camps have those numbers. If you don't believe me, let's go look. We don't even have to engage. Let's just see if there really are Fae being kept there still. Perhaps not all hope is lost."

Valerio's jaw worked extra hard, and she wondered if he was contemplating her words. He had to be, she couldn't accept anything else.

"There are too many camps."

"We will start with a small one," she urged. "There's one a few miles from here."

Uric's eyes narrowed, and his voice dripped with suspicion. "How do you know?"

"George told me."

He'd given her the locations to every single camp in existence all across Illyk because she'd asked. He'd marked them up on a map. A map she had studied just as fervently as she did the splintered ceiling. And when she had every single camp memorized, she burned the parchment and wept.

Their locations were still imprinted into her brain. She knew the size of every camp, their exact location. The only thing she didn't know was how many guards were watching and how many Fae they harbored.

She just wanted to prove to the prince she was right. She wanted him to shift his priorities. To save their people.

"You're a prince. You're supposed to care about the Fae."

"I do."

"Then prove it!"

Silence followed, filled with nothing but their harsh breathing echoing through the cold winter air.

Valerio looked like he was in deep contemplation. Uric sidled beside him, hovering, protecting, and glaring. Weylyn slipped to his other side and he was grinning at Iona beneath the broken nose she had given him. Like he knew.

Because he did.

She tried not to look into his golden, eerie eyes and instead focused on the prince.

"Our people need a royal to save them or they will never follow you in a war. How can you ask us to fight for you, if you aren't willing to do the same for us?"

Minutes passed and Iona's heartbeats measured the time. She held her breath, tapped her fingers to her thighs, and waited.

And waited...

And waited...

Finally, Valerio let out the softest sigh.

And Iona knew that she had won.

"Fine," he conceded, though the word was forced through clenched teeth. "A small one. We will pass by and observe, but not engage." Shock seemed to ripple through the group. Iona had to admit, beside the elation, she was shocked herself. She wasn't sure she'd ever convince him. "You better have a fucking plan, Iona," he growled. "Because I will not lose anyone here for a fool's errand, and you better pray to Mana that you're right."

She fought back the cheer she wanted to scream out. Shula stepped forward, her eyes blown wide and unsure.

"Are you serious?" she demanded, looking between Iona and Valerio. "You really want to do this?"

Valerio looked like he was holding back a snarl. "I gave the order, did I not?"

"I don't think this is a good idea..." She fiddled with the ends of her hair, pulling and pushing them away from her pointed ears. "The camps are dangerous—"

"We'll be careful," Iona interrupted with a sharp prick of annoyance. She didn't need Shula changing Valerio's mind after it had taken so much to get him to agree in the first place. She cut the fire Fae a glare.

"It's too dangerous," Shula argued, her voice rising to something that sounded similar to panic.

Iona fought not to roll her eyes and let the anxiety take over. She needed to be confident, or else Valerio would go back on his order. The Fae needed this; the Resistance would see the truth soon enough.

"The camps are made of iron. They'll block your magic—"

"Not ours," Iona said. "You burned the bars off a cage and melted iron beasts. We are stronger together, and even if we feel weak at first, we will overcome it."

Shula didn't look convinced. "Have any of you ever even been close to an iron camp?" When no one answered, she pounded her fist to her chest. "Well, I have! I watched my parents get taken to one. I felt the heat of their ovens. I watched the ash rise in the sky. Do you really want to go through that? Do you really want to take the risk that it could be any of us?"

"Don't be a coward," Iona snapped. It was too late to take back her words once they were out. She could see the moment they impacted Shula, and guilt consumed Iona's whole chest as the fire Fae staggered back.

Nothing hurt her more than to be considered a coward by the rest of the group. If there was one thing Iona had gauged during Shula's recounts of the events that led her here, it was that she didn't want to be considered weak. That she wanted to please.

Iona knew how to get her to go on board with just a few words. Even if she felt dirty speaking them.

"Enough," Valerio growled again. He glared at Shula. "Is everyone going to disobey my orders today? We have things to do. I suggest we all get started."

Valerio stared off into the darkness, his heart pounding up to his throat. He heard Uric's footsteps and did not bother to turn and greet his friend.

Uric didn't bother with pleasantries, either.

"You are making a mistake," Uric said gravely.

He hated those words. Hated how they pierced his chest and made him feel like a failure. He should have been familiar with them already, as his father spoke them more often than not. But to receive them from Uric had its own special brand of punishment.

"Then it will be my mistake to make," Valerio gritted out.

"You let her play you into making that decision."

Valerio closed his eyes and tried to find patience within himself. "My decisions are my own to make."

"She manipulated you!" His voice rose above a whisper, and Valerio riddled his friend with a glare.

"Am I or am I not your prince?" he asked in a haughty tone. He hated asking that as much as he hated feeling incompetent. He hated using his own noble blood to his advantage, to make others feel lesser.

Uric seemed surprised, blinking rapidly. His whole body tensed and the angry, vulnerable expression faded to hard lines. "You are." His jaw clenched.

"I am in charge here. You are nothing but my guard and my right hand. Anything else comes secondary. You are not my brother. You are not my father. And you are not my mate. You cannot presume to govern over me."

He knew he was hurting his friend with those words as much as he was hurting himself.

The truth was that nobody but Uric understood him. Nobody would stand beside him but him. And he feared if Uric thought he was making a mistake, if he was cruel about the decisions Valerio had to make, then he was truly everything his father had ever made him out to be.

"Noted," Uric replied, his voice colder than the night air around them.

Valerio wanted to grip his friend's arm and apologize, to explain why he felt the need to do this. Because Iona was right. No Fae would follow them if he did not have the bravery to stand up for them in this. Because he did not think he could live with himself if he passed by and pretended like they didn't exist. Because they did. And they needed their king—their prince—to help them.

He may not have been the prince his father wanted him to be, but he was a royal just the same. And he could have compassion, fear, veneration, and adulation in equal measure if he wanted to.

How could he explain to Uric that he was doing this out of selfish reasons? For his own peace of mind, his own sense of duty to the Fae he was trying so desperately to protect?

He knew his father would not approve, but his father never approved of anything Valerio did regardless of the circumstances.

Valerio couldn't handle it if Uric disapproved, too.

But before he could explain any of that, Uric was already turning and walking away. And there was something about his gait that screamed with finality.

Valerio tried not to feel like he'd just made the biggest mistake.

Ashes and Bone

The camp was miles away from the city. Iona guessed it was to keep the Esses taint away from the good citizens of Verdt. Maybe, as much as they professed to hate the Fae, even they couldn't stomach the screams of the dying and tortured.

Her teeth clenched in angry anticipation. Her body felt lethargic and she tried to fight off the effects of the iron building they were near.

The camp was exactly that. Iron wrought walls surrounded a smoking, iron building that spit ash from tall chimneys. Barbed wire circled the top threateningly, but when Iona squinted, she noticed they were ashwood thorns, crawling over like spectral fingers ready to reach for anyone who tried to climb to the other side for freedom.

Human guards wearing the colors of the Emperor of Illyk—red, black, and gold leathers with metal helms that hid their features—guarded the top walls. Swords gleamed at their hips, hitting against their thighs as they walked along from one place to another. They didn't appear alert; they looked lazy, bored.

There was something eerie about the silence in the air with nothing but the soft puffs perfuming through ever-thickening gray skies. No sound came from within those iron gates, like nothing but ghosts lived within those large walls. Iona knew better.

The close proximity to both iron and ashwood had her holding her breath, fingers tapping against her thighs. She tried to keep her mind focused on what they were there for, on the sights around them instead of letting herself get dragged back to the past. She couldn't go there, to the old war when there was a new one to be fought today.

She didn't have a plan. At least, not much of one. This was one of the smaller iron camps that spread throughout the empire of Illyk. There were so many more than this, this was almost as unimpressive as a chapel. Yet there were Fae in there.

She planned on getting them out.

The idea came to her. Something quick and straightforward. She counted the guards manning along the walls. She could scale them easily enough. If her magic didn't fail her, that is. It always debilitated her magic, but if Shula had melted iron in circumstances of extreme distress, then Iona could use her own Elemental magic for this.

They were only supposed to observe the camp, which was what they were doing in the shadows.

"There is nothing here," Uric growled, his whispering voice slicing through the silence.

Iona wanted to shush him, but she was focused, determined, *anxious.* Her whole body was overflowing with tension. This was the closest she'd ever been to the truth since she'd landed on the shores of Teg.

Behind her, Valerio sighed. "I cannot hear anything."

There was resignation in his voice. Like he was already retracting from the orders he'd given and was prepared to take them all away from this place. Iona couldn't let that happen. Not yet.

"It's the iron," she whispered back, hoping they couldn't hear the pleading note slip from her tongue. "It's weakening our senses."

"All the more reason to leave," Shula supplied.

Iona didn't turn a glare on the other woman, even if she wanted to.

"We need to get closer."

"Wait..."

Iona didn't stay to force herself to listen to his reluctance.

She was already moving.

Julius' heart thumped with equal parts fear and excitement. It beat through his blood with all the familiarity of the savage hoof beats of the little people of the wood, dancing against the forest floor.

Battle was akin to a wild song, one orchestrated by the Wild Hunt, Unseelie that danced across the skies and reveled in war and death. A legend older than even Mana. Where Mana ruled and connected Seelie magic now, there existed things even more ancient and powerful than that.

At least, that's what he'd been told. Legends, he thought, were funny little things. One could never be too sure what was true and what was a fabrication, weaved through with lies and overactive imaginations throughout the centuries.

Regardless, he felt that wildness inside. It expanded within him, rushed through his blood like the strumming of a lute in his veins, like the rumbling cries of the Hunt was his very heartbeat.

Fighting was innately engraved in his soul. It was an instinct, one he was too foolish to ignore. Not that he wanted to, not when his mate was breaking away from him and darting towards the iron camp.

A crescendo of sounds deafened him. Blood roared in his ears and his body came alive and urged him forward.

He took a single step before a hand trapped his bicep in a punishing grip. Prince Valerio's voice pulled him from the skies of the Hunt and what he imagined they sounded like in his mind.

"Your mate is going to get us all killed," he snapped. "I gave orders."

He felt the shame heat his cheeks, but he shoved it aside. He knew Iona was being impulsive and overzealous, that she was breaking their carefully constructed rules and placing him in a precarious position, caught between her and the prince. His mate and his leader.

The soldier within him wanted to apologize for what she'd done while the newly mated part of him wanted to snarl and defend her. It was a fine line he had to navigate, and he was unsure how to do that.

For now, all he knew was that his mate needed him, and it would take a lot more than his prince's ire to hold him back.

"We have to help her." Julius jerked his arm away and burst out of the security of the shadows. Valerio called out to him, but the rhythm had picked back up in his mind, and he could hear nothing, see nothing, *taste* nothing but the silence.

Right before the thunderous crash of death.

Valerio's sword unsheathed from his side. He brandished it in his hand, but his palm burned against the hilt of it like he was holding something forbidden. Not because he hadn't held a sword before. He had fought, killed, and this would be no different.

It was just that everything had gone straight to shit within a matter of moments, and it was entirely his fault. The sharp sting of his own idiocy stabbed behind his eyelids. He never should have trusted the Elemental. It was like the both of them had been sent to test his patience, and while Iona was entirely more willing than Shula had been, she was also too headstrong. Her inability to listen was going to get them all killed.

Had he not just had the exact same conversation with Shula days before?

Was every Elemental he met to be a thorn in his side?

Valerio could feel Uric's heavy gaze and the angry "I told you so" sharp on the tip of his tongue. Miraculously, he held it back because there was no time for that now. There would be later when they were alone.

If they even survived this.

Valerio gave the signal and their group was running, following after Iona and Julius, who had already climbed to the top of the wall and were engaged in a battle, surrounded at all sides. He made quick motions with his fingers that the others understood. After years of traveling together, they did not need words to communicate, only hand motions.

Uric was the only one who stayed behind.

"Can you open a portal?" Valerio cut to the chase.

Uric's jaw clenched, but he closed his eyes and the portal opened behind him. It flickered due to the heavy content of iron, and Uric's body withered with age as he grew weaker.

Seeing his friend wrinkle before his eyes made Valerio's feet move faster. He jumped into the portal, reaching back to grab his friend's hand and pull him inside.

They stumbled within the camp. There was nothing but darkness at first, their booted feet cushioned by something soft and pillowy. Valerio took a blind step, then two before his toes collided against something ivory.

His eyes adjusted to the darkness and he stared at the contents within the room. Anything he had eaten on the journey here suddenly soured in his stomach when he realized they were standing on a graveyard of their people.

Her palms were sweating, fingers shaking, but she couldn't stop her body from advancing. Adrenaline shot through her head and she was running,

She heard hissing whispers of her name behind her, but she didn't turn. She darted out to the building, her magic rippling through her blood. Her feet pounded against the gravel-covered ground, jarring through her skull.

Icy knives appeared against her fingertips and her hands shot out, the shards flying and hitting the humans against the sensitive flesh of their exposed throats.

They didn't even get a chance to scream before they went down.

The hood of her cloak fell back as she shot her magic out again, causing flat planes of ice to slam against the side of a wall, one atop of the other to form a staircase. Her magic wavered inside her, like the remnants of a fire sputtering to little bits of smoke. The ice held beneath her weight as she stepped against them, pounding up the steps.

She reached the top, jumping over onto the wall of ashwood thorns. They snagged against her cloak and crunched beneath her feet. With a feral grunt pushing past her lips, she landed on a crouch on the other side of the wall. As she stood, humans encased her from both sides, running towards her with their raised weapons. Iona's hands flew out, but her magic had dulled and the ice that shot from her fingertips like the shape of broken shards imprinted on her back were weak. Their swords twisted, breaking her ice apart into fallen snow.

They converged, running towards her at once. Her mind homed in on the fight. Just like it had so long ago when she'd burst from the doors of their small home, feet sinking into the sand of the Jade Court, while human soldiers marched their way through to kill everyone she knew and loved.

Her mind had blanked then. A mixture of fear and panic nearly choking her, but something rising even stronger from within her. Determination. Because her family had been out there. Helpless, without magic, fighting, dying.

It fueled her.

She willed a sword of ice to her palm. Weaker than the one she'd used to fight Julius, but it was enough to block the blade moving fast in her direction. They struck and ducked, whirling, pushing the human against his comrade where they nearly went down in a heap of steel and limbs.

Iona had little time before more humans came for her, and she had to know the truth of the camps. Of what they held within them. She blew out a breath of magic and ice crawled along the ground like a shadow. The humans cried out and scrambled away. But it never reached them. Her magic sputtered to a stop.

She felt the pain a moment later.

A blade sliced against her clothes, scratching her side. She cried out as the iron touched her skin, whirling with her own sword raised only to have it shatter against a single blow of an iron sword. She slipped backwards, staring into the eyes of a human beneath his helm. A cry burst past his lips as he swung again...

And then a fist met the side of his face, the blow so powerful, his helm and skull dented within themselves, his insides pouring from his nose and open mouth. His body crumpled to the side, falling from the wall into a broken mass of limbs below.

Julius jumped over the wall, his hands scraping against the ashwood thorns, boots crushing them, as he took the spot where the human had stood. She didn't acknowledge what he'd done for her with a smile, but she made sure the gratitude shone in her eyes.

The others climbed up the wall beside her as more humans appeared, wielding iron from head to toe as if that alone could stop them.

Maybe it had stopped them once. Maybe it had been the downfall of the Jade Court. But they were different now. *Times* were different now and Mana was a fiercer opponent than they could ever fathom. It had to be. They'd made them this way.

There was no holding back as swords and bodies collided, shoving off the sides of walls to fall to gruesome deaths. Iona fought her way past them, her legs screaming in pain as she ran towards the stairs.

There were rooms down below, and she meant to check every single one of them.

Her side agonized with each pounding step down the stairs. She hauled breaths into her lungs only to cough them out as a coppery scent stained her lips.

She didn't care though, not when she was so close to the truth. But as she neared the bottom, she found herself surrounded. Humans swarmed like bugs on an anthill, tripping over each other to try and kill her first. But she was no coward, and a trickle of magic slid down her back. Of Mana, telling her everything would be alright. She was sure of it.

So she met them head on, running down to them as they ran up. She didn't want to register the pain of their blades, but something inside her severed. It took a moment for her to realize it was the bond, and Julius was screaming through it.

She staggered back and slipped.

Then his pounding footfalls appeared as he all but slammed down the steps and into the wall of humans beating against Iona. He took them down, the heavy weight of his rage and muscle flattening their faces against the ground. A single blow wreaked death, and his anger threatened absolute destruction.

Iona pushed herself up on shaking feet, her hands trembling as she pushed away the mess of curls against her eyes, sure she was staining the silver red with blood. Her vision felt hazy with it, and there was a tugging against her magical self that she wanted to ignore but couldn't. It was something she didn't recognize, and it only took her a single moment to realize it wasn't her own pain.

It was Julius'.

Her mate fell to his knees. Blood bloomed across his abdomen, around the iron sword that was shoved inside his body. Iona wanted to scream at the sight, but her tongue felt heavy, leaden against the roof of her mouth. Her entire body trembled, and she wanted to take a step forward, but she felt frozen in more ways than one. Her legs wouldn't obey her command.

It was like living in the war all over again, watching those she loved died. Like waking up at night with her legs tangled around a ratty sheet, staring at horrifying images but unable to move. It didn't matter how much she commanded her fingers to tap against her thighs, they just wouldn't obey.

"Julius!"

The scream came from a voice that wasn't her own. Feminine, horrified, angry.

Something jostled against her body, rather, someone. Wavy, black hair trailed behind Shula as she darted towards Julius' crumpling figure, Clay and Ryker at her heels.

Iona watched as another woman bent towards her mate and helped sit him down on the ground. Her eyes flicked wildly, watching humans emerge from rooms, surrounding them. Iona was too helpless to stop it.

But then Shula Azzarh stood to her full height, and her rage was an almost palpable thing, burning like a blazing fire. No, not her rage, Iona realized. Her magic. Her entire golden-brown body began to glow like molten lava. Like rivers of it lived beneath her skin, flickering just below the surface of it.

Her eyes seemed to roll to the back of her head, consumed with orange. Like she was burning too hotly from the inside out. When the first licks of fire shot from her body, they caught against the nearest humans, incinerating them. Their screams pierced the sky like the ashes they billowed from their abominable chimneys.

Like a song of death Iona could never forget but hummed through her mind.

It broke her out of her stupor and her legs staggered forward one step, then two. Her knees collided to the ground in front of Julius, tears stinging against her eyes. She wanted to cup his cheeks, but she was too afraid to touch him. Too afraid her hands would shake and she'd hurt him more than her actions already had.

The blade pierced through his entire body. He looked more dead than alive, but she felt the life he was clinging to through their bond. She knew if they took the sword out, he would die.

"I can't lose you." Her voice was hoarse, heartbroken. "I can't lose you, too."

His eyes flicked over her face and he forced a familiar smirk to his lips, but it was entirely too strained.

"Julius..."

"Get out of the way!" Shula shoved Iona to the side, and she fell against the ground, her head jostling with the abrupt movement. She turned her glare to the fire Fae, nostrils flaring.

"You have no right to keep me from my mate." A fierce possessiveness rose inside her. One she thought only Fae males felt, but it was very much alive within her.

"Look what you did to your mate, Iona," Shula spat. "Take a good long fucking look." She gestured at the sword protruding from his stomach.

Julius looked like he was in excruciating pain, impaled and wheezing. Since the sword protruded from the other side, they didn't lay him down. Clay sat behind him, holding him up, while Ryker assessed the wound with a clinical eye.

"Just go do whatever you fucking came for so we can leave." Shula bent beside Ryker, whispering rapidly in his ear, asking if she could help.

Iona felt torn. She wanted to help but knew there was nothing she could do save hover over him. She wasn't a healer, but Ryker was, and she knew she'd only get in his way. The other part of her screamed to go check the rooms in the camp. To find what she'd set out to, just so this whole ordeal didn't feel like it was in vain.

"That will not be necessary," Valerio's tight voice joined them. She turned to the Seelie Prince. He was standing beside Uric, who was glaring daggers in her direction like he meant to kill her with a single stare.

She wanted that gaze to swallow her up. If only because the look in the prince's eyes and Julius' constant struggle to breathe made her feel like she made a colossal mistake. But she didn't want to admit that they'd been right.

That they never should have come here.

But she had to know, regardless.

"There is no one here, Iona," Valerio said, hatred bleeding through his words like Julius' life force was bleeding past the edge of the blade. "No one but these humans."

The words were like dying a slow death beneath the depths of waves all over again.

"I have to check—" She pushed herself to her feet again, swayed.

"Don't bother," Uric snapped. "We already did."

She looked to Prince Valerio for confirmation and found his lips set into a grim line of regret and anger "There is nothing," he said. "Nothing but ashes and bone."

Just like all those years ago, she knew she would remember this day as they marked another moment in her life while she wished otherwise.

A life slipping before her very eyes.

Ashes and bone.

Blood and steel.

Regret, bitter on the back of her tongue.

And worst of all, the sharp stench of death.

The Lies Fae Tell...

Getting Julius through the portal had been a challenge. Ryker instructed how to do it quickly and gently so as to not jostle the wound further.

"He's lucky to still be breathing," Ryker growled. "The sword is the only thing keeping him alive right now and preventing him from bleeding out."

Iona knew they were on a time crunch. It wouldn't take long for other human soldiers to show up. They had to get him through the portal without accidentally killing him. Just the thought made Iona sick to her stomach.

His usual ruddy, red skin had grown pale as they walked him across the mirrored surface of Uric's portal. They emerged on the other side, though Iona couldn't be sure where, as she could only pay attention to Julius and the way his skin kept paling further and further.

They sat him against the grass, Clay and Valerio propping him up from behind while Ryker bent to his front.

Shula shot Iona a glare and bent next to Ryker, placing a steadying hand against Julius' shoulder.

The simple touch was innocent, but Iona felt her own rage climb high up her throat. Because it was easier to be angry at someone else rather than at herself, like she should have been.

"Get your hand off my mate," she spat out from between clenched teeth.

It felt like everyone's heads snapped up to Iona, each wearing equal expressions of disdain except for Julius, who was struggling to breathe.

Shula shot to her feet, coming chest to chest with Iona. Her soft, beautiful features were contorted in a thunderous expression with as much rage as disdain. Her small hands pressed against Iona's shoulders and shoved.

Iona hadn't known Shula very long. She'd seen her use her magic to incinerate humans, but she'd never seen her truly angry before. Not like this, not thrumming with unbridled violence so her whole body shook.

"Fuck you, Iona!" she screamed.

Everyone seemed surprised by her outburst.

None more than Iona herself.

She'd felt a sort of kinship with the Fae. Mana calling to Mana. She never thought she'd be on the receiving end of something like this. Least of all with her.

"I don't want your fucking mate. But I am pissed. Pissed at all of you." Her gaze snapped to Prince Valerio's, bouncing back and forth between them. "You put us all in jeopardy for your stupid mission and now Julius is hurt. But you know what? It doesn't even matter to you. To any of you." She threw her hands up in the air. "You all run straight into reckless situations and you don't give a *shit* because you have your healer. You don't worry about wounds like this—" She gestured in Julius' panting direction. "—because Ryker is always fucking here to clean up your messes. But you know what? It's bullshit! None of you think about the consequences of your actions and what it does to him. Now he has to suffer because of your selfishness." She pointed an accusing finger at Iona then at Valerio.

"Whatever fucking reason you so badly wanted to go in there, I hope it was fucking worth it. Because now Ryker could be the one in danger. Not Julius, not your mate, but *mine.*"

Iona gritted her teeth, feeling her fingers tapping furiously. She wanted to block out her voice and words because they were true. She'd put them all in jeopardy. But it was hard to admit she was wrong. It was easier to lash out.

"You don't even want him as a mate," Iona whispered. She hated herself for the words, and all the intent behind them. "You regret your bond, so why does it even matter?"

"Iona!" Julius barked, the gravelly sound filled with rage. He winced as it jostled the sword still stuck inside him. "What the fuck?"

Clay glared at her. "Not cool..." he whispered, his hand whitening against Julius' shoulder.

Even Ryker stilled, his gaze going up to Shula, as if he could gauge the truth of Iona's words by looking to his mate, who stood rock still, her eyes wide and furious.

Iona wanted to take them back, but it was already too late.

It was Weylyn who broke the uncomfortable silence. "It was a shit show." His long, ringed fingers tugged at the end of his dark braid. "Perhaps now would be a prudent time to tell them the truth, Iona." His glittering eyes didn't hold mischief. Not since the first time she saw him. That was all they usually held. Now they flickered with annoyance.

"The fuck is he talking about?" Julius grunted as he tried to adjust his position.

Then, Weylyn's eyes *did* glitter brightly. "Shall you tell him or should I?" His lips pursed and his fingers flicked. Every gesture was calculated and cruel.

Her heart beat faster in her chest. She knew what he was talking about and loathed him for it. It was one thing to drag her secrets out before her in private, but to do it before the others was low.

His eyes flicked to the back of his head a mere second and then rolled back, a smile twisting his features. "Almost as low as you risking our lives for selfish reasons," he murmured, loud enough for everyone to hear.

Valerio stood, shoulders back, glaring with all the bearings of a royal. "What is going on?"

Iona couldn't bring herself to meet the prince's gaze. She couldn't bring herself to look at any of them. Not Julius, who was still paling, and staring at her with confusion and pain, as she could feel his gaze and his emotions down their bond. Not Shula, who glared. Certainly not Weylyn, who looked at her knowingly. Because he had a whole vial of her secrets gripped in the palm of his hand.

So she closed her eyes instead and took a deep breath, but there was a storm inside her. As perilous and destructive as the one that had nearly dragged her to her death. This felt the same. Like she was kicking her limbs and there was nothing to hold on to. The waves were a force to be reckoned with dragging her under, deepening, piercing into her mouth, her lungs, taking with it parts of her life and soul.

She tapped her fingers against her thighs as every memory, as everything came back to her. The stench of ashwood in the air, the rumbling ground as humans marched through the Herria Mountain pass to attack the Jade Court.

She remembered hiding, tucked against a wall with her sister and mother. She remembered the rest of it. The screams. The blood. Falling against the ground, a wound that should have been fatal, that should have taken her life pulsing at her shoulder. Her sister being dragged across the sand, nails clawing pointlessly against the ground, just before Iona fell into unconsciousness.

"Mana gave me a second chance." The words were whispered, but they felt right. Because she'd survived that day. She'd felt Mana in the air as her eyes opened, taking souls back where they belonged.

Leaving Iona alone in the aftermath of death, blood, and ash.

Iona's eyes fluttered opened and there were tears in them, even if she wanted to pretend to be strong. She wasn't anymore. She'd been selfish, had led her friends into danger without wanting to.

"I was there when the humans marched on the Jade Court. I watched it fall. I watched the human soldiers drag my sister across the sand kicking and screaming, and that was the last time I saw her." She looked at Julius, saw his understanding make way to confusion and betrayal.

She'd all but betrayed him by omitting the truth.

"I thought that if I joined the Resistance, I could get vengeance for my family and friends, but then we lost the war." She tried not to choke on her words, so they ended up rushing out of her like water cutting through sandy shores. "And I was on the boat, and then in Teg. I thought it was over. The Resistance was gone, the Fae were all scattered, the humans had won. I barely got through life as it was. But then I met George, and he gave me his theories. I didn't know if I should believe them, but Mana told me they were true. My sister was alive, taken captive in one of those camps because she had healing magic, but I had no way to get to her. Leaving Porir alone would have been suicide and I'd be no good to my sister dead."

Her sister's image rose to her mind. Her smiling, care-free face. Even when her skin clung to her bones in the aftermath of using her magic, she smiled through her pain. "Mana will make everything right," she would say.

After she was gone, Iona had tried to live every day a life her sister would be proud of. She'd tried to be optimistic, she opted to send out daily prayers to Mana in the hopes that they'd come true. And they hadn't.

Not until them.

"Then I met you, and I thought you could help..."

"Wait a fucking minute," Clay interrupted. "Is that the only reason you joined us, and why you did it so quickly without asking questions? That's why you manipulated us into going into one of those camps? Because you wanted to fucking find your dead sister?"

"She's not dead!" Iona shouted, pounding a fist against her heart.

"How do you know that?" Shula asked in a much softer voice. "She was taken to an iron camp one-hundred years ago..."

"I feel it in here." Iona tapped her chest, lighter this time. "And because Mana told me..."

Clay scoffed. "Great. We find the second Elemental and she's delusional..."

Julius growled a weak warning.

"I'm not delusional! Mana is an instinct that I follow, and when I met you all, I knew you were meant to help find her."

"So it was all a lie," Prince Valerio hummed, but there was something akin to death in his gaze, in his stance. "You lied to us all. You had us believe you wanted to save the Fae from death, but really you just wanted to find your sister." He turned that glare to Weylyn. "And you knew about it."

Weylyn smirked in response.

"What else do you know about that you do not tell us, I wonder? Did you know about Shula when she ran away as well?"

Weylyn just lifted his shoulders and tugged at the end of his long braid. That non-answer seemed to be answer enough.

"What the fuck, Weylyn? Are you even on our fucking side?" Valerio lost all his composure as he stepped towards the golden Fae.

But Weylyn didn't flinch under the prince's scrutiny. If anything, he seemed even more amused by it.

Humans had legends of devils. Beautiful creatures that provoked chaos and unrest. Weylyn reminded Iona of those stories. Of a deathly creature that resembled an angel, but who just wanted to watch the world burn.

"Am I to use my power for your every whim, my prince?" Weylyn taunted. "Should I reveal everyone's secrets just to make it fair?" His smile widened somehow, and for the first time since meeting him, Iona felt a sliver of fear down her spine. "Since we are confessing sins, should I tell them all why you really went after the Fire Dancer that night?"

Valerio seemed to pale at the very suggestion.

"No?" Weylyn laughed. "I did not think so, *my prince.*"

Valerio composed himself enough to growl at the mocking tone in his voice. "You know what? Fine. The only reason I agreed to go after Shula at the temple of the Brotherhood was because Davina led me to believe that Shula was my mate."

Ryker snarled.

Shula's face reddened.

But Valerio did not take his eyes off Weylyn. "You were using that information as leverage over me. It is what you do. You hoard secrets and taunt us with them because it makes you feel superior, but you forget you are just my father's dog." He stepped close until their noses were touching. "I am the prince here. Not you." He turned away from Weylyn, dismissing him. "And I will not be manipulated again." He glared at Iona. "You lied to me. To us. I will tell you what I told Shula. We are a group, and when one does not follow orders, we die. So take a good look at your mate, Iona Wylde. Because the next time I am disobeyed, his fate may be worse than a sword to the belly. The next time, he may end up dead. And that is a promise, because if you commit another act of treachery like this again, I will order Ryker to let your mate *die.*"

Then he nodded to Ryker, and he yanked the sword out of Julius. Blood bloomed and her mate let out an agonized cry. Ryker's palm covered the wound and glowed white, staunching the flow of blood.

But even as he healed Julius, Ryker still winced, groaning as his nostrils flared and he took on the pain of the wound to himself.

Shula hovered over him, her hair kissing Ryker's scarred cheeks as she bent. She whispered words of encouragement, but Ryker didn't hear them all.

Because he slumped to the ground and didn't get up again.

Promise

Shula swiped at Ryker's brow with a damp rag. It had been hours, and he still hadn't stirred after healing Julius. The others had all gone about setting camp and taking watch with tense postures while Shula tended to her mate. The only one who had stayed close was Ryker's familiar. The black cat sat vigil at his side, those bright eyes all but glaring at Shula as she worked, purring in a way that brought her a modicum of comfort.

Julius and Iona had disappeared. She didn't particularly care where the two had gone. Rage still seethed inside her chest. She'd told them going there was a bad idea, but they hadn't listened.

These were the consequences.

Tears prickled behind her eyelids, but she kept them at bay as she swiped over his brow once again. She hoped her proximity and touch could soothe him, bring him out of the unconsciousness he found himself under.

Shula was no expert on magic and certainly no expert on healing magic. She didn't know if this was normal for him, if the pain had just been too much and his body had shut down, or if it was something entirely worse.

She didn't want to contemplate if it was something worse.

She wrung out the cloth off to the side and when she turned back, Ryker's eyes were open and hard on Shula. For a moment, her movements stammered, her hand holding the cloth pausing just over the scars on his cheeks.

When he didn't speak or move, she swiped it over the sweat that had formed against his skin. She moved methodically, working in silence that somehow seemed to mean more than words ever could. Her heartbeat sped up with each stroke along his face, and when she finished with nothing else to do, she dropped the cloth off to the side.

Shula already had the pattern of his scars memorized, yet she traced them with her gaze just the same, wondering if she stared at them long enough would they be imprinted on her as much as Ryker was embedded into her soul.

His scars were a testament to his goodness. She'd always thought that. It was goodness and something else, too. A need to save the Fae like he couldn't save Mairin, his sister who had died brutally at the hands of human soldiers. The scars had been her last parting gift to her brother. Lines that zigzagged across a handsome face, distorting it entirely.

She pushed out a breath and her trembling fingers reached up to graze the edges of those scars. They bisected down his neck, disappearing into the collar of his jacket. So many littered his body like the pathways on a map. He'd suffered so much. Too much.

She couldn't fathom it.

"When will you stop punishing yourself for what happened to Mairin?" she asked, her whisper almost harsh, angry.

He didn't like to talk about Mairin. It had been months before he'd even confessed who she was to Shula, and within the same expanse of breath he used to explain his sister, he'd told Shula she was his mate and that he didn't want her.

Things changed since then. Because now she knew that he did want her, just like she wanted him. They craved each other so much it physically hurt. Sometimes she was still unsure if it was desire and love or pure hatred that tethered them together.

Ryker's displeasure at her question reflected in the pulling together of his brows. He grunted, clasping his fingers over Shula's to keep her hand right where it was. As if her touch brought him comfort.

They hadn't really touched much. She'd been avoiding him ever since their last painful encounter. When she'd told him they were a mistake. She didn't know if she still felt that. Her brain was still too clouded with the terrifying image of him falling to the ground and not waking up again.

"I'm not," he all but growled, his voice rumbling against the pulse at her wrist.

Shula fought back a shiver. "Are you sure about that? Because you keep putting your own life in jeopardy to save others regardless of what it does to you."

His touch against her softened as did his expression. "Contrary to what you might think, I do not wish to leave this life yet." He paused and brought her fingertips to his lips, pressing a soft kiss to each one. "I do not wish to leave you."

The sting of tears fell past her eyes and down her cheeks. He reached his hand up and caught a drop with his scarred fingers.

"What Iona said—" She broke off, sucked in a breath. "What *I* said before..."

Ryker grunted as he sat up, startling his familiar and making her hiss. Shula widened her thighs, and he pulled her towards him so she straddled his lap. Her thighs hugged his waist and his hands spanned across her lower back, keeping her pressed tightly to him.

"You were right," he said.

Shula blinked.

"Maybe we weren't ready for this." His eyes dipped between them. As if the bond that now interconnected them were somehow a visible thing. "Maybe we were just too fucked up to start something real. Maybe we never properly healed our own damaged minds like we were supposed to first."

Those were words Shula had more less told him before. But hearing him confirm it made her heart ache, because they were words she wasn't ready to hear, even if she needed to hear them. She wasn't ready for what would follow.

Her hands pressed against his chest and traveled lower, over his abdomen where she was sure if she would lift his clothes up, she'd find a brand new scar marring his skin.

"I'm not sure I can ever be what you want, Shula." He rubbed slow circles against her back, like that could somehow soften the blow.

Tears gathered against her eyes. How sad was it that they just found each other and now it felt like they were oceans apart? Their bonds were crumbling between them like the ashy remnants of her parents. Like the ash of everything Shula had ever destroyed in her life.

His fingers gripped her chin and forced her gaze up to his when she hadn't even notice she looked away. *Eyes on me,* he seemed to say. "But I want to be what you *need,* Shula." Her heart thundered. "We can heal apart, and we can heal together. It does not matter, but I *need* you more than I need air to breathe, more than I need the magic in my soul."

Her bottom lip trembled, and he traced it with his thumb. She leaned into the touch. "I need you, too."

She never realized how true those words were until she said them. They surged from her soul and back through them again, resonating deep in her bones. Not only did she need him, but she wanted him. Scars, temper, and all.

"If we want to heal, we need to be clear with one another, Shula. No more guessing, no more dancing around words. If you need something from me, you tell me. If I piss you off, tell me why. I did not choose to bond with you lightly. I want this to work, but we have to be honest with each other."

In response, Shula pressed her forehead to his, his scars scraping against her smooth skin, his beard tickling her chin.

"I want that," she whispered. "I *need* that."

He gifted her with one of his rare smiles right before he pressed his lips to hers. It was quick and chaste, and she didn't let it go further because she pulled away with a frown.

"Don't do that again."

"But—"

She pressed her finger to his lips, shutting him up. "It's my turn to speak. You said we need to be honest. I don't like when you heal others in that capacity." Her fingers touched the edges of his scars. "What if you can't recover from the next wound? How much longer can your body handle being broken and in pain before it gives out? It can't happen, Ryker. Promise me."

"I don't know if I can promise that." He sounded so sad. What she didn't know was if he was sad because he was thinking of the past—of Mairin—or of the future.

Her fingers dug into the roots of his beard, gripping his chin and forcing his gaze on her. "Promise me." The vehemence in the words were clear. "I can't lose you. Not like that. Promise me if you see a wound, you won't push your magic to the brink like that. You can help, but you have to know your limits."

They were both silent for a moment, their hearts beating in tandem against one another's chests, a rough push back and forth, a fight between their bodies while they waited.

Finally, Ryker sighed. "Fine," he said. "I... I promise."

Shula bent down and pressed her lips firmly against his. "Thank you," she whispered against his mouth. He reached for another kiss and this time their mouths opened, their tongues explored, and Shula no longer felt afraid.

Selfish Mistakes

Julius rubbed a big hand across his abdomen. He'd never sustained such an injury before. There had never been any need to be healed by Ryker, so it came as a surprise to feel the aftereffects of it. Phantom tugging of pain pulled where the wound had been, but when he tugged his shirt up, his skin was smooth and unmarred.

He took in a breath and raked his hand through his hair. That whole thing had been such a cluster fuck. He was usually levelheaded when it came to missions, but with Iona involved, he found he couldn't think straight. His possessive Fae instincts tried to overtake all logical thoughts, that combined with the blinding rage of using his magic made him irrational.

He'd charged into the fray without listening to his prince, desperate to get to his mate and help. It had landed him with an iron sword in the stomach and a painful truth he hadn't been ready to hear.

Like the fact that his mate had fucking lied to him. He didn't particularly know how to feel about that.

Fucked over.

Iona was his mate, and the fact that she hadn't confided in him about what she was thinking and feeling didn't sit right with him. If she didn't trust him, why had she even agreed to be his mate? Had she saw an opportunity in him to save her sister? Was she just using him?

He liked to think he understood women, that he knew them. You couldn't fake pleasure like the kind Iona displayed. But pleasuring her body wasn't the only aspect of being mates that mattered, and he'd been so fucking blind to the rest.

He sighed and raked a hand over his face.

Footsteps alerted him to another presence. Then came the scent of fur and drool, making him smile softly to himself for a brief moment before Iona and her familiar came into view.

He watched her familiar walk away and plop himself down near a tree and rest his head on top of his paws. His eyes remained opened and focused on Julius with a warning.

Julius shook his head and looked back to Iona.

She stood a few feet away from him, looking forlorn. Her hair was frizzy and pushed away from her ears, held back by a strip of dark leather. He noticed her fingers beating haphazardly against her thighs. From where he stood, he could hear her heart pounding rapidly in her chest and make out the way she swallowed tightly.

He was angry with her. In fact, he was fucking pissed. He had been lied to, and now he was questioning their relationship, their bond, when he shouldn't have been questioning it at all. Julius had no way to know what was real or fake. He wanted to lash out, break down a tree and snap the trunk over his knee. He'd done it before; it wouldn't take much.

But a bigger part of him realized that even though he felt betrayed, this couldn't have been any easier for her. He knew very little about the situation, except that they'd taken her sister. Julius didn't have any siblings that he knew of, but he knew what it was to fight for the things he wanted.

He'd grown up with the little people of the wood. They'd always taken the essentials he needed for survival. He'd savagely clawed his way through bodies to keep what he had or to get what they'd stolen back. He knew that a desperate need for survival could lead someone to do things they wouldn't be proud of.

He could never imagine what it was like to lose a sister like she had. So, Julius wanted to be understanding. Even if it hurt.

He took a breath and prowled towards her. He saw the fear in her eyes as he approached, but she didn't stagger back. It was perhaps a sign that she trusted him, or a sign that she thought she deserved whatever he wanted to dish out.

Once he was in front of her, he reached out and gripped both her hands, giving her a reassuring squeeze. That was all it took for the tension to melt out of her body. She drifted towards him, dropping her forehead against his wide chest and breathed in deeply. He did the same, burying his nose in her hair and inhaling.

She smelt sharp and sweet at once. Like mint and apples and ice. It was an intoxicating scent, something about it tranquil. Together, their scents mingled in a perfect pair. Like the woods during late autumn. When everything was ripe with fruits and ale, and wine permeated the air as the festivities to celebrating the upcoming winter began.

He didn't want to think about how well they fit, though. Because he wasn't even sure if they were going to last. Her heart beat faster and he could feel the pounding echoing against him, like she knew what direction his thoughts were taking.

Reluctantly, he pulled away, rubbing his thumbs across the pulse at her wrists.

"Iona," he began. "We need to talk."

⁂

Iona hated those words. She wished she could freeze them and drop them from a high building and watch them shatter against the ground. They spoke of dreadful things to come, and the burning look of betrayal in his eyes let her know this talk wasn't going to be pleasant at all.

She hated herself for putting that look on his face. Julius had been nothing but kind to her. He had accepted her without knowing the full truth. She couldn't imagine what he was feeling, and she didn't even know how to begin to tell him.

She sighed. "I'm sorry."

Julius didn't pull away but ran a comforting thumb down her pulse. His woodsy scent filled her nostrils and calmed her, took away her relentless need to tap.

"I just want the truth, Iona," he said tightly. "Was all of it a lie? Are *we* a lie?"

She jerked in his hold and pulled away only to grasp at the lapels of his jacket and yank him close. "Never," she said with anguish. "We aren't a lie, and I would never use you for my own gain."

"But you did." He sounded so broken that for a moment Iona's heart broke, too. "You used me—us—for something selfish."

"For my sister," she corrected. "Yes, perhaps it was selfish of me, but you have to understand. She's all I have left."

His eyes flared with injury. He grabbed her wrists and pulled her off of him, letting her go and taking a step back. That rejection hurt too much, too.

"Believe it or not, I understand what it is to fight for things in your life. I know starvation and humiliation as intimately as a lover." He shook his head and tugged at the end of his ginger beard. "I just wish you would have been honest with me from the start. It would have changed everything. Our strategy, Valerio's reaction... He will *never* trust you again."

She hated that she cared about that after everything he'd said, but she did. She revered the prince and was afraid she'd broken whatever relationship they could have built together because of her selfishness. She'd been blind by her own mission, and had treated everyone poorly. Especially the prince. Now, he probably wouldn't even want to be her friend at all.

"I was afraid," Iona confessed on a whisper.

"Of what?"

"I was afraid that if I told you about my sister, you wouldn't believe me and you wouldn't want to help. Or worse, that you saddled yourself with a mate who is mad." That would have crippled her, she thought.

Julius stepped forward again. "Why would I think you mad?"

She scoffed. "You saw how the others looked at me. Like I'm delusional because I had a feeling, given from Mana, that she was alive even after all this time. I couldn't bear for you to look at me like that, too."

Julius shrugged. "Crazier things have happened." He cupped her cheek. "And let it be known, I do believe you. I just do not like being lied to."

"I'm sorry," she repeated, not sure if she said it enough. He might not really forgive her, but she needed him to. He was her mate and she'd turned everyone else against her within a few hours. She needed him. Selfishly, perhaps, to not feel so alone in the world.

Julius smiled, soft and a little sad. "I forgive you. I know we jumped into being mates all too quickly and we will have to learn each other, but you can always be honest with me and I will always support you. I will always be here to help you. I don't give a flying fuck if we're new, or if I don't know much about you. I want to know everything, and I want to help with anything I can."

The tears she spilled were caught in the palm still cupping her cheek. "I was selfish," she whispered.

"It's okay to be selfish," he said, pulling her closer by the waist. "And it's okay to hope for the best, too. That's one thing living with the people of the wood taught me. But we are a group now, and we have to work as a team."

She groaned. "I have to apologize to Prince Valerio, don't I? And Ryker and Shula."

"Afraid so, mate."

She groaned and tugged him closer by the hem of his jacket. "Will you help me?" She wasn't usually nervous when talking to others, but just the thought of the confrontations ahead made her want to break her fingers against her thighs.

A deep, rumbling chuckle sounded from Julius' chest. "I think this is something you have to do on your own."

As much as she hated it, she knew he was right. She'd never relied on anyone to hold her hand in difficult situations before and she wouldn't start now, no matter how comforting Julius was or how much his presence helped.

This *was* something she had to do on her own. She had to own up to her mistakes and recognize when she was in the wrong. And she'd been wrong. She'd put her companions'—her friends'—lives in jeopardy over a rumor given to her by George. A rumor she'd held onto for years because she believed Mana was telling her it was true.

She still believed it was true, but she knew now the chances of finding her sister were slim. Because the Fae wouldn't trust her again, and there was no chance now that they'd go to another one of those places even if she fell to her knees and groveled.

Which, she suspected she would be doing.
Whether she liked it or not.

Like Sisters

Iona's feet dragged against the cold dirt as she made her way towards the water. Lake Degara had several rivers that spread throughout Orknie, even some that splintered off across the Ley Line and into Tir na Faie. They were filled with fish and clear water for drinking and bathing.

She found Shula at one of the riverbanks, squeezing water from a cloth and onto the ground. She was obviously in the middle of bathing the blood and grime off her body. Clad in nothing but trousers and a thin shift, her back was facing Iona, and Iona found herself staring at the scars marring along Shula's skin.

The image of flames seemed to be healing. Still fleshy, though they were no longer bright red and grotesque, and they were scabbing. They were dark against the Fae's golden-brown skin and could be seen through the sheer, clinging material of her wet shift.

At the sound of Iona's approaching boots, Shula whirled, her waist-length hair slapping against her skin. Her breath hitched up like she'd been startled, and she held the cloth in front of her like a shield.

When she saw it was just Iona, she lowered the material and scowled.

"I thought you were Weylyn," she said breathlessly. Her chest rose and fell, and there was the slightest scent of fear wafting from her pores.

Iona's feet skidded to a stop, brows pulling together. "Does he make a habit of spying on your while you're bathing?"

Her cheeks colored and the fear seemed to dissipate until all Iona could smell was the warmth embers and confections. "You'd be surprised at what he's done..."

"Fucking pervert. I should've kicked him in the balls."

Shula didn't snort with laughter like Iona had meant for her to. She was staring warily, her lips pursed and brows drawn together as if to ask, "What do you want?"

Iona tapped a rhythm, curled her nails into her palms for a second, and came closer to the riverbank, stripping her jacket as she went.

She was covered in grime as well, and it would be nice to have this conversation without blood on her hands.

She bent and cupped her hands in the river, shivering as the near frozen water touched her skin. She spread the water along her arms and rubbed at her neck then splashed some on her face. When she stood, she turned to face Shula. The water acted like some sort of barrier for Iona. One she desperately felt she needed to get through with this conversation. Now that she was clean, she could face her with a fresh start.

"Shula," she began. A shiver of nerves ran down her spine and her next words came out choppy. Not because she was afraid to say them; it was something else indescribable. "I'm sorry."

She'd hoped Shula would accept it immediately. That the almost meek, kind, and accepting female would make an appearance. But she sneered at Iona with a bit of disdain, and her tone was mocking when she replied, "For what? For almost killing my mate?"

Her fingers cramped. She closed her eyes, took in a steadying breath, and opened them again. "I miscalculated the situation," she tried again. "I didn't mean for any of that to happen. I know you might not want to forgive me, but I really am sorry."

Shula stared at her for a moment and Iona felt scrutinized, laid bare. Even with the hostility, their magic reacted to one another in that strange pulsing sensation. It was a clashing of energies that warred as much as they embraced.

When she didn't speak after a while, Iona picked up her discarded clothes in defeat and shrugged them on. As she started to walk away, Shula stopped her.

"Why do you think she's still alive?" she asked.

Iona turned.

"Your sister," she continued. "Why do you assume she's still alive? She was taken a hundred years ago."

One-hundred and two, Iona didn't bother correcting her. "Because Mana tells me so."

"Are you sure it's really Mana and not just your own hope clouding your judgement?"

Iona chewed on the inside of her cheek. She knew she would face this problem when she came clean. That they'd think her delusional.

"You know when you're decided and firm in doing something, but then your gut twists and you feel shivers down your spine? It's like something is whispering that your decision is the wrong one." She didn't wait for Shula to answer. She didn't need to. "When my sister was taken, that was the end. I thought she was dead, and I joined the Resistance to dual out my revenge. But it never felt right.

There was always this feeling in my chest like I was making a colossal mistake." Her fingers drifted to her curls then lowered once more.

"It's why I could never bring myself to cut my hair in mourning." At Shula's confused expression, she elaborated, "Hair is important to us. It's a way to connect, to celebrate. We used to spend hours braiding our hair as a family. When someone dies, it's customary to shave our heads to express our sadness. I didn't. That would mean accepting death, and I physically couldn't.

"I spent years drifting in Porir, never feeling truly alive. Then I met George, and he told me about the camps, and something seemed to snap into place. Like Mana was telling me something, and I knew she was alive."

Shula's fingers twisted against the wet material she held in her hands. "My parents were taken to the camps twelve years ago..."

Iona resisted the urge to reach for her and offer comfort. This was just another thing besides their Mana-given gifts that tied them together. An experience no one else could fathom. Good things could bring people together, but more often than not, it was the bad that was easiest to relate to. It was in tragedies where friendships were born.

"I was only twelve," she continued. "But I can assure you they are dead." She said it so coldly, though she noticed her bottom lip fought back a tremble. Grief was never as simple as a few spoken words. It always went deeper than that. As deep into the threads of things you could not see.

"How do you know?" Iona countered.

"Because no one who goes into those camps comes back out alive."

"But how do you *know*?"

"I tasted their ashes that day. The remnants of them clung to my cheeks. They weren't special. They weren't gift-given. What reason would they be kept alive? What reason could your sister have been kept alive all this time? The Emperor of Illyk mounts Fae on his walls like trophies. Your sister might have outlived her usefulness."

The words weren't spoken cruelly but they had the same effect as if they had been. She held back the sob that wanted to claw up her throat but pushed it down because she knew Shula did not mean the words to harm.

Shula must have realized the bluntness of her words because she fumbled with the cloth, dropping it to the riverbank. She took a step forward and drew in a shocked breath. "Sorry," she said. "I—I think I've been with them too long. They have a blunt way of speaking, but that was rude. I just..." She looked up at the sky as if the words would somehow magically fall onto her body so she wouldn't have to say them herself. "I was upset because of what you inadvertently did to Ryker. I was also upset because no one listens to me. *Valerio* doesn't listen to me."

The hurt in her voice was real. It made Iona observe her, *really* observe her. Just like it made her realize she didn't really know her. She didn't really think about what things were like before Iona had been accepted into the fold. There seemed to be a tension among Shula and Valerio. Not just because of what was confessed earlier; there was more to it.

"Why?"

"Because I'm a coward."

Iona blinked, too surprised at the words for a moment to come up with a coherent response. "Who the fuck thinks that?" she demanded.

"Everyone."

Her own problems forgotten, she felt a steady anger rise. "Did they not see you fight on that island? Did they not see you melt iron or incinerate about a dozen humans? Who the fuck thinks you're a coward? I will freeze the head from their shoulders."

Shula chuckled but the sound wasn't in amusement. "I gave them an image of me when I arrived and I think it stuck. I was always running away and *you* run towards trouble and I think sometimes they resent me for that."

Suddenly Iona understood the hostility between Shula and Valerio. She understood why Shula looked a bit self-conscious when they first spoke. Her wariness, the way she was looking at Iona now.

Iona had come and suddenly they had someone to compare Shula to. Iona had made things worse with what she'd done, putting both Julius and Ryker at risk. It gave Shula grounds to be pissed at her. Because they'd listened to Iona and she'd nearly gotten them killed. If they would have listened to Shula, none of this would have happened.

But she didn't want that to be their relationship. She didn't want the two of them in a competition set up by the Fae males in their group. She didn't want them to be compared because of their faults or what they lacked.

The world was shitty enough, and Elementals needed to stick together.

Like friends.

Like sisters.

Her throat tightened as she stepped towards Shula and took her hands in a firm grip. "You are the bravest woman I know," Iona told her, and she meant it. "I am in awe of you. You can melt iron and I don't even have that kind of control yet even though I've been using my magic for far longer than you. We don't have to be divided, Shula. It's not you or me, or my magic compared to your magic, or your bravery compared to mine. We are as different as the elements we wield. We aren't meant to be the same but to complement one another."

Tears glistened behind her amber eyes. She tilted her chin up. "You're right."

"Good. And I really am sorry for what I did."

"And I'm sorry for the crassness of what I said."

Iona squeezed her hands lightly. "It's what everyone's thinking. I don't blame you. I know it's far-fetched, but I have hope enough for all of us."

"Then I'll try to have hope, too."

"You're a good friend, Shula," Iona confessed. "The best friend I've had in a hundred years."

And between them, their bond strengthened. Like those were the words it'd been waiting to hear this entire time.

"Prince Valerio..."

The Seelie Prince was facing away from Iona, the dark ends of his hair tugging against the breeze. His hands were clasped tightly behind his back, his posture was rigid straight, and he was staring off into the afternoon sky. Iona couldn't see it, but she imagined his expression to be quite pensive.

He didn't reply.

She cleared her throat. "Prince Valerio," she repeated.

After she apologized to Shula, she'd apologized to Ryker, who'd merely grunted and rolled his eyes as if to say the apology wasn't necessary. Iona had saved the prince for last. This was by far the hardest apology she'd ever have to make in her life, she thought. She was already nervous, and Prince Valerio didn't even turn to face her.

"Prince Valerio, I came to apologize."

She could make out his elongated ears twitching slightly. They weren't obscured by hair, as the sides of his head were shaved to show off his pale skin. It made him look less like a prince and more like a dangerous mercenary, though she would never say that aloud because he was still *princely.* He reeked of command and power. She'd taken advantage of that, had intentionally exploited his weaknesses and obvious insecurities to get him to go along with her plan.

"I manipulated you and disobeyed direct orders and put the whole group in jeopardy. I am sorry, my prince."

He didn't respond and Iona didn't think he was going to. She was prepared to make a hasty retreat in shame when he angled his body towards her, regarding her with a curious expression and the slightest touch of a smile.

The smile unnerved her the most. If only because it wasn't a happy expression. Not really. It was something else. Not traced with malevolence, but different.

"I have been thinking about everything you said," he began. "Regarding the Fae, the war, and my duties as prince..."

She swallowed past the fear that was slowly building up her throat. "I misspoke..."

"Did you?" He pursed his lips, tilted his head. Every movement seemed almost deliberate and breathed of a great power she knew he wielded.

"I am no one to question you." She never would have before the war. But she'd been so lost in her desire to find her sister that she'd forgotten he was royalty and treated him like just another commoner.

"Do not apologize for being right, Iona."

She blinked, sure she'd misheard.

"The truth is you have given me so much to think about regarding my position as prince. Do you want to know what conclusion I came to?"

"What's that?"

He smirked. "That I have failed you all."

It hurt to admit, but the words came out of him regardless. For a moment, he was glad he'd sent Uric away. If only so he could have this moment with Iona in peace, without him hovering and glaring and scoffing at words that were true. Even if Uric could never stomach the admittance.

He could speak freely without him here, in a way that would make Iona understand.

The truth was, she had given him much to ponder. Like his life, his role as Prince of the Seelie Court, a court that has long since disbanded, the remains of it hovering within a broken castle in cold mountains. Waiting to be grand again.

Valerio did not feel like a royal anymore. At one point, he had relished in that life. But things had changed, and he was not as obsessive as his father about gaining back the riches they'd lost.

He realized what his father was doing. He was sending Valerio on a chase for the Elementals because having them on the side of the Fae would solve his problems quickly and easily. But if there was one thing Valerio knew, it was that nothing worth winning was ever quick and easy.

How could he call himself a leader of the Fae if he disregarded their suffering? Yes, he saved them. Helped them travel from camp to camp, only to shove them into the freezing walls of Castle Aileach and never hear from them again. That was not what a leader did. A leader stood up for his people. A leader freed his people from the tight grips of tyranny.

He was no better than his father. Following orders blindly to get to Elemental Fae just so they could join together and create a faster solution. Even if they found them, how would they even go about changing things?

War was inevitable.

And to go to war with the humans, the Fae needed numbers. Numbers they did not have.

"Prince Valerio..."

The ice Elemental—Iona, he amended, mentally berating himself for thinking of her like his father would—was staring at him almost worriedly. Perhaps she had good cause to, with the way he was speaking.

"I have helped Fae find our safe houses all throughout Illyk, but I have yet to actually save them. What is my worth, if not to help those in need? What legacy will I leave behind if not to save my race?" He turned to her fully, cocking his head to the side. "You were right to question me. How can I expect them to help me if I do not help them in return? I cannot rely solely on the Elementals because even though I have you and Shula, I do not know if the others will join or if we will even find them before the human emperor does. We need a backup plan in case we go to war."

"I agree," Iona nodded firmly. "But—and no offense, my prince—why are you telling me this?"

He smiled, though he knew it didn't reach his eyes. It had been so long since he last truly felt joy. Years, decades almost. His emotions had withered and died like the remnants of a once great past, and death clung to him with a permanence that reeked too sweet.

"Because you gave me an idea."

At that moment, the air beside Valerio shimmered. A portal opened that Uric and Weylyn both stepped through. It closed once again and Valerio flicked his fingers in their direction, commanding, imperious.

Uric shouldered past Weylyn and handed him a stack of parchment that he took from his withered hands and rummaged through. His eyes scanned over the contents quickly until he found the one he needed and pulled it out to shove it in Iona's direction.

She grabbed it and looked it over, her own eyes widening in realization.

"Is this—?"

"I made Uric and Weylyn go back." Though they'd found nothing within those foul walls, with death and ash at their feet, he'd had a feeling. An instinct.

Like Mana was speaking to him.

It was something he couldn't ignore.

"So it's true..." Her hand trembled as she lowered the page.

Valerio couldn't help but smile. "You were right, Iona. The Fae... they're alive."

She made a choking noise. "Will we—"

"Numbers win wars," Valerio said. "It is numbers we need. If the emperor has them, then I plan on getting them back and *keeping* them this time." He knew his eyes were sparking with the deeply rooted magic, begging to get out. Like everything else, he kept it tightly leashed so they could not see the true feral madness he kept within. "I will not let the emperor take anymore from us."

"The Fae will be broken," Iona whispered.

"I know."

"They would have suffered."

"I know."

"They will need time to heal."

"Then we will heal them," Valerio said. "We will train them. And when they are able, we will take back what is ours."

A Thirst for Death

"No." Shula's voice cut across the space between them as sharp as a dagger. Her lips were pressed into an angry, thin line, her eyes sparking with the beginnings of her flames as she stared down the Seelie Prince. "Not again."

Valerio's arms were crossed tightly against his chest, his whole stance obviously unimpressed with Shula's obstinacy.

The Fae were separated in two lines standing across from one another. Shula, Ryker, Clay, and Uric against Valerio, Iona, Julius, and Weylyn. As if they'd already divided themselves in different directions of warring sides.

"I did not ask your permission," Valerio said calmly, though Iona knew he was anything but. She didn't know the Seelie Prince that well, but his eyes told a thousand stories written many scriptures. The dark depths danced in shadows of anger and death and power.

She was almost afraid for Shula, but the Fire Dancer could hold her own in an argument. Heat surrounded her and sparks seemed to dance just beneath the surface of her skin, her magic responding to her distressed mood.

"Val," Clay began, cutting in before Shula could snap at the prince again. "I don't understand... A few hours ago, you said—"

"I know what I said. I said I would not be lied to or manipulated again."

Clay raked his fingers through his hair, looking confused. "I know, but we barely made it out of one camp alive. Why would you want to go to another one?"

When Prince Valerio had told the others his plan to storm another iron camp, it hadn't been met with the same acceptance as Iona had given it. She could understand after what they'd just gone through why they would be confused, but she hoped they would understand the prince's reasoning.

"We have hid in the shadows for far too long," Valerio said. "If we want to gain our lives back, we have to fight for it, because the humans will not hand it over lightly." He made sure to meet everyone's gaze to drive the point home, in their minds, hoping it would ingrain into their souls. "Even if we find the Elementals, there is no guarantee about what will happen after we do so.

While we journey, our people still suffer. If there is a chance that I can end that suffering, I will. Or else how can I call myself a prince?"

He said that last part with an innate sense of sadness and honesty that was damn near crippling. His voice a wistful, tired tune that spread over Iona and made the hairs on her arms stand on end. They were the words of a leader. Someone worthy of a crown, even when he felt it was too big for his head, everyone else knew it was the perfect fit.

Clay let out a sigh, scrubbing his face with his palm. "How do we even know there are Fae there?"

"Because..." Valerio held out his hand and Iona placed the parchment in them. Valerio unrolled them and passed them off to Clay. "The ashes and bones were of Fae they'd ordered murdered only a few days ago." He nodded at the contents in Clay's hands as his cousin read the same quick scrawl of the common tongue Iona had only moments before. "They keep a detailed inventory of the Fae they find, kill, or transfer to other camps. The Fae with powers appeared to be kept alive the longest. The reason the camp was empty was because they transferred them to a bigger one just a few miles from here."

Clay's brows pulled together as his eyes scanned the detailed notes. Shula and Ryker peeked over at them from either side of the Fae, while Uric stood to the side, his arms crossed, glaring at the Seelie Prince.

"Look at the date," Valerio whispered.

"They were transferred two days ago," Clay concluded, looking up from the parchment. His bright eyes seemed to burn brighter. "This camp is a two-day journey from here..."

"Which means they would still be alive right now."

"We need to hurry." Clay rolled up the parchment, shoving it into the pocket of his jacket. "We don't know how much longer the Fae have."

Iona kept her smile to herself and turned to look at Ryker. But the healing Fae was staring at his mate, the two of them having a conversation without words.

Ryker finally turned to Valerio and grunted. "We have to help them."

Iona could just make out the tightening of Shula's jaw and the glow around the edges of her body, her fire pushing to get out. She let out a loose breath, and the scent of smoke and burning embers grew more prominent in the air.

Valerio took a step forward, giving a respectable distance in front of Shula, though his muscles tightened and bunched under the confines of his clothes. Like he was barely restraining himself from reaching out to her, touching her. Whether it be to keep things between them neutral or out of respect for Ryker, Iona couldn't be sure.

"Shula, we have to do this. My people need us. All of us."

She swallowed. "Not me. You don't need me for that."

"Why would you say that?" Valerio sounded genuinely confused, and Iona wanted to reach over and slap him against the back of his head.

Idiot Fae, she grumbled internally.

Shula scowled. "You think I'm a coward. That I am only good for running away." Her voice came out a weak sound, too afraid to voice the same words she'd given to Iona in confidence before. For a moment, very brief, she looked defeated. Shoulders hunched, fire dimming to mere embers. But then her flickering gaze caught Iona's, and a single glance between them seemed to remind Shula what, and who, she was. Her shoulders tossed back, her chin tilted, and the fire in her eyes blazed with a challenge, a dare.

For the Prince of Seelie to try and tell her how weak she was, just so she could prove him wrong.

He must have sensed it because a breathless chuckle escaped from his lips.

"I apologize if I ever gave you that impression. You are not weak, Shula Azzarh. You are the only one among us who can burn iron. We need you to help us."

Shula didn't preen at his praise but took it like it was something she deserved, and it was. Given too little, too late, yet she deserved it just the same.

"That's not what you said before."

"Things are different now."

Shula scoffed, the sound holding no humor. "Different now because you want my help."

"Shula..."

"Fuck's sake!" Clay interrupted with impatience, throwing his hands up in the air. When he lowered them again, he was glaring at the prince. "Will you tell her the *real* reason you've been a dick to her? We don't have time for you to argue. We need to make a decision."

Prince Valerio scowled but didn't reprimand the little lord. His body went taut and she swore he looked uncomfortable as his fingers closed into fists at his sides. "I do not know what you are talking about."

Clay's eyes rolled. "Far be it for me to reveal other's secrets, but I might have to." He angled his body towards Shula. "He likes you but doesn't want to disrespect Ryker or you by liking you, so he acts like a dick to put distance between you." He shot a smug grin towards the prince. "There, I told her for you. Can we move along?"

They stood in a brief moment of stunned silence that shattered when Ryker growled, the sound possessive.

"Of course, I like her, fool, as much as I like any of you here. Can we drop this subject now? Shula, will you help us or not?" The sharp angles of the prince's cheekbones colored with a tinge of pink. His words were clipped, abrasive, and Iona found herself smirking at his deflection.

Given the confession earlier and the fact that the prince had believed she would be his mate when they went to save her, Iona assumed being a dick was his way of separating those confusing feelings.

"I—It's too dangerous," Shula argued, fingers gripping the hem of her jacket. "I am not saying it because I am afraid, though I am, and I'd be a fool not to be. I say it because if this camp is bigger, it will have more soldiers. We don't know what we are up against."

"That's the thing about life, Fire Dancer," Julius cut in, his voice rumbling with amusement. "We never know what we're up against. But as long as we face it together, there's nothing we can't do."

She took her bottom lip between her teeth, chewing furiously on it. Her eyes danced with indecision, doubt.

"What if it was your parents?" Valerio asked, not cruelly, but the way Shula jumped made it seem like she'd been slapped. "What if your parents were the ones there right now? Alive, suffering, wishing for death? Would you help them then?" His words were similar to the one's Iona had given Julius before. They were carefully calculated, just the slightest bit manipulative, yet effective.

Shula's eyes flickered and for a moment, it looked like streaks of fire slid down her cheeks in the shape of tears. Smoke billowed out of her nostrils as she took a breath. Her eyes flicked up to Iona, and the indecision was still there, though she caught fire crawling along the edges of her vision, burning away her inhibitions.

When she finally spoke, it was minutes later. Minutes that had felt like hours. "I'd burn the camp to the ground to find them."

"Will you help us then?"

This time, Shula didn't hesitate but spoke with conviction and vengeance, and Iona knew she was picturing her family. Her mother and her father, taken by the emperor's soldiers to die.

Fire blazed behind her eyes until the golden-brown color was consumed entirely by an inferno of her rage and loyalty...

... and her burning thirst for death.

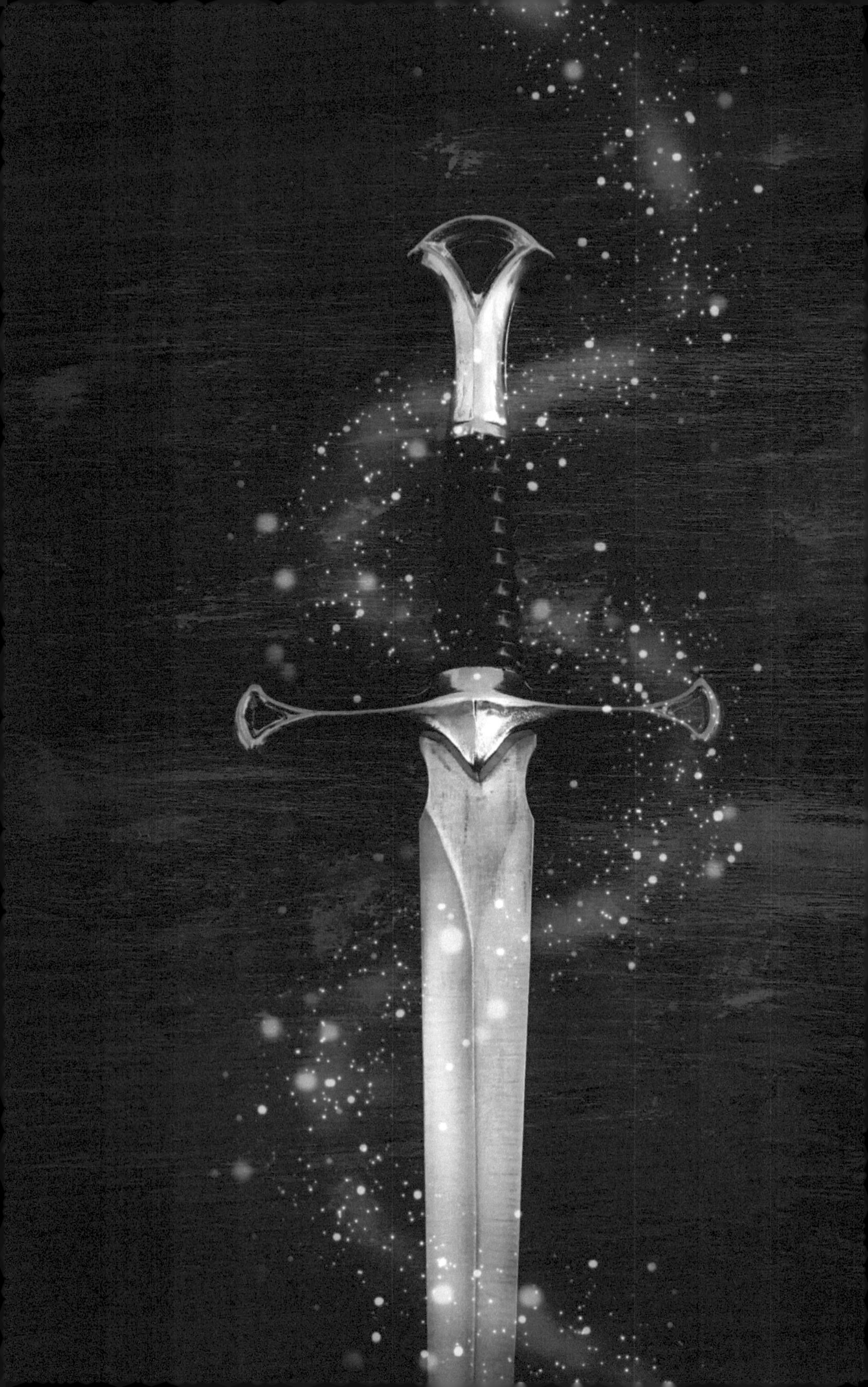

Consequences

Uric's rage was a beast in chains, subdued without a fight.

Like always, he kept a tight lock against his emotions, for they served no purpose in the grand scheme of things. It was no hardship to let the mask fall into place. His life, after all, had always been a play, everyone around him pretending. And he was just another lie among many.

Feigning was easy. That hard mask he wore, even easier to slip into place. Though, there were things he could not control. Things he never thought would be factors in his life.

Like how weak Prince Valerio Ashera made him.

The Nova family were lords and silent assassins in equal measure. They believed in presenting the façade of nobles, while cutting through the courts with efficiency and precision. Giving their youngest son to the Ashera family to be the young prince's companion had been a calculated move on their part. To learn the Seelie Court's weaknesses. To learn the *prince's* weaknesses.

What they never could have predicted was that Uric was to be the one to fall weak.

Weak for a kind smile, a comforting hug.

A friend.

Secrets had ceased to matter, and then their world had gone to shit and spying mattered even less. Yet old habits died hard, and Uric still found his mask slipping into place. But, these days, Uric found it harder and harder to keep the pretense up.

For years, he'd felt this breathlessness, the pounding beat of his heart, the smiles that twitched at his lips as the only evidence of what he felt. His loyalty had been an undying thing.

Ever since this endeavor, given to them by King Ashera, Uric felt his friend slipping away. He was becoming reckless. While he was a good prince, with a big heart, no good could ever come from this.

"You are angry." Valerio didn't seem amused, or upset. Just curious.

As if sensing his thoughts, Valerio gestured with a flick of his fingers. "Your tightening jaw, your eyes... You forget that you are my best friend. I can read you as easily as I can read myself."

No falser words had ever been spoken.

See, Valerio did not know himself as well as he thought he did.

He did not recognize that the only reason he was doing this was because he burned to have his father's approval. He ached to be recognized as a good ruler, without having realized that he already was.

If only Prince Valerio could see himself through Uric's eyes, then he would know what the Fae saw when they looked at him. They saw a prince worthy of leadership while they counted down the days until his father's death.

Why did he think the king insulted him so? Because Valerio had been born to rule the Seelie, while his father got by on fear and cruelty alone.

He had always been that way, even before the fall of their courts.

Valerio had never seen it before, though. He thought the cruelty was new, born of the desire to earn back all they'd lost. Oh, he knew his father was implacable the way kings were supposed to be, but he didn't know the full extent of it.

That the King of the Fae was no better than the human Emperor of Illyk.

"Say what you want to say, Uric." Valerio huffed a breath. "We are familiar enough with one another to do away with subtleties."

Uric made a gentle sound of irritation. He did not like speaking his mind, if only because he learned early on in life that his words could be used against him. But Valerio was his friend.

Even if he was acting more like his tyrant father these days.

"This is a bad idea," Uric whispered, low enough so only the prince could here. He did not like feeling like others could hear him. Bad enough to have Weylyn eavesdropping on their every thought, he did not want the others to know what he said aloud.

"I know you think so—"

"I know so. Tell me, what will the king have to say about this detour?" His question was met with silence. "Precisely. You know as well as I that he will not be happy about this."

"I will deal with my father."

At this, Uric snorted softly, earning himself a glare from the prince. Uric shrugged but didn't stop walking. "I am afraid this infraction is not too small a thing. He will feel slighted, his ego bruised." He turned to face his prince and looked him in the eyes. Black on black, though if one looked close enough, they would see that Prince Valerio's eyes weren't black at all, but a dark brown with the slightest flecks of gold. "This time, there *will* be consequences for your actions." He forced his gaze back forward, lest his own vulnerability slip through the already flaying cracks of his armor. "And I pray to Mana you can live with them."

Ice Statues and Shattered Iron

They arrived at the camp just as the sun began lowering in the sky, bathing Illyk in ominous shades that blended into the smog of the sky. Shadows were beginning to spread across the ground, and the lone camp was stark against the landscape. Black smoke billowed from their chimneys, filling a foul taste in the air that stuck against their bodies in a thin, grimy layer.

Ash pressed against Iona's lips and tongue as she breathed it in. She tried not to gag at the thought of what she was inhaling. At *who* she was inhaling. The remnants of what were likely Fae bodies threatening to choke down her throat.

Vines of ashwood twined and twisted across the top of the camp like barbed wire, soldiers manning the walls like at the previous camp. The sentinels walked back and forth, the only sound that echoed through the air was the clattering of their armor against brick and their steel swords against metal.

The proximity of the iron made Iona's throat itch, but she pushed away her own physical discomfort, even though she couldn't push away the anxiety. Her fingers tapped against her legs in a choppy rhythm and broken pattern. Only this time, Julius was too distracted to place his hands over hers to calm her. She needed this focus. Needed to trace patterns while she thought of all the possible outcomes and scenarios.

There were Fae in this camp. People they could save. People they could help.

And maybe, just maybe, her sister would be in there, too.

She wasn't sure what the odds against that were, but she sent up a quick prayer to Mana that she would find answers within those walls.

"No more running off on our own," Valerio whispered the harsh order, his voice jerking through the shadows. Though he didn't speak directly to Iona, she knew the words were for her. "We go in together." He turned to Shula, his lips twisting at a hint of the tenacious malignancy he kept so tightly bound. "Melt the gate."

"Watch out for the archers," Julius said, his big hand pointing along the most invisible parts of the wall, where Iona could just make out dark figures hunkering down like specters.

"Good catch." Valerio nodded in his direction. "Iona, cover above our heads with your ice. Julius, Weylyn, and Ryker will take the front lines, Clay will get anyone that slips past them. The familiars will stay behind and Uric, you will open a portal into every locked room so we can save the Fae." The prince turned his dark gaze back to the door. "I know they're there. I can smell them."

Shula's heart was caught in her throat, and she feared her magic would sputter to its death. She tried to focus, calling on a darker, more dangerous part of herself. She'd made the connection eventually. Every time she'd been able to melt iron had been under extreme duress.

She called forth that familiar pain now.

She let her memories invade. Of her life before. Of her Papa, of Mama. Of the soldiers catching Shula as fire danced from between her fingertips. The way her parents had stood up to them.

Shula could still feel her mother's cold fingers gripping her forearm and shoving her through a hole in the gate on the reservation. She remembered her clothes and arms snagging against the thin, iron fibers, making her bleed. She remembered turning and watching her Papa jump in front of the soldier with his hands up to stop him.

She remembered the blade he took to his shoulder, the hilt of the sword that came down against her mother's head just as she screamed at Shula to run.

Those memories overpowered almost everything inside her, coming to the front of her mind until it felt like she was in that moment again. A barefoot child, afraid, her heart pounding as she ran. She'd been a short, skinny girl for her age and had easily hid from the soldiers. It had been her mistake to circle back and watch them haul her parents off to a camp.

Feet bleeding as they scraped against rocks, sticks, and gravel with every pounding step she took, Shula's tears didn't stop flowing as her parents were tried as traitors and pulled through the gates for hiding a magical Fae.

All hope she'd had of their survival had died as their screams had pierced the sky that night. They'd been shoved into a door, and then the heat was an overwhelming force until their screams of agony became the echoed memories of a terrifying song, and ash rained from the sky and clung to Shula's body.

The last touch her parents would ever give her.

In hindsight, it was a morbid thought.

But everything about that day had been morbid.

And that's what she summoned to her as she stepped from the shadows with her Fae companions at her back. She summoned the one truth she hadn't yet given them, given Iona. Her friend had been honest about her feelings, had tried to give Shula hope that her own parents might still be alive. Little did she know that *that* particular hope was a dead thing. Because Shula had watched them die that day.

Her companions made their way towards the gate of the camp, and Shula imagined it to be the same entryway that opened the doors to her parents' deaths. Her fire raged. It enveloped her in its fury and shot out with licking trails against the ground until it crawled up and consumed the iron gate.

The iron was oppressive, but not as oppressed as the Fae, and her own memories melted the thing off its hinges. She channeled every bit of pain she'd felt then, her arms rising until she felt consumed with it herself.

The rusted gate turned red, dripping from the top down like lava squirting out of a volcano. She could hear humans shouting from a distance, the whoosh of arrows and ice magic, but the roaring in her ears grew louder until it was a deafening force.

And all she knew was fire.

Fire and melting iron.

Iron pooled against the ground, a hot river that made the very earth look like it was bleeding.

Iona cut through Shula's line of vision, their magic warring against one another for a fragment of a moment before Shula's magic pulled back into her. Iona bent, her arms poised in front of her, fingers spread wide. Ice struck from inside her and covered the ground to cool the heated earth.

A moment later, they were running towards the entrance. Arrows flew and Iona ignored the pulsing discomfort of iron to create a canopy above their heads. The flying weapons struck, splintering against the strength of her magic. There were shouts and rushing footsteps, the clattering of metal uniforms, a horde of humans appeared.

Then the battle began.

Her sword formed against her palm, the force jarring against steel with every swing of her arms against her enemies. Humans fell around her, one after the other in heaps of scattered and frozen limbs, charred flesh, and screaming pain.

It wasn't quick. The battle waged on. When one human fell, another materialized as if born of smoke. Determination was the only thing keeping Iona on her feet. She couldn't make out her companions around her, but she got glimpses of them, flashes of hair and flying magic.

She whirled with her sword in hand, cutting through a human's exposed neck. Her gaze snagged against Weylyn, fighting his way through humans. His laughter rang out, manic and vicious, above the screams of the dying. With a swift raise of his sword, he sliced through armor and skin, the entrails of a human dangling from his blade, swaying with the wind like a chime that brought good luck. Blood splattered against his face, staining his white teeth. He resembled a rabid animal, a devil from legends of terror.

Despite the direness of their situation, Iona found herself rolling her eyes at the crazy Fae while she fought through the melee. Bodies dropped left and right, blood flew, and from the chaos, an enormous human charged at her. He was easily the same size as Julius and strong for his race.

He barreled into her. Their swords clanged together, the force so great that her weapon shattered in crystal shards.

She gritted her teeth, then cried out as his hilt came crashing down against her. The iron had her weakened, and she slid against the ground, falling on her ass away from him. The human loomed, prowling towards her. His arm raised and the sword came swinging down.

With a cry, she whipped her hand out, a new sword forming and blocking his weapon inches from her face.

Her heart pounded up to her throat, her every muscle screaming with fury. Her limbs shook, his strength pressing her back, back...

The blade was centimeters from her face, the iron singeing the skin at her cheek.

For a moment, everything felt hopeless. Like this was the end. A finality lived in every inch he swallowed between them. She wouldn't find her sister or liberate the Fae from the cages they found themselves in. She wouldn't fulfill the will of Mana because she found herself staring down at the last fragile moments of her life.

This was where it all ended.

Where Mana would take her soul and she would be reunited with her family once again.

As soon as the thought spread through her mind, something else ripped through it in harsher increments. Louder. Demanding. Pulsing. A feeling she was intimately familiar with. A whisper of magic, of Mana.

One that told her not to give up.

Because there was still so much more she had to accomplish.

Magic exploded, her sword shattering between them. A flurry of snow and ice and sparks clouded between her and the human, and it rippled through her veins. It was a power unlike anything she'd ever felt before, born of her need to survive.

She opened her eyes just as the human's sword swung a second time. Only now, she wasn't afraid when it came crashing down against her skin...

Only to shatter in a thousand pieces.

The iron blew apart the moment it connected to her body. A body that glowed the same blue as her ice. Iona's skin hardened, became a scintillating, indestructible force around her. A statue of blue, she rose to her full height. Her skin glowed, her magic becoming a force to be reckoned with. Like Shula's fire against iron, she became impervious to it. Mana evolving within her, born from a need to protect.

Her sister needed her.

The *Fae* needed her.

And she would help save them all.

The human stumbled away from her new form, the acrid scent of his fear piercing through the air, rising above smoke, burnt flesh, and death. It only grew more prominent each step she took towards him. The reflective surface of her skin shone in his eyes beneath his helm.

She made a terrifying image. Like something out of legends. Like a goddess.

Like Mana given form.

He didn't fight back as she stepped in front of him. Like he knew it was useless to even make that attempt. And it was. Because Iona wasn't going to let him walk away alive.

She pressed her palm against his chest, raking her nails across his armor and willed her magic forth. The tips of her nails became knives that pierced through the metal, killing the human almost instantly.

Blood slid against her icy fingers and spread down her arm. She pulled away, her hand the only thing keeping him upright, and as soon as she stepped away, his body crumbled to the ground.

She didn't spare his body another glance and turned. Her purpose pushing her feet forward. Dozens of doors spread across the camp. Rooms, whose blueprints she'd studied as easily as she studied the webs on her ceiling. Just another gift from George.

As if her mysterious Fae friend had prepared her exactly for this moment in time.

As if he knew she would use her gift to break down the bars of these prisons.

While the battle continued behind her, she ran towards the vaulted jail of her people. Her foot lifted and connected to the iron. With a strength she didn't know she possessed, she dented it and tore it off its hinges.

She stepped into the room. Darkness greeted her from within. Slivers of light crawled across the ground in skinny beams that did nothing to illuminate the despair within the bowels of the cage. The stench of feces, piss, and vomit penetrated her nose, and inside, rail thin, malnourished bodies huddling together in a corner?

Fae.

Their frightened shouts reached her ears, dying into whimpers as they took in the sight of her. The glow of her skin illuminated their expressions. Fear, haggard and starving, their eyes wide, the skin pressing in a thin layer against their skulls. They were nothing but skeletal figures leaning against death.

And beneath all that despair and terror, hope.

She released a breath and with it, the powerful magic enveloping her. It sucked back in her body, rivers of glittering blue through her blood until the ice settled back into that special place beside her soul.

A cold breath clouded in front of her, disappearing as she stepped forward, holding her hands in front of her to appear as nonthreatening as possible.

"Don't worry," she whispered to them. "You're safe now." She took a step further into the room. They recoiled from her presence like spiders scuttling into the darkness, and she froze mid-step.

Iona reached up and pushed aside her curls to show her ears, knowing it was the one thing that would make them trust her. Because her magic hadn't been enough. Perhaps they thought it was an illusion, a trick of the mind. Among the fucked up things they'd seen, it was her ears these Fae would trust.

Gasps rang out as they took them in, and she tried to give them a soft smile.

She felt a shimmer in the air behind her and then the warmth of two different bodies. She didn't need to turn to know who breezed in. It was obvious in the powdery scent below steel and magic of Uric, and the soft scents of a campfire and confections, and Shula's surprised voice cutting through Iona's senses.

"Oh, sweet Mana..." Shula's hand closed against Iona's shoulder. "It's true. They're *alive*."

A brave Fae crawled towards them, his skin clinging to the fragile bones of his body, his limbs shaking as he pulled himself against the dirty floor, his voice a raspy whisper in the darkness. "Who are you?"

Iona, Shula, and Uric shared a look amongst themselves, but it was Iona who answered, tilting her chin up. "We are the Resistance," she said. "And we are here to free you."

"My mate." The voice was a rasp of broken glass scraping against a floor, the sound filled with pain, edged with desperate hope. Weak hands grasped at Iona's arms, dull nails pressing against her skin.

"H-h-help m-my mate..." Tear tracks slid down grime-covered cheeks as the man all but wept in her arms.

Iona's hands gripped his fragile shoulders, as weak as the broken wings of a baby bird, to keep him upright so he didn't fall at her feet. He grasped at her arms in return, nails sliding helplessly against the material of her dirty, cut up coat.

"M-my mate w-was t-taken..." His lips trembled and he stuttered through every word.

"Ssh," Iona soothed. "It's okay."

Shula and Uric were escorting the Fae from their prison to their freedom in a single line. The humans had been subdued, most of them dead, but those that were still alive had been tied up in the center of the courtyard at the camp.

They'd only been spared momentarily because Prince Valerio wanted to question them before their executions.

The Fae locked up here were weak, tripping over clumsy, shaking feet, crying out as the last glimmers of sunlight in the sky hit their eyes. Then this Fae had fallen into Iona's chest, begging her to find his mate.

He was Unseelie, with skin that was a pale pink. His head was shaved, showing one pointed ear and the other nothing but a scrap of twisted flesh, scarring that spread up the side of his head and down his neck. The evidence of torture he'd endured.

She could feel his heart pounding against his delicate ribcage, through the thin scrap of cloth that passed for a shirt. It beat faster than it should, and for a moment she feared it would burst right out of his chest.

"What's your name?" Her hands squeezed his shoulders with the slightest bit of pressure. She was almost afraid his bones would shatter beneath her grip.

"Larke," he replied.

"Larke. Can you take a deep breath for me?"

He complied, taking in choppy breaths of air, coughing through the first few before he fell into a steady rhythm of breathing.

"Good." She smiled. "Now, can you tell me what happened?"

"The soldiers took my mate a few days ago... I—I *think* it was a few days ago..." His head cocked to the side, his eyes darting around the prison.

Iona's heart broke for him. To lose all sense of time, with no way to watch the sun rise or fall, to not know how long the love of your life had been taken away. When one minute could feel like an eternity instead of the quick inhalation it should have been for the Fae.

"Do you think your mate is still..." She hated to ask the words, but they were necessary.

Larke's fist closed over his shirt, right where his heart beat. "I feel my mate in here." He scratched at his chest, like he could tear the bond out with his bare fingers somehow. "The bond is still here."

"What does your mate look like?"

Larke blinked slowly. "Namir h-h-has h-h-ho-horns and b-b-b-black-k-k skin..."

She tried to imagine Julius missing and failed to conjure up the image. Swallowing past the sudden lump in her throat and breathing in deeply, she slid her palm reassuringly against Larke's arm. "Don't worry," she reassured. "We haven't opened the other doors. We'll find her."

Before Larke could reply, she pulled away and left the prison.

"We need to open the rest." She grabbed Shula's arm in passing, tugging the fire Fae towards a second door. "There's a Fae named Larke looking for his mate. He says they took her away. Her name is Namir. There could be more Fae hurt here."

Her heart pounded as she thought of her sister. A part of her prayed her sister was here. Alive. Another part prayed she wouldn't be. Not as the image of Larke's ears flashed in her mind. Cut off, twisted, scars spanning across his pale, bruised skin. Head shaved, given nothing but a shirt.

Dignity didn't exist in a place like this.

She had the sudden urge to tear the place to the ground.

Shula followed her towards the next door. The lock was made of iron, and if she touched it with her bare hands, it would singe her skin. Iona pressed her hand to Shula's chest, pushing her lightly back.

She called magic to herself, along with that same familiar feeling of wanting to protect. She siphoned the magic to her fist. Even with the iron in the air, her will to save others was stronger than her weakness. A fresh coat of ice spread across her hand like a glove. Her whole fist hardened like it was made entirely of solid ice. She pressed her fingers into her palms and swung at the lock, the strength behind the blow breaking it.

Then she was kicking the door in, hearing the shouts of fear on the other side.

This room was full of Fae. Filled to the brink of piles of bodies, more than the last one. The Fae inside whimpered and crawled over one another to get away from Iona.

Rage swelled inside her at the broken sight of them. She had to turn away so as to not frighten them further.

"Get them out of here," Iona gritted out to Shula, who was staring at the scene with heartbreak prominent in her eyes. "See if you can find Larke's mate."

She walked away to take a breath, pressing her palms against the tops of her thighs as she bent over and heaved in deep breaths. The air burned through her nostrils, stale with the acidic taste of ashwood and iron, so it did little good.

She composed herself after a moment. She couldn't let the Fae see her break. As part of the Resistance, she had an image to maintain. The image of someone brave and fearless, even if her heart was threatening to ride up to her throat and choke her. Even if her fingers itched to cramp against her thighs.

She turned around the courtyard, looking at the angry faces of the humans kneeling on the ground. Julius and Clay were watching over them while Ryker and Prince Valerio went to the Fae to heal and to reassure them, while Shula and Uric helped them file out of their prisons one by one.

Her eyes caught on Weylyn. Blood splattered against his skin, and his smile was a manic thing pulling at his features. Innards and broken off body parts were skewered against his sword, and he began waving them in front of the humans with taunting laughter and quiet jokes.

Crazy fucking bastard.

She'd always known he was a bit feral, hiding it under that quiet gaze. This just seemed excessive. Not that she really cared that the humans were looking green at the sight of so much gore of their own. They deserved it for what they'd put the Fae through.

Seeing Weylyn seemed to help her feel more composed. She took a final deep breath and went to the next door. As her hand hardened to ice, Shula came up behind her.

"Larke's mate isn't there," she whispered. There was a trace of uncertainty in her voice. Like she was hoping for the best but expecting the worst.

"Then I will break down every fucking door in this place until we find her."

"Iona..."

Her fist shot out and broke the lock. More Fae were freed. She kept punching through doors, and Shula kept pulling more Fae out. Hundreds trapped in a single camp. Her eyes frantically searched through everyone's faces, looking for bronze skin and a face not unlike her own.

But there was nothing.

Even when they broke down the last and final door, there was no sight of her sister at all.

Tears stuck behind her eyelids, but she refused to let them fall.

"I can't find Larke's mate," Shula whispered, oblivious to Iona's turmoil. "There's not a single female name Namir here." Her hands tugged at the ends of her hair, pulling it forward and pushing it back again. "What do I tell him?"

Iona felt her own heart break. For Larke. For herself. For the sister she feared for even more now than she had in the past.

"I'll tell him," she said firmly. "It should be me."

She weaved her way through bodies until she found Larke. He was in the middle of the courtyard, standing on the tips of his toes, obviously searching through the sea of faces to find his mate.

And Iona was coming to tell him that his mate wasn't here.

"Larke," she called out.

He turned towards her, stumbling. She rushed to catch him before he fell. "Did you find my mate?" he demanded, his voice a whistling whisper.

"Larke, I'm sorry." She willed the tears to freeze before they fell, but it didn't work. Fall they did, crystal ice rolling down her cheeks. "We can't find your mate..."

She watched his expression crumble, and then he was shaking his head back and forth fervently. "No," he denied. "I feel the bond. I—"

"I'm sorry, Larke."

"No! It can't be true!" He crumbled to the ground, and this time Iona wasn't strong enough to catch him. She fell to the ground with him, holding his fragile body in her arms as he wept, screaming his mate's name at the sky. Like a blessing. Like a curse.

Iona wanted to do the same. She wanted to shriek her sister's name across the heavens and maybe then Mana would hear. Maybe then Mana wouldn't disappoint.

She'd prayed. She'd begged.

And still her wishes were not granted.

"Larke?"

A soft, rasping voice cut through the screams and sobs. Iona and Larke whipped their gazes upward at the figure who spoke.

A figure with skin the color of tourmaline and two horns sheared down to stumps against his forehead. His eyes were red as they stared down at them on the ground, and his palms went to his mouth. Where claws should have been, Iona noticed they'd been ripped off entirely.

"Namir?" Larke extricated himself from Iona, nearly elbowing her in his haste. He jumped to his feet and wobbled towards the Unseelie male. "You're alive?"

The Unseelie smiled a nearly lipless gesture. He was more animalistic than anything, and yet the love shining in his red eyes was as vivid as magic.

"Idiot," he whispered. "Couldn't you feel me down our bond?"

Then they were embracing, kissing in a tangle of weak limbs and tears.

Iona watched from the ground and felt her jaw drop open until Shula appeared next to her. "So, his mate was a male, not a female," she whispered, as if they should have considered this in the beginning. Which, they should have. They should have asked. They hadn't, and Iona had caused Larke unnecessary heartache because of it.

Mating bonds were strange and mysterious. It made Iona wonder just how Mana chose the bonds and between who. What other combinations existed out there? Male and male, female and female, Seelie and Unseelie, Unseelie and human. Maybe there were even the possibilities of several bond mates, though that was probably extremely rare.

"Bonds of the heart know no gender or race," Shula whispered like the words were a revelation of some kind. "Like Orna and Des." Her gaze pulled away from the mated pair and found Ryker among the fray, a small smile pulling at her mouth. "Like Ryker and I." There was an ache in those words, a longing for water after so long in an oasis, of a breath of fresh air after being submerged for so long in the waves.

Shula's feet were weightless against the ground as she all but glided over in Ryker's direction. Her cloak trailed behind her like a shadow, flittering against cold whips of wind. The crowd seemed to part for her like she was a ghost they were making room for, leading her down a pathway to her mate.

She didn't throw herself into his arms like Iona half suspected she would. Ryker was speaking with a Fae, his eyes flicking over the bruised male's figure, assessing the damage. Shula didn't dare interrupt that, but when she arrived at his side there was a spark of awareness pulsing between the two. Ryker leaned in her direction, their eyes meeting for a fraction of a second before turning back to the Fae.

Iona found herself smiling at the discreet display. She realized that love wasn't always loud and boisterous. It wasn't always screaming from sandy shores or throwing your arms around one another even in the midst of the chaos and the dying.

Love was quiet, too. It was alive and vivid even within the simplicities of leaning towards one another. Love whispered between the spaces of firmly clasped hands.

Love existed in the silence of words that went unsaid.

Iona pushed herself up from the ground, dusting off the backs of her pants as she went. Her eyes scanned the growing crowd for Julius. She suddenly needed to be next to her mate. He would understand the toll today had taken on her mental state. He would understand without her saying that her fingers were hurting, cramped. She longed for the feel of his rough pads soothing out the muscles of her hand like he could cure all her aches away with a single touch.

She needed it as desperately as she needed her next breath.

She caught sight of him and took a single step towards him before she was intercepted.

The Fae in front of her was gangly and broken. Wings that looked like torn sheets were folded weakly against his back, the bottom of the sheer, ripped wings dragging against the ground. His whole body was skeletal, his eyes wide and round, and he was staring at Iona like he'd just seen a ghost.

His mouth opened and closed, over and over again like he wanted to speak but couldn't bring himself to.

Iona's brows rose. "Is everything alright?" she asked.

Then his mouth opened, and a sound keeled from his throat. "Mm-ahhh-hhi-ii-hha..."

It was then that Iona noticed he did not have his tongue.

Horror, disgust, and a frightening anger roiled in her gut.

"Mm—mmaahiiha!"

"I'm sorry," she began, swallowing past the lump in her throat. "I don't understand you. Are you okay? Are you hurt? I can get Ryker, he's our healer..."

He shook his head vigorously and gestured at her with his hands. "Mmm-aa-hii-hha..." When she stared blankly at him, he gestured, growing more agitated the more she misunderstood. He repeated even slower the sounds. They rolled off his lips until...

Iona's breath caught in her throat.

"Malika?"

His eyes lit up, and he nodded.

"Yes?"

He grasped for her weakly, hands sliding up and down her arms, and he kept repeating it in his mumbling, broken sounds. But Iona understood, and it was like everything falling into place in a single instant.

She grabbed his wrist, trying to keep her touch light even while her body suddenly vibrated with anticipation. She pulled him towards the Fae, marching him straight to Weylyn, still covered from head to toe in blood.

With her other hand, she grabbed his wrist and hauled him away from the line of soldiers and their small group of Fae watching over them. When she found a modicum of privacy, she turned to Weylyn.

His golden eyes were glittering, his lips tilted up in a sneer.

"Fuck off with that look," she growled at him. "I need you."

His dark brows rose, and he leaned towards her. She'd never realized how tall he was until he was looming above her. She was tall herself, and she'd dismissed

Weylyn as unimpressive before because when compared to Julius, he was like a mere fragment of an ice cube next to a solid block of ice. Besides, the last time they'd been in close proximity, there'd still been space between them.

He seemed threatening now.

"Oh, my sweet Iona, as delectable as you are..." His fingers gripped her chin, and she felt her skin stain with blood. "You are just not my type."

Iona jerked away from him and that eerie voice of his. "Will you quit with the fucking jokes?" She wasn't in the mood for his games. She felt like she was balancing on the very delicate edge of the precipice of the truth she'd been searching for, for years. "I need your magic," she clarified, gesturing at the broken-down Fae next to them. "I need you to use your magic on him and ask him mind-to-mind how exactly he knows my sister."

A Ghost of the Past

Weylyn straightened, smoothing out the front of his jacket. His posture was too leveled, his gaze too sharp. He looked like he was a lord holding court, but the only royals among them were Valerio, Clay, and maybe even Uric.

His gaze snapped over to the Fae, and there was no word of warning before his magic pounced. It struck like a force of lightning, and Iona didn't have time to cry out before she was enveloped in a foreign sensation. Her vision blanked and she was swallowed up by the darkness until it was all she could see. It felt like she was suspended in nothingness, like her soul had been hauled straight from her body and was dangling over a cliff.

And then she heard a voice.

Weylyn's voice.

"Speak, Fae. How do you know her sister?"

The sound came from everywhere and nowhere at once, pulsing around her. The worst part of this magic was that she could not see where it was coming from. She was completely blinded with nothing other than her hearing.

"She was kind to me," a voice replied. The old Fae's. His inner voice thankfully still intact. It was a tremulous, dusty sound. "They brought her here. I thought you were her, because you look so alike, but she was thinner. She did not have hair."

Somewhere beyond this sensation, Iona could feel tears prick at her eyes at the declaration.

In her family, their hair had been a sense of pride; even her brother and father had long locks. Iona had inherited her father's silver hair, and so had her brother. Her sister's hair had been dark like their mother's, and she'd kept it in thin braids. To think of her being degraded like that was crippling.

"They took her away because she had healing magic. They said she was needed. I have not seen her since."

"How long ago was it?" Iona's own voice echoed through the space; it was cracking and full of emotion.

"I... I do not know. Years, it feels like. Time flows differently in the dark."

"Thank you," Iona said, because there seemed like there was nothing else to say, nothing more he could give her than he already had. "I appreci—" She didn't get the rest out because she was slammed back into her body. She gasped for a breath, her vision slowly returning to her. She looked around, her gaze wild for a moment.

Weylyn had already recovered, staring at her like her reaction to his magic was amusing. "Do not think this is a gift freely given," he said in his strangely accented voice that was full of cruelty and malice. "It was a favor, and I expect you to give me one in return."

She gritted her teeth.

Bastard.

As if he could hear her thoughts, he smiled. "As to when I plan to collect?" He leaned forward, fingers swiping at the blood she knew was on her chin. "It will be when you least expect it." Then he was prowling away.

She didn't watch him go but turned back to the Fae. He was breathless, like he was just as overwhelmed by Weylyn's magic as Iona had been. She grasped his hands and gave them a reassuring squeeze.

"Thank you so much," she whispered. "You have given me hope."

After leading him back with the other Fae, Iona decided she needed to find out where they'd taken her sister.

She knew she wasn't dead. In fact, any time she tried to conjure up those negative thoughts, it felt like Mana was inside her, tearing them down before they could even fully arise. Because it couldn't be true. Her sister was *alive*. And she'd been here. At this dreadful place where hope was dead and the Fae were broken.

She should have felt closer to Malika, but all she felt was dread as she took the steps to the upper levels of the camp where there were doors to what looked like human offices.

The first one she broke into was wide in space with side doors that Iona assumed were the bathing rooms or connecting offices. It held a long metal desk that she circled, using her magic to break the locks on the drawers. She yanked them open and found stacks of papers inside.

She didn't hesitate to pull them out and start reading.

Hours. It felt like she was sitting there for hours, her gaze scanning every page. Every detail of every Fae they ever harbored and everything they'd ever done to them. They'd been degraded. Reduced to magic and numbers and pain.

Her heart hurt like every word on the page was piercing her own soul. Like everything she was reading was happening to her instead.

Then she came across the words that would haunt her.

She read them over and over again until every single word was memorized, starting with her sister's name—*Malika Wylde*—and further down. To everything the humans in this place had ever done to her.

Broken ribs.

Pulled nails.

Broken nose.

Missing toes.

"Subject does not break under measures of extreme torture."

"Subject's magic has depleted and has outlived her usefulness. Tomorrow she will be transferred to the camp in Ojor, Ielwyn, where she will be evaluated before her execution."

Execution.

"No."

Her legs gave out from under her, and she came crashing down against the edge of the table. Everything on top clattered to the ground in a commotion that felt similar to the one raging in her own chest. A storm roiled inside her, and her magic responded to her emotions. Snow began to rain down from the ceiling, fat chunks freezing against her skin like the winds in the northernmost parts of Illyk.

Executed.

The word rolled over and over in her mind like a song that had no beginning and no end. She tried to shove it away, to pray to Mana that it wasn't true, but her own turmoil couldn't help her see past what was already staring her right in the face.

She tried to summon that feeling of Mana, of instinct, that would tell her that it was all a lie. That her sister wasn't dead. That she hadn't been executed in a camp in Ielwyn like the papers said. But there was nothing. No sliver of magic jolting down her spine, no magic to knock the idea out of her head before it even grew.

It was like Mana had hidden away, gone silent in the face of the lies it had led Iona to believe. It made her wonder if Mana had ever really been there at all. If it had all been Iona's own imagination just like everyone had said.

It was easy to believe in rumors and the impossible. So when George told her his theories, she'd held tightly onto that shred of hope. Because it was the last and only thing she ever had in her life to look forward to. Everyone had died that day on the beach. When the possibility had been spoken of her sister being alive, Iona had grasped for it with shaking fingers. Because in a world that was ever-changing, full of violence and a never-ending loneliness, she needed something to believe in.

And it had given her delusions.

Mana had never really been alive, whispering in her ears at all.

Maybe that had been her own imagination. Her own hope breaking through logical reason and thought.

Which meant that her entire journey had been for nothing. She'd put everyone else's lives in jeopardy chasing a dream.

One that quickly melted into a nightmare.

"No!" The word ripped from her throat on a painful cry. She grabbed the evidence of her own delusions—of the single ghost from her past that really *had* been a ghost all this time—in her fingertips, and she ripped it down the middle.

Her rage knew nothing of logic or calm. It stormed and came out of her mouth in screams and cries. Like prayers she'd wasted for so many years on things that could never come true. She cursed Mana and the emperor until her voice was hoarse in her throat and the paper was nothing but thin, ripped up strips in her fingers. Even then, there was no calming what lived inside her.

She needed more. She needed an outlet for her rage. She needed to get it all out in any way she could. Her hands met the edges of the desk. She gripped it and used all her strength to send it flying backwards.

Then she tore through the room, destroying everything in sight, kicking chairs and files that held years of cruelty and despair. If she could eradicate the haunting memories with a blast of magic like she could the pages, she would. But even the whispers of the camp's terrors slid between the empty spaces of these walls.

Iona screamed until her throat ached. Then she slumped to the floor, pressing her palms tightly against the cold iron. It singed and hurt, and she welcomed the pain as she buried her face against the tops of her hands and wept for the sister she'd hoped to find. For the sister she realized wasn't even alive at all.

Her heart broke in that moment. It shattered, and her fingers itched to tap against something, but she couldn't find the energy to piece herself back together again. Down the mating bond, she felt Julius' essence and reached out to him. She needed him. Needed his grounding strength. She could admit that at least. That she was tired of being alone. Tired of dealing with the uncertainty and fake positivity that she'd only opted in place of her missing sister.

Because being happy was like having a part of her sister alive and by her side. If she was happy, then it meant her personality still shone as bright as the wishes of stars in the sky.

Maybe deep down the whole time she knew she would never find Malika alive.

And that's what hurt most of all.

A door creaked open from somewhere in the room. She sniffled. "Julius?"

But the footsteps that sounded on the floor weren't his. They were unfamiliar and metallic and reeked of iron.

She turned on the ground.

And Iona didn't even have time to scream before the sword came crashing towards her head.

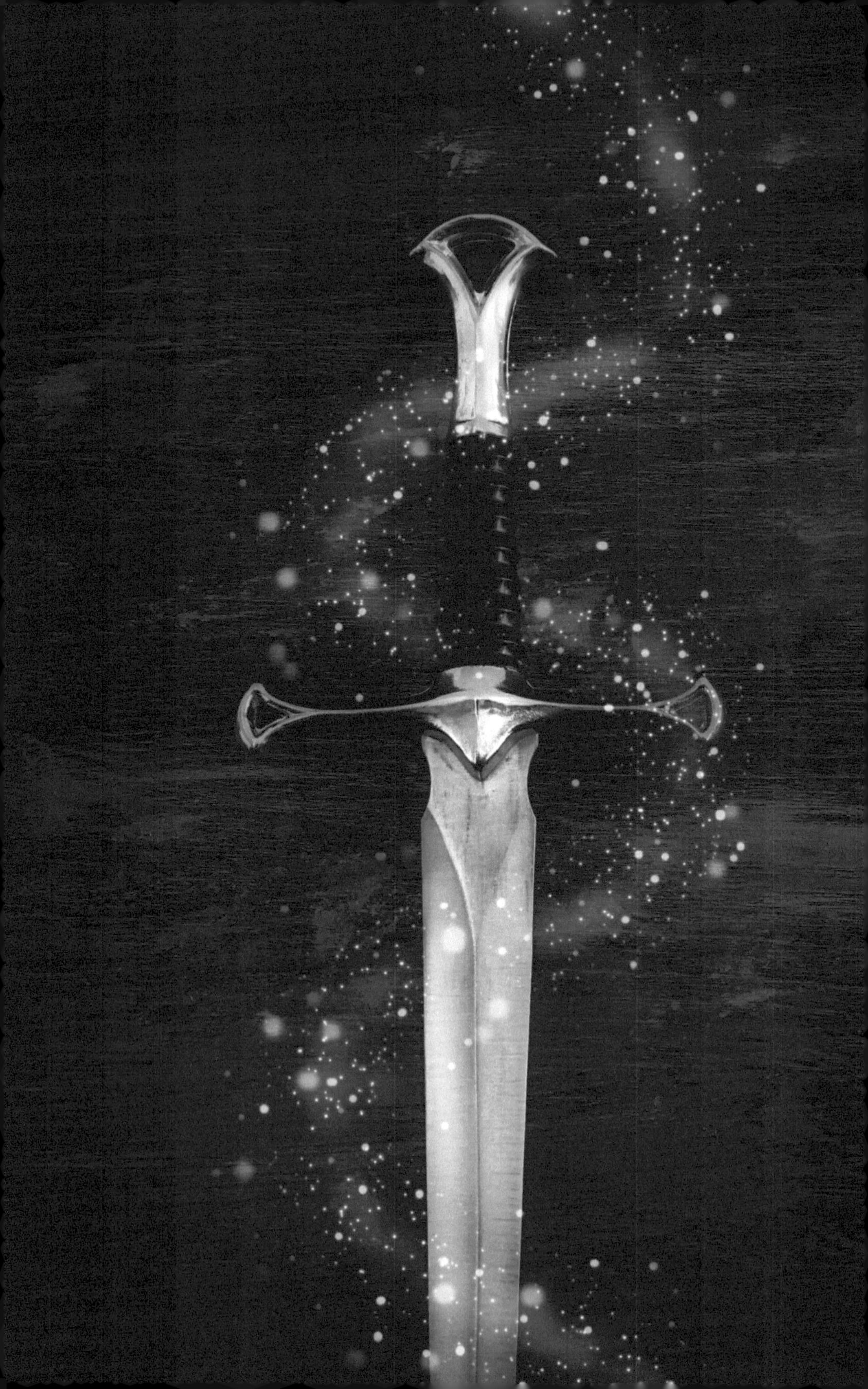

Snowfall and Blood

Julius' green eyes glared at the humans they'd subdued. They were on their knees, clasped in the same manacles they used against the Fae. The only difference was, the iron didn't burn them, didn't hurt.

But soon they'd all be screaming their pain to the skies.

He turned to Weylyn, who prowled down the line of humans with a wide smile and glittering, devilish eyes. It wasn't so often they caught the more feral side of the Fae.

Julius didn't know a lot about him. Like where his family was from or what drove him to do the things he did. There was something about death and killing that made him almost effervescent.

He was little more than a wild animal.

Sure, he kept himself tightly contained, but Julius figured that had to do more with the fact that he was the king's lackey, and therefore had an image to maintain out of orders, rather than because he actually cared about what image he portrayed.

Then again, everything Weylyn did seemed calculated somehow. Like he couldn't even move his fucking pinky finger without analyzing what others would think of it first.

He wanted people looking at him, just as much as he wanted to frighten them.

He was succeeding in frightening the humans with his demeanor. That and the fact that he was covered in their comrades' blood. Weylyn had all but bathed in their entrails earlier, swinging their innards around by the blade of his sword while laughing maniacally.

If that wasn't an image that would haunt the humans for the rest of their short-lived lives, Julius didn't know what would.

His smile had been sharp-toothed and stained red. He still hadn't cleaned the mess from his body, though he did let his hand graze across the humans occasionally, staining them in the blood of their friends.

It made them recoil and whimper in fear.

Julius chuckled at the sight. Even if he hated Weylyn and didn't understand the fucker, he knew he wasn't going to let them get away anytime soon. Which meant Julius could go in search of his mate.

He pushed through the crowd of Fae, searching faces. The last he'd glimpsed of her she'd been here in the crowd helping the others. He saw Shula and Ryker, and then his gaze caught on Valerio and Uric. He shouldered his way gently over to them and caught the last vestiges of their conversation.

"We will open a portal and take them directly to Castle Aileach."

"Your father will not be pleased."

"I will deal with my father. The Fae need medical assistance, more than just what Ryker can provide."

"And the humans?" Julius asked as he approached, cutting into their conversation.

"We will execute them in due time." Valerio flicked his fingers with disinterest in Julius' direction. Like he didn't care at all for the fate of the humans. Not that Julius blamed him. Those who worked at these camps did not deserve sympathy.

"Have you seen Iona?" Julius' gaze scanned across the faces but didn't see her.

"She went upstairs," Uric answered with barely concealed annoyance. "Perhaps you should keep a leash on your mate to better keep track of her whereabouts."

If Uric was hoping his snarky words would grate on Julius' nerves, he was wrong. He snorted and leaned towards the silver-haired Fae with a smirk held firmly in place. "Careful with your words, Nova. They reek acrid of jealousy." His green eyes flicked over Uric's form, then back and forth between him and the prince before settling on Uric again. "You will never find your own mate with all that pining you do."

The blade slashed towards him, but because he was expecting it, his forearm came up, bumping against Uric's wrist and curving the knife in a different direction. Julius grabbed Uric by the front of his clothes and shoved him back lightheartedly.

"I'm not blind, Uric. I see you looking at my mate. Wishing you had what we have. Pining does not look good on anyone, friend."

Uric blinked, his impassive stare focused on Julius' face. The man was hilarious. Julius had seen him gut a man with an entirely blank expression and flick the blood off his cuffs without an echo of emotion. Unlike Weylyn, who relished in the cruelty and laughed at death.

"You are a fool," he finally replied.

"Takes one to know one, yeah?"

Uric's expression warped, and Julius opened his mouth to let out a roar of laughter, but before he could even get the sound out, he felt it.

A tugging down his mating bond. A rippling shock of agony splitting through his chest, busting apart his soul.

He grasped at his chest and doubled over, a roar of pain and rage rumbling past his lips that didn't even feel like his own.

"Iona..." His feet stumbled forward, his body colliding against Uric's. "Something's wrong..."

His friends were instantly alert. "Physically?" Valerio slid his sword from his sheath.

Julius took a breath. "No... it's... something else." His eyes scanned the top level of the camp, his gaze closing in on where he sensed Iona. A door was cracked open a fraction, and he could just make out her shadow moving from within.

"Julius..." Valerio began, his voice slow and cautious.

"Yeah?"

"We did not search those rooms."

Fuck.

Iona.

They ran towards the stairs, Valerio's quick, lithe form moving ahead of Julius, his sword drawn and gleaming. Julius swallowed up the steps towards his mate in long, stomping strides. The stairs shook beneath his furious weight, and his heart pounded as a fresh spike of grief, anger, and fear jolted down their bond.

His every instinct screamed at him to protect his mate, but Valerio made it into the room first, his foot connecting against the iron door. It flew open, hitting the wall and nearly slamming back closed gain against Julius' face. His fist connected with it, knocking it off its hinges. By the time Julius and Uric were stepping into the room, it was to be greeted by the sounds of clashing metal.

And the crisp, cold scent of snowfall on the ground.

Snowfall.

And blood.

The sword connected against a thin wall of ice that shattered upon impact. Crystalline shards sliced against Iona's face, and the sword sliced down, its pathway diverted so it grazed the side of her cheek.

Blood swelled and dripped against the blanket of snow beneath her body. A product of her grief and fury.

Iona rolled on it, and the blade followed. Slicing with little finesse, its only purpose murderous rage. The human attached to the end of the sword followed, his cries of fury silenced by the whistling swing of his sword. Iona dodged by a hairsbreadth every time, flinging weak magic as she crawled away, her nails scraping against the ground.

Her hoarse voice seemed stuck, a lump so tight in her throat that she could barely wheeze past it, let alone scream. Everything that had happened within the last few moments had made her energy deplete, the overuse of her magic and the proximity to iron already wearing on her. Down the bond, she screamed, but there was no response.

As if she'd been abandoned not only by Mana, but her mate as well. Like this was her punishment for the sins of her past, for her delusions.

She sobbed at the treacherous thoughts as she slid against snow. The blade snagged against her leg, cutting through the material of her pants, too close to her flesh. The flat part hit against her leg, sending a limping agony through her muscles.

She waited for the blow, her eyes squeezing shut. She wondered if it would be prudent to send a final prayer up to Mana. Not for herself, but for her familiar, for Julius, for the others.

Just as soon as the prayers were about to fly from her mind, the door to the office was kicked open and steel rang against steel. There was a loud crash, stomping, familiar footsteps. Then she was in someone's arms.

The familiar smells of ale and grass and leather enveloped her like a blanket of comfort.

"Iona." Julius' hand cupped her cheek, but her eyes remained firmly closed.

Then the sharpness of blood cut through her senses, and her eyes flew open.

"Fuck!" Prince Valerio shouted. Blood welled from his chest and dripped down the human's sword.

The first drop didn't even have time to hit the ground before Uric was in front of him, merely a blur cutting through shadows. Within the next moment, his blade was embedded deep into the human's gut.

The sword clattered to the ground, and the human soon followed. His breaths came out in gasps as the life began leaving his eyes, the process slow and agonizing.

Iona predicted he would be dead within the hour.

"It is just a scratch." Valerio pushed Uric away, who hovered over him, his fingers reaching for the wound. The blood on the Seelie prince had stopped flowing, and Iona caught a flashing glimpse of his chest beneath the cut in his shirt. It really did not look like just a scratch.

Valerio shoved Uric aside with his arm, taking a step towards the human, slouched against the ground. He was wheezing, blood staining his lips that sprayed against his front with every gasping breath he took.

Valerio's foot connected to his side. "Scum," he sneered, while at the same time looking completely composed. "I should kill you where you lay for attacking a prince."

The human let out a strangled whimpering noise, which only caused Valerio to smile.

"Do not worry. I think you deserve to feel the pain you have inflicted on the Fae you have harbored here for yourself. Which means a slow, torturous death. Uric." He snapped the Fae's name like a command.

And Uric knew exactly what he meant.

He stepped forward and ripped his blade from the human's gut so he'd bleed out agonizingly slowly.

"Iona."

Iona's gaze caught the prince's. He was all hard expression and slashing lines, yet she detected a hint of softness around his features that was surprising. "Are you well?"

She couldn't bring herself to answer so she gave him a terse, slow nod that she was sure nobody believed.

Because she wasn't okay.

But she was functioning, and that seemed good enough for the prince.

He nodded once and turned, leaving them to follow. And as they made it down to the courtyard, Iona limping and Julius carrying most of her weight, Valerio snapped his fingers and a shimmering portal opened beside him and his silver guard.

"It is time to leave," he announced. "A better life awaits those who wish to follow."

One by one, the Fae gratefully piled into the portal.

"Weylyn," the prince said, his gaze going to the golden Fae. The silent Fae smiled, and it was a look that was absolutely savage. It was like Valerio had given him a silent command that he was all too eager to follow. He turned and began chopping through humans. No one paused to watch them be butchered, because that was how little they mattered.

When they were down to the last few Fae of their own little group, Valerio turned to Shula and ordered, his voice a whip against the night, "Let it burn."

Shula Azzarh's eyes responded in kind, brightening like embers as she turned away from them. She looked over her shoulder, her gaze meeting Iona's, and she held out her hand. Like she wanted Iona to do this with her, or like she needed the strength of a friend.

Whatever it was, Iona limped forward and took Shula's hand, the weight of her palm warm, grounding, and fueled with the magic of Mana.

"Let it burn, fire Fae," Iona whispered as a single tear slipped down her cheek.

"What is it?"

The words almost stuck in her throat, but Iona found herself confessing anyway. "My sister was sent to her execution."

Shula looked at her sadly. "She could still be alive." But there was doubt in her voice.

It broke Iona even further.

She didn't bother to contradict the Fae. Instead, she flicked her gaze over this cursed place and hatred rose up inside her to stay. She turned, holding out her free hand to Julius.

"Your dagger," she croaked.

He didn't question her and quickly placed a blade in her palm which she turned on herself.

"What the fuck are you doing?"

Iona ignored her mate's panicked question, slipping her hand away from Shula's so she could grab that first curl and snipped it away.

The lock floated to the ground, and once she began, she couldn't stop. She sawed through the tight spirals of her curls, shearing the hair near her scalp with a quick desperation. Her sobs and heaving breaths were soon the only sound to be heard, an echoing song of her grief that she couldn't stop.

When the final wisps of curls had been chopped, her hand gripped tightly to Shula's wrist. "Burn it, Shula," she whispered as her tears froze against her cheeks. "Burn it to the fucking ground."

Then the fire consumed, crawling across the ground like demons from nightmares and wrapped around the iron prison and ignited, blazing up the sky, shadowing it with ash and dark and light like they'd done to so many Fae before.

And for a moment there was nothing to do but watch solemnly.

As the whole place fucking burned.

The Blood of a Prince

Black smoke spiraled towards the sky, staining it with a darkness that spread throughout the entire city of Wyrshl. The fire had long since died, leaving nothing but embers and ash in its wake, along with the broken structure of a once great camp.

The parts that had been made of wood and metal had twisted, crumbled, while other parts melted into a molten pool against the earth.

A group of humans rode up to the charred remnants of the emperor's precious camp and dismounted the horses, their metal armor the only noise piercing the air.

The tallest of them all led the group forward, his boots crunching against ashes and fragments of bone and flesh, clinging to the metal of a uniform. He kicked at it with disgust and continued to prowl through the debris.

"Captain!" the voice of one of his soldiers called out. He turned and saw the man waving at him from across the camp. "Come look at this, sir!"

He took his time closing the distance between them. Once he did, he was able to see what the commotion was about.

Men gathered around him, gasping and gagging at the sight.

The captain didn't. He was used to the unpleasant scent of charred flesh and the sight mangled bodies. Of blood and innards hanging from slit skin. He'd seen battle, had fought in many.

A burnt, still alive and wheezing body was hardly reason to lose the contents of your stomach over.

"Can you speak?" he asked with something that sounded like bored disinterest. At least, it did to the men at his command. He could all but feel the looks they gave one another behind his back.

They all thought their captain unfeeling, sometimes a bit manic.

The truth didn't lie in either of those things.

"H-h-hy-e-sss." The wheezing reply was enough for him.

"What happened?"

"F-F-Fae..."

"Well, that much is obvious." His eyes darted around the camp. Why else did the dying fool think he was here? To save his life? Surely not. No, the captain was here for someone far more interesting.

A female with fire dancing in her veins.

He almost smiled at the thought of her.

"S-Seelie Prince."

The captain's gaze slammed back on the dying man. He observed him more closely. The grotesque flesh melted to muscle and the smallest hint of bone beneath. Metal was already pooling against his body. Just a single glimpse was enough to tell the captain that this man didn't have very long to live.

"You have served the emperor well with this information," he said. It would please Emperor Laurel to know that his precious fire Fae Elemental was being harbored by the Seelie Prince.

His hand lowered to graze against the still hot, ashy ground.

And she was being unleashed.

The dying man began wheezing, and the captain thought they were his last breaths until he realized it was laughter.

"I-I-I g-got it."

The captain's brows pulled together. Was the man falling into hysteria because of the pain? He wouldn't be surprised. It had happened often enough in situations like this.

It was a soldier at his back who asked, "Got what?"

"H-h-his blood!" His fingers twitched. "I g-g-got the Seelie Prince's blood."

The captain's eyes widened, and something that felt a lot like success and malice came alive in his veins. It was a feeling of rebirth and conquest. Of good things yet to come.

"Where?" he demanded softly.

The man's fingers twitched again in the direction off to the side. He didn't have to bark the order out for his men to know what to do. They began digging through the debris, wincing and exclaiming as the hot embers touched their skin. But eventually, they emerged with a sword that was still intact. It was charred in a few places, but it had been buried beneath enough debris to remain safe.

And there, on the edge, the captain could make out a darkened blood stain. It was slight, more burned along the edge than anything else, but it was there nonetheless.

"G-g-get th-the t-trackersss..." The man groaned as the pain started to take him under.

"Of course, I'm going to get the fucking trackers," the captain snapped with impatience, making those around him flinch.

But the captain did not apologize, nor would he, even to a dying man. He was stating the obvious and he did not tolerate insubordination or stupidity. From anyone.

Besides, what kind of a fool did the man take him for?

The trackers were Fae, gifted with the uncanny ability of finding any thing or person or Fae, so long as they had a single fiber of them. With that, they were traceable anywhere.

With the blood of the Seelie Prince, they could cut off the head of this so-called Resistance.

"Give me the sword," he ordered. Once the hilt was placed in his gauntleted palm, he tied the thing to his waist and then inclined his head towards the dying man. "Now put him out of his misery."

"T-t-thank you, sir."

"You have served Illyk well." A flash, and then a sword came crashing down against his body. "Unfortunately, it was not well enough."

He turned away and walked back towards his horse and mounted. He gave one last lingering look on the destruction wreaked by the infamous Fire Dancer of Piriguini's Circus and smirked.

He would never admit it aloud, but he was looking forward to this chase. He was looking forward to the moment when he had her in his grasp again and punished her for daring to leave.

He was looking forward to the moment his blade would meet the soft flesh of her body in punishment for daring to run away from him.

With that thought in his mind, Captain Brannon of the Emperor's Royal Guard turned his horse and sped away.

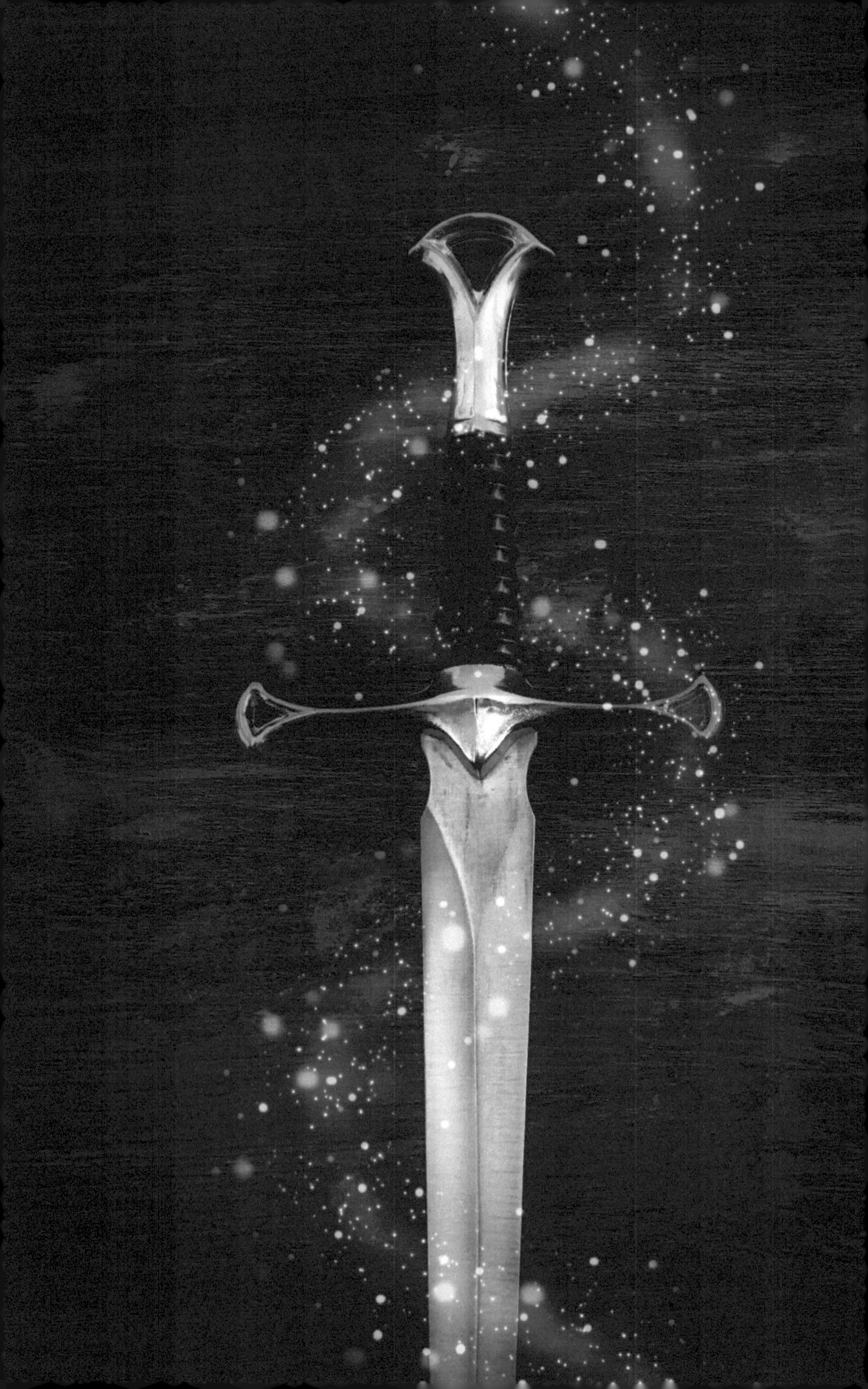

Shadows Given Form

A storm of ice and snow greeted them on the other side of the portal. Wind slapped against their faces like the quick slide of icy knives. Iona stumbled knee deep into snow, her leg twinging with pain that almost had her buried within it. A hand clasping the back of her jacket jerked her back up.

She landed comfortably against Julius' chest, his big hands wrapping around her waist to hold her steady. She turned over her shoulder, pressing her lips gratefully together, hoping he could understand the brief expression. She focused her attention back against the slicing wind in time to see her familiar running through it with glee emanating down the bond they shared.

She chuckled lightly at the sight. A brief moment of happiness stolen in the cold winds on a mountaintop, surrounded by other Fae who looked as equally broken as Iona felt inside. But for a single moment, she could cast that aside and enjoy the simplicities of her familiar's glee.

"Where are we?" she asked, her voice shouting over the wind.

Julius guided her forward, kicking their way through the snow. Ahead of them, Prince Valerio and Uric led them up a slope, where the turreted peaks of a broken-down castle came into view. Made of stone with flickering lights glowing in the glassless windows, it was a crumbling structure, bare bones of where she imagined a once-great castle used to stand.

"Castle Aileach," Julius answered. "The home of the new Resistance."

If the home of the new Resistance was a reflection of how much heart they had in this fight, then Iona was disappointed. She tried to push those thoughts aside and think positive, but something stopped her. That positivity had been her sister's influence. A sister who was no longer alive, and she couldn't bring herself to summon that part she kept close, if only because she recognized it for the lie it was.

Her grief must have tugged down their bond because Julius' grip tightened reassuringly. He leaned down, the wind whipping his tresses of flame hair against her face. "I don't know everything that happened in that room," he said. "But when we have a moment to speak alone, will you tell me?"

Her heart skipped a few beats, but she managed a nod.

He didn't say anything else the rest of the way. He just held her, guided her in the dark towards a castle that loomed higher with each step they took towards it until they made it to the grand entrance of the place.

Inside, dozens of Unseelie Fae greeted them, fluttering on rapid speeding wings, and clomping quickly on hooved feet, to and from the arriving Fae. Almost as if they knew and had been waiting for them all to show up. They carried blankets, towels, pitchers of water, and platters of food.

They sped through it like a routine that had happened before. Ryker and Shula, along with a few of the Unseelie, began leading the injured Fae from the camp up a winding staircase, Ryker barking orders along the way.

Glittering faeries illuminated the space, their entire bodies buzzing above their heads like little floating lights. A hearth burned with a bright fire that filled the room with warmth, even while stray wind and snow pilfered through the broken windows.

A flying Unseelie approached, draping a towel around Iona's shoulders. She smiled her thanks, though the expression felt more like a grimace. A warm tankard was placed in her hand with a liquid that tasted strongly of herbs and ale, and it warmed her insides.

Fae started dispersing, being led from the foyer and up the staircase to their rooms. When it was empty, with no one but Iona's original companions and a few stray Fae by the fire, a far door opened and brought in the cold along with a group of High Fae.

Julius' hand tightened on her waist, but she couldn't gauge if it was in warning or not.

The group approached, the male at the head of them was the one that caught Iona's attention, because his whole demeanor commanded it. It was in his posturing that screamed, "Look at me. I am power here."

He radiated it. Not magically, though she felt the smallest wisps of some Mana-given gift emanating from him. It was more in his stance, in the devastating expression he wore that was familiar.

She knew this Fae.

She'd seen him before, sitting on his gargantuan, black stallion, wearing the beautifully bright colors of the Seelie Court while he commanded in the war. That had been her first and last memory of King Amos Ashera of the Seelie Courts.

Now here he was again.

His beard was dark, long, and braided with golden gems. His hair was pushed back, his clothing of fine make, but obviously worn with age. He had the same grave features of his son. Except where Prince Valerio wore a staid, almost subservient expression, his father wore one that bespoke of killing rage.

"Boy," the king addressed him, the tone of his voice disrespectful enough to make the Fae behind him appear uncomfortable with the acknowledgment.

Iona had always respected royalty, yet there was something almost abnormal about him. Something mocking in the way he said the word, and it made her hackles rise.

She knew that this moment would come. When she would see the king and her actions would reflect badly against Valerio. She felt the premonition of the moment slide deep down her spine, and it filled her with dread.

"Your Majesty." Valerio swept into a graceful bow that the others—Uric, Weylyn, and Clay—mimicked. Even Julius pulled her down by the waist into a much less elegant version of one.

He kept them there, frozen in that moment until Iona's back began to cramp.

"Rise." The word tore through them powerfully, and Iona was grateful to stand, but less grateful to find the king's gaze on her instead of his son.

She wanted to wither under his attention, but she found it within herself to tilt her chin up high.

The king's eyes flashed, as if he didn't like the way she was staring at him at all. It was not to be purposefully disobedient to royalty, but to establish her own worth within their circle.

Even if she'd fucked up and had been chasing delusions her whole life, she was still an Elemental. She was not born of royal blood like them, but she was still powerful in her own right and deserved the respect her position entailed.

"So, you're the Elemental," he crooned, his lip pulling back with what looked like distaste.

"Iona Wylde, Your Majesty."

"Hmm. Very well, then." He dismissed her easily, turning back to Valerio. She almost breathed a sigh a relief to have his attention diverted from her, then but recoiled when his eyes narrowed on his own son. "Boy, I will have words with you and your..." he sneered in Uric's direction. "...right hand."

Then he was turning, a sweep of billowing cloaks following behind him like phantoms. Valerio and Uric trailed a respectable distance behind as they disappeared down the door from where they came, the king's own group staying behind.

Iona caught a flash of nervous energy emanating from them. That worried her. If the king had gone off by himself with Valerio and Uric, it meant there wouldn't be an audience.

She hadn't known him that long, but she knew cruelty when she saw it. It lived in the eyes of Petey, in the eyes of the jailors on the West Isles. It was something that was too familiar.

Guilt crawled up her throat, and she hauled in a breath. It was her fault Prince Valerio found himself in this position. If she hadn't been insistent, if she hadn't been stubborn and disobeyed...

"There is nothing you can do," Julius whispered in her ear. "It is something he must deal with on his own."

"Right..." But it still didn't let her breathe easier. If anything, it hurt more.

As if sensing her thoughts, Julius dug his fingers into her waist and tugged her away.

"Let's go," he said. "Let me show you around Castle Aileach."

Valerio could hear his father's heart beating in his chest. It pounded a rapid, furious rhythm, and Valerio found himself measuring the seconds with the beating of that black heart.

Ba-dump.

Ba-dump.

His father's fist came crashing down against the table in his provincial meeting room. The wood splintered beneath his knuckles and split the skin on his hand. He didn't seem to notice or particularly care, as he slammed his fist down a second time.

Like this could somehow prove a point and show Valerio just how displeased he was with his actions.

It was not new.

His father was always displeased with him. From the very moment Valerio had been born into existence, he had been nothing but a disappointment to the great king.

Oh, perhaps there had been a time when he had been loved by the man, but if such a time existed, it was one Valerio did not remember.

It was the love of his mother he recalled the most. Before that too had been tainted by the darkness in King Amos' heart.

"The orders I gave you," the king began, low and deadly. "What were they?"

"Your Majesty—"

"What were they, boy?" He did not need to raise his voice to a shout. Not when the venom came across on a whisper just the same.

Valerio had long since stopped flinching when facing his father. A prince never flinched. A prince never showed weakness. Even when faced with his own creator.

So he stood tall and let out a soft, quiet breath. "To find the Elementals."

"What else, boy?"

"To not go to the camps and release the Fae."

"You deliberately disobeyed my direct orders."

Valerio tried not to grit his teeth. "When I discovered the truth, I had to save them."

The king sneered at him. "Oh? Why is that?"

"Because I am their prince."

"But I am your king!" The words echoed off cold stone, pulsing in dangerous vibrations. King Ashera sighed and pushed himself away from the table, swiping away the blood on his knuckles with his fingertips. "You are a blight in my life, boy prince," he continued. "Disobeying the orders of your king brings with it consequences, as you well know." His cruel, black eyes found Valerio's. Eyes that were a reflection of his own.

He wondered if, when people looked at him, they found the same things Valerio saw in his father. If they saw a well of cruelty and obsession, a willingness to draw blood and do whatever it took to gain what he'd lost.

The thought almost pained him, because he knew the truth. He knew it was exactly what he was like. He had become his own father, molded himself into that image, and still it was not an exact replica.

"What are those consequences?"

He just wanted to hear Valerio say the words, to balk at them with fear.

What King Ashera did not know was that Valerio did not fear the words any more than he feared his devil of a father. For words were just that. And he'd suffered a crueler fate at Mana's hands by having this monster's blood running through his veins.

"The consequences are death."

He could feel Uric behind him shaking with barely concealed dark energy. He would be a fool not to know what it meant, and his own body tensed a fraction. He knew what Uric would dare to do if the king came at Valerio with a blade.

His friend would kill the king before he even got that far.

Just thinking the words were treasonous. One never placed the words "kill" and "king" next to each other unless it was to discuss *who* the royal meant to kill. Not the other way around. He was lucky Weylyn was not here to pry through his thoughts.

He would consider himself even luckier if Uric decided not to do anything stupid.

Like attack his father for carrying out the law.

And Uric would do it, this Valerio knew as surely as he took his next breath. Uric would throw himself within the path of destruction for his prince.

"Unfortunately, you are my only heir, and I cannot kill you." Valerio hated how he sounded so disappointed by that. "However, I cannot let this slight go unpunished."

"Father, I did what was right."

A snarl ripped from the king's throat. "You will address me as 'Your Majesty', cretin. We are not equals, and you are no longer a child sniveling behind your mother's skirts. You had no respect then, and it seems you have no respect for my authority now." He rounded the table until he was before Valerio.

The prince had been expecting it, and yet the slap still caught him off guard with its sting.

"Useless." The king sneered at his face. "The fact of the matter is you have ruined the carefully constructed plans I have laid out. The emperor will see this action as a slight against him, and the Fae will suffer for it because of you."

"We are *already* suffering—"

"I know very well what my people are suffering. Do you really think me so foolish as to not know what is happening? Do you really think I do not have my own infiltrators feeding me the emperor's plans of destruction?"

At this, Valerio froze.

"You have spies in their midst?"

The king's lip pulled back. "Not that it is any concern of yours, but yes. I have managed to slip a trusted Fae in the soldiers ranks."

Valerio blinked.

For years, he thought his father had done nothing but sit behind the walls of Castle Aileach, sending Valerio on missions to find Fae and hop them from safe house to safe house, if only to build his numbers back up and go back to his former, rich glory.

He never imagined he was actually plotting for a war behind the closed doors with his advisors and the other High Fae. That he had actually set something in motion.

"Why did you not tell me?" he demanded, feeling sudden anger surge through his system. "If you included me in your plans—"

"My plans are my own, boy. You need to know only what you are told."

"No, you need to include me in this!" Valerio finally lost his temper, found his words rising. "Had I known—"

"You would have followed orders?" His father stepped back and snorted. "You should do that anyway."

"But—"

"Shut up," he hissed, whatever vestiges he had of patience left were fraying. "I grow tired of this conversation. You are a child, Valerio, and still act like one.

Which leads me back to the point. Punishment. I think a whipping should do very nicely."

Valerio gritted his teeth together. He wanted to scream at his father a little bit more, but it was useless. Talking to him was useless because he didn't understand what things were really like out there. Even if he was plotting, he was doing it without really going out and living what the Fae were living.

It was easy for him to exclude Valerio from his plans, because he feared Valerio was right.

Yet he could not say that. He had already surpassed the line that lay between them, the one that separated the great King Ashera from his lesser offspring.

He had questioned his father; even worse, he had disobeyed a direct order.

Now, he would suffer the consequences.

"Fine," Valerio conceded. He began to shrug off his cloak and shirt.

"Wait," Uric interjected. "Let me take the punishment in his place, Your Majesty."

Cold swept over Valerio's body until he felt like he was burning and shivering at the same time from the inside out. His hands froze against the strings of his shirt. "I am the one who gave the order," he said, careful to keep his voice neutral, lest his father hear what he was really feeling.

Though judging by the widening of his smile, Valerio feared he was too late.

He'd always been careful to keep what he loved away from the king, but it was obvious to anyone by the way Uric followed that he'd grown to mean something to the prince.

It was why he'd always tried to keep his feelings at bay with anyone he came in contact with. It was why he always seemed so cold and aloof when the reality was, he was anything but.

"A punishment is meant to hurt," his father said as he began rolling up his own sleeves up to the elbows. "To ensure you do not disobey me again, I will make it agonizing for your friend. If only to get my point across."

"Your Majesty..."

"Undress!" he barked at Uric. "Now."

"No."

But Uric was already moving without complaint, pushing past Valerio, shrugging his jacket off as he went. It dropped to the ground, followed by his shirt until he was standing there in nothing but his pants, his pale skin on display.

The latticework of blue veins that spread across his body like the rivers of a map somehow made him look more vulnerable than the sharp jut of his shoulder blades did. His silver hair fell across his back that he turned so it was facing the king.

"Father," Valerio tried pleading once again, but he realized his mistake as soon as the word left his lips.

He was pleading, trying to appeal to the king's compassion.

And his father had none.

"Watch what the consequences of your foolery brings, my son," he said. Magic sparked against his fingertips, a whip of shadows forming in his hand like something ethereal yet real at the same time. His magic taking hold.

For the King of the Seelie Courts could mold shadows into solid form.

"Father, *please.*"

But his words fell on deaf ears as his father's hand arched back and the whip in his hand snapped.

Uric's dark eyes found Valerio's own, and a wry smile twisted his face as if to say, *"Do not worry, my prince."*

But the king's arm came whipping down, and the first lash struck against Uric's back, and his body convulsed.

And Uric's blood flooded the halls.

The History of Castle Aileach

Fae wine hit her system like a jolt of raw magic, making her skin buzz. Every nerve ending felt alive and primed for something Iona couldn't quite grasp no matter how hard she reached.

Her tankard became a bottomless pit. It seemed every time she neared the end, it was being filled all over again by Julius.

"I have a feeling you're trying to get me drunk," Iona said, feeling her words slur and her cheeks heat.

Julius smirked at her. "That obvious, mate?"

"Ha! You think you're so smooth, but you're not." As if to prove a point, she grabbed the tankard and downed the contents within seconds, then slammed it back against the rickety table. Julius' hand darted forward, but before he could dump more wine from the pitcher into her glass, she pushed it away and watched it go crashing to the ground. "Ha, beat you," she teased.

"So you did..." A twinkle glossed over his bright green eyes, and a second too late she realized it for the mischief that it was.

"Julius..." Her voice held a note of warning that he didn't heed. She stood from her chair, and it toppled to the ground. She stepped over it, her palms up as Julius followed like a prowling predator. "Think about this..."

His mouth twisted up into one of his growling, mocking smiles.

That was how she knew she was in trouble.

She didn't bother talking anymore. Instead, she turned and ran through the foyer of the castle, crying out when he caught up to her in just a few strides. His arms wrapped around her waist and lifted her from the ground. Her feet flailed and she pounded against his forearms while laughter trickled out of her throat.

Eyes turned to them, and she watched the fire from the hearth dance against the color of their irises before Julius started spinning her in his arms. Her stomach pressed up tightly against the muscle of his shoulder when he flipped and flung her over it. The air left her in a single breath at the quickness with which he managed that. Then she was laughing again as his palm slapped against her ass.

"Put me down, brute." Her fist walloped against his back, but he didn't even wince. She was a bit offended by that, so she struck harder. "Brute!"

"Tsk, tsk, tsk..."

Julius stopped spinning, and when he did, Iona's eyes caught on Clay standing behind her mate. Julius turned, pulling her gaze away from the Fae, but a moment later he was sliding her down his body, and she was turning to face him again.

"Didn't anyone ever tell you that's no way to treat a lady?" There was a grin on his face, the kind that made the little indent on his chin just that much more prominent. He looked freshly showered, his cheeks heated a soft red with what Iona could only assume was Fae wine. His light brown hair was curling, wet strands stuck against his forehead and cheeks in a way that made him look almost boyish and endearing. On his arm, a female Unseelie Fae clung.

Iona's eyes slid over her for a second. Her skin was bright pink and flushed a deep purple, her hair long, orange, and braided. She looked like a field of flowers, or a sunset across a horizon.

Julius snickered. "Don't let his big talk fool you into thinking he's any better at treating a woman than I am," he told the female on his best friend's arm. "He's trying to make himself look good by making me look bad."

Clay scoffed in mock objection while Iona snorted.

"Trust me, I have 'how to treat a woman' down to an art form." He pulled the female close, but his hand never strayed anywhere but her side. If anything, his touch was respectful, not roving or demanding or sexual.

"You keep telling yourself that, when you only last three thrusts."

"Oookay, I do not need to hear this. That is disgusting." Iona elbowed Julius' side, and he busted out laughing at the look of abject horror on the Unseelie woman's face.

She started to slowly pull herself from Clay's hold, and he let her go reluctantly, but still chased her as she ran away, glaring at Julius over his shoulder a second before calling out all the reasons Julius was a liar.

Iona's own laughter bubbled out until tears were slipping from her eyes, and she had to hold herself up with her palms against her thighs, wheezing breaths rolling into quiet sobs that she couldn't stop.

All the elation she'd felt only moments before suddenly disappeared entirely. Sorrow took its place, wriggling its way around her chest like happiness had never really lived there at all, like it had burned away back at that flaming camp.

She pushed herself up, straightening and smoothing down her shirt.

Fingertips wrapped around her shoulder. "Do you want to talk about it?"

"Yes."

The fluttering of wings had her looking up to see a swarm of pixie-like bugs hovering above her head. She hadn't noticed them before, the way they floated, their tiny gazes intent with mischievous curiosity. When she caught their expressions, they began chattering animatedly in a language she didn't understand.

She frowned at them and looked back at Julius. "Let's go outside."

He allowed her to take his hand and guide him out of the castle and to the knee-deep snow of the mountains.

The wind was sharp and painful and sobering, but Julius didn't complain. She caught sight of her familiar running through the snow, biting at the swirling snowflakes.

"Let's go over here." She led him far enough away from the castle where there wouldn't be prying eyes. Eyes that would likely report everything back to the king. She didn't know why she didn't particularly trust that monarch when she trusted his son.

She believed there was a lot you could discern about a person by looking into their eyes. It was in the eyes where you could find someone's story. It lived in a single, quick glance. Enough to know if someone was trustworthy or not.

She'd seen a lot of dead eyes set on living corpses during her life, almost as much as she'd seen true malice.

King Ashera was something else entirely.

"You going to bury my body in the snow?" Julius inquired, his voice holding only a tad bit of wariness.

"If I brought you out to kill you, trust me, you'd know." She dropped his hand and raised her own. The wind whipped against her clothes as her own magic surged through her system and zapped out. Blocks of ice began forming, stacking upon each other until they coalesced into an igloo with a doorway big enough to fit Julius' massive form.

"Wow," Julius exclaimed, taking in the surface. It sparkled like crystals from a royal's treasure chest. Glittering white and blue like it was made of diamonds.

She offered him a small smile. "I used to make these all the time on the beach when I was little. We used to play in them before the heat of the sun melted them away." The memories brought a sharp moment of pain against her chest that she wanted to shove away but couldn't. It enveloped her until she felt like she couldn't breathe.

Iona pushed her way inside the igloo, and once Julius was inside as well, her magic swallowed up the empty entryway, covering it with ice to ensure their privacy.

Even though the place was made of ice, it protected them from the wind, and therefore the sharp bite of cold.

Not wanting to sit in a thick layer of snow, Iona put her magic to work until two high-backed chairs had been formed of her ice. She went and took a seat, gesturing at Julius to take the one next to her.

He chuckled, thumb swiping against his bottom lip in a gesture that was all too sexual, flashing white teeth. The sound of his amusement rumbled through the space of their small enclosure.

"What?" she demanded, pressing her thighs tightly together.

"Nothing, mate." He dropped his hand and stalked forward, pressing a kiss to her cheekbone. "You just look like a queen on her ice throne, is all."

Her face warmed at the declaration, but before she could reply to him, he was already taking his own seat beside her, angling his body so their knees touched.

"Talk to me?" He framed the words like a question, giving her the option to do so if she wished, and also the option to deny him if she didn't feel like bearing her heart and soul.

It was because of that she knew without a doubt that he was *made* for her. Julius would never push or pressure her into doing something she didn't want to do, even if it meant leaving him in the dark about her feelings. Even though she could feel his curiosity burning down their bond, he didn't press.

"For once in my life, I'm not sure where to begin." A tear slipped down her cheek, and she batted it away impatiently. "Ugh, and I can't stop crying. It's disgusting."

Julius leaned back against his seat but didn't say a word. She knew he wouldn't until she poured her own feelings out.

"She's dead, Julius," Iona blurted. "Malika's dead and Mana abandoned me. For a second I thought you had abandoned me, too. It's a mess. I did all of this to find her because I was so sure she was alive. I put everybody at risk. I put *you* at risk. Fuck—" She broke off, hands clamping against her head. It was a strange sensation to not feel her curls there anymore, to feel nothing but the soft fuzz against her scalp. Tears came anew at the realization, but she pushed on. "I put the new Resistance in danger. I put the prince in harm's way while I was busy chasing a damn dream."

She pushed herself up from the chair and paced the small confines. Her fingers nearly broke against her thighs with the force she began tapping them.

She probably sounded and looked manic, she knew. She could feel her mate's worry for her down their bond. She tried to rein in her instability, but her words came out short and choppy.

"The Fae recognized me. I look like my sister. Well, she looks like me. And Weylyn pulled me into his mind with that weird power of his and—" Her fingers cramped. She closed her hand into a fist then opened it again. "She was taken.

So I looked through their records. They tortured her. They cut her hair." Her fingers scraped against her scalp.

Julius stood to his full height, and still he didn't interrupt.

"Our father and mother used to braid our hair together. I preferred to leave my curls, but it was a sense of pride for us... That seems so small compared to broken bones and missing toes, but it got to me the most. Like they were trying to take away her identity..." A sob choked her. "She was sent away from the camp and to her execution."

That was what broke her.

Iona crumbled within herself, her knees giving out. The ground seemed closer suddenly as her body fell towards it. But then she was in Julius' arms. He caught her before she fell into the snow. He pulled her up to his chest, wrapping his arms around her back to keep her in place. She was too weak to wrap her arms around him, but he had strength enough for the both of them.

He picked up her and cradled her to his chest as the sobs racked her body.

"The feeling was gone!" she shouted into his jacket. "I tried to find it inside of me, but Mana didn't respond. What if Mana was never there to begin with? What if it was all a lie? What if it was part of my own delusions? What if the voice I'd been hearing this whole time had been nothing but my own hope?"

"Iona..." Julius began. "Who the fuck cares?"

She pulled away, shock marring her expression as she took in his own pulled brows and flashing eyes. "What?"

"Who the fuck cares if the voice in your head was your own hope?" His arms squeezed her for comfort. "There's nothing wrong with having hope. So what if it wasn't Mana? So what if it was you this whole time? What does that matter?"

"It means... it means I was alone this whole time."

"That's bullshit and you know it, Iona. When one has hope, one is never truly alone." His thumb swiped against the cheek he'd kissed moments before. "I am sorry about your sister. I am sorry the records in that place silenced the hope inside you." His palm spread on top of her short hair, the pads of his fingers scraping along the bits she'd missed.

She suddenly felt self-conscious about the fucked up way it probably looked. She was never the kind of Fae to fall for the allure of her own reflection, though she'd known she was attractive. Her hair had been her favorite part of herself. Not because they hid her ears, which were now on display, but because it had reminded her of the life she'd had before.

Now that, too, was gone.

"You did this to honor her," Julius surmised. "To remember her."

"I would never forget."

"No. You wouldn't." His thumb swiped against her cheek again. "I have seen soldiers fall in combat and others tattoo the names of their friends on their bodies in ink. Even if it is something they could never forget, they need the reminder."

Iona took a deep breath. That's exactly what it had been. She'd taken the knife to her curls to remind herself of her sister's suffering.

To remind her why she fought in the first place.

"I don't think Mana abandoned you, Iona."

The words made her heart squeeze painfully, which he must have felt down their bond. His fingers gripped her chin and tilted her head up to look at him.

"You've been searching for the truth about your sister for years, Iona." His breath fanned across her lips. It was warm and smelt strongly of wine. "Mana gave you hope so you could find out the truth, and that's what you did today. You discovered the truth, or else you would have spent your entire life wondering what had happened to your sister."

His words sunk in her chest, calming the ache inside her. She wanted to argue against them but... they made sense. Perhaps he was right. Maybe this quest had never been about finding her sister alive at all. Maybe it had been about something more. About truths.

About saving Fae who couldn't save themselves, and in them, find the spirit of the sister she so desperately loved.

She hadn't been able to protect Malika, but she could protect others. She could save them from camps. She could fight in the upcoming war, for a war *was* coming.

And Iona meant to be on the side of good.

She meant to fight the Emperor of Illyk.

And kill whatever hateful humans who got in her way.

Her fingers gripped his jacket. "Thank you," she whispered, feeling all the tension leave her shoulders. The ache was still there, and it was something she knew almost instinctively would never go away.

"I will never abandon you, Iona," he whispered. "No matter if your thoughts try to convince you otherwise, no matter how hopeless you feel, I will *always* be here. I'm in the bond tethered to your soul, the quiet spaces between the loud beating of your heart. Whenever you need me, I'm just a kiss away."

Iona wasn't sure who reached for who first. One moment Julius was speaking and the next her body was wrapped around him, feet hooking behind his waist, heels digging into his back, while their mouths devoured one another in an attempt to get closer.

As if close could never be close enough.

Space didn't exist between them. Her fingers trembled as they reached for his clothes, pulling the shirt from his pants and reaching for the strings that kept them tied together. When his pants loosened, she reached her fingers inside to grasp his aching cock.

He groaned when she jerked her wrist, tugging at the velvety skin of him.

"Fuck, Iona, wait, fuck—"

"I need you."

An animalistic growl rumbled from deep within his chest. Then she felt him turning, and a moment later she was dropped to her feet in the snow. Before she could cry out at the fact she wasn't touching him anymore, he gripped her by the hips and whipped her around so she was facing her makeshift chair—or throne, as Julius would have it—and bent her over it.

He palmed her ass, squeezing the globes in his big hands before his hand snaked around to her front to cup her through her pants.

She didn't need to see him to picture his wild expression as the groan was ripped from her lips. She didn't need foreplay. When it came to him, her body was always primed and ready.

His fingers tugged at the drawstrings of her pants until they loosened. Then his fingers were inside, sliding up her wet folds in a teasing motion.

"Julius..." she groaned, jerking her ass back in his direction. She needed him desperately. She wanted the pleasure he could bring. She wanted the eradication of her memories. She wanted to get so lost in his thrusts that she couldn't remember her own fucking name.

As if reading her desires down the bond, she felt his own pants loosen from behind her and slide down until his skin was warming her skin.

"Hold tight, Iona," he ordered.

A moment later, her fingers were grasping fruitlessly at the ice. It slipped in her grasp until she wrapped her hands around the edge of the chair and dug her nails in tightly. Cold wanted to encase her body, but Julius chased it away with the warmth of his body against hers.

One hand against her hip, he used the other to guide his cock against her ass and down until he found the wet slide of her folds.

"Fuck, your ass is perfection." A slap proceeded his words and she yelped. Wetness oozed from her legs, her clit pulsing with a screaming need for attention.

"Julius, stop fucking around." She pushed back into him and he chuckled.

"Fine." The head of his cock pressed inside her and he stopped, balancing at that edge, giving her just a fraction of what she wanted so she'd beg for more.

"I swear to fucking Mana if you don't—" He slapped her ass, abruptly cutting off the words she was about to say.

"Don't threaten me, little mate. You won't like it."

"Then stop teasing and *fuck me.*"

He slammed inside her to the hilt, his body doubling over hers. She almost slipped, but one of his hand's clamped down on hers, keeping her tethered in place.

"Fuck, you're so tight; always so damn good."

He thrust as if to the prove a point, and she squeezed his thick length inside herself. He eased the desperate ache of desire he'd caused in her, but it still wasn't enough. She wanted more. She wanted rough friction, she wanted him pounding her body against the ice.

"Is that what you want?" he purred near her ear, causing a shiver to roll down her spine.

"Yes," she croaked, knowing he'd felt what she'd thought down their bond.

Nifty, that.

"Then hang on."

And Julius began to thrust. The furious glide of him in and out of her body pushed her harder and harder against the ice chair until she was all but plastered against it. He closed her against it, his hips pushed against her own, pressing her clit against the slick, cold surface with every move of his body.

She groaned at the sensation, at the unexpected desire it caused inside her, pushing her higher and higher to the edge where she wanted to drop. Before she could reach that sudden release, Julius pulled her back, his hand splaying against her stomach, taking away the cold friction and replacing it with the warmth of his fingers.

The sudden change of temperatures made Iona cry out, hand slipping. His thumb swiped against her clit and a finger slid inside her, stretching her even fuller. He played with her folds, spreading them wide open for every deep, hard thrust inside her channel.

"Fuck," she gasped. "Fuck, Julius, I'm so close."

"I know." His hips pounded harder against her. "I can *feel* you, squeezing me with that tight little pussy."

"Julius..." she warned, but the word fell on deaf ears. He spoke, each word filthier than the last, promising pleasure beyond imagining in that rumbling, seductive voice until he all but shoved her over the edge, and she was falling.

She screamed her orgasm, and the sound echoed through their little igloo, cut off from the rest of the world, if only but for a moment. She prayed to Mana that there would be more moments like these. More stolen times before the war began. Before everything else was doused in the cold uncertainty of what the next day would bring.

For now, at least Iona could have this.

She could have pleasure, spiraling through her body.

She could have Julius' punishing thrusts as he reached his own peak.

She could have his lips, pressing against the soft lobe of her ear.

She could have his words, whispered with a certainty she felt down to her soul, and she could say them with equal conviction.

"I love you."

*

Stars scattered across the sky in blinking clusters that framed the peaks and spires of Castle Aileach like a crown.

Iona supposed it could have been grand, once upon a time. But it was nothing but a hollow, crumbling structure with broken windows now that promised temporary safety for the Fae.

She breathed out a sigh at the melancholy turn of her thoughts, and it puffed in front of her like a cloud.

"What's the deal with this place?" she asked quietly.

They were laying against the side of her familiar in the whispering cold of the mountains, staring at the sky. The cold usually bothered her, but in this tight huddle, she barely felt anything beyond her own storming thoughts.

"What do you mean?" Julius' fingers stroked down her shoulder absently.

"I mean where did you find this place? What is this place?"

"Basic Fae-human history, mate," he teased.

"Enlighten those of us who didn't have such an excellent education." She shoved her elbow into his side, making him grunt.

"Castle Aileach is a human-Fae stronghold," he began. "I'm not sure when it was built, but it was a place where humans and Fae came to delegate treaties and peace, long before the war and discord had ever begun. According to legends, it sits on a Ley Line of its own, and these mountains are infused with magic."

Iona's brows rose. "Magic?" she echoed. "Impossible."

Human lands didn't have magic. Not in the same sense as Tir na Faie did. While it was ripe with elements that they themselves were destroying, there couldn't possibly be raw, uncurbed *magic.*

"The legends say otherwise. Remember how I said I was raised by the people of the wood?"

"Yeah?"

"They taught me a few things, songs and legends from the Unseelie Court that we never learned in the Seelie."

Iona cuddled closer to him, curious to hear this story.

"There was one, I can't remember the words exactly, but they basically said that the Unseelie broke the rules of human-Fae separation and opened portals to the human lands and kept them there."

Iona lifted her head. "Portals? What kind?"

"Stone circles, mushroom circles, that kind of thing. Because of this, magic bleeds through the human lands through these portals. When this castle was built for human-Fae negotiations, the Unseelie opened a portal in these mountains, one big enough to fit a whole court through. No one knows where it's at, but they think magic lives and breathes within these mountains, just like slivers of magic live and breathe throughout the human lands as much as it does in Tir na Faie."

"Do you think it's true?"

He shrugged. "Probably. I wouldn't be surprised. Years ago, things were different. There might have been peace, but there was still a distinct difference between the two races that a safe, neutral territory was obviously necessary for them to meet. But then years passed, things changed, and this castle sits here all but forgotten by the humans."

"So how did you find it?"

"Fae live longer than humans, and we don't forget things quite as easily. This was all but a relic lost in time until Weylyn mentioned it to the king."

"Ah. Weylyn. Where is he even from?"

Julius chuckled. "Sneaky rat bastard, that one. He's from the Gold Court. He was adopted by a poor farming family or something, but we don't know much about them. He was found by lords of the court and sent to the king where he's been ever since." He paused, his chest moving in a steady beat. "We're lucky we have this place or else we'd be lost. There's nowhere else we could keep this many Fae."

A sudden feeling of unease coiled through her belly. Julius must have picked up on it because he tugged her closer.

"What's wrong?"

"Julius... what happens if the humans find this place?"

His body tensed. "Mana, I hope that never happens."

"But if it does—"

"If it does, there are secret tunnels beneath the castle that lead out to a new mountain here in Tuath. We would lead everyone there and pray we can get away in time."

Silence pressed between them after that, and Iona hated that she'd ruined the mood between them. But if she knew one thing, it was that they couldn't be safe forever. Being in Porir had proved that. Soldiers had invaded then, and there was a possibility that they could invade now.

She didn't want to think about all that, but as the night wore on, the feeling that an impending doom lurked beyond the shadows of the night remained.

The Pain of Unrequited Love

The door clattered as it closed, while King Ashera's footsteps echoed through the cavernous room. He walked steadily, as if he had not just dealt a cruel punishment. As if there had been no price to his malevolent magic at all, save for the blood that pooled on the stone floors.

Valerio could not watch the king leave. Still he waited, and as soon as the cruel bastard was gone, he dropped to his knees. His pants soaked through with Uric's blood, and his friend did not stir at Valerio's proximity.

His eyes raked over his friend's broken body. At the pale flesh stained with blood, his skin flayed open in violent slashes across his back that looked like the spread wings of a bird without feathers.

He was almost too afraid to touch him, afraid he would hurt him further.

The ends of his hair were matted crimson and curling against his cheeks. It was for the hair that Valerio reached, pushing it away from his cheeks to find Uric's eyes already opened and staring at the prince.

Valerio suddenly felt angry. "You fool," he spat, unable to control his fury. "Why are you always doing such foolish things?"

A hoarse chuckle escaped from Uric's mouth. The sound was bitter and entirely without humor. "You know why."

It was in those words that Valerio felt his heart clench in a pain he never thought he would feel. As much as he wished they had not been spoken, they had been, and there was no turning back once it was said. He almost wished he could place the blame on Uric's pain, on the gashes flayed open against his back that were making him delirious.

But he had expected this for quite some time. He had dreaded the day it would come.

The day he would have to hurt his one true friend.

The truth must have reflected on his expression, because Uric's eyes darkened even further, and he let out a mirthless laugh. He moved, grunting as he rolled.

"Do not—"

Valerio's words were useless because Uric rolled to his back anyway, a sharp hiss of pain pushing past his clenched teeth.

"Your wounds..."

"Fuck my wounds," Uric whispered the words, but they savored bitter and dark. Valerio knew what they really meant. He was good at reading the silence between the spaces of Uric's lies and gauged the truth easily enough.

He ran a hand through the ends of his hair, only to realize they were stained with his best friend's blood. Blood that smelt as sharp as Uric did, with the softest undercurrent of vulnerability. It was a perfect scent to sum up what Uric *was.*

As sharp, defensive, and deadly as a blade. But once you cut yourself to get past those defenses, you found something newer beneath that. Something you would never expect to find for an Obsidian Court Fae.

Something he would rather die than show.

Yet he *had* almost died. Rather, he had suffered a great deal. What Uric did not seem to comprehend, was that by offering himself in place of the prince, showed more than he could ever know.

The king had realized it. He had known it for years now. Valerio did not doubt that his bastard of a father had been lying in wait, searching for the perfect opportunity to somehow expose them both, to take his anger at Valerio out on someone else.

And because Valerio cared about Uric, that made the Fae the perfect whipping boy.

And because Uric was in love with Valerio, it meant he would martyr himself every fucking time.

"We should get you to Ryker." Valerio eyed Uric warily as the Fae forced himself to a sitting position. He flinched and hissed at every tug and strain his movements caused against his backside. "He will heal you quickly..."

"No," Uric cut in, in a voice that made Valerio blink with surprise.

Uric was never one to deny the Prince of Seelie what he wished. That did not mean Valerio was ever demanding; he never felt as pompous as other royals. While Uric did not hold back from voicing his displeasure sometimes, or his wariness of certain situations, he never outright *denied* him.

"Your back—"

"Will cause Ryker unnecessary pain and arouse questions neither of us need to answer." He stood to his feet, his hand grasping for his discarded shirt as he stood to his full height.

Valerio stared up at him from his kneeling position and watched as he methodically began pulling on his white shirt, only to soak it through with blood. It plastered against his back in a way that must have been painful, but Uric was careful to keep his expression as inscrutable as always.

He raised his arms and flicked back the long length of his silver-white hair, causing blood to fly and hit Valerio's cheek. It made him realize what position he was in. The pressure registered in his knees a moment later, and he was all too aware that they were both covered in blood.

Valerio slowly got to his feet, his eyes never once straying from his friend.

"They will have questions anyway," Valerio pointed out, nodding at their haggard appearances.

Uric did not appear to be listening. He buttoned up his shirt with cold precision, as icy in his demeanor as Iona's magic. When he finished, he reached for his jacket and shrugged that on before he started walking away.

Valerio felt dumbfounded at his attitude and followed.

"Uric..." He grabbed his arm, and Uric whirled, his nostrils flaring.

"What would you have me say, Valerio?" he demanded. He did not need to shout to get his point across. His voice was deadly enough in its low timbre.

It made Valerio's hackles rise at the audacity of his insubordination. "I will have you obey my requests, as I am your prince."

A brief strike of disbelief crossed his dark depths before it was replaced with a hardness he only ever reserved for others.

It made Valerio feel like a cad.

"Of course, my prince," he gritted out. "How could I ever forget that my only purpose has ever been to serve you? That is why I was given to you in the first place."

Valerio reeled back as if the words had slapped him. It was the truth, and yet they still felt wrong. "It is not like that," he defended. "You know we are not like that."

His brows furrowed. "Then what are we like? Friends?" He scoffed. "You have kept me at arm's length for years and have made it clear that you do not wish for anything more."

Annoyance flared through Valerio's blood. Suddenly, the entire weight of the things he had been carrying for so long toppled over into being too much.

He had never given in to tantrums as a child, much less as an adult, however he felt like snapping now, so he did.

"What more do you want from me, Uric?" He took a step forward until their chests were touching. Until the scent of him was sharp enough in his nostrils that he wanted to sneeze. "Define *more.*" When he did not speak, Valerio cocked his head to the side. "No? Then I shall do it for you. You want to fuck me and be fucked by me; you wish that I loved you the way you love me, but you know I do not and cannot. I will not *ever.*"

Uric did not suck in a breath. He did not reel back or twist his features in pain. He straightened, his expression completely impassive, and smoothed his palms down his jacket, only to clean the blood from his fingers.

This was almost worse than if he would have shouted, but Valerio should have known better. Uric did not shout. He did not show emotion. Not like others. Yet Valerio could read him perfectly just the same.

"You have coveted feelings for me for far too long, my friend," Valerio said, if only to soften the blow, while putting as much emphasis on the word friend as possible. "You know we can never be. I am waiting for—"

Uric gave him a stiff bow, interrupting him. "If that will be all, prince?"

Prince.

Not *my prince.*

Prince.

It was what Valerio wanted, to set himself out of that emotional box Uric had placed him in, and yet it still hurt. Not because he was playing with Uric and wanted him to secretly harbor feelings for the rest of his life.

But because Valerio hated hurting the best friend he had ever had.

Because the pain of unrequited love was sharper than the blade he had taken to the skin hours earlier, and he could feel it reflected in Uric's eyes.

There was so much more he wanted to say, but he held the words in the back of his throat and straightened himself.

Arm's length.

It is what Uric said he always gave, and he would not stop now.

"That will be all, Uric," Valerio snapped, ever the imperious royal. "You are dismissed."

Darkness flashed in Uric's eyes once again, but before Valerio could read more into it, he was turning, and leaving the way King Ashera had gone.

And when Valerio was alone, he turned and stared at the pool of Uric's blood and told himself that all he had said and done was for his own protection.

That it was for the best.

The Invasion of Castle Aileach

Stars bled across the sky, leaving behind streaks of white against an endless expanse of darkness.

"Humans make wishes on those," Julius supplied, his arm wrapped tightly around her shoulders. "They think they'll come true." He sounded incredulous.

"Humans are a strange race," Iona said in an almost lazy tone. "They'll make wishes on stars like it holds magic, but they'll kill us for the same thing."

Julius laughed, the sound loud and throaty. "That's what I said, too. But not all humans are bad."

"Oh, I know. Henry wasn't." She smiled as she thought of the old man, and her heart ached with the sensation of missing him like she had every day since he'd died.

Julius pulled her close. "Will you tell me about him someday?"

A smile tugged at her lips. "Someday."

Not today. She'd already shared so much, and he realized that right now she felt drained. She didn't have much left to give, and that was okay.

"And I'll tell you all about what it was like growing up with the little people of the wood." His fingers grazed across the sharp jut of her ear, causing her to shiver and burrow deeply both into him and her familiar.

The air had gotten colder in the mountains, and still they hadn't brought themselves to go inside the castle. Surrounded by dozens of eyes that were spying for the royals had no appeal to her. It was one of those times she felt grateful she hadn't been born into royalty and had instead been born a fisherman's daughter. The courts played games that Iona didn't want to understand. They were cruel, and there was an obvious lack of love in those circles, the crown merely a competition they were all vying for. It seemed like it could grow old really fast.

No, thanks.

As she buried herself in her thoughts and the warmth of the two she cared about above all others in this place, her thoughts were suddenly scattered as her familiar lifted his head and began to growl.

Julius was instantly alert, his body tensing as he turned in the direction her familiar was growling at. He was staring beyond the copse of frozen trees and in the darkness beyond.

A feeling of unease slithered down her spine like a snake as she stared into the darkness as well, her ears twitching as she fought to catch the slightest sounds that didn't belong.

But she couldn't hear anything.

"Strange," Julius voiced her own thoughts on a perilous whisper. His eyes narrowed, and her familiar kept rumbling.

Then, there in the darkness, Iona caught the glean of something shining.

Like ice.

Like a blade.

Julius pulled her to her feet. She could feel the tension in his body, and he kept one hand against her familiar as if to calm him, and his other hand wrapped tightly against Iona's.

She was aware of the way he slowly pried his hand away from hers. Of the way his hands went to the sword that was still tethered at his hip. The slide of the blade against the sheath was loud, but not loud enough to be heard above the shrieking wind. It made Iona nervous.

Adrenaline pumped through her blood and pounded through her ears. She willed her magic out to her hand and a sword formed. But as she formed it, there was a dull pulsing rushing through her temples.

She tilted her chin up and sniffed the air. Ice and snow, and something else. Something that felt strongly of magic and metal.

And beneath that, something she recognized and always would until the end of her days.

The wind carried the smoke towards her, and it stung her eyes, making them water.

"Ashwood," she whispered, dread tightening her gut.

Julius let out a low curse. "We have to run."

Iona couldn't find it in her to move.

Her mind was betraying her once again, yanking her back to the place on the beach, with the sun and darkening clouds, with the taste of ashwood prominent and heavy on her tongue.

Her body trembled as memories assaulted through her mind, and she felt like she was reliving them.

"Iona!" Julius' voice snapped her out of her reverie.

She turned to look at him and the grave lines of his features.

"We have to run and warn them," he growled. "We have to *run*."

Her limbs unstuck, so many emotions storming through her. But she didn't waste another moment as the three of them turned...

...and ran.

It had taken hours to care for all the injured of the camp. By the time they'd gotten everyone settled, well rested, and healed without the aid of Ryker's magic, both Shula and Ryker were exhausted. Still, they'd made their way down to the foyer of Castle Aileach instead of slinking to their room to rest.

Their hands were firmly clasped together, Ryker's thumb tracing circles against the top of Shula's. He didn't release her, even as they made their way over to the bar and ordered their tankards full of Fae wine before they made their way to sit before the hearth.

They were pressed tightly together, their thighs and shoulders touching. It was the closest Shula had ever felt to her mate, which was ridiculous considering he'd been inside her not long ago. But holding hands, sitting in the quiet, seemed much more intimate somehow.

After taking a sip of her wine, she angled her body towards him. "How are you feeling?"

He grunted in response, and she could read it as easily as if he'd said, "Fine."

She took another swallow, and the buzz of wine combined with the magical element of the drink flowed through her system, making her tongue feel heavy and her words loose.

"I want cake," she blurted, feeling her stomach cramp with hunger. It'd been hours since they'd last eaten, and it had been on dried bread and a few bites of jerky on the road. "I miss kabobs," she said again. "I hope wherever the next Elemental is, they sell kabobs there."

Ryker chuckled, the sound foreign and endearing. "Do you still have the map?"

She guarded it like a precious treasure along with the six stones. She knew the stones were unnecessary, but they felt symbolic somehow. Like the weight of them in her pants pocket connected her to the Fae they still had yet to find.

Pulling it out, she smoothed over the edges of the parchment, staring down at the map of Illyk. Her eyes trailed down to the Ley Line, over it to Tir na Faie.

The land covered in iron, whose beauty she would never see.

Her fingers traced over the symbols of the courts.

She could feel Ryker observing her face, the way she took her bottom lip between her teeth as she stared at the different places. One of those should have been her rightful birthplace, but because of the war, she'd been born in Orknie, her parents ushered into reservations that were supposed to keep the Fae happily contained. Where they were supposed to live peacefully with their own kind and their culture intact.

How wrong it had been.

"I'm from the Crimson Court," Ryker supplied, his finger pointing at a spot on the map just below the Ley Line. "Mairin and I were born there and lived there our whole lives." His voice was gruff and thick with emotion.

"What was it like?"

"There was a mixture of races who all lived there. Since we were so close to the border that separates Tir na Faie and Orknie, humans were always trading goods with the Fae there. All courts are special, I suppose, and each court's name suggests what you will find there. The Crimson Court was the court of healers and blood letters. The streets were paved with red gems, and when the sun reflected off of it, it looked like the entire city was bathed in perpetual sunset."

"And the other courts?"

"The Jade Court, where Iona is from, had glittering green oceans and were ripe with fruits and vegetation. The Gold Court, that's where Weylyn is from, I think, they were miners and mined the gems for the king. The Sapphire Court, that's where Clay is from originally, is famous for Nach es Forest; the trees and leaves are blue, and the sap bleeds green and tastes like wine. The Obsidian Court, where Uric is from, is full of permanent darkness and shining stars. They reside in the dark and so they are the dark, according to them, anyway. The Seelie Court is the one that keeps the rest of the courts together.

"Every court has a High Lord, yet there can only be one king, and that is King Ashera. He resides over all of these courts."

"And the Unseelie?" Her finger pointed further south, past the Obsidian Court where the Unseelie Court lay in the corner of the map like a forgotten specter. "And Nymph Island?" She pointed to the island in the Black Waters, where she imagined more Unseelie lived.

"That is beyond King Ashera's jurisdiction. The Unseelie are ruled by their own cruel king."

Her fingers grazed the edges of that territory again. "He is confined to so little space, while the Seelie Courts take up most of Tir na Faie."

Ryker shrugged a shoulder. "That is how it has been since as long as I can remember. There has always been unrest between the Seelie and the Unseelie. Even a war with the humans has not changed that. They always used to fight over territories, until King Ashera pushed the Unseelie King back to the south. It is also why the Unseelie did not come to the Seelie King's aid when the humans invaded, even if we are all trapped beneath the emperor's tyranny."

She tried to imagine a world where the Fae didn't help each other and was surprised at the vivid image her mind conjured up. It wasn't a difficult feat. Just because they were fighting on the same side did not make all Fae inherently good, just like not all humans were evil. If the Unseelie had abandoned the Seelie, even while their own Fae residing further north had been captured, what did that say about the Unseelie King?

"What happened to the Unseelie in the war?" she asked.

"We don't know. They did not come to our aid, and they did not fight the humans either, despite their own being captured in the war. You saw the state of Tir na Faie. My only guess is that the iron expanded and killed the Unseelie, scattering the king's court."

It made sense. The iron had been too heavily planted in the ground. Being in there for hours had made Uric vomit blood. They'd nearly *died.*

She couldn't imagine what a lifetime of iron could to do a Fae.

Carefully, she folded the paper back up and put it in her pocket.

"Not going to take a peek at where the next Fae is?" Ryker inquired.

"Not without Iona."

It felt like something they had to do together. A sort of ritual that could help the two of them bond. It was probably ridiculous, Shula thought, but she wanted to do this with someone else who understood what it was to be an Elemental. The importance of their existence wasn't something they could rightly ignore.

She'd been normal before, hadn't thought herself special. On the contrary, a part of her loathed what she was if only because it spelled imminent death, should anyone find out. And while the death part of that was still true, she no longer felt that same burning hatred, that painful ache in her chest that reminded her she was supposed to be uncomfortable in her own skin.

Now she felt strong. Now, she knew her worth as an Elemental, as a Fae, and more importantly, as herself.

It was Iona who had made her realize it.

"You look different," Ryker commented, his voice low. It rolled over her like the slow slide of melted chocolate, the kind that tasted like lust and a stronger, darker emotion.

Shula's head tilted in his direction, her eyebrows raising. Her fingers pushed a long lock of hair behind her ear. "Do I?"

"Hmm..."

She knew what he meant. The past few hours had changed so much inside her that she *felt* different about herself. "I guess I don't feel so... worthless anymore."

Ryker's expression darkened into a frown that pulled at the scars on his face, making him look grave. "You were never worthless."

The words warmed her more than the Fae wine did. She found herself leaning towards him and kissing a scarred cheek. When she pulled away, his expression had smoothed out a fraction.

"It's a hard feeling to describe," she said, bringing the tankard to her lips for another sip. She swallowed the last of the drink and bent to set the cup on the ground.

"Is it the wine?" He eyed her warily, which made her bark out a soft laugh. She remembered the first time she'd tried Fae wine, how off-kilter she'd felt around Ryker. It hadn't been the first time he'd made emotions rise in her, and she was sure it wouldn't be the last. But that particular time was burned in her memory.

"No. I just feel... better?" She shrugged, unsure how to describe it. "About everything. About me." She paused, tilted her head slightly. "About us."

Ryker threw the tankard back, downing the rest of the contents before dropping the cup. His hands snaked around her waist, and then he was pulling her closer.

Her entire body warmed.

They were always careful around each other, treating each other like broken pieces, edging past the invisible line they'd both drawn around the other. Their touches were always demure, almost shy and *contained.* Like he was afraid, not to break her, but of breaking himself by caring with her.

He placed her so she was straddling his lap, and her fingers reached up to trace the contours of his scars. They went over the pulled flesh of his cheekbones, over his nose, and stopped shy on his lips.

Her whole body buzzed in a way that had nothing to do with the wine. It was all Ryker Valda. Touching him made her feel this energy that threatened to burst her chest into thousands of little pieces. Like he was somehow breaking her apart and putting her together again with the simple brush of his fingertips, and she was addicted to the destructive force they made.

They were a bomb, the seconds counting down until they ignited and caused chaos.

His eyes flashed, and she wondered if he could feel her thoughts down the bond they shared.

His fingers lifted and shoved aside her long hair, pushing it behind her shoulders so it didn't curtain her face. Ryker let his thumb graze across her cheekbone, over her nose, down to her lips. Just like she'd done to him.

Her breath caught in her throat at the intimacy that pulsed between them.

She wasn't sure who moved first. Maybe they moved at the same time, because a moment later they met in the middle, their lips fusing together, their bodies burning, igniting with a mix of magic and something so much more primal.

Their cheeks kissed, his beard and scars scraping along her skin. He groaned into her mouth, his hands spanning against her waist.

It came to a stop all too soon as he pulled away. His breaths were heavy, his eyes hooded with desire.

"We're a bomb," Shula voiced, the words panting from her lips.

Ryker opened his mouth to reply, but words never came.

But chaos *did.*

Boom!

The entire castle shook, rocked by an explosion. Stone crumbled from the ceiling to the ground, and part of Caste Aileach caved in.

The resonance of the destruction echoed in Shula's ears. Her body swayed, and the only thing keeping her upright were Ryker's hands, pulling her to his chest, where she felt the rhythm of his rapidly beating heart.

Rock and dust rained down against her head, and her ears rang loudly. The quiet after the chaos settled, and in it Shula felt like she couldn't breathe, like she couldn't catch her breath.

Ryker's hand engulfed her cheek, shoving away her hair.

"Are you alright?"

She wasn't sure how to answer that, and she wasn't sure Ryker was expecting an answer anyway. His eyes assessed her quickly, and then he was lifting, pushing them both to their feet. Her legs wobbled, but Ryker's firm hold kept her from falling.

She swept her gaze around, her breaths wheezing out of her as she observed the destruction. Brick of the castle had smashed through, crushing Fae beneath their heavy weight. She could make out feet, hands, *blood.*

Bile shot to her throat and she forced it back.

"What—"

A moment later Iona, Julius, and Iona's familiar were bursting through the caved-in part of the castle, panting. Their eyes barely registered the destruction and death, but they caught Shula and Ryker.

"We have to go now!" Julius shouted.

"What the fuck is going on?" Ryker growled, his voice barely concealing his confusion.

"Humans," Iona panted. "They've found Castle Aileach."

Shula felt like the ground had fallen from beneath her and she was suspended through nothingness, going at dizzying speed.

"No." She felt the word leave her lips but didn't register it until Iona's eyes found hers, the sadness in them undeniable.

"They're here," she said firmly. "And we have to leave before it's too late."

Uric's back ached.

Not surprisingly, since he had just taken the whipping of a lifetime from King Ashera. The wounds inflicted to him by the cruel monarch was nothing compared to the pain his own family had put him through as a child.

He had trained for things like this. But he had not been prepared for how different the magical whip the king had conjured would be in comparison to what his father had used. It was raw power flaying through his skin.

He had not cried out, though, and perhaps his father could be proud of him for that much at least.

Had his father not been fucking dead.

He realized his thoughts were taking a dark turn for someone who was currently getting his cock sucked.

The skin of his back stuck to his tunic and jacket. Blood seeped through the material; that, combined with the fact that he was pressed up tightly against a stone wall had him gritting his teeth tightly. It had nothing to do with the Unseelie male who was currently on his knees before him, worshiping his cock like it was some holy gift from Mana.

The sucking slurps that echoed through the stone room irritated Uric more than they turned him on. Still, his cock was hard, and he needed that friction of release.

So he pushed past the pain and gripped the long black hair of the Fae man in his hands, pushing it aside enough to see the tips of his pointed ears, but not enough to see the features of his face.

The face he did not care about. Because if he looked at it, he would know it was not the male he truly wanted.

Tonight, he did not want to feel any more pathetic than necessary.

He gripped the male's hair tightly in his fist and began pumping into his mouth until his dick hollowed into the back of the Fae's throat. He set a punishing, unrelenting pace, his anger bubbling over in this moment as he pictured imparting this cruelly onto someone else.

Onto the fucking Seelie Prince.

"Bastard," Uric groaned, dropping his head back against the wall, his hips never stopping their punishing force. He did not particularly care that he was all but choking the other Fae or enjoying the moans of pleasure that came from his throat. He ignored that. He ignored everything but his own fury and humiliation as he took it upon himself to give those useless emotions to someone else.

Here he did not worry about his back hurting. Here he could block away the pain in favor of something else.

His fingers caressed the silk strands of dark hair, pulling in a demanding tight-fisted grip and began shoving his cock down the man's throat, faster and faster until he felt himself reach his release.

Uric groaned and shoved the Unseelie away, turning so he did not have to watch him clean Uric's cum from his mouth or smile at him as if what they just did was going anywhere else. Or, Mana forbid, he thought Uric would reciprocate pleasure.

A selfish lover, Uric had always been. He did not particularly care that it made him look cruel or like a bastard. He relished in the image. Let them all think what they wanted.

He was familiar enough with the courts and observing people to know they did it anyway.

Once the Fae stood to his feet, he made the mistake of reaching for Uric. Uric dodged his hold, a blade appearing in his fingers and pressing to the man's throat before he could even blink. It had become instinct now. To threaten others with the edge of a weapon.

"Get out," Uric ordered. "And do not ever presume to touch me without my permission again, lest you lose your hand."

The Unseelie blinked, then smirked a wicked smile. Uric ignored it and began undressing, toeing off his boots. All the while, he was alert, gaze watching the Unseelie slowly walk towards the door. When he left, Uric felt his body sag with relief, though a bit of tension remained as he took off the rest of his clothes.

Taking off his tunic felt like he was ripping the skin at his back all over again. He bore through it, clenching his teeth until it was done, and then doing it again as he slipped on fresh clothing and bent to lace up his boots.

It was an easy thing, to compartmentalize the pain and suffering. Even easier not to ask Ryker for help like Valerio had all but ordered him to do. He was smarter than that. To give his bare back to someone he did not entirely trust.

Yes, Ryker was a trustworthy Fae, but Uric did not trust anyone. That was one thing he had learned from the High Lord of the Obsidian Court, at least. To never trust.

Yet Uric trusted Valerio.

More the fool, him.

He stood to his full height and began stretching. He would heal within a few days, and he would have no need for the healer to look him over. He could care for his own wounds well enough. He did not need the prince looking after him. He did not need him to pretend like he cared.

He certainly did not need him telling Uric all the ways they could never be, because he was awaiting a mate that might never show up for decades yet.

If he wanted to spend the rest of his days pining after someone who might not even exist, then he had every right to do so. Royals always did whatever the fuck they wanted anyway, without regards to who or what destruction they left in their wake.

His back was proof enough of that.

So was the ache in his chest that Uric refused to acknowledge.

Uric needed a fucking drink.

He made his way towards the door, knowing full well that Julius was likely monopolizing all the Fae wine for himself like it was some addiction. Fucking bastard. Uric was very much on edge and predicted he would be pulling his knife on the other male over a single tankard soon enough.

The thought almost made him chuckle...

But then everything around him exploded.

He wobbled on his feet as the castle shook around him. His head rattled, and old stone crumbled into soft debris that rained down over his head.

His body moved on instinct, summoning his magic until a portal opened in front of him. The toll it took on his already weakened body made his bones creak like an old door. His smooth skin wrinkled, his fingers bent, and it was a challenge just to step to the other side and come face to face with Prince Valerio.

The prince's eyes were wide. "We are under attack," he breathed.

Despite what had happened, Uric wanted to take his friend's hand and offer a modicum of comfort, but he kept his arms pressed tightly to his side. He hated how they were under attack and his mind was still wandering on things they should not have been.

Like how easily it was to fall back into place at Valerio's side.

As if nothing had happened after all.

"We need to find the others," Valerio commanded. "Quickly."

Uric nodded and opened another portal.

"Beautiful, beautiful Flora." Clay's hands caressed the side of the female's pink cheek. It elicited a giggle that made her skin glow with bright luminescence, lighting up the dingey halls of the damp and broken castle.

"Yes, Clay?" She smiled up at him like he was a gift from Mana, and he bit the inside of his cheek to avoid laughing at the thought.

It hadn't taken much convincing on his part, after Julius had nearly ruined his chances at bedding the female. A few smiles here, a few delicate touches there, the right words, and she was ripe for the taking.

"I had such a beautiful time." He pushed aside a lock of suddenly glowing hair as she beamed at the praise and threw her arms around his neck, smooshing her body to his.

He let her hold him and held her back with a delicate press of his own arms.

Every touch and smile was genuine because Clay Valentino fucking loved women. He believed in treating them like actual people, not just as holes he could sink his cock into. To treat them like they should be seen and heard, because that's what they were. They were fascinating, beautiful creatures. He didn't think anyone could ever truly understand the love he had for them.

That he didn't just say lines to get them into his bed. He was genuinely interested in them, in their thoughts, their minds. And he liked to think they appreciated being seen by him as well.

"I wish I could spend the night," she whispered in his ear.

He pushed her gently away, lightly enough to pry her body off his, but not quick or hard enough to offend her with the gesture.

"I know," he replied, pressing a kiss to the corner of her mouth. "But I am nothing if not honest, and you know I cannot sleep beside anyone."

She pouted. "I know, I know. It's just... I had a wonderful time as well."

Of course, she had.

Clay had made sure of it.

He always made sure the females in his company enjoyed themselves. Whether it be with his face buried between their thighs or when they wanted something *deeper*. Like conversation over a tankard of ale or a cup of tea. Whatever they wanted, he was happy to oblige.

"I am afraid this is where we must part, my dear." He tilted her chin up with his fingers and saw the awe and happiness shining there. "Goodbye."

"Farewell."

He watched her hips sway as she left, biting his bottom lip until she disappeared around the corner. When she did, he turned the other way and began walking, a tune humming past his lips. As he rounded the corner, he froze as he spotted something curious then ducked back around the corner to peek over the side of the wall.

Weylyn was obscured in the shadows, though Clay could just make out the glittering gold of his eyes in the dark, bright like a cat's. His voice whispered, too low for Clay to make out the words.

Before him, there were Unseelie Fae. One of them, a pixie, fluttering above his head as if offering illumination. The other Clay recognized immediately as Veles Riel, a purple-skinned half-breed High Fae in King Ashera's court.

It was not odd to see them together, as Weylyn was the king's lackey. It was suspicious, however, to see them both whispering about in the dark. Clay wondered if it was some sort of message from the king and strained to hear, yet he could no longer make out any words.

He dared another glance back, but when he did, the two Unseelie were no longer there. But Weylyn was, and his golden gaze was focused brightly on Clay.

He stepped out from the shadows, the rings on his fingers glittering as much as his eerie eyes. "Eavesdropping?" His deep voice pooled against stone.

Clay didn't feel a need to hide anymore, so he stepped out to face Weylyn fully. "Of course not. I was on my way down when I saw you. I did not wish to interrupt."

Weylyn's gaze flicked over Clay and Clay recognized the look. It was the look of someone gauging how much of a threat their opponent was. It was positively predatory and filled Clay with a sense of unease.

Finally, Weylyn's lips twisted into that familiar smile. "Of course," he said. "Shall I accompany you?"

Clay didn't really want to be anywhere near the Fae, but it was impolite to reject him. If he were Ryker, he would have growled at him to fuck off, but Ryker was a barbarian even on his better days. Clay had been raised with propriety, and that meant dealing with people he didn't particularly enjoy.

"Sure," he said, walking. He was careful not to give Weylyn his back, though, and walked side-by-side. They went in silence down the hallways. Voices echoed across stone, coming from the long line of rooms on either side of them.

A door to Clay's right opened and an Unseelie Fae stepped through. He stuttered to a stop, his eyes taking in Clay. A moment later, he bowed low.

Clay felt himself chuckling in amusement. "I am merely a High Lord. I am not the king. You may stand, Fae."

The Fae stood and something in his eyes flashed. He opened his mouth to speak, but the words never came out.

Because a second later, the castle was ripped apart as a gargantuan rock plummeted through the side, squashing the Unseelie beneath the boulder. Bones cracked and blood sprayed, and Clay could taste it in his mouth.

Then the rock was falling, tearing down with it a portion of the castle, leaving a gaping hole in the side. Clay felt his feet slip against crushed stone, and then he felt himself falling a moment before an arm snaked around his waist and pulled him back to hug the wall.

"Fuck," he cursed, looking down at the rock and snow below. "That would have been such a shitty way to go." He turned a smile he didn't quite feel towards Weylyn, only to find the other male's eyes rolled to the back of his head. "Great," Clay said. Because that was exactly what he needed right then. "Please don't fucking fall."

Weylyn blinked a second later and turned to look at Clay. "The humans," he explained. "They are invading."

Fallen King

Another boulder caved in the ceiling. Enormous chunks of broken brick rained down. Iona was barely able to cocoon them within a wall of ice before it hit against the surface layer of their protection. A moment later it crumbled, ice and snow dropping beneath their feet.

The whole front side of the castle had been destroyed, its remains squashing the inhabitants. The scent of blood and broken bone was strong, but not more prominent than the burning scent of ashwood, and the snow and wind drifted into their nostrils.

The humans had marched closer, and in the darkness there was the brightness of flame as their iron ovens burned bits of the poisonous plant and sent smoke billowing across the sky.

Iona's throat closed up, and she was already feeling the dizzying effects of it, and so were her friends.

"We have to do something!" Julius' shout was cut off as he went into a coughing fit, staining blood against his pale palm.

Another boom ricocheted across the mountain, a boulder hitting another side of the castle. They staggered from the force of the explosion, Iona falling against her familiar's side. Shula let out a cry as her feet slipped beneath her, regaining her footing with a few quick twists of her feet.

Rocks pelted against Iona's head from above, and her gaze sailed upwards to see the night sky blackening against wind and smoke, blocking out the sight of the stars.

"We're almost out of time," Ryker growled.

In the ensuing chaos, Iona's mind wandered. It didn't go down the dark path of her past, but through different emotions that threatened to meld together in a maelstrom through her mind. Her eyes squeezed closed, her heart raced, and panic threatened to settle deep in the roots of herself.

Mana, please, she felt herself praying. *Help us.*

She waited for a reply with bated breath, but none ever came. No sign, no sensation of raw magic zinging down her spine to let her know that Mana was listening.

Because Mana had never been there.

But... maybe that wasn't quite *right.*

Mana was in all things, both living and intangible. It was the magic in a star streaking across the sky, in the elements, in a mother's love, in a Fae's wrath.

Maybe what Julius had said before was true, and Mana had been inside Iona all along.

In a funny little thing called hope.

Iona's eyes opened and she straightened, renewed vigor pumping through her blood and pushing away the panic in a forceful shove.

"Shula..." Her voice came out as a broken shout. Blood dripped down her chin as she spoke, but it didn't drown out the fury of the magic inside her soul.

The fire Fae's panicked gaze cut to Iona, and she must have seen something in her eyes because she staggered towards her, the embers of her depths burning with her emotions.

"What do we do?" she asked. Her lips were cracked and bleeding, her eyes a wildfire.

"We're the only ones who can protect the castle."

If they'd been able to melt iron and harden themselves against it, then why should ashwood be any different?

Their hands met in the middle, fingers interlacing. A surge of magic siphoned against their fingertips and their eyes held. There was fear in her friend's eyes, but there was fear in Iona's too. And maybe, just maybe, it wouldn't be so bad when they were together.

Shula's fingers tightened. "Lead the way."

Iona began leading her outside. Broken bits of brick crumbled as they stepped past the entryway of the stronghold now in pieces, their hands tightly clasped, their magic humming together. Their feet pushed against the snow as they stepped out into the fray. Into the chaos of metal armor clanking, of screaming winds blowing ash and snow against their skin.

It took Iona back to when sand billowed just the same way the ash did.

She'd been petrified then.

So petrified that she'd allowed herself to be ushered into hiding with the women and children. Where she'd sat in a corner, her fingers clasped tightly between the spaces of her sister's.

Things were different now. She was no longer the same frightened female she'd been a hundred years ago. And in her hand, she no longer held her sister's, but a friend's.

Then, she'd given strength to Malika, even as she trembled herself and tears burned behind her eyelids. Now, she stood tall in the face of a situation she was intimately familiar with, one branded deeply inside of her.

The ashwood in the wind burned against her skin. The two Fae shivered against it but started forward anyway.

"Where are you going?"

Iona heard the voice shouting at her like it was a distant memory, one that fogged around the edges and she couldn't quite grasp. It was like reaching with phantom fingertips or hearing garbled voices from beneath the water.

It was something far away, too far to comprehend when all that was within her grasp and focus was the marching feet that rumbled across the pillowy earth.

Catapults lined the front of them like pawns in a chess game, releasing boulders straight in their direction.

Iona reacted on instinct. Her hands raised and ice rose from the ground and collided against the boulder, stopping its trajectory. Ice and rock shattered into pieces, but where one was released, another emerged, and soon, the castle was covered in the percussive sounds of whistling winds, ice colliding against rock, the reverberations of metal armor, and the pounding of Iona's heart. Blood dripped against her lips as it slid down her nose.

It tasted sharp like magic and fear that weren't solely Iona's.

The roaring of fire soon followed. A line of orange and green flames streaked across the ground, cutting a line through snow and earth. It separated them, the edges of the flames licking the humans and their weapons until they were engulfed and the fire reached to the sky. Their magic touched, a collision of raw, unmitigated power that exploded across the darkness to let the humans know one thing.

That they weren't weak.

That they had hope.

"Never thought I'd die like this." Clay's fingers grasped at the wall behind him, nails chipping the already crumbling structure even further. His feet were balanced precariously against the ledge, toes hanging over the edge. A single movement would send him toppling over to his death. His body would be greeted by the debris below, his every bone would splinter into thousands of pieces until he was an unrecognizable mass of flesh and blood.

He cringed to think of the wounds Ryker would try to heal.

If Ryker was even alive right then.

Maybe his friend had found himself in a similar situation as Clay and Weylyn currently. The whole side of this castle had caved in, and they were stuck balancing on the edge of what had once been the hallway, their backs pressed tightly to the wall. There was nowhere to go, as everything had disintegrated on either side of them.

They were well and truly fucked.

"We are not dead yet," Weylyn purred.

Clay wanted to turn sharply to the Fae at his side, but the only thing keeping him from doing that was that the brisk movement would cause him to plummet to his demise. But he swore he heard the hint of fucking delight in the bastard's voice, and he knew if he looked at his expression, he'd find his eyes glowing brightly.

As if anything about this was fucking amusing.

"Key word being 'yet'," Clay spat. His eyes kept darting downwards, and it threw him completely off balance.

"Do not look down."

"Great fucking advice, Weylyn."

"I am being helpful."

"It would be even more helpful if you found a way to get us out of this mess." His eyes flicked on the horizon, his stomach sinking, and not just because of what he found marching from the trees; rather, *how many.*

Well and truly fucked, he thought.

Weylyn snorted. "What manner of fool do you take me for?"

Clay bit his tongue instead of replying to that. If only because what he had to say wasn't anything pleasant, and he didn't appeal to the thought of bearing the brunt of Weylyn's anger or mischief.

Instead, he focused his gaze across the horizon and winced, his nails grasping frantically at the wall, when another boulder hit the opposite side of the castle, rattling it from its roots. It made Clay's stomach tighten with nausea. When the feeling finally subsided and a new scent hit his nostrils, he almost choked.

"Ashwood..." The word scraped from his throat, caught, and when he coughed, he felt the slightest tang of blood in his mouth. "Great. Just what we needed."

"Silence," Weylyn growled.

"How the fuck are we getting out of this?" His eyes had already darted around the moment he'd found them in this position. There was nothing to help them, nowhere to go. The beam above their heads jutted out, and Clay wasn't sure he could reach it without falling, and he wasn't sure if it was even fucking safe anyway.

"Silence," Weylyn repeated.

"Fuck you, asshole," Clay snarled. "I am so sick of your shit."

"Will you be silent and *listen*?" The harsh tone of his voice had Clay shutting up instantly.

He'd never heard the cadence of that particular tone. So he tilted his head a fraction to the side, and that's when he heard it.

Meow.

Clay's head jerked up in the direction of the single beam overhead. Balanced along the edge sat a little black beast with wide, almost demonic eyes.

It stared at Clay and whined, *meow.*

Clay's head thunked against the wall. "How are we supposed to get ourselves out of here alive *and* help Ryker's familiar in the process?"

"You are the one with the clever ideas."

"Now is not the time to display this sarcastic side of you, asshole."

"It is a lucky thing, then, that I have the powers that I do."

"What the fuck are you talking about?" This time Clay did turn to look at Weylyn and nearly lost his foothold doing so, only to catch that grin of his marring his face. Bastard.

"It means I am not so foolish to leave the future of my existence in the hands of a Fae man from the Sapphire Court who has an irrational fear of heights."

"You'd be scared too if you looked down and saw all those fucking rocks down there." Clay's hairs prickled with offense at Weylyn's comment. "Shit, at least I got to bury myself between someone's thighs before I die."

Weylyn hummed a sound that was amusement and rancor both.

"Fuck off, Weylyn."

"If I did that, then who would save us?"

Meow, meow.

"Surely not you with that useless blood magic of yours?"

Clay's jaw clenched. "It won't be so useless when I make you squirt blood from your asshole, will it?"

Weylyn chuckled, and the sound was so startling, Clay found himself nearly slipping. His fingers cracked and bled, but he felt his momentum pushing him forward. He cried out, bent his legs and made a leap.

His legs flailed. His fingers brushed along the edge of the beam and missed. His heart caught in his throat, and he knew this was the end. Even as Ryker's familiar made a swipe for his hands with her claws, like she meant to hang to him for dear life so he wouldn't fall.

But it was too late.

Clay didn't even get a chance to scream as he hurtled towards his death.

The portal opened to hover over empty space.

Uric's hand shot out, colliding against Prince Valerio's chest before he stepped out and fell to his death. The move had been instinctive, protecting him so. It grated on Uric's nerves to be so weak as to protect the man that had obliterated his heart.

Yet did it he did.

And he pushed the prince back just in time as a figure came hurtling in their direction.

Normally it took a lot of energy and concentration to keep a portal open. With his back screaming, with his body weak and broken, it took a lot within him not to shutter it closed but reach out and grasp at the figure as he came colliding against his chest.

Their arms grasped for one another, and Uric felt a muscle pull as he was hauled down, his feet slipping. But he was yanked from behind, hanging halfway out of the portal, holding onto Clay while Prince Valerio held onto him.

He gritted his teeth, his back burning as if he were being torn open all over again. An involuntary cry pierced past his lips as he used every ounce of strength he had left within him to haul Clay up by the arm and into the portal, on the other side, where solid ground lay.

Clay flopped inside on his belly, his mouth kissing the floor. "Thank fucking Mana." His whole body melted, his breath coming out in short pants. "Fuck, I thought I was going to die."

Uric echoed the sentiment, though not exactly from the attack but from the pain slicing down his spine. He barely managed to turn in time to see Weylyn make the same jump that Clay had with much more finesse. His fingers grabbed the beam and hung tightly before he made a noise that had Ryker's familiar prowling over to him and perching herself on his shoulders. He did not wince even as the beast stuck her claws into his body, and he wriggled his way closer to the portal, one hand in front of the other.

Weylyn did not ask for help and Uric did not offer it. He watched as Weylyn swung his legs with ease and moved to the side in time so the Fae could land on the other side.

Uric's control faltered, and he closed the portal. Already, he could feel his skin shriveling even further, wisps of hair gliding down his shoulders like a fish cutting through water. His vision blurred a fraction, and he wanted to scream.

He despised the weakness his magic left him with. His vanity took a blow, and even worse that everyone was witness to it. The only way he could pretend it did not bother him at all was acting like it did not.

"We got your message," Valerio declared while Weylyn smoothed out the front of his shirt. The cat still perched on his shoulder and did not move, as if she belonged there and not by Ryker.

"I would assume that was the case, otherwise you'd not be here at all," Weylyn pointed out dryly.

Uric's weak, bent fingers closed into his palms, and he gritted his teeth at the tone. Defiant, as if the Prince of the Seelie were beneath him, a mere lackey for the king. The insolence in one so insignificant was astounding.

Valerio, having more experience with the Fae's comments, did not take it as personally as Uric did, and merely turned away. Uric wanted to do the same, but he found himself captivated by Weylyn's gaze and the smirk he wore just below it.

Like he was intimate every thought within Uric's head.

"We have to find the others," Valerio snapped. "And then we will find my father. Uric—" His prince turned to him, a pleading in his eyes that had not been there before. "Can you open another portal?" His gaze slid over the wrinkled imperfections marring Uric's skin.

Uric wanted to cringe away from the stare. Fae were not meant to be this, as fragile-looking as a human. They were proud and beautiful, not blights or marred flesh or weak hands and knees.

As it were, Uric was too weak. His magic barely flared to life within his chest. He should refuse. He *wanted* to just to spite his friend and reeled back the thoughts because there were more important things at stake.

Later, he would let the prince suffer for all he had done and said. Later, he would spite him in the cruelest of ways.

For now, Uric found himself too weak to resist as he closed his eyes and opened another portal.

Shula fell to her knees in the snow, a cry ripping from her throat. Try as she might, she couldn't keep the weakness at bay. It consumed her as surely as her own fire consumed the humans. Yet her magic still sputtered to a stop and her throat closed up as the tinge of ashwood in the air invaded her orifices and started to cripple her.

She was no match for this.

She'd melted iron before, but this seemed even worse than other times because the humans were relentless in their pursuit.

And they were closing in on them.

Fear slid through her body along with the sharp pricks of cold. She couldn't move, couldn't fight back. She dropped to all fours, taking in heaving breaths. Blood spit from her nostrils and mouth, staining the snow.

It felt like an omen.

Iona's ice still battered against their iron, shattering beneath the steel weapons. She wanted to fight, refused to give up, even as her movements became more sluggish. As her feet tripped and she fell forward. She got up every time until she couldn't.

Then, Julius was next to her, pulling her into his arms and running back into the destroyed remnants of the castle.

Soon Shula felt arms wrap around her waist as well and haul her upright. Familiar hands pressed into her stomach as she was pulled backwards. The titillating press of magic warmed her veins, and she groaned against her mate, feebly pushing his hands away.

"Don't," she warned. But it was too late. Energy filled her while at the same time depleted from him. He sagged, his legs wobbled as he walked her backwards. When he stopped, Shula stood, turning and wiping the blood from her face as she went.

Ryker's face looked haggard, and she glared in the face of his pain.

"It's useless," Julius said breathlessly. "We can't fight them. There are too many."

Iona growled her displeasure at the words, her body unable to do more than grasp weakly at her mate.

"We have nowhere to go," Shula argued. Not with death right across the line and gaining on them by the foot.

"The tunnels..." Iona whispered.

"What tunnels?"

Another catapult hitting the castle cut off Julius' reply. This time, Shula lost her footing from the impact. She fell forward, throwing her palms out to stop he collision against the floor. Instead of hitting the ground like she predicted, a silver mirror appeared before her. Her panicked reflection shone back. Then she was going through it and landing solidly against the waist of the Fae walking out.

She looked up at the same time Prince Valerio looked down at her in that familiar grave expression she'd come to associate with him.

She hated the relief she felt sear through her chest, but it was there.

She dropped her forehead to his stomach for a brief reprieve, taking in a sharp breath before he was helping to pull her to her feet.

Shula stepped back as Valerio stepped out, followed by Weylyn and the cat on his shoulder, Clay, and a haggard-looking Uric, who had more creases on his face than the crumpled up map in her pocket.

Her relief at seeing them all, particularly Clay, had her launching forward and wrapping her arms around her friend.

"I was worried about you!" she cried into his neck.

Clay's arms wrapped around her waist and pulled her close. His breath pressed against her neck as he exhaled his own relief. "Thank Mana you're okay," he whispered. When he pulled away, the beautiful lines of his face were in a tight frown. "Fuck, Shula—"

"We have to go find my father and quickly," Valerio interrupted. He turned to Weylyn. "Contact him."

The Fae's eyes glittered before they rolled to the back of his head.

Shula felt a tug on her own mind as she was ripped from her own consciousness and sucked into the void.

"Father! Where are you?!" The echo of Valerio's voice was suspended over nothing and pulsing against everything at once. He could feel many bits of subconscious' flittering through the connection. It tethered them together, Weylyn's magic. All of them.

Why he'd allowed so many in at once, Valerio did not know.

But his father's voice cut through his question and instilled a coiling sensation low in his gut that he tried to fight off.

"What are you still doing here, boy? Take the Elementals and go, get to safety!"

The panic in his father's voice was evident, and it filled Valerio with an unease he was not accustomed to, for he had never heard that particular brand of urgency in the king's voice.

"Father, where are you?"

There was a long pause and magic in the empty space seemed to flicker in and out. And then, "I was hit."

Valerio felt his consciousness reel back from the revelation. To admit to even that... the king's injuries must have been severe.

He did not know how to feel about that. He did not know what he should feel, so his body decided for him. His stomach dropped in what felt like a pit even darker than the one he was currently in. His throat tightened, and the next words Valerio said felt like they were forced, ripped from somewhere in his chest.

"Tell me where you are. I will bring Ryker and—"

"Foolish boy," the king cut him off. His voice sounded weak, like it was flickering in and out. That did not bode well, and Valerio felt his eyes burn. "You know as well as I that we cannot be found together."

"We will not be," he said vehemently. "Father, tell me where you are!"

The panic was unexpected. It choked like a noose around the neck. He had never imagined any circumstance in which he would be in this situation. His father hurt; on the verge of death, he could not be sure.

Valerio had lost one parent. He thought he would not care if his father died, yet when faced with it, it felt like much too hard a concept to grasp. Like it did not quite belong within the confines of his mind.

It was something he could have never pictured, and even when it was there in the tone of his father's voice, he did not want to accept it.

The King of the Seelie Courts could not die.

Valerio would not let him.

"We would be caught together and killed. Our lineage severed," he continued, as if Valerio had not interrupted in the first place. Like he usually did. "Is that what you want, boy?"

It was in those words that Valerio knew how dire the situation truly was. It was in those words that Valerio realized he would not be saving the king, the leader of the Resistance.

His father.

"Your Majesty..."

"Nova, get my foolish son out of Tuath, and boy..." He paused, and Valerio wondered if he was contemplating what he was going to say. If this would be their final goodbye. If he would never say the words he had held in for the entirety of his life. "Find the Elementals, and this time, do what you are fucking told."

His voice drifted further away, and within one second and the next, Valerio was slammed back into his body. He sucked in a harsh breath, blinked open his eyes to find he was still in the castle. Debris till pelted their bodies. The humans were still approaching.

Everything was still moving.

So why did it feel like things within his mind had stood still?

"My prince, we must leave." The voice felt far away, but he would recognize it anywhere. The way it scratched against his throat like speaking hurt because of the toll of his magic.

Uric.

But not even his friend could break him out of his reverie. He took a staggering step forward, his whole world imploding in on itself. His father, a man he had hated his whole life, a man who probably had his own wife murdered, was dying.

And Valerio did not want him to.

"My father." He stepped forward. "I have to go to him." He found his path suddenly blocked, firm hands gripping him. He blinked and made out Weylyn's features.

"The king said we must leave."

Valerio stepped back from him and turned in a circle, looking for another way out. A way to find his father, to help him. He could not die, because the Resistance needed him. And, despite his hatred, despite anything else, Valerio needed him, too. He was not ready to face what was out there in a world without the King of Seelie. It meant ascension, and Valerio had proved before that he was not ready for such a task.

He took a step, and another, and another.

Then Uric was in front of him, blocking the way while he opened a portal at his side.

Valerio eyed it warily. "I am not going."

"My prince..."

Another crash, another boom.

"They're getting closer! We have to go, now!" Julius ushered his mate and her familiar through the portal. Ryker and Shula followed at a much slower pace, and still Valerio could not bring himself to move.

"We have to leave." There was an urgency to the rasp in Uric's voice, but the prince did not want to acknowledge it. He did not want to acknowledge anything beyond his own panic, his own hurt. He pushed at his friend's frail soldiers.

"Get out of my way."

He was surprisingly steady for a Fae who looked ready to keel over from his age and did not so much as budge. Valerio pushed him again.

"I have to save my father. I have to!" The hysteria in his voice rose. His eyes burned. His gut clenched. His fingers danced towards the sword at his side and unsheathed it, placing the tip against his friend's throat. "As your prince, I order you to step the fuck away and let me go to my father."

He saw the sadness reflected in Uric's eyes off the steel blade. He did not move, but he did place his gnarled fingers against Valerio's shoulders.

The compassion in his gaze nearly gutted the prince.

"Kill me if you must," he whispered, his throat bobbing against the tip of the blade. "But I will not watch you run to your death. My only job is protecting you with my life. If you wish to take that away, then so be it."

Valerio lowered the sword a fraction, his heart splintering, his mind a mess he did not understand.

"It is time to go," Weylyn said.

And before Valerio could protest, his arms were grabbed from both sides and he was being shoved into the portal.

Leaving his people, his father—the fallen king—behind.

King Regent

Valerio's knees hit the grass on the other side of the portal. He fell from the tight grace he usually kept himself trapped in, forehead kissing the earth, nails digging into the dirt. He did not scream or cry out, but his emotions felt like a storm roiling across the horizon.

Something they could all see coming but weren't exactly sure when it would hit. The grief, the anger, and everything else that accompanied a loss.

Iona should have known better to expect such a thing from someone as tightly composed as him. Not a moment later, he pushed himself to a standing position, his hard mask in place, his jaw tight, his hands clenched into fists.

Iona watched like it was a spectacle as he took a deep breath, smoothed his palms against his shirt, and turned to face them all.

Death had a way of hollowing a person out. It was what Iona felt when she'd discovered her sister's execution. She and the prince were clearly not made from the same cloth.

If anything, death had made his dark eyes more vivid. They looked dark brown, rather than black, and they danced with all the violent things he so obviously wanted to do.

His gaze swept across the line of them, taking in their current state of what was left of Castle Aileach.

Ryker slumped against the ground with Shula looming over him as he breathed in fresh air free of poison.

Clay and Weylyn stood off to the back; Clay worrying at his bottom lip, Weylyn's fingers stroking along the fur of the cat against his shoulders.

Julius held tightly to Iona against the ground, while her familiar leaned against them.

And Uric had fallen like a sack filled with potatoes straight to the ground. His hair fell from his shoulders like slices of ribbons, and he groaned but made no attempt to move.

Prince Valerio swallowed as he seemed to memorize their features. Haggard and broken down, hope and magic depleted.

His gaze came to a full stop on Weylyn. The golden Fae must have known what the prince was silently asking because he shook his head back and forth slowly, flicking his long braid over his shoulder and holding the end with his ringed fingers.

"I cannot," he said. "The connection was severed."

Iona was familiar enough with his magic to guess what that meant.

If there was no connection, then it likely meant the king was dead.

Emotions warred against Valerio's features, and everyone kept quiet, giving the monarch a chance to process everything that had happened.

"How did the humans find us?" he asked finally.

"They should not have," Clay whispered. "Castle Aileach was supposed to be safe."

"Nowhere is ever safe," Iona cut in. "Don't you understand that? It won't be. Not until we battle the humans and earn our freedom instead of hide in the shadows."

"Any hope we had of building an army has just been decimated," Clay whispered gravely. "Fighting them is impossible now."

Shula lifted her head. "Not impossible, just very, *very* difficult." Though Iona didn't think she sounded convinced.

The hope that had blossomed in her chest during that vicious battle was subdued within her.

She hadn't been fond of the king. He'd seemed cruel, vicious, yet it had still been Valerio's father. And all the people they'd just saved? Her heart ached for them. To be freed from one prison only to find themselves at the end of a blade, crushed beneath rocks.

Tears burned behind her eyelids and threatened to fall, but she held them back. There would be a time to mourn their losses, but it wasn't now.

Emotions swirled inside her and had her standing to her feet. She wobbled, her gait uneven as she went to Prince Valerio. When she was before him, she dropped to her knee and bowed her head.

There was magic in the gesture. Or maybe it was hope ringing to life again inside her despite everything. Like it was just a part of her now, something she didn't think could ever die.

"I am with you. I will fight for you, whatever you decide. My magic is yours." The words felt right. Like sliding broken pieces home where they belonged, and they clicked into place. "I will be your sword when your arm cannot carry your own. I will be the hope when yours has died out. I will be the magic when yours has depleted." She dared a glance up at him through silver lashes. "I am your warrior, my king."

Prince Valerio staggered back like the words were a physical blow that threatened to gut him. The truth often felt like that.

Iona would know.

"My king." Julius kneeled next, bowing his head beside Iona, burying the hilt of his sword in the earth. "I will follow you to the death."

One by one, the Fae kneeled before their new king.

Clay.

Ryker.

Shula.

Uric, grunting in pain, his limbs weak and gnarled like the roots of an old oak, kneeled as best as he could, looking up at Valerio through white lashes, dark gaze flashing. "My *king*," he whispered with reverence.

Weylyn... Weylyn cocked his head to the side, taking in the prince, the *king*, with curiosity. Like he was deciding if it was worth it or not to pledge his allegiance to him. They stared at one another, energy cackling between the space that separated the two. Eventually, Weylyn stepped forward and dropped to one knee, though he did not speak, and he did not bow his head.

It was as much subservience as Valerio would get from him.

There would be no coronation, no crown or ceremony to commemorate the new King of the Fae.

But there would be war.

There would be blood.

It would be Valerio picking up the broken pieces that had been left behind, trying to put together the scattered courts and armies meant to protect them.

This small group was all he had. It wasn't much; there were only eight of them plus two familiars, but it was *enough.*

It had to be.

Valerio visibly swallowed, his throat bobbing up and down. "I cannot be your king," he whispered, an echo of heartbreak slipping past his lips. "I cannot yet accept that my father is gone. Not without proof." He turned to Weylyn. "If you feel him with your magic, you will tell me. Until then..." He looked at the line of them. "I will be king regent, until we know for certain that my father is gone." He pivoted on his heel then and briskly walked away from them, heading towards a copse of trees and vanishing into the darkness.

Iona's ears strained.

He didn't go far, as she could still make out his footsteps in the darkness, and when his breathing grew heavy, she forced herself to her feet and turned away, as did everyone else.

Valerio needed a moment to collect himself, to come to terms with everything that happened. They would let him mourn in peace, and when he was ready, they would discuss what came next. They had to, despite how difficult it was. The mourning could wait; their sorrow at all that they had lost pushed to the backs of their minds to make way for other thoughts and other things.

Iona walked towards Shula, touching her arm. "Do you still have the map?"

Shula pulled it out of her pants pocket, unfurling the folded edges. "I do." Her eyes darted around. "Do you want to look for the next Elemental now?"

Iona shook her head as she took the map from the fire Fae's fingertips. "I want to know where we're at, first." What she didn't say was that an idea had begun forming in her mind, and she needed to confirm something.

"We're in Tuath," Shula said.

"How do you know?"

Shula gave her a pointed look. "I was with Piriguini's Traveling Circus, remember?" Her gaze did a sweep of the terrain. "I recognize certain places almost instantly. We are still in Tuath. The sky has more smog here than anywhere else because it's the kingdom with the highest number of iron camps. The earth here has blackened over time." Her foot nudged against the ground, scraping away the dried grass to reveal the dark earth underneath.

Iona found herself tucking away that information for later. "What would we do without you?"

Shula pressed her lips together like she was trying to avoid laughing. "Ask Uric where he deposited us?"

"Ha, ha, very funny, Azzarh. Now, show me what other tricks you have up your sleeve and tell me if you remember anything worthwhile about the kingdom of Tuath."

"Like what?" She didn't lean over the map like Iona rapaciously did, biting her bottom lip as she stared at the cities scattered around this kingdom. The capitol was nestled towards the east, closer to the Lagnh Sea.

Iona knew the emperor ruled over Illyk and that he'd given free reign over the kings of Illyk. Each one resided over a kingdom, each one implementing their own rules, all the while following the supreme law of the emperor.

The King of Teg had been a spoiled brat, focused on pulling riches into his own castle while ignoring the rest of the kingdom. It was why Porir had been awash with Fae that lived right under his nose, and why it'd been such an impoverished city to begin with.

She didn't know anything else about the rest of the kings or kingdoms, but maybe Shula did.

"In your travels, did you ever see soldiers?" Iona asked.

"All the time. They were everywhere."

"And their camps?"

Shula blinked. "I'm confused, I thought you knew about the camps."

"I know about the camps where they keep the Fae. I don't, however, know where the soldiers keep court."

Understanding dawned in Shula's eyes, along with a bit of wariness, but she still leaned over the map and pointed. "A couple of miles away from Seirz, where the King of Tuath holds court in his castle, there's a military camp."

"Keeps his soldiers close to protect him, huh?" Iona mused. Then she was folding the map back up. "Can I borrow this?" But she was already pocketing it, even as Shula was nodding, her head tilted a fraction to the side.

"What are you thinking?" Her arms crossed against her chest.

Iona didn't know what to tell her. She didn't want to be dishonest with her companions ever again, much less with someone she was considering a friend. But she didn't want to talk about her plan just yet, if only because it was still in the beginning stages, and she wanted to go over the finer details of it first and get her mate's input.

Still, she answered as honestly as possible. "I'm thinking it's time we start to even the score."

Before Shula could ask anything else that Iona wasn't ready to answer just yet, she waved her off with a promise that she would tell her later and walked over to Julius, who was starting a fire. He turned to look at her as she approached and must have read something on her expression that she hadn't even been aware was there at all.

He dusted his hands off as a fire sparked to life and stood with a lopsided grin twisting his mouth. "What crazy idea have you come up with now, mate?"

The tightness in her chest eased a fraction when she was near him. "What makes you think I have a crazy idea?"

He swiped his thumb against the tip of her nose in a sweet gesture. "I know that look, and I know *you*. Something's on your mind." His arms crossed against his chest. She tried not to be distracted by the bulge of his muscles flexing. "And I want to know what."

Prince Valerio—or King Regent Valerio, as it were—leaned against a tree when Iona stepped into the woods to speak with him.

He had expected nothing less, though he had predicted that Uric would have been the one to come find him instead of the ice Fae. An ache pressurized his chest because Uric had not come to him, but as quickly as it formed, he pushed it away.

Just like he had pushed Uric away hours earlier.

If he was alone, really, he only had himself to blame. He could not even be cross with his friend for giving him the space he had desired.

He used the brief time alone to pick through his thoughts and compartmentalize them into boxes he did not want to open or look through. The loss of his people and death of his father were first and foremost. But as much as he wanted to avoid the heartache those brought, he forced himself to think of them.

He was king regent now, so decisions fell on his own shoulders. After so long of dreaming of his coronation, of taking over for his cruel bastard of a father, he could not seem to fit into that metaphorical crown now. It was a strange sensation, to realize that you could never fill the spaces of the one who came before you.

It felt like he was being chipped apart from the inside. Like his soul was given solid form and was being chopped away in thin layers, and there was no substance strong enough to put those pieces back together again. Somehow, he had to.

There were Fae relying on him now in the absence of his father, but he had not the minimal idea what he would do. He felt hopeless, like he was drowning and there was no air.

Not until Iona stepped in front of his line of vision, bringing with her what felt like a soft breeze of cold that slapped against his senses and pulled him out of the sweet darkness he had been trapped in.

She pushed away the darkness with her sharp scent of apples and ice and mint. Then Shula appeared and he startled, straightening as he took her in, her scent of confections and embers warming him.

These two females, they woke him up. Shula especially. He regretted the thought as soon as it formed. He thought of Uric, the feelings he harbored like a carefully guarded secret that was not a secret at all.

For a single moment, he had been able to relate to Uric. In that single instance when Davina had convinced him that his mate waited for him, he had felt that surge of happiness, a surge of love for someone he had not yet met. It all came crashing down when he had come face to face with the fiery Fae, only to realize she belonged to another.

It was why he tried so hard to push her away. To separate her from the delusions he had let himself fall under when they had gone to save her. Because when he looked at her, he was reminded of what he did not have and everything he had ever desired.

He did not want the desire for a mate to turn into desire for the wrong female.

His eyes narrowed on her presence, and he despised the way she tensed near him. Like he was someone she had to be wary around.

"King Valerio," Iona began, and Valerio tried not to visibly flinch at the words that hurt more than his father's cruelty or magic ever could. "I have an idea..."

They could not have given him more time to come to terms with the fact that he was supposed to lead them? All his life, he had taken orders. Sure, he had commanded servants and his own small group, but his father had never allowed him to be privy to his plans of war.

How was he supposed to deal with that?

With his head held high and his mask in place, that was how.

He lifted a brow, gaze flashing between the two Elementals. They were pressed close together, a united front in the face of their newfound ruler. He stared at Shula, but she did not recoil from his gaze, so he turned to Iona.

"I am listening..."

This is War

The streets of Seirz bustled with activity and colors that Iona hadn't seen in years. She breathed it in, her throat closing from the flecks of iron and ash in the air, with a curiosity that pressed into her bones. Porir had never been this lively. In fact, she'd assumed every human city was as melancholy as her previous home.

It was strange to see that not everyone lived in the poverty she'd imagined they did. The streets were ripe with riches and a gaiety she'd not felt in a long time. Street urchins weaved their way through roads and stalls of street vendors, their sticky fingers slipping up to steal oranges and apples and pocket their wares.

After spending so long traveling from place to place, from quiet woods to a hollow castle, Iona was glad to see something lively, even if it wasn't her own home or her court. There was something about this place that was as freeing as it was deadly.

Deadly, because if the humans found out that Fae were hiding in plain sight, they wouldn't hesitate to call their soldiers and have them executed.

"Come one, come all, and catch a glimpse at the world's last polar bear!"

Clay's shout drew in clusters of humans. They surrounded them, whispering their eagerness down the line. Children pushed their way to the front, bouncing on the balls of their feet, smiling through gapped and missing teeth. They were there, as captivated by Clay's energy as they were about the promise of a polar bear.

He seemed like he'd actually been raised in a circus, Iona thought, peeking at him from behind a single sheet they'd hung between twin posts in the city's center. A simple change of clothes, stolen by Shula Azzarh's own sticky fingers, and Clay appeared the part of a ringleader. The top hat on his head covered the tips of his elongated ears, and the tail of his jacket whipped with every quick move he made down the line of viewers.

He entranced them, pulled them in with accidental glamor, and they were too weak to resist his beauty.

"The beast is behind this curtain! But beware his teeth, little ones... lest he gobble you in one ferocious bite!" He made a growling sound near a group of children, who jumped back in a fit of giggles. Then he straightened and walked backwards towards the curtain, grabbing the edge in his fist. He yanked. "Behold!"

Iona's heel dug lightly into her familiar's side where she was mounted on his back. He growled and stepped forward as the curtain was ripped away, and they came face to face with the crowd.

They gasped, jerking back as Iona and her familiar walked into the circle.

The music came next, a song that trailed from Shula's throat and echoed around them. It rose and fell through the crowd in a beautiful melody that Iona found her body moving to. She threw her leg over her familiar, falling at his side in a flurry of thin skirts.

Never before had Iona worn so little in the human lands. In the Jade Court, wearing thin, white skirts that reached their thighs was normal because of the heat. Seirz wasn't warm. In fact, it was rather chilly. Her ears were safe from the piercing stab of the wind thanks to the scarf she'd wrapped around her head. The bright blue scarf covered her ears from view and trailed down her back against the scars.

Everything else felt entirely too exposed. The skirt she wore was merely twin scraps of fabric that covered her front and back, yet left the sides open to show the toned, smooth skin of her legs. Her feet were covered in flats, and bangles slid up and down her ankles and wrists.

If this was what Shula had worn every day at the circus she used to work for, Iona couldn't fathom how she'd stayed. It was terrible attire to be forced into.

But she did it.

She moved around her familiar in quick steps to the rhythm of Shula's rising voice. They moved like a unit until Weylyn burst from the crowd, surprising them as he joined in on the dance. He moved like he belonged in the wilderness, with savage abandon.

Shula had planned this choreography; half of the plan had been filled with Shula's ideas. Valerio had stared at Shula when she'd mapped out the details, as if surprised she'd ever been capable, and Iona had to force herself not to look so smug about it. How could he ever had any doubt that Shula was anything less than amazing?

Weylyn was in nothing but his pants and boots, his bronze chest on display. The long braid at the end of his head twirled and danced with his own movements like it was its own entity. He was hypnotizing, like his glamor was on full force, and that magic lived within the light steps as his feet flicked against the ground.

They made quite the show for the next few hours. Humans came and went, and soldiers passed never the wiser, dropping coins into their purses as they slowly made their way across the city, until night finally fell and they packed up their things.

The city was a busy place. One they never would have been able to slip through undetected. There were no trees to hide them, the buildings clustered too close together to keep them in the shadows.

It had been Shula's plan, really, and subject of grand debate. How to slip through the city undetected.

"By hiding in plain sight."

Her own face had been hidden behind scarves as she sang her way across the city so no one would recognize her as the wanted Fire Dancer from Piriguini's Circus that was on every poster they passed.

And because humans could not see what existed right beyond their noses, they hadn't noticed she was the Fae the emperor wanted at all.

It helped them breeze through the night as word of them traveled fast throughout the city, so that when it finally slept, they made it exactly where they needed to be.

They waited all night, their fingers moving quickly, quietly, as they stripped of their circus-like clothing and donned their uniforms of war.

All except Shula.

So by the time morning came and the light was bleeding against the dark, swathing the sky in hues of pink and light blue, Shula was walking into the military camp.

It wasn't such a difficult thing to do. After all, they were strong, and no one would dare break into their poorly guarded stronghold. Julius and Clay took care of the guards who'd fallen asleep at the entrance, rendering the entryway free for Shula to step through.

She walked in alone, though not without backup. The others waited at the entryway while Shula stepped into the light. Clad in a similarly styled skirt that Iona had been wearing before, her golden-brown legs all but glowed as rays of sunlight sliced against her skin. Her arms raised and the bangles decorating her wrists slid down to her elbows. Slowly, making a show of it, she unwound the scarf from around the bottom half of her face and let it go so it drifted towards the ground.

"Hey! What the fuck are you doing here?!"

Shula smiled and pushed her hair back away from her ears. Their gasps cut through, sharper than wind, as they recognized the female from the wanted posters before they started forward, Shula began to dance.

Her feet moved across the ground in dexterous, seductive movements. Her body undulated, and danced like cresting waves of the ocean, falling to the shore. Her every turn was practiced and yet borne from somewhere deep in her soul at the same time. Like she ripped it straight from a place of pain and sorrow and spoke without saying. She cried without tears and laughed without noise.

In her dance she whispered the beginnings of a story.

And when the first human approached her, she lit him on fire with her words.

He screamed as he burned, metal melding into his flesh. Others soon followed and Shula didn't need to open her eyes. Her senses saw for her and fire consumed, licking along the ground and reaching for anyone who dared to come too close.

The rapid succession of the flames chased along iron beams and tore through doors and walls. Soon, weapons were drawn and aimed, and they went flying at the fire Fae, only to be caught against a wall of solid ice.

Iona made herself known by then, creating weapons of blue and sent them flying from her fingertips as the magic consumed her from the inside. Her skin glowed blue, and she was encased in ice. A statue, an Elemental. Beside her, Shula's own skin glowed and bled like fire as it danced from her veins.

Together, they tore through the military camp, their rage silent whispers between them, while their magic screamed and tore through the place, ripping it off its hinges. Iron melted and broke against fire and ice. They cleaved it apart layer by disgusting layer until the whole place shuddered and fell apart. Their magic was explosive, destructive. Just like the humans had been. As Castle Aileach crumbled, so did this place. Like the Fae were crushed beneath the rubble, so were they.

And when it finally ended, the chaos finally subsiding, Iona took her friend's hand in her own, interlacing their fingers, and something akin to hope flashed through their blood like Mana whispering words of promise and destruction.

This is war.

To Dana

Valerio stared at the setting sun, the breeze soft as it pushed his hair away from the sharp jut of his cheeks. A storm rolled within his chest while his manner appeared calm and collected. His mind waged thoughts of war and his body longed for rest, for peace.

"We have officially declared war against the Emperor of Illyk." He had heard Uric's footsteps before the Fae's voice came to him. He did not turn to greet his friend but stared straight ahead.

The sun dipped beyond the horizon. Crests and valleys decorated this part of Illyk. Lush green grass, a bright sun, and a sky free of smog reminded him for a single second of home. Of Tir na Faie.

"Good," came his curt reply. "I want him to know who did that to him. I want him and his kings to bleed like they have bled us for years."

They had left a single survivor in that camp. They had hammered his still breathing body to an iron pike with his arms spread wide and a message to be delivered past his stuttering lips.

"This means war."

Ice wrapped around the human's legs, keeping him upright, and Shula Azzarh had danced her fingers along his armor, leaving fire in its wake until he smoldered and screamed. She had put it out so as to not kill him, but just enough to leave a message.

"Is it wise to let the emperor know that you have the Elementals?" Uric questioned.

Valerio huffed a breath. "This is why I value your friendship so," he said, and Uric tensed. "I know you do not want to hear these words, but you question me when very little do so." For once, he lost the perfectly composed expression and dragged his fingers through the ends of his hair. "Perhaps it was a mistake, but then again, perhaps the emperor knows already that we have them. How else could he have found us at Castle Aileach?"

He had been asking himself that question since they stormed past the tree line and pelted the castle with boulders. They had been found somehow, the Emperor of Illyk had found them.

"I do not know," Uric answered, his voice laced with shaking anger.

"If he found us once, do you think he will find us again?"

Uric contemplated before answering. "After that display in the military camp, yes."

"Good."

Uric seemed shocked at the profession, though he covered the expression with ease.

"Let him find us. Let him come. We have hidden in the shadows for far too long, and if this is the way we must play the game in order to win back our freedom, then so be it. I will unleash my wrath upon every fucking camp in the empire. I will break out every Fae he holds hostage and keep my own armies to fight his until he is dead and buried and we have a place to call home again."

And Valerio would do anything, *anything,* to keep that promise. At the cost of his own happiness, at the cost of his own *life.*

Uric pressed a hand to his shoulder, the touch gentle and barely there before he pulled away just as quickly. "You are a good man, my king," he whispered. "I have no doubt that with you, we will find the freedom we so seek."

Valerio blinked away the burning in his eyes and took a deep breath.

"I hope so," he whispered. "I really fucking hope so."

"Are you ready?" King Valerio inquired.

Iona and Shula sat cross-legged across from one another. The map of Illyk was spread out between them, held down on its four corners by stones so the wind didn't blow it away.

In her hands, Shula held six stones of her own. Each one represented an Elemental, including herself. She held them tightly, her lip pressed tightly between her teeth while one hand tugged at the end of her hair, pulling and tucking, pulling and tucking.

Iona's fingers pressed against her leg in a slow rhythm while she made an attempt to control her breathing, as if that could somehow dissipate the nerves that were rolling in her stomach.

She wasn't exactly sure why she felt so nervous about what they were about to do, but she was. It felt... strangely... intimate. They were going to toss the stones and search for the Fae Elemental they would need to find next. Another one of them. Another friend, or another foe, they couldn't be sure.

A friend, something whispered through her mind, and she tried to push that voice away because the truth was, she wasn't sure what she would find, and she didn't want to give in to her own hope only to be disappointed again. Even when everything inside her screamed that she needed to keep that light alive. The light of her sister that had bled into Iona's personality for so many years.

Her eyes met Shula's and held. The Fae men were in a circle around them, hovering, *waiting.*

"Are you ready?" Iona repeated King Valerio's question. Her voice was breathless, strange, echoing in her own ears.

Shula swallowed, the sound audible. "I'm ready." Her chin wobbled as she spoke.

"Then let's do this."

Iona held out her hands, palms facing up. Shula's hands hovered over her own and turned, dropping the cold stones onto Iona's skin quickly before her own hands came down, and they were tethering the stones in the middle.

A surge of power zapped through them like a bolt of lightning across the sky. Iona and Shula both arched into it, gasping. Their fingers tightened almost painfully a fraction before they pulled away and let the stones fall.

Iona's eyes opened, though she hadn't even realized she'd closed them, and watched each stone drop, one right after the other, on different locations on the map.

Two fell side by side in Orknie, right at the edge of the Arcana where they currently were. The others scattered all around.

In the north, on a spot named Valley of the Dead in the kingdom of Vellm.

In Ielwyn.

In Dana.

And the final stone jumped around the map like it had a life of its own. Iona was hypnotized by it for a single instant before glowing lines in different colors spread across the map like veins, bright and humming.

"Holy Mana," Iona breathed.

"Right?" Shula agreed.

"What?" Clay demanded, shuffling behind Shula.

"You can't see it because you are not an Elemental," Shula told him. "But the map is glowing. Like it's showing us where they are. Like it's telling us that we're connected."

Iona and Shula shared a look before staring back down at the map.

"So?" Julius placed his hand on her shoulder. "Where do we need to go next?"

A line of dark blue brightened against the map like it had heard Julius' question and was responding, leading a line towards the kingdom where they needed to go.

In unison, Iona and Shula's fingers slammed down against the map and they called out, "There!"

Their eyes met once again.

"You feel it, too, right?" Shula whispered.

"I do."

"Feel what?" Clay asked.

"A sense of foreboding. Like something is *wrong*."

"The Elemental needs our help." Iona pulled her finger off the map, staring at the place they would be headed to next.

"What Elemental is it?" Julius bent. "Earth?" He cocked his head to the side.

"No," Shula answered. "Not that."

"Want to place bets?" Clay's grin didn't quite reach his eyes. "Male or female? Element?" His eyes flicked over the males. "Who's mate it will be?"

"Enough!" Valerio barked with a hint of irritation. "Get some rest, for we have much to do." His eyes stared down at the map, and Iona swore she caught a flash of longing in them, but it was gone as quickly as it appeared. "Tomorrow we begin our fight to freedom and our war against the humans." He turned and his voice trailed after him as he walked away, a phantom in the night. "Then we will go to Dana and find this Fae."

Shula began picking up the stones reverently, pocketing them one by one. Then she took the map ever carefully, her eyes on the glowing lines before she folded it up and pocketed that again. "What are you thinking?" Her fingers gripped the sides of her pants, clasping over the map and stones in her pocket.

"I'm thinking about this gut feeling I have..."

Julius' brows rose, and when Iona didn't elaborate, he swiped his thumb across her cheek. "Talk to us, mate."

"I can't *explain* it..."

"I can," Shula interrupted, her eyes wide and far away. "You saw where the stone landed, right?"

Clay whistled. "I couldn't see much beyond that stone on the Valley of the fucking Dead." He shuddered. "I have heard stories..."

"We all have," Ryker growled. "Now shut the fuck up and let her speak."

Shula reached for Ryker, letting his hand envelop her own like she was trying to find strength in her mate. "It landed in Port Bay, Dana."

Just hearing her friend say the words had Iona's stomach tightening in knots.

"*Soo...* what about it?" Clay asked.

"You don't recognize that city?" When no one nodded, Shula sighed. "It's the capital of Dana..." She swallowed. "It's located near the king's castle."

Silence.

Then, "Oh, fuck."

The feeling of unease only incremented until Iona's fingers cramped against her thighs. Not even Julius' hand squeezing hers eased the ache.

"May Mana keep you safe and well, Elemental." Iona whispered. "Hold tight because we are coming for you. We will find and protect you. But *hold on.*"

No one else spoke. Silence ensued like they were waiting or echoing their own thoughts out to Mana, hoping, *praying* that the wind would take the words where they needed to be.

Maybe Iona could no longer believe in the magic of prayer and Mana like she used to, but she could put her inhibitions aside for this. For an Elemental in dire need of a prayer and a friend.

In need of a little, magical thing called hope.

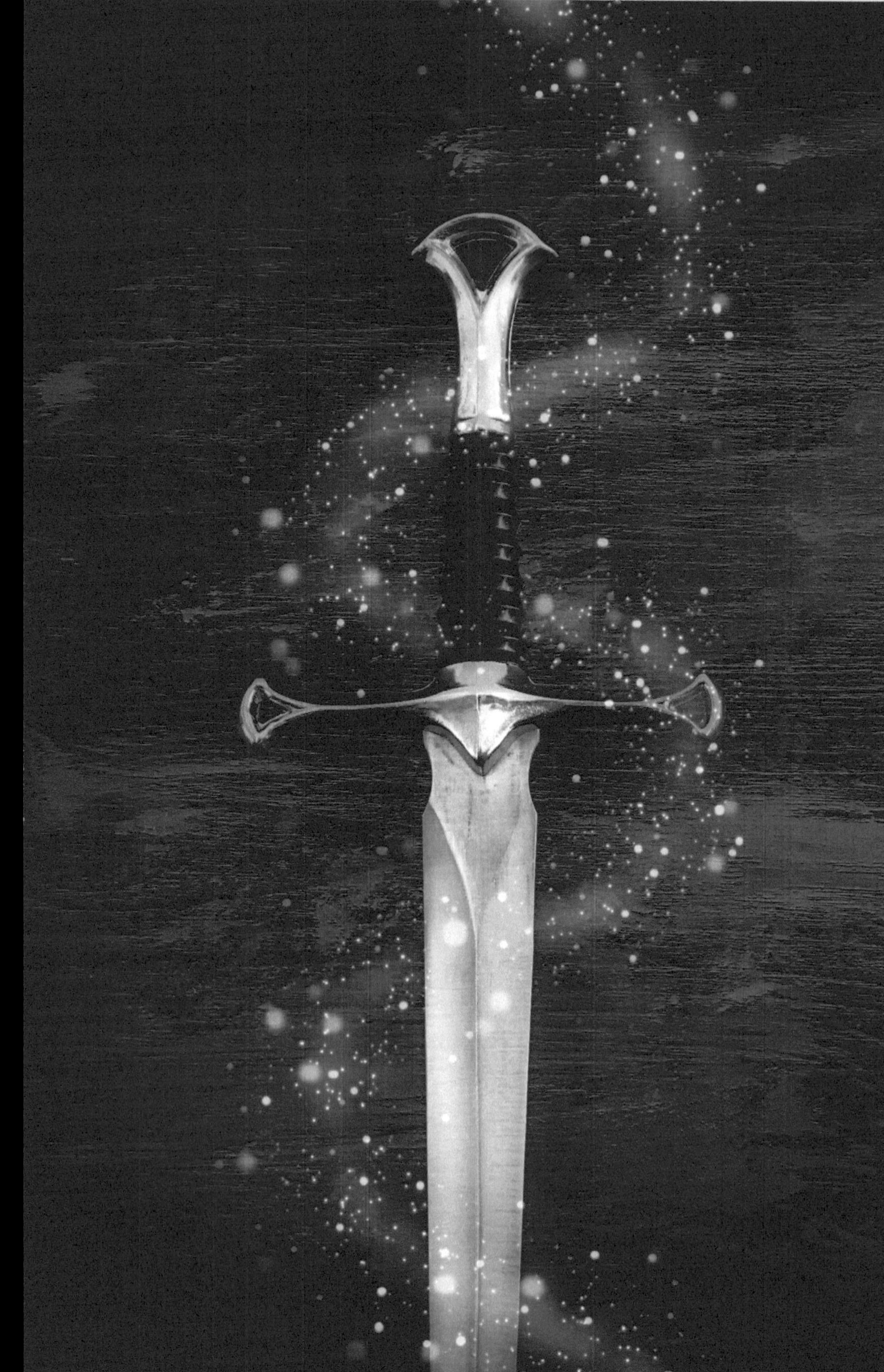

Acknowledgements

Wow. It's alive. Book two is seriously *alive.*

This entire series has been a journey I never expected, and I am eternally grateful for the team who helps me to make my dreams come true. Thanks to Lisa Nieves-Taylor for helping me edit these thicc books and perfecting them and just lecturing me on all the repetitive words and phrases I use, haha.

Thank you to my cover designer, KD Ritchie over at Storywrappers for bringing my main characters to life with your spectacular cover art.

Huge thanks to my pack, for dealing with my thousands of teasers in our group chat and helping me flesh out details when I was confused.

To my lovely beta and ARC readers, I adore you all.

My lovely Cheerreaders (Char, Haidee, Katie, Zoe) your encouragement these last few months have meant the WORLD to me. I don't think you understand how something like "Your writing is so good, can't wait for the next book!" can mean so much when your self-esteem is down. You have helped when I've felt like I wasn't good enough, and for that I can't thank you enough. ALSO, thanks for helping me pick out names when I was too lazy to google.

Finally, but obviously never less importantly, thank *you*, dear reader, for picking up this book and giving my Fae Elementals a chance, a space on your shelf and in your heart. I know we aren't supposed to pick favorites as authors, but this series is my favorite. It has taken so much of me, all the best and worst parts of my soul and has become something so personal. When you all message me and tell me how much you loved reading this? It warms me and reminds me of why I started writing in the first place.

About the Author

Aleera Anaya Ceres is the USA Today Bestselling author of several series including the Origins of the Six series and the Daughter of Triton series. Like most introverts, Aleera prefers to curl up with a good book, listen to music, paint, read tarot cards, and snack on the tears and heartbreak of her readers. A proud Mexican-American from the state of Kansas, Aleera currently resides in Tlaxcala, Mexico with her husband and children.

You can find/contact her here:
aleeraanayaceres.com
aleeraceres@aacbooks.com

Also by Aleera Anaya Ceres

Adult Fantasy Series
Fae Elementals

A Dance With Fire

A Sword of Ice

A Shield of Water
The Dark Waters series

Riptide

Reverse Harem Series
Royal Secrets

Secrets Among the Tides

Whispers Beneath the Deep

Caresses Between the Sand

Death Beyond the Waves
Royal Lies

Slave to Ice & Shadows

Princess in Frost Castles

Queen of Frozen War
Origins of the Six series

Academy of Six

Control of Five

Destruction of Two

Wrath of One

A Daughter of Triton series

Triton's Academy

Triton's Prophecy

Triton's Legacy

A Daughter of Triton Box set

Reverse Harem Standalones

Queenie & the Krakens

Lourdes & the Mafia

Paranormal Romance Series

Deep Sea Chronicles

Fall in Deep

Siren Queen

The Blood Novels

Love Bites

Blood Drug

My Master

Last Hope

Young Adult standalone

The Last Mermaid

www.ingramcontent.com/pod-product-compliance
Lightning Source LLC
Chambersburg PA
CBHW020245030826
48979CB00030B/2620/J
* 9 7 9 8 9 8 6 9 5 4 6 5 3 *